How to Charm a Beekeeper's Heart

Candice Sue Patterson

D1246617

This is a work of fiction. Names, characters, places, and incidents either are the product of the author's imagination or are used fictitiously, and any resemblance to actual persons living or dead, business establishments, events, or locales, is entirely coincidental.

How to Charm a Beekeeper's Heart

COPYRIGHT 2016 by Candice Sue Patterson

Contact Information: customer@pelicanbookgroup.com

Scripture quotations, unless otherwise indicated are taken from the King James translation, public domain.

Cover Art by *Nicola Martinez*

White Rose Publishing, a division of Pelican Ventures, LLC
www.pelicanbookgroup.com PO Box 1738 *Aztec, NM * 87410

White Rose Publishing Circle and Rosebud logo is a trademark of Pelican Ventures, LLC

Publishing History
First White Rose Edition, 2016
Paperback Edition ISBN 978-1-61116-856-3
Electronic Edition ISBN 978-1-61116-855-6
Published in the United States of America

Dedication

To my amazing siblings—Joe, Missy, Brock, and
Aaron. Because I just can't say it enough: I love you.

Acknowledgments

Every book is a group effort; therefore, I'd like to
thank the sisters of my heart--The Quid Pro Quills--
Robin Patchen, Pegg Thomas, Kara Hunt, Jericha
Kingston, and Marge Wiebe. Thank you ladies for your
support, prayers, wisdom, and honesty.

Marti Chabot, I treasure our friendship and
appreciate your insight and experience as a true
Mainer. Thank you for watching for errors in my
stories. Any found are entirely my fault.

A big thank you to my hubby, Adam, who
provides the inspiration for my stories. Your support
and willingness to help brainstorm at times, as well as
enduring my endless chatter about characters and plots
is appreciated more than you'll ever know.

To my little men--Levi, Silas, and Hudson--you are
wonderful boys, and I'm blessed beyond measure to
hold the title "Mom."

Above all, I thank the Lord Jesus Christ for my
salvation. He has blessed me beyond words and I'm
grateful to Him for allowing my dream of writing to
come to fruition. All honor and glory goes to Him.

And thank you, reader, for taking time from your
busy life to spend it with my characters.

What People are Saying

Candice Sue Patterson delivers another sensational romance for readers of Christian Fiction. Awash with compassion, Patterson lets us walk in the boots of one without Christ, in the high heels of one trusting Christ, and in the hearts of both.

~Jericha Kingston, author

Candice Sue Patterson knows how to write. Period. This author's descriptive abilities are phenomenal, as is her insight into matters of the heart and emotions.

~Delia Latham, author

Sixteen ounces of honey requires approximately 1,152 bees to visit 4.5 million flowers.

1

This was one sick, twisted joke.

Huck Anderson stared through his reflection on the glass storefront, rubbing his temple where a headache pulsed. On display, an oak frame supported white satin that gleamed in the sunlight. A yellowing guest book was propped in the corner window next to a vase of fake flowers. The breeze kicked up, lashing the American flag behind him on the courthouse lawn, the fabric snapping in the air. Uncle Marty's grating laughter carried from somewhere on the wind. Good thing the old man was dead, or Huck just might kill him.

He ground the toe of his boot into the sidewalk. This hadn't been on his agenda for today. In fact, he'd rather fight a rabid moose with a cap gun. But according to the will, this was what Uncle Marty had left him, so he'd honor the man's wishes. Even if it stripped his dignity.

Huck ripped open the door, his neck and shoulder muscles threatening to snap like tightly coiled springs. His dusty boots met worn, purple carpet. A strong flowery stench made him sneeze—the smell of death. He curled his upper lip, searching the room for the owner or director, whatever they were called.

No one. Not a sound.

Catalogs stacked high sat to his right on a rough oak table. Sheer pink-and-white fabric hung over a full-length mirror opposite him. Looked like this place was in need of an undertaker too.

A beat-up cash register swallowed the glass counter to his left. Frilly business cards caught his attention, and he lifted the girlie stock paper.

Yesteryear Bridal Boutique, Pine Bay, Maine.

The scuffed walls were as naked as his pride. What in the name of Uncle Sam was he supposed to do with a bridal boutique?

So he'd gotten into some trouble when he was younger. Nothing he'd put Uncle Marty through was worth this. He wasn't a pink-shirt-wearing, sissy-voiced, *Say Yes to the Dress* kinda guy. He'd seen the commercials. He didn't have a feminine side.

High-pitched giggles echoed from the rear of the building. A stout redhead in a huge wedding dress marched from the narrow hallway into the room. A gaggle of women followed her to the mirror, going nuts over the ugly thing. They didn't even notice him standing there.

He continued reading the card. *Arianne Winters, Owner and Bridal Consultant.*

According to Uncle Marty's lawyer, the woman hadn't paid rent in almost a year. Now was the perfect time to turn this nightmare into something the town needed, like a sporting goods store or a bait and tackle shop.

A petting zoo. Anything but this.

Cameras clicked, and through the ruckus, he managed to pick out bits of conversation about blue garter belts, the flower girl's hair, and what lingerie the bride planned to wear on the honeymoon. The word *romantic* had him eyeing the door. He needed to get out of here, could feel the testosterone leaching from his veins.

He stepped forward and held up the business card. "I'm looking for Arianne Winters."

"I'll be with you in a moment." A voice came from somewhere within the mass of women.

A petite blonde, kneeling on the floor, stood and faced the bride. "Take all the time you need. I'll be right back." She stepped toward Huck. "I'm Arianne. Can I help you?"

Her full, red lips parted in a smile. Huck surveyed his reneging tenant. Blonde hair, curvy build, attractive in a classic way that drew him in.

"Are you Joelle Bellman's fiancé? She said you might be in today to get fitted for your tux."

He almost laughed. Him? A groom? Never.

"No, I'm Huck Anderson." He offered his hand along with the famous Anderson dimples.

She pressed her soft palm against his. Lightning flashed in her navy blue eyes, and her pretty smile faded to a pout.

"I need to speak with you, but if now isn't a good time, I can come back."

"You have no idea who I am, do you?"

He studied her heart-shaped face.

"Arianne…"

Those eyes. Something about her seemed familiar.

Seconds later, those red lips twisted in a smirk. "Of course. How could I expect the great Huck Anderson to remember me?" She tucked a strand of hair behind her ear, her cheeks turning pink. "We went to high school together. I was your English tutor. And math and science…"

Arianne Thompson. Wow. Twelve years had taken her gangly build and filled in all the right places. A fistful of shame walloped him in the chest, making his skin hot. He rubbed the back of his neck. He'd never expected to see her again. If there was one thing in life he could rely on, it was karma.

"Is it all right to try on a veil?" the bride barked from the mirror.

Poor guy. Whoever he was.

Arianne craned her slender neck to see over her shoulder. "Of course. Let me know if you need any help."

Now what? Old insecurities crept into his gut. Maybe she'd forgotten. Though judging from the pinched look on her pretty face, she remembered.

He did, now that she'd dredged up the memory.

So he was pond scum. That didn't change facts. She couldn't pay her rent, and he wanted no part in a bridal boutique. "I'm here about the building."

"I don't own the building."

"I know. I do."

Arianne blinked. For a minute, he thought she'd stopped breathing.

"Martin didn't tell me he was selling."

"He didn't. He passed away last month. I'm his nephew. Left this building to me in his will."

Huck removed the folded papers from his back pocket and offered them to her.

"Martin's…gone?" Her creamy skin turned ashen and her eyes pooled with tears. She'd done this once before. He'd been the cause then too. With Arianne, he was always the bad guy. He lowered his voice to a whisper. "It appears you've had trouble paying rent.

4

Ten months."

Thumbnail tapping her bottom lip, Arianne stared out the display window beside them, past the mannequin holding up a monstrosity of a dress. "He told me not to pay rent until business…picked up."

"There's no mention of that agreement in his will." Huck pushed the papers along the countertop with his finger so she could read the contract terms.

Arianne wilted onto a nearby stool. She raised weighted eyelids and hit him with a pained look so raw and desperate, it twisted his gut. "What are you going to do?"

Honey bees are vulnerable creatures threatened by mites, chemical exposure, poor nutrition, and bad weather. Bees are also very strong creatures, adapting to their environment, capable of carrying pollen and nectar equal to their body weight.
—*NOVA,* Bees: Tales from the Hive, *produced for PBS, January 4, 2000*

2

Arianne clasped her trembling hands in her lap. Huck towered over her. He scratched his whiskered jaw. Intense brown eyes stared back at her with all the velvety smoothness of brushed leather. After all these years, he and that lazy southern drawl still turned her insides to mush.

The term "devil in disguise" fit him better than his worn jeans and the white T-shirt straining around his chest and arms.

Arianne steeled her spine. She wasn't seventeen and naïve anymore. She had a daughter to support and didn't like the way he'd strutted into her shop like he owned the place.

Even if he did.

Huck scrubbed the back of his neck. "I'm not sure what your circumstances are but—"

"We found the one!" Sara, the bride-to-be, waved a veil above her head as though it were an Olympic medal. "I'll take it."

Finally, a sale. Too bad the good news couldn't obliterate Huck's unspoken words. Or Huck.

Arianne forced a smile. "Great. I'll draw up the papers while you change. Just leave the gown on the dressing room hook, and we'll set a date for alterations."

The women made their way down the narrow hall, staccato chatter echoing off the walls. Arianne pulled in a deep breath and stood on shaky legs, supporting her weight against the glass counter.

Huck would not get the best of her again. "You were saying?"

He pocketed his hands and shifted his weight to his other leg, one foot slightly askew. "The accountant provided me with the financial report for this building. Since you haven't paid rent in so long, I came prepared to evict you."

Her heart dropped to her toes. "But Martin and I had an agreement."

"Your agreement isn't in writing, and I can't afford to let you stay rent free."

Heat flooded her cheeks. If Huck evicted her, they'd be homeless. It wasn't her fault the economy had affected business and she was barely scraping by. Martin had understood that. Huck would too, if he wasn't the Tin Man.

"Mommy!" Emma burst through the front door. Tears stained her cheeks.

Arianne's heart lurched and she dashed around the counter. "What's wrong, baby?"

She knelt beside her daughter and thumbed the moisture from Emma's face.

Emma revealed a bloody, dirt-encrusted knee. "I

fell."

Arianne glanced at the door. "Where's Aunt Missy?"

Emma hiccupped. "Outside."

"It'll be all right." Arianne wrapped Emma in a hug. "Let's get you fixed up."

She stood, noting Huck's raised brows, as if he hadn't considered children as part of this twisted scenario. And was that *remorse* in his eyes? Hard to tell since she'd never seen him have any before.

"Huck, this is my daughter, Emma."

He nodded.

"Come on, baby." She tugged Emma toward her office and the First Aid kit.

"I can't, Mommy. It hurts." Emma's lips pooched to twice their normal size.

"All right. You keep Mr. Huck company. I'll be right back."

If she'd have thought Huck posed any real threat to her daughter, she wouldn't have left them alone. The only perceived danger was that Huck would charm his way into Emma's affections the way he had every other female on the eastern seaboard—and judging by the child's dreamy eyes when Arianne returned with the First Aid kit thirty seconds later, the damage had been done.

He'd lifted Emma onto the counter. Both were smiling so wide their dimples sank into their cheeks, and Arianne suspected she was the cause for their humor. "What's so funny?"

"Nothing." Had the answer not come so quickly—and in unison—Arianne might have believed them.

After cleaning and dressing the scrape with two flesh-colored Band-Aids, the reality of Huck's visit and

Martin's passing returned. Arianne gazed into her daughter's navy blue eyes, which she'd passed down the gene pool, blinking away the moisture threatening to give her emotions away. She couldn't let her daughter down. All they had was each other and this store. She'd fight him if she had to.

Emma squirmed on the counter. "Can I have a juice box?"

"I'll get you one in a minute."

"I can get them myself, Mommy. I'm four."

"And independent." Arianne helped her daughter to the floor.

Good as new, Emma strode to the office.

Arianne closed the latch on the First Aid kit and faced Huck, her eyes still burning with unshed tears. "I'm sorry for your loss. Martin was a good man."

Huck swallowed. Hard. "Look, maybe...maybe we can work something out."

"We're ready." The singsong voice interrupted Huck as Sara approached the register, her family close behind.

Six purses plunked on the counter, one octave at a time.

"Now's obviously not a good time." Huck raked his fingers through his chestnut hair, spiking it into a hot mess. "Can we meet tomorrow?"

"I have alteration appointments all day."

"How 'bout Friday?"

"Friday's are swamped."

"Saturday?"

They could play this game all night, and she'd find an excuse for the next 365 days. "Saturday's fine. I close at three."

"See you then."

Emma peeked around the office door, wearing a conspiratorial smile. "Good-bye, Mr. Huck."

"See ya, kid." His gaze flickered to the women at the register, and his dimples made another appearance. "Ladies."

He nodded in expert cowboy fashion, causing Arianne to wonder what he'd look like in a leather hat and chaps. The image, as appealing as it was, made her want to find the nearest cliff and chuck herself straight into the ocean.

Huck moved toward the exit.

Arianne's sister rushed in, head down, thumbs moving over her phone, and crashed into his chest. The phone hit the floor. Missy bounced off him and gripped the doorframe.

Huck didn't flinch. He reached out to steady her. "Sorry." Then he picked up her phone, winked, and disappeared down the sidewalk.

Missy blinked, smoothed her shirt and hair. "You got Emma?" she asked, gaze still following Huck's movements down the street.

Arianne sighed and pulled out a sales slip. They'd discuss this later. "Yeah. Thanks."

And with that, Missy was gone.

"Who's the hunk?" Katherine, the bride's mother, wiggled her perfectly sculpted eyebrows.

"No one worth swooning over." Arianne rang up the dress.

"Ex?" Katherine's eyebrows arched.

Arianne's throat went dry. "No. An old…" What—*friend, first love?* "Acquaintance." She accepted Katherine's check and handed the paperwork to the future Mrs. Shaw.

The bride's grandmother slid her purse off the

counter and threaded her arm through the strap, a sharp whistle escaping through her false teeth. "If I were your age, I'd make sure he was more than an acquaintance. I'd catch that boy and—"

"Tell you what, Grandma." Mallory, the bride's sister and maid of honor, picked up her purse as well. "If you don't finish that sentence, I'll buy you some ice cream."

Grandma agreed and left the shop without another word.

What the woman didn't realize was that Huck Anderson couldn't be caught. He might resemble the noble hero in a classic western, but he was really the villain. And she'd been his victim.

Huck the acquaintance, she could keep at a safe distance. Huck the landlord, however, would be a whole different story.

~*~

Bees flew in and out of the fascia boards of Widow Haywood's peeling, orange, Cape Cod. She'd called Huck in a panic the night before, terrified her house was infested. Said their buzzing interfered with her hearing aid, and she could smell honey seeping through the walls.

The woman had been fifty-two cards short of a full deck before her husband was abducted by aliens. Bee infestations were a common problem, but there was no way they interfered with her hearing device.

Huck strapped his tool belt around his waist and climbed the extension ladder, slowly approaching the hidden hive. Bees smacked into his veiled helmet and buzzed around his arms.

He ignited the bee smoker and pumped it, sending a cool white cloud through the nozzle. With gloves in place, he sprayed the entrance to the hive with a few short puffs. Dazed bees scattered. The aged, brittle boards moaned as he detached them from the studs. Normally, bee droning relaxed him, but nothing in the past two days had erased Arianne's face from his mind.

Why couldn't his uncle have left him something practical, like his fifty-state spoon collection or antique lobster buoys? Huck would've gladly accepted the mint-condition Chevelle. He hadn't even known Uncle Marty owned real estate. Why leave the building to Huck?

A man owning a bridal shop was the stupidest thing he'd ever heard. Well, he didn't own the business, but owning the building was bad enough. Uncle Marty knew how Huck felt about marriage. The whole thing was nothing but a bad excuse to spend money and eat cake.

Six stepdads proved his point.

He rolled his head from side to side to ease the tension in his neck. How bad was Arianne's financial position? Her last name had changed. Didn't she have a husband to support her? 'Course, there'd been no ring. Yeah, he'd noticed. Along with her hourglass curves and distrusting blue eyes, all of which he'd like to see a little closer.

And the kid. A tiny copy of her mother who'd looked at him with wonder, like he was a celebrity or something. The same way Arianne used to, until he'd blown it. Big time.

If only his new tenant had been a stranger. Anyone but Arianne. He couldn't evict her now.

There'd be tears involved. Maybe he could help her find a new location, or offer a good price if she'd buy the building.

With the swarm captive and secured in his truck bed, fascia boards back in place, he loaded the ladder, running through his options before his meeting with Arianne tomorrow. He cursed under his breath. If he hadn't witnessed his uncle's struggle with pneumonia, he'd swear the man had died on purpose.

After the death of Queen Elizabeth I, England's economy plummeted. The poor and unemployed were encouraged by ministers and political leaders to start over in The New World. This exodus was referred to as "hiving off."
—Bees in America: How the Honey Bee Shaped a Nation *by Tammy Horn, The University Press of Kentucky, 2005*

3

The rickety wooden chair groaned as Arianne leaned against it and studied the sketch in front of her. She squinted and tipped the paper one way, then the other. The charcoal pencil dangled loosely between her fingers as she studied the dress: sweetheart neckline, beaded bodice, ball gown silhouette with multiple layers of tulle. She slipped her thumbnail between her teeth.

Something was missing.

"Mommy, I'm hungry." Emma sat amidst her Barbie collection, the majority of which had been Arianne's when she was a child. Their rubber legs were chipped and scuffed. A few dolls sported spiky hairdos from when Arianne had decided to try her hand at hairdressing. Edward Scissorhands would have done a better job.

"All right, precious, give me a few more minutes."

Arianne curled her leg beneath her and continued to examine the sketch. "Bibbidi Bobbidi Boo" filled the room, disrupting her creativity. She tucked the pencil in her bun and shifted her attention to the small television, where Cinderella's fairy godmother waved her wand and transformed the girl's rags into an exquisite silvery blue gown.

That's it! Arianne yanked the pencil from her hair, bringing loose strands with it. She grazed the charcoal across the paper a few more times then brought out her pastels. With a feathery-soft touch, she added the slightest hint of robin's egg blue to the hem, giving the bride her "something blue."

The front door slammed. Arianne jumped, dumping her pastels on the carpet. Missy barreled into the room, shuffling through a stack of white envelopes. "I'm famished. What's for supper?"

Was that all she was good for around here? Though she didn't mind feeding Emma, waiting on her loafing sister, who was capable of fixing her own supper, and finding a job if she really wanted to, was a whole different matter.

Arianne opened her mouth to say as much, but swallowed the words instead. It was her fault Missy acted the way she did. Arianne pulled off her glasses, set them on the desk, and rubbed the bridge of her nose. "I was just getting to that."

"Ooh, my hair salon has a discount on highlights this month." Missy held up a postcard and smiled.

Where did an unemployed, single woman find money for highlights? Arianne touched the loose tendrils escaping her messy bun. She hadn't had a haircut in almost a year. Her thick, natural curls had slackened into waves as it grew. But when she'd have a little extra cash, Emma would grow four inches overnight. It was either her hair or her daughter.

She glanced at the little stinker, encircled by an explosion of miniature eighties outfits and tiny shoes. Emma focused on the television, her legs stretched in front of her. Her jeans ended an inch above her thin purple socks. It was time to go shopping again.

"Here's your mail." Missy handed over the stack. "There's a final notice for something in there."

Arianne closed her eyes and drew in a patient breath. "Thanks for the good news."

"Someone's sassy today." Missy sank onto the couch and sprawled her body the length of the cushions. With a dramatic sigh, she lowered her lids as if she'd just returned home after an exhausting day's work.

"Forgive me, but you seem a little too eager to drive that final nail into my coffin."

Missy yawned. "What's your deal? Did you have another bride back out on you or something?"

"Well...yes. Among other things." *Like the fact that there's more month than money, Huck's trying to close me down, I've gained six pounds, and I'm noticing fine lines around my eyes.*

She stared at her twenty-five-year-old sister. Missy's jeans formed to her perfect, lean legs. Her flawless tan complexion glowed against her walnut-colored hair. No glasses, pimples, wrinkles, or cellulite. Enough to make a supermodel jealous.

Arianne's stomach howled. Supper—a problem she could fix. She put away her art supplies, tucked her dreams back into the compartment of her heart marked *Maybe Someday,* and patted Emma's head on her way to the kitchen. As Arianne filled a stock pot with water, she let the sound of rushing liquid from the faucet wash over her. Time for plan...what letter was she on now, G?

Missy entered the kitchen and went to the fridge, scanning the miniscule selection. "So what excuse did they give this time?"

"What do you mean?" Arianne turned off the water and set the pot on the chipped stovetop to boil.

"The lost bride. What reason did she give?"

"Same excuse as the others." Arianne twisted the burner knob to high. "She kept looking and found her dream gown at a couture salon."

Missy shuffled through the fridge and pulled out a soda can. "Last one. Can I have it?"

Arianne's shoulders drooped. Diet Mountain Dew. Her one splurge. "Sure."

The can hissed as Missy popped the tab with her French-manicured, artificial nails. Arianne looked down at her own blunt fingernails, barely revealing any white. She sighed and turned her attention to the bubbles skimming the bottom of the pot.

"You have that problem a lot. Have you ever considered carrying higher-end designs?"

Arianne rolled her eyes. "No, it never crossed my mind." She pulled uncooked spaghetti noodles from the dingy yellow cabinet. "Of course I've thought about it. But that takes money I don't have."

She retrieved a skillet and set it on the stovetop. "The gowns aren't the problem. The problem is that brides don't know what they want. They think they have an idea, but they really don't have a clue. I work hard to find a vintage dress that fits their style and personality. Then they walk into a couture salon and get enchanted by a modern Italian label with a diamond-encrusted bust line."

Missy leaned against the counter and slurped the

carbonation from the can's rim. "Don't take this the wrong way, but it might be because your dresses are so…old-fashioned."

Arianne spun to face her sister. "Vintage. My dresses are *vintage*. There's a difference. And what woman in her right mind wouldn't want to look like Elizabeth Taylor on her wedding day?"

"Apparently, lots." Missy clicked her fingernails on the dull, Formica countertop. "Your original designs are a perfect blend of modern and *vintage*. Why don't you start making your own gowns and selling them in your shop?"

Did her sister think her incapable of coming up with a good idea on her own? She'd only dreamed of that since she was five. "I'd love to, but again, that takes money. Money for materials, money to pay employees to run the shop while I sew, money to pay a skilled seamstress to take over alterations on the ready-made gowns…the list goes on and on."

"You'll get there someday."

"Doubtful." Arianne added salt to the boiling water, followed by the noodles.

The aluminum can clanked against the countertop. "What's this, the eternal optimist throwing in the towel?"

Arianne fetched a package of ground beef from the fridge and dropped the thawed meat into the skillet. It sizzled, like the sound of her life going up in flames. "I'd rather quit on my own terms than be forced out by cowboy Casanova."

"What?"

"I think I'm losing the boutique."

"What are you talking about?" Missy leaned her elbows on the counter, standing close enough for

Arianne to smell the freesia scent weaved into her clothes. Had Missy been into her perfume again?

"Martin Billings, the man who owns the building—"

"He's not going to start making you pay rent again is he? You guys had a deal."

Arianne shook her head. "Worse. Do you remember Huck Anderson from high school?"

Her sister chuckled. "Who could forget Huck? He was every girl's southern fantasy."

"Turns out he's Martin's nephew." Arianne planted a hand on her hip. "Huck inherited the building when Martin passed away last month. I just found out a few days ago." The browned beef blurred in her teary vision. "I feel awful for not attending his funeral. Martin was so good to me."

She sniffled, and Missy pulled her into a hug. "There, there. You didn't know..." Missy rubbed her palm on Arianne's back. Her sister might be flighty, but she was always there when Arianne needed her.

"So what makes you think you're losing the business?" Her soft voice reminded Arianne of their mother's.

"And this apartment. Huck came by the other day to tell me about Martin. He brought up the rent issue several times. He clearly wasn't happy."

Missy pulled away. "But you had a deal."

"Not in writing."

Her sister's expression looked as hopeless as Arianne felt. Then her eyes widened and her lips curled. "That was Huck I ran into when I dropped off Emma the other day?"

Arianne nodded.

"Wow. It was like hitting a brick wall."

Arianne stirred the noodles, ignoring the visual of perfectly sculpted muscles her sister had just put into her head.

"I didn't think he could get any hotter."

Agreed, but Arianne wasn't about to admit it. "Please. The guy's a celebrity in his own mind." She rubbed her nose. "He was going to hand me my death sentence the other day, I could feel it, but we were actually busy for once and kept getting interrupted. He wants to meet with me after work tomorrow to discuss it. Can you watch Emma for me?"

Missy crossed her arms and cast a mock glare. "What do I look like, a nanny? I'm already watching her for your date tomorrow night."

"Actually—my jobless sister who crashes on my couch several times a week, eats my cooking, wears my perfume, and drinks my last Diet Mountain Dew—you do look like a nanny."

Missy smirked. "Wake me up when supper's ready."

The quiet kitchen amplified Arianne's gloomy thoughts. She'd wanted to carry her personal designs in a shop she owned for as long as she could remember. Her dream lingered on her tongue, but she couldn't fully taste it. She glanced around the run-down kitchen. This wasn't where she'd imagined herself on the precipice of thirty.

Then again, she hadn't imagined her husband running out on her three years into their marriage, either. How she wished she could go back and see that one coming. Love truly was blind. And clueless.

When supper was ready, she placed the ice-filled glasses, bread and butter, napkins, silverware, and spaghetti on the table. The trio gathered around the tiny, round table. The only thing absent was a chocolate cake.

"Mommy, Mommy." Emma pushed from her chair and sprinted back into the living room.

Arianne put down her glass and followed her daughter's enthusiasm, wishing she could grasp pieces out of the air. "What's up, pumpkin?"

"Watch, Mommy, it's our favorite part."

Little fingers hooked around her hand, and together they watched Cinderella and Prince Charming burst through the church doors and climb into the horse-drawn carriage, love and happiness plastered on their faces. While the mice cheered, the royal couple rode off in the sunset to their happily-ever-after.

Arianne sighed. Why couldn't her love life be as sweet as those fairytales?

~*~

Foamy waves crashed against jagged boulders, churning the greenish water. The color reminded Arianne of the jade Depression glass her grandma used to display on shelves in the summer kitchen. She missed the security of those days, the sun's warmth washing over her through the windows at sunrise, bouncing prisms of light off Grandma's collections.

She paused for a moment to enjoy the scenery, and inhaled a deep breath to steady the orchestra of nerves playing a grand concerto in her stomach. The woodwinds carried the melody of anxiety, mingled with brass notes of nausea. Then the string section played the slow, mournful tune of what loomed in her future. It would be beautiful music, really, if it wasn't her life's song.

She climbed the natural granite steps up the hill, moving aside for customers who made their way back to the parking lot. *Lord, please give me the strength to get through this.*

Picnic tables dressed in blue and white gingham were scattered along the level plateau. The Atlantic stretched for miles, disappearing on the horizon. The smell of lobster and buttered corn on the cob made her mouth water, and she brushed her fingertips along her mouth to make sure no drool had escaped.

Huck stood from his seat at a table as she neared. He smiled, revealing straight, white teeth. His dimples carved deep canyons in his tan cheeks. It wasn't fair. He was better equipped for battle.

"Arianne." He nodded, touching the bill of his ball cap.

Her heart tripped. She enjoyed, way too much, the way her name rolled off his tongue, warm and soft like fresh cotton towels from the dryer. He was still every bit the small town celebrity—tall, muscular build, a little scruff, and just enough suave to be dangerous. Not to mention the twang.

"Huck."

"Where's the kid?"

"With the sitter."

"How's her knee?"

"Fine."

He scratched his neck. "Oh. Well, I don't know about you, but I'm starvin'." He patted his gut, which she knew, thanks to Missy's description, felt as rock hard as the ground they stood on. "Order whatever you want. It's on me."

"Thanks, but I'm not hungry." Actually, she was famished, but Travis was taking her into Bar Harbor tonight for dinner, and since fine dining was a rare occasion for her, she wanted to have an appetite.

"I'll be back, then." He swaggered to the order window, lifted the hem of his black shirt, and pulled his wallet from the back pocket of his boot cut jeans. He'd never adapted to the layered, outdoorsy fashion of true Mainers. He epitomized the traditional southern male, charmingly good manners with a side of wild—a dangerous combination for any east coast girl.

She lowered onto the wood bench, hating herself for being attracted to the goon, and closed her pink cardigan sweater against the cool breeze blowing off the water. The late-May sun blazed warmer than normal for this time of year, but it was still chilly.

She'd always loved this place, though as a teenager she enjoyed it with her family, as opposed to the popular kids who'd used it as a local hangout. That crowd had made a sport of overlooking her, making her feel invisible. Until the day she found Huck leaning against her locker.

With his sexy drawl, he'd begged her to help him study for his math and English finals, to which she reluctantly—and delightedly—agreed. She was shocked that the football star even knew she existed. Then one night, after cramming for weeks, he looked up from his book, and all doubts that he saw *her* vanished. Huck leaned closer and—

Plunk! She jumped as a basket of food dropped on the table in front of her. The memory fled as quickly as she had from Huck on prom night.

He sat across from her and wasted no time digging into his meal. The vibrant red of the steamed lobster shell made her regret turning down his offer. She

Candice Sue Patterson

concentrated on the roaring waves slamming into the cliff below instead of her growling stomach.

Huck took a sip of his soda and ran a napkin over his lips. "So how'ya been, Arianne?"

Making small talk before he cut her throat. Nice tactic. "Fine. You?"

"Good. Been real busy." He tugged his long sleeves up to his elbows, revealing tanned forearms. A result of his southern DNA, she was sure.

For the next ten minutes, in between bites of juicy lobster meat, he filled her in on his wonderful life since high school. It was just what she wanted to hear. Felt like old times.

"What do you do now?" Arianne tucked a wayward strand of hair behind her ear and scolded herself for carrying a grudge over something that happened so long ago. People change. She had.

He finished his bite and rested his elbows on the table, his perfect lips shiny with butter. "I'm a beekeeper. Run my own honey farm in Summerville."

Made sense. He'd always been able to charm anything into doing his bidding.

"What about you? I mean, I know you run a bridal shop, but I heard you'd left Pine Bay for good."

Ah, her favorite tale. One with such a happy ending she read it to herself before bed every night. She plucked a French fry from his basket and popped it in her mouth. "I did."

"College?"

"Harvard Medical School."

His brows shot upward. "Wow. I always pictured you at a place like that. But you're a— What brought you back here?"

She glanced at her clasped hands. On the way

24

over, she'd chewed her thumbnail down to the nub. "Got married. Dropped out. Divorced." This was the part where everyone always remained silent, waiting for the details, which Huck would not get. "It just didn't work out."

She seized another fry.

His expression grew serious, and he watched her chew. "Sorry to hear that."

Arianne nodded. Not as sorry as she was.

He slurped the last of his soda through the straw and pushed his remaining fries toward her. He leaned in, elbows on the table. "About the building…"

Here it comes. She snatched another fry.

"I don't know what you had worked out with my uncle, but between the taxes and insurance, I can't afford to let you to stay there rent free. I'm sorry, Arianne."

She lengthened her spine, raised her chin. "How much do you want in rent?"

"The market says it's worth a thousand dollars a month."

Her lids widened until she felt her eyes bulge. She'd be lucky to cover a quarter of that amount. "Outrageous!"

Huck shrugged. "Let's work something out, then. I can lower the rent to seven hundred and you can make the repairs yourself as needed—with my approval, of course. Or, if you can swing a thousand, I'll take the extra three hundred and put it toward repairs, then you can purchase the building with a loan, and I'll deduct the repair costs from the price. That's a steal considerin' you live there, too. What'd'ya say?"

Arianne opened her mouth, but no sound escaped. She closed it, blinking back tears. She couldn't afford either option. "I can't."

Huck looked away. "Buy it on contract? Balloon payments?"

She couldn't do anything other than what she was already doing. "No."

Huck dropped his head and let out a breath. "Then I can't help you."

Bile burned her throat. "What do you plan to do with it?"

"Turn it into something the town needs. A bait and tackle shop. Offer sporting goods supplies, kayaks, fishing nets, et cetera."

She studied his face, waiting for a grin. His mouth didn't budge.

Arianne tilted her chin and leaned closer. Anger burned her cheeks. She knew it wasn't fair to expect him to let her stay for free, but a roof over her daughter's head was more important than fishing poles. They were about to become *homeless*. "You think Pine Bay *needs* a bait and tackle shop?"

He frowned at her harsh tone, his old quarterback scowl coming out to play. "No less than a store dedicated to marital bliss, where, once the honeymoon's over, the happy couple runs to the nearest courthouse for a divorce."

A slap across the face would've hurt less.

Huck cleared his throat and glanced down at his wadded up napkin. "Sorry. I wasn't referring to...I didn't mean you, just..."

And there was that melody that played through all her disappointments. In came the percussion section, only this time it was in her head, the beat in her temples so violent, she could feel her pulse.

He stroked his forehead. "It's a bad location for a

bridal shop, anyway. Why don't I help you relocate?"

Did the buffoon still need a math tutor? If she couldn't afford rent, she couldn't afford to relocate. She'd never find a place cheaper than what he offered. "I can't do that either."

Huck's patience was waning as fast as her future. "If it helps, you can continue to rent the apartment upstairs for, I dunno, let's say two-fifty a month until you find another place."

"I…" She swallowed. "Thank you."

He scrubbed a hand down his face and blew out a loud breath. "Sorry I can't do more."

Reaching into his back pocket, he produced a folded document. The contract she'd signed with Martin. She skimmed the pages, skipping the legal jargon. *Thirty days to vacate the shop.*

Thirty days? The ramifications of this news hit her like a speeding train. She'd have to liquidate, practically give away her inventory, since she didn't have room in her shoebox apartment for storage. Find a way to pay off her creditors, her student loans. Let go of the last piece of herself she swore she'd make successful after Adam left. Prove her father wrong. Give it all up for what? To become a school janitor or a gas station attendant? She was a bridal consultant!

She tried to steady her voice, but her emotions betrayed her. "Please, Huck. I helped you out once, remember? Twelve years ago, when you begged me to tutor you so you could graduate. I had better things to do back then, but I took pity on you so you wouldn't be left behind, so you could better yourself. And you never came through with your end of the deal."

He seemed to consider it for three whole seconds then lowered his voice to a whisper. "I'm sorry,

Arianne. For then and now."

She stood from the bench. "That's it?"

He rose and palmed her cheek, eyes intense, full of something she couldn't decipher. At the moment, she didn't care. She was sick of things never working out for her. And how badly she wanted to fall into his arms right now.

Arianne jerked away and ran to her car.

All worker bees are female and specialize in a number of different tasks, such as foraging, caring for the queen, cleaning the hive, and converting pollen and nectar into honey.

4

That went as badly as he'd expected.

After Arianne disappeared into the parking lot, and the feel of her soft skin disappeared from his fingertips, Huck pitched his drink and uneaten fries in the trashcan, along with the pink camouflage Band-Aids he had stashed in back pocket, calling himself all kinds of idiot. Though he'd never shopped for anything pink in his life, that's what the kid wanted. And he'd promised her the day she fell that he'd bring them next time he saw her so she'd stop crying.

Female tears were bad enough, but when they came from something so small, it was torture.

He jogged down the steps to his Harley. The last thing he wanted to do was hurt Arianne again, but that pleading look in her eyes, the one that said she could see past the guy he was to the man he could be, had scared the spit out of him. Imagine *him* spooked by a five-foot bookworm. He'd helped birth calves bigger than she was.

He wasn't the man Arianne wanted him to be, plain and simple. Sure, the building was paid for, and he had a decent cushion in his savings account, but the taxes were a killer and he didn't have any obligation to support her financially. Plus, he refused to get too involved with a woman who had a kid. Arianne could stay in the apartment until she made other arrangements. She was smart. She'd get by.

He threw his leg over the seat and straddled his Harley, shoving away the guilt.

"Huck?"

The pubescent voice came from Matt, a thirteen-year-old giant from the Downeast Big Brother program. Husky jeans hung from the boy's skinny frame, paired with a faded sweatshirt that needed a good scrubbin'. How many times had he told that boy to wear a belt?

"Hey, buddy." Huck offered his fist and Matt bumped it. "What are you up to?"

Matt hiked up his pants with one hand and pointed to an older couple behind him with the other. "My grandparents are visiting from Ohio. Grandpa taught me how to change the oil in Mom's car today, and since I did such a good job, he's buying me dinner."

That explained the grease stains. "That's an important thing to learn."

Huck introduced himself to Matt's grandparents, Doreen and Ben.

"We've heard a lot about you," Doreen said, patting Matt's shoulder. "Thanks for volunteering. We're so glad to learn that both his grades and attitude have improved."

Heat rushed into Huck's neck. He was the furthest thing from a father figure, but he could at least be Matt's friend. "He's a good kid."

"Are we still on for Monday's game?" Matt's pants

started to slip, and he hoisted them up by the belt loops.

"You better show up with a belt."

"Yes, sir. Prepare to get creamed."

"You're crazy."

Matt's changing voice hit a high note. "I've mopped the floor with you the last four games."

OK, so basketball wasn't his thing. "Dream on, midget. Big Brother rules state I have to let you win."

Was he really trash talking with a teenager?

Matt stood taller. "How about a wager?"

"Depends. What'cha offerin'?"

Fuzz on the kid's upper lip shifted as Matt twisted his lips. "If I win, you let me ride your Harley."

Please. "If you win, I'll let you *sit* on my Harley."

"What?"

Huck shrugged. "Take it or leave it."

"I'll take it."

"Good. If I win, you do the dishes for your mom for a week."

"A week?" Matt groaned. "Deal. You won't win anyway."

After helping the kid off his ego, Huck left them to their dinner and drove south to Bar Harbor. The thirty-minute drive was just long enough to haunt him with images of Arianne in his arms, those red lips—he couldn't get past the red lips—smiling at him, her eyes trusting him for once. And that cute way she dropped the *R*'s when she spoke.

Even in her wallflower, tutoring days he'd had a thing for her. Still did. Something about her gentle nature, her quiet strength told him if a man was willing to let her, she'd make him her whole world. That was intimidating to a guy like him.

He turned at the light and squeezed into a small space between two parked cars. The Crabby Tavern, more restaurant than bar, was wedged between Whitley's Bookstore and Moby's Attic, an antique store that sold nautical items.

Uncle Marty had frequented the tavern for years. Being friends with the owner, his passing had earned him a memorial on their menu—Marty's Monster Burger. A half pound beef patty with all the fixin's, fried pickles, and a side of heart attack. Huck didn't have room for any more food, but he'd promised Don, the owner and chef, he'd stop by soon to see the picture of Uncle Marty that they'd put on the Wall of Fame.

He removed his helmet and ran his fingers through his hair. It wasn't right the old man was gone. Huck officially had no family.

The blue door of Whitley's Bookstore opened, and a brunette in skin-tight pants and high heels stepped onto the sidewalk empty-handed. Huck relaxed against the seat, one palm gripping the handlebar, the other resting on his thigh. She had his full attention.

Her head gave a double-take when she spotted him. Her dark eyes, almost black, drank him in. Her lazy smile told him she liked what she saw. He motioned her over with a nod. She stopped next to his bike and introduced herself. Giada.

An exotic scent clung to her olive skin.

Her low-cut blouse teased him.

Gorgeous.

They talked for a while, and Huck wasn't a bit surprised when she agreed to a ride. They always did.

He gripped the helmet and placed it on her head. His thumb brushed her soft chin as he secured the strap. Swinging her leg over the bike, she scooted close and wrapped her arms around his waist.

The Crabby Tavern could wait. Huck started the engine and revved the motor. The beast trembled beneath them. He backed out and snaked through town, opening full throttle when they reached the highway. Giada tightened her hold.

If he'd learned one thing from his string of stepfathers, it was this: the best way to forget one woman was to move on with the next.

~*~

Lights danced on the water. The full moon illuminated the entire night sky. Piano music floated through the air, weaving among the low hum of dialogue. Silverware clinked against fine china. Arianne hadn't been treated to a dinner this nice in…well, ever. She should be relishing this moment. But she wasn't.

Travis offered his arm, and Arianne hooked her fingers around it, noting the feathery touch of his expensive dress shirt. The silver hue brought out the gray threads around his ears. He smiled down at her as they followed the hostess to their table, the lines around his eyes deepening. He looked handsome.

She forced a smile, regretting her three-inch heels as she did her best not to walk like a duck. She hadn't inherited her mother's gracefulness.

Travis pulled out a mauve chair and slid it beneath her with perfect timing. They'd gone out a few times now. She liked him, but he wasn't *the one*. Then again, what did she know? Her ex-husband was *the one* and that time-bomb had exploded in her face.

The smell of melted butter and warm herbs filled the dining room. Everything on the menu looked delicious—and expensive. Would anyone actually pay that much for stuffed flounder?

After they ordered, Travis slid his hand across the cream tablecloth and folded it around hers. "You look ravishing tonight."

She glanced down at the red dress Missy had insisted she borrow. Arianne was still surprised it fit, though it was a little shorter and fit snugger around her hips than she liked. "Thank you. You look dashing yourself."

He asked about her day, concern knotting his brows. Apparently her acting skills needed work. She answered but omitted her eviction notice. She shook every time she thought about Huck Anderson. Once again, he'd killed her dream, making her feel the fool. She was. His touch was so warm and electrifying she'd almost given into it. Weak, stupid woman.

Travis listened intently as she answered his questions, joining the conversation instead of nodding with a blank stare like most men. In the flickering candlelight, she welcomed his rendition of what he called "a boring week." She craved boredom. The drama that had become her life was exhausting.

Travis told a really bad physiatrist joke, and she chuckled, even though she didn't find it funny. He laughed until his face turned purple, deepening laugh lines that didn't fully disappear with his smile. He might be older than she preferred, but he was stable, secure. Everything she wanted and needed. The smooth-talking, gorgeous types who promised adventure only left her heartbroken.

Could she make Travis be the one? She studied

him closely. There was something about him that nagged at her. Something she couldn't quite put her finger on.

The waitress brought their meals. Travis worked on his stuffed flounder, while Arianne picked at her shrimp linguine the way Emma did with broccoli. The pasta tasted divine, but every time she thought about Huck, which was every five seconds, her appetite vanished. No matter how romantic this date was, she couldn't unwind her brain from around her dilemma.

Chin up, Arianne. Things can only get better from here.

"Don't you like your meal?" The skin on Travis's forehead wrinkled.

Arianne smiled. "It's delicious, just very filling."

Thirty minutes later, the waitress left with their plates, promising to return with the leftovers. Arianne was wiping her mouth when a forty-something blonde in a fitted, sapphire dress approached their table. The woman's pulse ticked between her skeletal collarbones, and her thinning hands trembled as she glared at Travis.

His face drained of color. "Patricia."

The woman pursed her lips. "A patient emergency, huh?"

He fumbled for words. Pasta worked its way back up Arianne's throat. She didn't like where this was going.

The woman scowled at Arianne. "Exactly how long have you been seeing my husband?"

Arianne's heart lurched. *Husband?* That couldn't be right. She'd never date a married man. Wouldn't even flirt with one.

She glanced at Travis, waiting for him to introduce the woman as one of his mental patients who'd escaped the psych ward. When he didn't say a word, but answered with an embarrassed look laced with regret, she knew.

Boy, she could really pick 'em.

An eerie laugh filled Arianne's ears for minutes before she realized it was coming from her. Why was she laughing? This wasn't funny. Something had possessed her, and if she didn't laugh, she'd spontaneously combust in the middle of this restaurant.

Was this what it was like to go insane?

Travis and his wife watched her episode, mouths agape. Arianne needed to leave before Travis whipped out his license and had her committed. Arianne rose from her chair and turned to go.

Travis pushed back his chair and stood. "Arianne, wait."

The waitress returned, and Arianne swiped the box of fattening pasta from the woman's hands. She'd need some comfort when the shock wore off.

Weaving through the tables as fast as she could, attempting to escape an Oscar-worthy performance, her ankle twisted in her ridiculous heels, and she steadied herself on the passing sommelier. Chilled wine soaked the front of her dress.

And the award goes to…Arianne Winters.

Warmth flooded her cheeks, and she fled the restaurant. The cool night air brushed across her heated skin. She sucked it in like a fish gasping for water. Dare she wonder if this day could get any worse?

"Arianne." Travis's voice trailed behind her.

She wouldn't look at him. Couldn't.

His footsteps pounded closer. He touched her

elbow, and she jerked away.

"Arianne, I'm sorry."

Ahh! If one more person said that today, she'd commit herself. "How dare you, Travis? I am not that kind of woman."

The corners of his eyes and mouth drooped. Was he disappointed by his actions, or that she wasn't a floozy?

"We're technically separated. I filed for—"

"Save it!" She hobbled down the sidewalk and dug through the junk in her purse for her cellphone.

"At least let me drive you home."

No way was she giving him the opportunity to try to talk his way out. Arianne shook her head and continued limping, ignoring the stares from other couples entering the restaurant. Missy would rescue her.

It went straight to voicemail. Twice. Her shoulders wilted. She'd walk home if she had to. Stilettos and all.

An hour later, a cab driver deposited her safely at her front door. She'd refused to look at the meter on the way home, afraid the dollar amount would make her vomit in his backseat. The haul from Bar Harbor would cost a small fortune she didn't have. "How much do I owe you?"

"Nothing. Someone called the station and pre-paid before I picked you up."

Travis. Well, it was the least he could do.

"Thank you." She tipped him and exited the car.

"Have a good night."

She shut the door, and he pulled away from the curb, leaving her alone in the dark with the chirping crickets. "Too late for that."

On her way to the door, her heels clacked the

pavement, one scraping the concrete with every limp. Her ankle, now double in size, throbbed. Why not add lameness to this tragedy, too?

With a bump of her hip, the door unstuck from the frame. She stepped inside and turned on a nearby lamp. Missy was snoring like a hibernating bear, arms and legs sprawled all over the couch. Luckily Arianne hadn't inherited that.

She kicked off her heels and considered throwing one at Missy for persuading her to wear the absurd getup in the first place. But she didn't have the energy to argue, or recap the day's events. All she wanted to do was slip into her pajamas and bury herself under her blankets with a gigantic, triple-layered chocolate cake.

*Drifting: The return of field bees to colonies
other than their own.*

5

Steam lifted from Huck's coffee mug, and the young waitress offered a shy smile. She turned and weaved between the too close tables; the white ribbon in her hair bounced with her ponytail. Huck dug his fork into the cheesy hash brown casserole. Mmm, just like Mama never used to make.

Giada nibbled her unbuttered whole-wheat toast. No wonder the woman was as skinny as a porch post. In the two weeks since they'd met—and they'd been spending a lot of time together—she'd hardly eaten a thing.

The man next to them vacated his table, leaving behind a few dollar bills and a newspaper. Lips pressed against the mug in his left hand, Huck stretched across the tabletop with his right, sliding the paper toward him as he read the front page headline.

Couture Bridal Salon's Grand Opening in Bar Harbor.

He relaxed against the padded booth, skimming the article. Arianne had serious competition. Like he'd told her before, Pine Bay wasn't a good location for a bridal shop. He'd given her several options, and she'd refused them all. He was done feeling guilty. He wasn't cut out to be anyone's knight in shining armor.

Least of all hers.

"Find something interesting?" Giada sipped her skim milk.

He tossed the paper aside. "Not a thing."

She glanced down at the paper. "Well, look at that." She pointed to the picture accompanying the article.

The photo showed headless mannequins in wedding dresses. Giada's long, white-tipped fingernail rested on one in the middle. "That's my wedding gown."

Huck choked on his last bite of maple pancakes. "You're married?"

She didn't wear a ring. He always checked for a ring.

Giada laughed. "Not yet. But when I do, that's the one." She continued tapping the dress with her fingernail, her face dreamy.

Huck ran a hand along his neck. "You've picked out a dress before you're even engaged?"

"Of course." She took another sip. "I've been planning my wedding since I was five."

He crumpled his napkin beneath the table.

"Don't look at me like that, Huck. All girls do. It's perfectly normal."

Normal? Planning from childhood the million ways to make a man miserable wasn't normal. The process never took his mother that long. She could ruin a man from start to finish in less than a week.

"When the right man comes along, a girl wants to be ready."

Time to go.

Throwing his head back, he downed his remaining coffee. "I've got to get back to the farm."

She placed her hand on his arm as he stood to go. "I didn't mean to scare you off." She pulled him down next to her. "I wasn't proposing, you know."

"Good thing."

"And why is that?" She leaned close, brushing the end of his nose with hers.

He hooked a finger below her chin and gave her a quick kiss. "I'd have left you disappointed."

She laughed as if she didn't believe him.

"Meet you outside." He tossed the tip on the table and joined his favorite waitress at the cash register. Her blue uniform enhanced the blue flecks hidden in her gray eyes, their edges weary and wrinkled. He'd never known his granny, but he imagined she was just like Marge.

"This is the third time you've treated her to breakfast this week." Marge hiked her chin toward Giada. "You plan on keeping her around awhile?"

He twisted, looking across the diner at Giada, who was finishing her milk. Why did she have to go and mention marriage? They'd been getting along so well.

He passed Marge a twenty.

Gorgeous or not, he refused to sleep on floral bed sheets with lacey pillows or shower with fancy monogramed towels. "You're my favorite girl, Marge. I can't go givin' my heart away to just anyone."

Marge plucked the bill from his hand, and the register popped open. She grinned, revealing a pink lipstick smudge on her teeth. "Flattery will get you everywhere, Huck. I haven't been a girl in over fifty years." She stretched across the counter and squeezed his forearm. "Thank you, handsome. You made my day."

He winked, refused his receipt, and then turned

the knob on the toothpick holder.

"I hope you settle down one of these days. Though I expect it'll take a very special woman to win you over."

He popped the wood sliver into his mouth. "I pity the woman who tries."

She cackled. "Me too."

The only woman who'd come close was living in his building, reminding him of everything he wasn't.

As Marge vanished into the kitchen, Huck noticed her worn tennis shoes. The widow worked hard for not much pay, he presumed. He tugged an extra twenty from his wallet and dropped it into a glass jar labeled *Marge*, where customers could leave notes and extra tips for the veteran staff.

He stepped through the door and into the sun. Huck straddled his bike and slipped on his helmet. The Harley's black leather seat warmed his thighs. It was a perfect morning for a ride—cloudless sky, sunshine, the freedom of the open road.

Freedom.

Giada joined him, her black bag secured diagonally across her loose white shirt. She kissed his cheek, put on her helmet, settled on the seat behind him, and wrapped her arms around his waist.

He fired the engine. The bike rumbled out of the parking lot. They coasted down the narrow two-lane highway, gliding along the smooth blacktop. Wind wrestled his T-shirt.

The road dipped and curved around a small cove. A pebbled shoreline bordered the water, reflecting pine trees on the glassy surface. Mountains covered the distance on both sides.

Marriage. Though Giada's hands only gripped his

waist, he felt them tightening around his neck too.

Nope. When a man shared his name in matrimony, his freedom was gone. He refused to give this up for anyone. Better not to commit to a woman at all than to change his mind later.

The speedometer climbed. They raced toward Somes Sound, leaving all voices of commitment and regret in the wind. He didn't need anyone or anything. He controlled his own life, his own destiny.

He and he alone.

The engine zipped louder. Adrenaline surged through his veins. He gripped the handlebars and hugged the curve.

The grill of a black Cadillac. In his lane. His pulse switched gears.

A rock wall flanked his right. He jerked the handlebars left and skidded into the next lane. Screeching tires slid onto loose gravel. He lost control. The bike flipped. The stench of burning rubber filled his nose.

They slammed into the guard rail. Indescribable pain shot through his body. His skin was on fire. For a second, he went airborne then hit the pavement. Metal crunched. A scream pierced the air right before his world went black.

Women became prominent beekeepers during and after the Civil War, when their men returned wounded. Or dead.
—Bees in America: How the Honeybee Shaped a Nation *by Tammy Horn, The University Press of Kentucky, 2005*

6

Arianne climbed the steps outside her shop to her second-floor apartment. Her feet weighed as heavy as her heart. She struggled with the door that had swelled in its frame from the summer heat and stopped the complaint rising to her lips. At least she still had a home. With a bump of her hip, the door gave way easier than expected, and she dropped the mail to the living room floor.

"Mommy!" Emma threw her arms around Arianne's knees.

Arianne gripped the doorknob for support and rubbed Emma's head. "Hey, princess. What'cha been up to?"

"Watching *Beauty and the Beast*." Emma bounced on her tiptoes. "Aunt Missy let me paint her toenails."

"She did?"

"Uh, huh. She said I make a great bootishan."

Arianne stepped into the room and closed the door so the air whirring from the window air conditioner didn't escape. "Maybe after supper, I'll let you paint mine."

Emma beamed. "Yay, but you have to sit still." She gestured for Arianne to lean her ear closer. "Aunt Missy's not very good at that," she whispered.

"She never has been," Arianne whispered back.

Mrs. Potts's voice floated from the TV while Belle twirled around the ballroom in a golden gown.

"How'd it go?" Missy entered from the kitchen with cotton balls wedged between her toes. The pristine bubblegum-pink paint was too perfect to be Emma's handiwork. Missy grabbed the remote and tuned to an entertainment news program.

"Exactly how I thought it would." Arianne picked up the envelopes off the floor and tossed the stack on her desk. "They turned down my loan."

Missy scrunched her face. "Bummer." She returned her attention back to the TV. "I can't wait to see Matt Damon's new movie."

Not quite the word Arianne would use to sum up the predicament, but, yeah, *bummer*. "Who cares about movies when there's real news going on in the world?" She seized the remote from Missy and flipped to a local news station.

Missy scowled. "What are you going to do now?"

Arianne had two weeks to make a decision. Stay and fight, or go. She had a valid case in court, since Martin had allowed her to stay rent-free for almost a year now, and she had an eyewitness to their verbal agreement. Problem was a lawyer would want payment for his services. Money she didn't have. "I don't know yet."

"Well, I started supper, but you'll have to put it in the oven. I've got a date." Missy inspected her fresh pedicure.

"Hope it goes better than mine did." Arianne sank onto the couch.

"A date with Hannibal Lector would go better than yours did."

Arianne frowned. "Thanks for your support."

The humiliation of her date with Travis was still so fresh, it was like pouring turpentine on an open wound. A couch spring bore into her tailbone, and she shifted to find a more comfortable spot. "What'd you fix for supper?"

"Lasagna." Missy smoothed her khaki miniskirt.

Whatever Hannibal served for dinner had to taste better than Missy's lasagna. She was an even worse cook than Arianne.

Arianne waved. "Good luck."

Missy knelt to buckle the thin ankle strap of her new sandals then plucked out all the cotton from between her toes. "Look at it this way, your next date has to go better than your last one."

Next time? There wouldn't be a next time. Arianne had officially given up. Her Elvis had left the building.

Missy left, deserting the cotton balls on the carpet. Arianne's gaze roamed the small apartment. Dirty laundry overflowed the hamper and spilled into the hallway. Was it asking too much of her sister to help out? She'd babied Missy far too much when their mother died, but her sister had been just a toddler at the time, and Arianne had known Missy needed her. Except now, Missy relied on everyone to do everything for her.

Arianne leaned her head against the back of the couch and closed her eyes. The voices on TV mingled with her exhausted emotions and beckoned her closer to sleep.

How she craved a man's strong arms right now, a deep voice to whisper assurances that all would be fine as long as they had each other. To know at the end of a long, hard day, she had someone to come home to. Of course, she had her precious daughter, but motherly love couldn't fill all the rooms in her heart.

Would she ever know a real family again?

"Mommy, can I take a bath? Aunt Missy said I could use her new vanilla bubble bath."

Arianne opened one eye.

Emma clasped her purple skirt and danced on her toes. Gold curls bounced around her cheeks.

"All right, but when you're done, you have to pick up your toys."

Emma hung her head, and her shoulders wilted in a dramatic performance. She released a long, exasperated sigh. "Yes, Mommy." In slow motion, Emma trudged to the bathroom.

"Drama queen." Arianne forced her legs to stand and listened to the news anchor on TV discuss the wreckage lying behind him. The guardrail was mangled, and the black Cadillac was completely smashed in on one side. Motorcycle parts lay strewn across the highway.

She cringed. On her way to the bathroom, she silently prayed for the victim's safety. The words "Huck Anderson" stopped her cold. She raced back to the television. Her fingers fumbled to increase the volume.

The camera faded to a female reporter at the station, who reminded viewers the clip was filmed earlier that morning and that Highway 233 was now clear and open for traffic. Another news anchor began an interview with the new superintendent for Hancock

County schools.

What about Huck? Arianne's heart raced as she sped through the channels, searching for another news station reporting the accident. She fought the urge to shake the TV.

Her heart stumbled over the thousand questions running through her brain. Was he alive? She recalled the metal pieces that littered the road and winced. It would take a miracle to survive that.

Tears burned her eyes. She'd wanted an escape from the eviction, but this wasn't the solution she had in mind.

~*~

Disinfectant and bad cafeteria food assaulted Arianne as she walked the cold hallway toward the ICU. She hated hospitals. Every experience she'd had in one always ended with a loved one dying. Memories of her beautiful mother lying pale in a hospital bed, wrapped in thin, white blankets, clinging to life, soured her stomach.

Huck's alive. She'd comforted herself with those words repeatedly since yesterday morning. After Channel 5 reported that Huck was air-lifted to Bangor Regional Hospital, she'd called a hundred times until she spoke to a nurse willing to at least admit he was still breathing. She thanked God again for His mercy.

Huck's passenger, however...Arianne's heart broke for the woman's family.

Goosebumps crawled along her skin. She shivered and rubbed her palms up and down her arms. Hospitals were always so cold. Why hadn't she brought a sweater?

A nurses' station came into view at the end of the hall. She passed an empty gurney. A small family stood in a patient's doorway, weeping. Death was evident all around her.

Would they let her see Huck? Was she ready to see him?

She inched to the nurses' station. "I'm here to see Huck Anderson."

The nurse looked up from a stack of charts and slipped a pencil behind her ear. Arianne recognized her instantly. Lucy Cosgrove, former head-cheerleader and homecoming queen. Still slim, still gorgeous. The blonde highlights in her dark hair reflected the fluorescent lights. "Name, please."

"Arianne Winters."

Lucy plucked a chart from a metal divider and opened it. "I'm sorry, but you're not listed as—" Her eyes narrowed and she leaned her head to the side. Then her brows arched and crinkled her forehead. "Arianne, from Ellsworth High? "

Arianne nodded.

"Gosh, it's been a long time." Lucy plunked down the chart and sped around the desk, her mouth gaping as if a dentist were about to inspect her molars. "Look at you. What a transformation."

Was that a compliment? Arianne resisted the urge to pick Lucy's chin up off the floor.

"I just can't believe it. I hardly recognized you."

Heat filled her cheeks, and Arianne swallowed the rising anger. "Thank you." *I think.* She was surprised Lucy remembered her at all. The pair had been best friends until the fourth grade, when Arianne's mother died. After that, they grew apart. Lucy was never unkind to Arianne, but she didn't pay her any attention, either.

"Do you think Huck's feeling up to visitors today?"

Lucy finally gained control of her mouth and curled it into a smile. "That's right. I forgot you two were related. Cousins or something, right?" She went back to the desk and opened Huck's chart, writing something in with the pencil she'd removed from behind her ear.

Arianne had no idea what Lucy was talking about, but knew the ICU wouldn't allow her to see Huck unless she was family, so she chose to remain silent. Maybe Lucy was offering her a little grace.

"I wrote your name down so you won't have any trouble getting past the desk from now on. He's in room 204. Follow me."

A buzzer sounded and a large automatic door swung open. Lucy stepped through with Arianne at her heels.

"I'm so glad you're here, Arianne." Lucy picked lint off her black scrubs. "He's really bad. The doctors rushed him into surgery as soon as he got here, and he's been in a medically induced coma ever since. He's got two more surgeries scheduled this week, if his internal swelling subsides enough."

Tears filled Arianne's eyes, but she blinked them away and focused on Lucy's tennis shoes squeaking against the floor. "So, he doesn't know that the woman with him died?"

They'd reached room 204, and Lucy gave her arm a gentle squeeze. "No." She stared at the floor as if trying to control her emotions as well. "Don't stay too long or Nurse Vivian will run you off. She's worse than the National Guard."

Lucy walked away, leaving Arianne alone in the open doorway. The hospital walls shrunk around her, and her head buzzed and swam as if she'd taken something awful.

What would she see when she walked in? Would Huck live through all this?

She swallowed and stepped inside. A blue curtain engulfed the corner, hiding him. Her gaze followed the maze of tracks on the ceiling. She tugged at the curtain enough to see the patient.

A mummified Huck filled the narrow bed, his limbs cradled with pillows and slings. Tubes ran in and out of him like tunnels of a tiny subway system. Black eyes framed the white medical tape on his nose. Arianne's insides folded.

Huck's chest rose and fell to the rhythm of the ventilator. Arianne stared, her stomach turning at the thought of a machine keeping him alive. She tip-toed to the bed and dared to stroke her fingertips along his knuckles protruding from the full arm cast. His skin was clammy. She ran her hand along the thin blanket spilling over the mattress. She'd be sure to ask a nurse for another one.

The curtain rolled in its track. A tall, skinny man with white hair stood with a stethoscope in his hand. Teal scrubs extended from the knees to his matching rubber shoes.

"I'm sorry. I didn't realize he had company. I'm Doctor Reynolds." He draped the stethoscope around his neck and extended his hand. "And you are?"

She placed her hand in his. "Arianne Winters."

He nodded. "Do you know of anyone else we need to contact? We've had a difficult time locating family members."

To her knowledge Martin never had any children, so she wasn't sure if Huck had real cousins out there somewhere or not. His mother was deceased. Had he ever met his dad? The thought brought fresh tears. How horrible to almost die alone. "I'm all he has."

The doctor nodded.

"Is he going to pull through?"

He checked his watch. "At this point, there are no guarantees. It'd be easier for me to tell you what isn't damaged than to go through the list of what is. I'm scheduled to be in surgery in ten minutes, but I wanted to come by and check on him. I'd like to meet with you tomorrow morning to discuss his injuries and a plan for long-term care. Will ten o'clock work for you?"

"I can arrange it." *What am I doing?* She had no authority to make medical decisions for him, or to be involved in any way for that matter. But if she didn't do it, who would?

"If you have any questions in the meantime, please see a nurse."

He left the room and her attention shifted to the monitors. Rainbows of light flashed his vital signs. Daylight filtered in through the thick blinds, spilling over this larger-than-life man a breath away from losing it all. What a long recovery ahead.

Huck's eyelids quivered. Arianne prayed that his dreams brought him comfort.

"He is not worthy of the honeycomb, that shuns the hives because the bees have stings."
—William Shakespeare

7

Had he swallowed sandpaper? Were his eyelids taped shut? Every bone in his body screamed in pain. That must've been some party. This was, by far, the worst hangover on record.

Huck forced his eyes open and met toes peeking from a cast. His eyes crossed as he focused on the white spot on his throbbing nose. He tried to pull it off, but his arm was restricted by a sling. Tubes snaked from his arms to machines beside his bed. Was he in the hospital? His muscles tensed, adding to the agony.

"Good. You're awake." A woman in black scrubs entered his line of hazy vision. She scooted a chair next to his bed and leaned her elbow on the mattress. "Remember me, Quarterback?"

Quarterback. Now it made sense. He'd been injured during a game. Except he didn't remember playing a game. With as little movement as possible, he assessed the damage to his body again. The guys on the other team must've been huge. How would this affect his scholarship?

She patted his arm. "It's fine if you don't remember. I'm Lucy Cosgrove. We went to school together."

Went. So, this wasn't a football injury?

She held up a Styrofoam cup. "Thirsty?"

She had no idea. He gave a stiff nod, disappointed when she spooned ice chips into his mouth. He wanted water. A gallon.

After another spoonful, she placed the cup on the table. "That's enough for now. You're scheduled for a swallow test first thing tomorrow. If you pass that you can have water." She turned and added something to his IV. "This will help with any pain."

Lucy removed the oxygen tube from his nose, which made him want to howl. "Your oxygen level is good, so I'm going to give you a break."

From the look of things, he didn't need any more breaks.

She paused beside his bed, frowning at him, hands on her hips. "Do you remember why you're here?" Her voice was low, cautious.

He barely shook his head. His nose burned with a sneeze, and he held his breath, willing it to pass. A sneeze might kill him.

"You were in a motorcycle accident twelve days ago on Highway 233. The driver of the other vehicle had a heart attack and veered into your lane. You swerved to miss and lost control of your motorcycle."

Screeching tires rang in his ears. Memories slammed into him like a sledgehammer—the diner, the wind, the black Cadillac, his body contorting through the air.

Giada.

He closed his eyes and nodded once.

"You remember. That's an excellent sign." She touched his arm. "You're lucky to be alive. Good thing

54

you were wearing a helmet."

He looked at her. What about Giada? Was she wearing a helmet? He couldn't remember.

"Your cousin, Arianne, was here earlier." She walked to the dry-erase board covered with medical code and checkmarks. The marker squeaked across the board's slick surface.

Cousin? He didn't have any cousins. Huck spoke Giada's name, but it came out like a hound dog with a mouth full of mashed potatoes.

Lucy's smile fell. "I know you have questions, but right now you need to rest." She pulled the blankets up to his neck. "Hang in there. I'll be back to check on you."

What about Giada? Dread crushed his chest.

The room got blurry.

She patted his shoulder and left. He tried to call after her, but fire shot through his bottom lip. He worked his tongue over the roughness. Stiches?

The torture in his body eased, and his head clouded in a thick fog. Giada filled his mind as his heavy eyelids closed.

~*~

Arianne stared out the bridal shop window, gnawing her thumbnail. Fingers snapped in front of her face.

"Earth to Arianne. Hello?"

She turned to Missy. "I'm sorry. What did you say?"

Missy studied her. "What's up with you?"

"Nothing." Arianne straightened the business cards and sale flyers behind the register. Anything to distract her mind from the mess she was in.

Her sister leaned against the glass counter, palms spread wide. "Yeah, right. Spill it."

"I just cleaned that. Now your fingerprints are all over the glass."

Missy rolled her eyes. "The first customer that walks in here is going to mess it up anyway."

Arianne glanced around the empty shop. *If* she had any customers today.

"Look, I'll clean it up while you tell me what's wrong. Beside the fact that you're OCD."

Arianne plunked the cleaner and a roll of paper towels onto the counter and shoved them at her sister. "I've made a bad situation worse."

Missy pushed up her silver bracelets and sprayed the counter. "You're going to have to elaborate."

"I visited Huck in the hospital last Tuesday and let the nurse assume I was his cousin so she'd let me in the ICU. While I was there, the doctor came in, and I was afraid he would kick me out, so I let him believe I was Huck's cousin, too."

A dramatized gasp escaped Missy, and she covered her mouth with her hand. "You lied?"

"Omitted."

Missy rolled her eyes and chuckled. "Is that what's got your granny panties in a knot?"

Arianne snatched the window cleaner and pointed to the counter. "I *don't* wear granny panties. And put some elbow grease into it. I don't want any streaks." She returned the bottle to a cabinet beneath the register. "A lie is a lie, Missy. No matter how it's presented. But no, that's not the entire reason I'm upset. That's just what started it all."

Missy made a rolling motion with her finger,

signaling for Arianne to get to the point. Then she scrubbed the paper towel over the counter once more.

"Huck doesn't have any other living family members, and they think I'm his cousin, so the doctor gave me the information regarding his care. The nurse called around noon and said Huck woke from his coma yesterday—which is wonderful—but the doctor wants to meet with me again tomorrow to discuss further treatment and give instructions on how to care for him once he's released."

She shivered. "And Huck still doesn't know the woman riding with him died."

Missy wadded the paper towel and tossed it in the trash can. "I'm still failing to see the problem here."

Arianne gripped the glass counter in frustration. "Aren't you listening? They think *I'm* going to take care of him when he's released. Huck's going to be livid when he finds out I lied, and the doctors have shared all his personal information with me. I'm supposed to have everything out of here by the end of next week." She drew a deep breath and exhaled slowly. "And on top of that, the doctor wants me to be there for moral support when they tell him about his girlfriend, or whoever she was."

Missy swatted Arianne's hands. "I just cleaned that, you know."

Arianne stormed away and went to her office to check on Emma. Her sister could be so insensitive sometimes. Arianne complimented Emma's picture of a princess, kissed her cheek, then lumbered back into the shop to fluff the mannequin's dress for the hundredth time.

"You might have something going here." Missy turned from side to side, admiring her reflection in the floor-length mirror. Her red-and-white, nautical-style shirt matched perfectly with her white shorts and gold sandals.

"What do you mean?"

"I mean, this situation could work to your advantage."

"A woman died, Missy. I have no desire to *work it to my advantage*."

Missy waved her hand. "I'm not talking about that part." She joined Arianne by the mannequin. "Think about it. *You* need Huck to let you stay here. *He* needs someone to care for him when he leaves the hospital."

Arianne released her hold on the lace veil and raised her brows.

Missy smacked her forehead. "For a brainiac, you can be so dense sometimes. Make a deal with Huck. Tell him you'll take care of him if he'll let you stay."

Arianne gazed around the shop. Missy's suggestion was looking like her only option. Huck had no one, and if he tossed her out, she'd be homeless. Maybe they could help each other. Of course, they'd tried that once before, and he didn't keep his end of the bargain. But they were adults now, and he had offered other scenarios in lieu of eviction. She could trust him this time around. Couldn't she?

E.B. White, author of children's classic Charlotte's Web, *wrote a poem in* The New Yorker *(1945) criticizing the development of artificial insemination of queen bees.*

8

Huck jolted awake. His heart slammed against his ribs. Sweat beaded his temples. As his surroundings became clearer, he took a deep breath and pushed the crash's replay from his mind.

If only he could do the same with his injuries.

He turned his head to the dry side of the pillow. Arianne perched at the edge of a chair in the corner, ankles crossed. Pink flip-flops matched her wrinkled shirt, and her jeans had a small hole in the knee. A messy pile of curls was secured on top of her head. The only thing he could imagine looking better was a T-bone steak. If those nurses didn't start feeding him some real food around here...

Arianne stood and approached his bedside, rubbing her palms across her thighs. Her fingers trembled. A strange look that bordered on guilty crossed her face, puckering the skin on her cute little forehead. "How are you feeling today?"

Huck cleared his throat and eyed the cup beside his bed. "Like I've been hit by a car."

"Can I get you anything?"

His stomach gnawed his backbone. "Yeah, a 12-

ounce steak, medium rare, a baked potato with butter and sour cream, and a dozen yeast rolls. Can you do that for me?"

She bit her bottom lip and shook her head.

"Come on, have a heart. All they've fed me the past twenty-four hours is ice chips and chicken broth. I'm starving."

"I'm sorry, but it's liquids only right now."

"How 'bout a beer then?"

Another no. Why did she ask if she was going to deny every request?

He shifted to relieve his stiff muscles and released a groan. The morphine kept him fairly comfortable, and he'd done nothing except sleep. At the moment, he'd give everything he owned to get out of this bed.

When Lucy—he finally remembered her—had checked his vitals this morning, she told him they'd start weaning him off the morphine and start him on a lesser controlled substance. Every nurse who made an appearance dashed in and out, dancing around his questions as though they had something to hide. The boulder in his gut told him he didn't want to know the answers.

"Come to inspect the damage?" The skin beneath the medical tape on his nose itched.

Arianne swallowed, and for a moment he wondered if she was going to get sick. "Huck, please, don't be mad." She licked her lips. "I—"

A doctor burst into the room. Tall, lanky, covered in blue scrubs.

"I'm Dr. Reynolds. I've been overseeing your care since you arrived. How are you feeling?"

Couldn't everyone tell just by looking at him? "Peachy. Although, I'd feel even better if you'd remove this catheter."

"That'll come with time." The doc pulled up a vacant chair as if he intended to stay awhile.

"So, what's the damage, Doc?"

A rustling noise came from the corner. Arianne was back in the chair, clutching her hands together so tightly her fingers turned purple. The scared look she'd given him earlier intensified. What was going on?

Doc explained the three surgeries he'd performed and went through Huck's injuries in a medical language he didn't understand. What did a spleen do anyway? His brain reeled. He'd really lost twelve days of his life in a coma?

"Your left fibula gave a clean break, along with a hairline fracture to the femur. Your pelvis—"

"Enough mumbo-jumbo." Huck couldn't process any more. No matter how bad the news was, he needed answers now. "How much longer until I'm back to normal?"

Doc glanced at Arianne. "Best case scenario, six to nine months to a full recovery, including physical therapy. Possibly longer."

The room tilted. He'd go insane lying in a bed for six months. "How long before I can walk?"

"Unassisted—four to five months. If your healing continues to progress, we hope to release you by the end of next week."

Huck exhaled a loud breath. What about his bees? The honey? The farm?

Matt. Who would watch out for him?

The doc nodded at Arianne. What weren't they telling him?

Arianne stood and paced, thumbnail between her teeth.

Giada. The weight of a semi-truck settled over him. "What is it?"

Doc leaned forward, palms on his knees. "What I'm about to tell you isn't going to be easy to hear. I asked your cousin to join us today since she's agreed to oversee your recovery. Every patient needs moral support."

"*What?*" Huck shot a glance at Arianne. She winced.

"The passenger with you that day," Doc said. "What was your relationship to her?"

Acid burned his throat. "We were dating." He forced himself to ask the question. "How is she?"

"She was pronounced dead at the scene. I'm sorry."

His gut twisted and he leaned his head over the side of the bed to puke. Doc rushed at him with a bed pan, but there was nothing in Huck's gut. He dry-heaved.

Huck caught his breath, fighting the pain.

Doc patted his back. "I'll give you some time to process this. We'll set you up with a counselor, and we've got a full staff if you need anything."

The door opened then closed. Huck shut his eyes.

He'd killed someone.

Giada would never take another breath because of him. He should've died instead. She had a family. He didn't.

A tornado howled inside him.

Fingers brushed through the hair at his temple. He turned to find Arianne at his bedside. Tears glazed her cheeks. "Are you OK?"

Anger replaced despair. He'd forgotten she was here. He didn't like the piteous way she watched him, how exposed he felt right now. "What's your angle, Arianne?"

She flinched at his growl. "What do you mean?"

"Don't play games with me. My cousin? Why did you tell the doctor you'd see to my care?"

"We don't have to talk about this now."

"Yes. We do." Anything to take his mind off death.

She lowered onto the mattress. The warmth from her hip seeped through the thin blanket into the part of his thigh that wasn't casted. "You don't have anyone else. Do you?"

Her words were soft, careful.

He turned away at the brutal reminder. She touched his chin and gently turned his head back around.

"I thought we could help each other."

Here was the catch.

"I'll see you through your entire recovery. All I ask is that you let me stay in the shop in the meantime. I'll still pay rent for the apartment and help in any other way I can. Give me time to get back on my feet, and I'll help you get back on yours."

Huck's skin heated. No way. He could barely look at her after what he'd done. "I'll hire a nurse."

She wrapped her arms around her middle. "I made it halfway through medical school, so I'll make as good a nurse as anyone. The price of in-home care is outrageous, and with me you won't be out any money."

Like he was worried about money right now.

She folded her hands together. "We worked toward a goal together once before and succeeded."

Somehow he always managed to hurt those around him. He couldn't chance it. Not with Arianne.

The kid. What if… His eyes watered. Nose burned. "Get out."

"Huck…"

He turned his head away. "Get out!"

The mattress lifted and so did the warmth. The door clicked shut behind the curtain.

~*~

"Thanks." The phone threatened to slip from Huck's splinted fingers.

"You're welcome." His nurse pointed to a button on the keypad with a picture of a microphone. "If it's easier, you can press that and it will go on speaker." She dialed the first of two phone numbers she'd looked up for him earlier then left the room.

It rang three times before Jude answered. "How'ya doing, Huck?"

Jude was an expert beekeeper who worked closely with the local college. They'd met through Maine's Beekeeper Association a few years back and had taught some workshops together.

"I've been better." Asking someone to run his farm really stuck in his craw. He'd combed every possibility the last three days, and since he'd come to the conclusion he didn't have a choice, he wanted a man he trusted. Jude knew his craft, and Huck would recoup easier knowing his farm was in seasoned hands. "Listen, I'm gonna be down for the next six months or so and wondered if you'd be available to run things for me 'til I get back on my feet."

"Six months?" Jude paused. "What in the world happened?"

"Had a motorcycle accident a few weeks ago. Doc

says it'll be Christmas before I'm running any marathons."

"Man, I hate to hear that. Say, you're not talking about that accident at Somes Sound?"

Huck glanced at his mummified body. The memory of Giada's scream piercing the air made his stomach roil. "That's the one."

"I'm sorry. I'll help in any way I can. Sherry and I were on vacation when it happened. We heard about it when we got home, but we hadn't heard it was you."

Huck swallowed. "I had everything caught up before the accident. If you could just give all the hives a once over in the next few days, I'd really appreciate it."

Huck gave him the address, told him where to find the spare key and where he kept his tools and supplies. "Doc plans to release me from my cell sometime next week, so we can talk more then. In the meantime, if you need anything, call me at the hospital." He rattled off the number.

"Will do."

"One more thing. You don't happen to know any nurses in need of a job do you?"

"Sure don't. Why?"

"Never mind. I've got someone taking care of the house, and me, once I get home. If you see a blonde woman with a little girl, they've got my permission to be there."

"Got it."

"Thanks, Jude."

The phone disconnected in Huck's ear.

He groaned against the rage and despair crashing against his insides like waves during a hurricane. Why did this happen? It should've been him.

His vision blurred and he blinked to clear it.

Yawned. Best to get this over with before the morphine took full effect and he started making all kinds of crazy promises. With clumsy fingers, he dialed the number and brought the phone to his ear.

"Hello?"

Huck's throat closed. He couldn't do this.

"Hello? Is anyone there?"

He forced his teeth to unclench. "Arianne."

A pause. "Huck?"

"We've got a deal."

"If you want to harvest honey, don't kick over the beehive."
— *Abraham Lincoln*

9

Arianne still couldn't believe it.

Huck wasn't thrilled with the arrangement. He'd made that clear over the phone. Well, she wasn't either, but neither of them had a choice, so they'd find a way to survive.

The morning sun burst through the passing rainclouds, bathing the earth in gold. Moisture still saturated the pavement, and she slowed the car as the road looped around Somes Sound. The guardrail to her left was mangled. Broken glass still lay on the highway's shoulder to her right.

She cupped her hand over her mouth. *Thank you, Lord, for keeping Huck alive.*

Summerville was farther from her shop than she preferred, but if it gave her almost a year to get her affairs straightened out, she'd gladly drive the extra twenty-five miles. She'd only been through the village once, on the way home from camping with her dad at Seawall, Acadia National Park, when she was twelve. What had brought Huck way out here?

A few miles down the road, a wooden bench rested on a grassy knoll, tucked peacefully in the corner of an inlet. Sea hawks scavenged the ground, slicing through the morning fog. Across the water, a roofline peeked from a pine grove. She pulled over and rolled down her window, inhaling the salty air. The landscape was straight out of a storybook. Surely this wasn't Huck's place.

The number on the mailbox matched the one he'd told her, and the names Anderson and Summerville Honey were hand painted on the side. She flipped on her turn signal and started up the gravel.

The driveway was a bridge with a white-washed railing built across the marsh. A two-story, white, vinyl-sided house with black shutters reflected off the water. Red geraniums spilled from the window boxes. She checked the address again. It was too beautiful to be real.

An old pickup, a perfect blend of sea foam green and rust, was parked by the back door, advertising *Summerville Honey* in black script. She pulled next to the vehicle and stopped, staring in disbelief. A curved footbridge started behind a garden shed that looked like a miniature version of the house. Beyond the bridge lay a field dotted with buttercups.

Arianne glanced in her rearview mirror at Emma sleeping in the backseat. For the next half-year at least, they'd live in a real home, not a cramped apartment that froze in winter and suffocated in summer. Emma would have a place to run and play.

She rolled down the other windows, turned off the engine, and exited the car. Her heels caught in the gravel as she walked to the front door. They'd woken early that morning to attend Sunday school. With a nice breeze blowing and the car parked in the shade, she'd let Emma sleep. It wouldn't take long to gather the items Huck had asked her to bring.

Two doors welcomed her on the front porch, separated by a single rocking chair. The home was a duplex, more or less, the way Huck described it. Separate sleeping quarters and bathrooms and a shared kitchen. He'd said it was built by Colonel Sanders in 1765 with the east wing built to accommodate his widowed mother-in-law. Huck had begged her to bring fried chicken too, so she'd assumed that was the medication talking. Different Colonel Sanders.

A spare key waited beneath the welcome mat, just as Huck had said. Unsure which door was hers, she picked one, unlocked it, and stepped inside. Beige carpet stretched down the hall and up the stairs. The rooms were furnished with utilitarian furniture, and the closets and cabinets were empty. This must be her and Emma's quarters.

She explored her way to the other side and halted as she reached the kitchen. Crusted, dirty dishes overflowed the sink, stacked like an abstract sculpture made by cavemen. Newspapers, honey jar labels, and an empty pizza box littered the countertops.

"And Huck enters stage left," she mumbled.

A quick survey of his living quarters proved once again that her new arrangement wouldn't be easy.

One glance at his bathroom and she closed the door, afraid it would cause nightmares. His bedroom wasn't any better. A twisted mass of sheets and blankets on the bed. Dirty laundry covered the floor. She tip-toed to the dresser for his things in fear a living creature might emerge from the mess and nip her ankles.

Yes, she was being dramatic, but she'd forgotten how messy men could be.

Despite disaster, the room smelled like him—a mix of earth and women-find-me-irresistible cologne. After she gathered his requested belongings, she made a mental note of all the chores that needed to be done. Seemed she had a date after all—with Mr. Clean and a large can of disinfectant. Huck couldn't come home to a dirty house and risk infection.

As she passed through the living room, a huge, dark object loomed to her right. She turned and screamed, throwing her hand to her chest. A big, ugly moose head hung from the wall, glaring at her. Good grief. Why did some people feel the need to hang dead animals in their homes?

Arianne hurried out the front door, returned the key, and tossed Huck's things into her trunk. Emma slept, releasing a light snore. This gave Arianne time to investigate the footbridge. She walked along the stone steps and ambled to the middle of the bridge. Leaning her elbows on the railing, she stared down at her reflection. She could picture herself sketching in the field, drawing inspiration for her gowns from nature.

What a breathtaking spot for a wedding.

She inhaled the aromatic summer air—salt and flowers. This whole place baffled her. The man who didn't believe in happy endings lived in a storybook.

The weak spot she had for him throbbed. He was like a lost, drenched puppy she'd found in an alleyway and, though she knew he'd be nothing but trouble, she couldn't stop herself from taking him home.

Dummy.

She gazed at the field of buttercups, bending in the breeze. Honeybees hovered from flower to flower. Maybe this wouldn't be so bad after all. They'd tolerate each other then go their separate ways. Perhaps by the time it was all done, they might even become friends.

But she couldn't shake the feeling she'd stepped right into a hornets' nest.

~*~

Huck rolled his achy head to the other side of the pillow and forced himself to wake up. A blonde imp with big blue eyes stood beside his bed, gaping at him like a science experiment.

The kid strangled a plastic doll in the crook of her elbow. "Hi, Mr. Huck. Are you ready to go home today?"

Arianne stepped away from the window. "Give him room to breathe, Emma."

The kid wasn't the problem. It was how good Arianne looked in that black-and-white cotton dress that made his pulse stutter. This arrangement would never work.

She looked at the clock. "The doctor's finishing up some paperwork, and then you're free to go."

Emma tapped his arm and grinned. Son of a gun, there were two of 'em. He'd never survive.

"What happened to you anyway, Mr. Huck?"

"I got hit by a car."

Emma's mouth dropped open. "And you lived? You're like Superman."

And you ladies are my kryptonite. The awe in her tiny voice made him more uncomfortable than his itchy cast.

An hour later, they were on the road with a grocery bag of pills at his feet, and his new wheels in the trunk. He barely fit into the Micro Machine Arianne had the nerve to call a car. He'd shed his gown for a T-shirt and shorts and promised to never take clothes for granted again.

Arianne glanced his way, and the wind from the open window blew loose curls around her face. "You're frowning. What's wrong?"

"You're not driving Miss Daisy. Could you speed up to at least forty? I'd like to get home sometime this week." He couldn't wait to sleep in his own bed.

"I'm trying to be gentle. I don't want to hit any bumps and put you in more pain. That happened to me as a child when I broke my arm. It's not fun."

Huck shook his head. "I'm glad your broken arm can sympathize with me." If she wanted him to die a slow, agonizing death, her driving would do the trick. As well as the off-key humming from Emma in the backseat.

His neck muscles stiffened as they approached Somes Sound. The overcooked bacon and eggs he'd eaten for breakfast rolled in his gut. When they reached the accident site, he cringed at the mangled guardrail. His body hurt just looking at it. Had Giada died on impact, without pain? Why did the other driver have a heart attack at that very moment?

Arianne reached over and squeezed his hand. "I'm sorry, Huck. If there was any other way to get you home, I'd have taken it."

"I'm fine." The bite in his voice proved otherwise. He ripped his hand away and hitched his thumb toward the backseat. "Can we cool it with the noise? I have a headache."

She pursed her lips and glanced into the rearview mirror. "Emma, honey. Huck isn't feeling well. Can you hum a little quieter, please?"

"Yes, Mommy. Sorry, Mr. Huck."

Jerk. It wasn't her fault. He concentrated on the pine trees flashing past.

The engine coughed as the speedometer climbed. They moved down the straightaway to the inlet where his roofline appeared.

Arianne turned into the driveway. "Your place is gorgeous. How did you come to live here?"

He shoulders relaxed. "It's not mine. The acreage is owned by Mount Desert Island. The municipality allows me to rent it in exchange for my bees."

Arianne slowed to a stop behind the house. "I don't understand."

"Bees are vital to crop production. They pollinate blooms so farmers have something to harvest. I ship bees all over, but mostly rent whole hives to blueberry farmers in Machias. I deliver the bees and get the hives set up, then collect them again after harvest."

Being home lifted his spirits. "Farmers help stabilize Maine's economy. The crops are bought not only for food, but from businesses that make soaps, syrups, jellies, wines. Those products are sold to tourists in Bar Harbor and online. They provide the land, I provide the bees."

A corner of Arianne's mouth turned up.

"What?"

She yanked the door handle. "Nothing."

Arianne got out and lifted the trunk. A moment later, it slammed, and she came to his door with his unfolded wheelchair. He curled his fists. Thirty-two was too young to be pushed around like an old man.

She knocked on his window. "Ready?"

He studied her navy eyes then trailed down her nose over her red lips to her stubborn chin. He needed to get over the red lips. But it was hard when they looked like they came straight out of one of those makeup commercials. Doomed to failure this was.

He opened his door and scooted to the edge of the seat. The movement sent a sharp pain through his ribs. His stolen breath kept him from any swearing. He managed to swing his leg out. Arianne scooted close and wrapped her arms around his waist. The cottony scent of her shampoo filled his nose. This would never work. A twig couldn't hold the weight of an oak tree. Even if her body did feel right against him.

Jude walked out of the shed. "Hold on, girlie, I'm coming."

Arianne released him. Jude hooked his arms beneath Huck's armpits to pull him up. The two men bear-hugged to the open wheelchair. Huck preferred the softness of Arianne.

Both men groaned as Huck's weight dropped into the chair. It hurt to breathe. Jude wiped his sweaty brow, panting. "You OK?"

Huck nodded. "Jude, this is Arianne," he said through gritted teeth.

Jude wiped his hand along his jeans and held out his hand to her. "You think you can handle this guy?"

Arianne smiled and unbuckled Emma then shook Jude's hand. "We'll manage."

"And who's this little lady?" Jude bent, and his stomach folded over his belt.

"This is my daughter, Emma."

Emma jumped like a jackrabbit. "We're moving here, and I'm going to have a place to play!"

Arianne laughed. "As you can tell, she's very excited."

Emma lost her balance and almost fell into Huck's broken leg. "Are you excited, Mr. Huck?"

"Thrilled." The scant amount of energy Huck had used to get home was exhausted. He yawned.

"We'd better get you to bed." Arianne pushed the wheelchair. "Come on, Emma."

Jude held the door open. The chair's front wheels caught in the doorway.

Ouch.

With an *oomph,* Arianne shoved his chair into the kitchen. Was this his kitchen? It was so...clean. The countertops sparkled and the room smelled like cinnamon and apples.

"I'll be finishing up outside if you need anything." Jude squeezed Huck's shoulder and disappeared out the door.

Everything was fine. Now that he was home, things would get back to normal.

"Your bedroom's all ready for you." Arianne steered through the kitchen. "Your dirty clothes have been washed and put away, and I put fresh sheets on the bed."

"You cleaned my room?"

"Someone had to. It looked like a nuclear warzone. You can't afford to risk infection."

The idea of her going through his things rankled. They entered the living room, and his blood pressure spiked. "What is that?"

A large blanket draped over his moose.

"I got tired of Bullwinkle's eyes following me everywhere I went. It scared Emma, so..."

"Whatever." He'd deal with her later. Right now, he was too weak to argue.

She struggled to get the wheelchair through his bedroom door, but finally managed. His bed was made, and he could see his carpet. The room smelled like fabric softener.

Arianne tugged down the blankets and wheeled him as close to the bed as she could. Emma stood beside the mattress. "Thank you, Mr. Huck, for letting us live with you. Do you have a swing set?"

"No."

"Can I see your bees? Will you teach me how to make honey?"

Arianne knelt in front of her daughter. "Huck's had a long day, and he's very tired. Would you please get a water bottle out of the refrigerator and bring it to me? He needs to take his medicine."

"Yes, Mommy." The kid skipped from the room.

Arianne fluffed his pillows. "You ready?" She walked in front of him and her cheek touched his as she hugged him close. With his good arm and leg, he helped push his weight up. He teetered, but she held him steady. She fit against him like a puzzle piece.

They maneuvered to the mattress and he fell onto the bed, taking her with him. Something he would've enjoyed had the pain not made him nauseous.

Emma returned with the water, and Arianne held a finger to her lips. He clenched his teeth as he lowered onto the pillows. The ache in his ribs snatched his breath.

"Pain?"

He nodded.

Arianne retrieved a pill and twisted the cap off the water. He downed the capsule along with most of the liquid.

She tugged the blankets up to his chest. "Get some sleep. I set up Emma's old baby monitor, so let me know when you're ready for supper. Just talk into it and I'll hear you."

How ridiculous. A few minutes ago, he'd played the part of an old man. Now he was a newborn baby.

Arianne shooed Emma out and turned to go. He grabbed her wrist. "Thanks."

The contact sent a spark of heat through him. He'd almost died, and in that moment he realized how much he wanted someone to care. But Arianne couldn't care. He needed to keep his distance so he wouldn't hurt her too.

Nurse bees care for the developing bees as they undergo metamorphosis, from egg to adult.

10

Arianne peeked inside Huck's bedroom door. The setting sun glowed through the sheer curtains and cast a pinkish hue over the room. He faced the window, making it hard for Arianne to determine if he was asleep. The sight squeezed her chest, like witnessing Samson after his battle with Delilah. A strong, capable man weaker than a newborn kitten.

He turned to her, eyes glazed.

"Ready for supper?"

"Sure." He tried to sit up, but his lips twisted in pain.

She moved to his bedside.

"I can do it," he growled.

Arianne inched to the bed and put her knee onto the mattress. She bent and put her arms around him. "Let me help you."

His thick back muscles flexed beneath her palms. She pulled with all her strength. Her pulse raced as she fluffed his pillow against the headboard with one hand and held him tight with the other. She clung on longer than necessary, to comfort him more than anything. He'd been through so much. It had nothing to do with her silly crush or that delicious smell of soap and...Huck.

He eased back against the headboard, breathing heavily. "I could've done it myself if you'd have given me a minute."

She ignored his grouchy tone and retrieved his food from the kitchen.

"Please tell me the food doesn't jiggle." He frowned at the tray.

"Jude's wife sent over homemade clam chowder and blueberry muffins. How does that sound?" His stomach answered with a rowdy grumble. She laughed and straddled the tray over his lap.

Huck reached for the spoon but failed to grasp it, restricted by his finger splints. He tried again. After the fourth failed attempt, she sat on the bed and reached for the spoon.

"Drop it."

"Let me help you."

"I can do it." He scowled at the bowl. His jaw flexed. The skin around his eyes was jaundice from the healing bruises. Despite the fact that his hair was shaggy and he needed a good shave, he was handsome in a wild mountain man kind of way.

Just yesterday she'd sat behind him in math class, staring at the back of his head, daydreaming he'd profess his undying love. Yet twelve years separated yesterday and today.

She loathed the way he stirred her blood. "Will you please let me help you?"

He glared at her. "I can feed myself."

"Fine." She stormed out the room and shut the door. If he ate cold soup, so be it.

After a late supper, Arianne tucked Emma into bed and checked on Huck one last time. His bedroom light blazed, and the tray sat on his bedside table, most of the food wasted. Muffin crumbs sprinkled his blanket and soup stains dirtied his shirt. Stubborn mule.

She tip-toed into the room for the tray and turned off the light with her elbow as she left, chasing away the disappointment that he didn't want her help.

~*~

The next day, Huck woke to the sun in his face and the scream of a bald eagle outside his open bedroom window. He pressed his hand against his ribs and pushed his weight up and back against the headboard. His body trembled and he took slow, steady breaths.

A knock.

"Come in."

The door opened to Arianne with her hip against the doorframe. Bare feet peeked from teal-and-purple-striped pajama bottoms. "Hockey Fights Cancer" stretched across her too big T-shirt in purple letters. Hair that hadn't made it into her ponytail framed black horn-rimmed glasses.

There was the Arianne he used to know. She'd been there the whole time under a different alias.

She smiled. "Good morning."

"Morning."

"Breakfast is ready. I didn't know what you liked, so I made about everything I could think of. What can I get you?"

A bathroom. He needed to go so bad his eyes were crossing. Huck stared at the wheelchair. How was this going to work?

She cocked her head.

He scooted to the edge of the bed, swallowing

curses. His good leg wouldn't hold him steady as he tried to stand, and he dropped back onto the bed. Arianne rushed to his side and tucked her little body beneath his arm.

"I'm not helpless." He bit down the rest of his growl.

She assisted him to the wheelchair anyway, her soft body pressed against his. "Doctor Reynolds has you scheduled for physical therapy in a couple of weeks. Things will get better."

Would they? He'd killed a woman. Which made his need to get closer to this one impossible.

Gripping the wheel, he pushed forward and swiveled straight into his nightstand. Son of a gun. The urge to go was maddening, and he stared at the bedpan on his dresser. He'd fight a swarm of African Killer Bees, unarmed, before he'd use that thing with Arianne in the house.

"Careful. Would you like to eat breakfast at the table?"

He was starving. The spoon never would cooperate with his finger splints last night and a muffin only went so far. "Please."

She wheeled him from the room and down the hall. As they neared the bathroom, he grabbed the left wheel and jerked the chair to the right. The foot pedals crashed into the doorframe. *Torture.*

"What are you—? Oh. Why didn't you say so?" Arianne realigned the wheelchair and pushed him near the toilet. Her cheeks flamed. She scratched her forehead. "Um, how are you…"

He remembered the plastic urinal the nurse had put in his bag that hung from a nearby hook. "Don't worry about it."

She crossed her arms. "Awkward, yes, but I can get you whatever you need and—"

"What I need is a strong cup of coffee, so see to it, woman." That'd raise her hackles, but if it got her out of this room, so be it. Another minute and his bladder would burst.

Her lips twisted in a smirk, and she slammed the door behind her.

Once his business was done and his vision had cleared, he maneuvered the chair to the door. It opened toward him, so until she returned, he was stuck in here. One thing was certain, these finger splints wouldn't make him go hungry again. He ripped them off, tossed them in the trashcan, and glimpsed his haggard appearance in the full-length mirror. He looked as terrible as he felt.

Arianne knocked, and with his permission, entered the room and wheeled him to the kitchen.

The room smelled of vanilla and cinnamon. A smorgasbord of food lined the countertop, making his mouth water. She pushed him to the table next to Emma.

"Good morning, Mr. Huck." Propped on her knees, she fiddled with her pink bathrobe. Curly hair stuck out in all directions.

"Hey, kid."

"Did you sleep good, Mr. Huck? I did. I got to sleep with Mommy. I really like it here."

He wanted to tell her not to like it too much, they *would* be leaving, but he didn't want to hurt her feelings.

"Can I see your bees today?"

Arianne patted Emma's back. "Honey, why don't you let Huck wake up and eat his breakfast before you attack him with a million questions?" Arianne smiled at him. "Coffee's ready. Cream and sugar?"

"Black."

She returned with a full mug and a plate piled with food. Huck picked up his fork, stabbed his scrambled eggs, and lifted it to his mouth.

Emma placed her hand on his wrist. "You can't eat yet, Mr. Huck. We haven't prayed."

He glared at Arianne across the kitchen.

She frowned. "What happened to your finger splints?"

"I took them off."

"You can't do that."

"I did."

"Men." She spat the word and poured another cup of coffee into his favorite mug. "Don't push yourself too quickly. Your body won't heal and then—"

"If I wanted to be nagged, I'd get married."

She scowled, stirring cream into her coffee. "You can't push yourself too hard."

Ignoring Emma's rule, he popped eggs into his mouth. "Appreciate the concern, Mom."

Emma giggled. "She's not your mommy. She's my mommy, silly."

"Well, she's trying to be mine too."

Arianne's chest rose with a deep breath and her eyes darkened. "Emma, say grace, please." She tossed him a dirty look before bowing her head.

The kid folded her chubby fingers together and shut her eyes tight. "Dear, Jesus, thank you for this food. Thank you for this day. Please, help Mr. Huck to feel better. I really want to see his bees. Amen."

"Amen." Arianne mumbled, refusing to look him in the eyes.

No one had ever prayed for him before. It was sweet, genuine. Too bad there was nobody there to hear it.

"Mommy, can I play outside today?"

Arianne swallowed her bite. "Sure, honey, but I have some alterations I need to finish up first?"

"OK."

Huck chewed the charred bacon. He preferred it floppy, but wouldn't complain. He was hungry enough this morning to eat the stinker out of a skunk. "Who's running the shop for you?"

"My sister." Her tone was curt and she still wouldn't look at him.

"Oh yeah, I forgot you had a sister. What does she do?"

"Nothing."

"What do you mean nothing?"

She rested her fork on her plate. "I mean *nothing*. She never went to college, she's currently unemployed, and I'll be lucky if my shop is still standing by the time I'm able to get back to work."

Her voice cracked on the last sentence. She left the table and stormed out of the kitchen, dabbing at her eyes.

What was that?

He looked at the kid. She held her palms up and shrugged.

The joys of a female mood swing.

~*~

Arianne cleaned the table, scooping stray crumbs into her hand. A cartoon theme song played from the living room where Emma was coloring. The girl was amazed by the 54″ screen. Huck had insisted on spending time in his office, though she couldn't imagine him getting any work done.

She glanced out the kitchen window to the sparkling water beneath the footbridge. She had to pull herself together. Her emotions teetered between *I can't do this—my shop's not worth it* and *Toughen up! Prove them all wrong.* Huck made the simplest things difficult and was grouchy enough to scare away an angry bear. She didn't want to be here anymore than he wanted her here, so why couldn't they make the best of things and move forward?

Missy running the shop worried Arianne the most. Sales were bad enough without adding her sister's flightiness to the mess.

A red sedan rolled into the driveway and parked next to the shed. Jude emerged and walked toward the house, carrying a pan covered in aluminum foil. She met him at the door. "Good morning."

"I see you survived the night." Jude's dark eyes danced. His weathered face bunched in a wicked grin. She guessed him to be somewhere in his sixties.

"Barely. Coffee is still warm. Would you like a cup?" She stepped aside.

"Sure." He passed her the glass pan. "Haddock casserole, compliments of my wife."

"Sounds divine. Please, thank her for me."

"I will." Jude followed her to the coffeepot. He took the mug she offered and poured a cup. "How's the patient?"

Cold air from the refrigerator hit Arianne as she slid the pan inside. "Cranky. It doesn't matter what I do to help him, he gets mad."

She didn't usually open up to strangers so quickly,

but something about Jude told her he'd understand.

He laughed. "I think I can help you with that one." He took a sip and leaned against the counter. "See, us men don't want to be the victim. We want to be the hero. I'm sure Huck doesn't like having to ask for help. I know I don't."

So this was all some stupid male pride thing? Men really were from another planet.

"Don't coddle him," Jude said. "And just between you and me, if there's something you want accomplished, it's best to trick him into thinking it's his idea. My wife does this to me all the time." He winked. "It always works."

She considered this. "Thanks, Jude. I think I understand."

The clock read nine. Alterations for two bridesmaids' dresses awaited her, and she needed to get started while Emma was occupied. "I better check on Huck before I dive into my work."

Jude put his mug on the counter. "Let me do it. We've got business to discuss anyway."

"He's in his office. Second door on the right." She pointed toward the hallway.

Jude sauntered that direction.

She rinsed out the mug and put it in the sink. Huck had suffered a loss most people never experience. He'd confessed that he only dated Giada a few times, but had he loved her? The thought bothered Arianne, which was insane. Not to mention disrespectful. Maybe she needed more sleep. Her new bed was like staying in a hotel suite, and she'd forced herself to climb out of it this morning.

So, with Huck she needed a different tactic. Strategy wasn't her forte. Her life was proof of that.

But if Huck wanted to play the hero, she could fill the role of the damsel. Though it went against her inner girl power.

If all men would go back to Mars, her life would be so much easier.

~*~

Knuckles rapped on the door. Huck brushed his fingers across his eyebrow. He wanted to be alone. Couldn't she respect that?

Jude poked his head in.

Huck sat straighter. "Come on in."

Jude shut the door behind him. "Got a few minutes?"

"I've got months." Huck gestured to his leather office chair. "How's the farm?"

"Good. You run a tight operation here. In the end, you may be sorry you asked me to take over." Jude dropped onto the chair and laced his fingers over his paunch.

Humility was one of Jude's best qualities. "I doubt that."

He gave Huck a long look. "How are you getting along?"

"Fine."

The man's lips curved, but he appeared to be fighting it. "Good. Seems you're in capable hands."

"Hmm." Arianne was capable all right. Capable of making this the longest year of his life. "How's the missus?"

Jude laughed. "Bossy as ever."

Weren't they all? Even the little ones. He remembered Emma's comment earlier about praying.

"Sherry sent over her famous haddock casserole."

One of his favorites. "She didn't have to do that. Y'all are helping so much already."

Jude glanced out the large window and shook his head. "She loves it, gives her something to do." He leaned forward and rested his forearms on the desk. "Women like to feel needed. They're built that way."

Not all women. Huck's mom had been a taker, not a giver.

"I know this situation isn't ideal, but the fact is you need help—whether you want it or not—and Arianne's willing to do the job. Be gentle. Women have these things called emotions. Make her feel needed, and time will pass more smoothly."

He didn't need anyone.

Huck scratched his chin. He did, however, need a shave. "What brought all this about?"

Jude stood. "Just a little advice from one man to another. I'm willing to help out in any way I can, but at some point, you're going to need to bathe, and that's where I draw the line." He moved to the door, pausing with his hand on the knob. "She's not so bad, you know. Quite the looker too."

Since when had Jude become Cupid? "Is she? I hadn't noticed."

A raspy chuckle escaped his friend. "Yeah, right."

Jude left, and Huck stared at the closed door. Arianne was a looker all right, but that's not what drew him. It was her sweet, giving heart. Her determination to succeed on her own, though she clearly needed help. A vulnerability that pressed him to protect her, shelter her. Only he was the one she needed protection from. His tainted past spread like a deadly virus, and he'd done enough killing for a lifetime.

The waggle dance is performed by worker bees to let their sisters know a food source is farther than 295 feet from the hive.

11

Arianne threaded the last stich on the bridesmaid's dress and rubbed her sore fingertips. She zipped the gown into a garment bag and hung it in her bedroom closet. Her whole apartment could fit in here. She definitely could get used to this—living in a real home with a backyard and a faithful hot water heater.

Emma's snore drifted from the bed. Arianne shut the closet door and stared at her daughter. The girl's hair lay in damp ringlets across the pillow. Covers pulled to her chin, the corners of her mouth curved up. After lunch, they'd played outside, chasing butterflies and tumbling down the hill. Halfway through her bath, Emma's eyes had grown heavy, and she'd fallen asleep as soon as her head hit the pillow.

Arianne yawned. It was late enough that Emma would sleep through the night. After getting Huck fed and settled, she'd turn in early herself.

She went to the kitchen, took the casserole dish from the refrigerator, and preheated the oven. Lemon scent permeated the air from when she'd mopped that afternoon. The sheer curtains danced in the breeze. Clouds hid the setting sun and cast shadows over the landscape.

Huck's room was quiet. She peeked in and found him leaning against the headboard, staring at the laptop she'd placed on a tray over his lap earlier. "I have some things I need to take care of at my shop tomorrow, but Jude said he'd stick around until I get back. I'm heating up the casserole his wife sent over. Until then, can I get you anything?"

He looked up from his laptop. "I'd like to take a shower."

Arianne blinked. The nurses had instructed her on how to give a sponge bath, but the idea had seemed unfathomable at the time, and she'd pushed the thought from her mind. Figured she'd burn that bridge when she got there. Now here it was, a dangerous swinging bridge with fire blazing at both ends, and she was on it.

He turned all dimples. "Your face is red, but you look as green as your sweater. Like a Christmas tree."

This was not funny. Her stomach tied a sailor's knot as she glanced down at her mom's old cardigan. She couldn't give him the satisfaction of knowing he'd embarrassed her.

He chuckled. "Calm down, Arianne, I've no intention of corrupting your morals. I researched how to bathe with casts. I can do it myself. I just need you to fetch two trash bags and the plastic stool in the shed for me."

Arianne fled to gather the items, fighting to control her nerves. Why was she so rattled? It made perfect sense that he'd want to shower. He'd been home for over twenty-four hours and still wore the same shirt and shorts he'd left the hospital in. So why did this surprise her? She could cope. She'd encountered worse things than this during medical school. Even seen some patients in the nude.

But those patients weren't Huck Anderson with a buttery southern drawl and the ability to turn her stupid.

The stool fit in the tiled, walk-in shower with room to spare. Arianne tested the angle of the showerhead to make sure the water would fall in the right place. She retrieved a towel, washcloth, and the topical antibiotic the doctor had sent home. Then she hesitantly returned to Huck.

He sat on the edge of the bed, face twisted in pain. "Are these ribs ever gonna stop hurting?"

"It'll get better. Give them a couple more weeks."

He slipped his arm from the sling and yanked his T-shirt with his good hand, holding out his un-splinted fingers. He turned and tugged, but the shirt wasn't coming off. Arianne's teeth dug into her lower lip, and she reached for the worn cotton, inching it around his cast and over his head.

Her breath caught.

Bruises and scrapes marred his sculpted chest. His ribs were blackish-yellow. Pink road rash covered his right shoulder blade and continued down his back and around to his washboard abs.

He glared at her. Heat flooded her cheeks when she realized she'd been staring—as much at the grotesqueness as the beauty. He looked at himself in the mirror on the closet door behind him. The skin around his eyes frowned along with his mouth.

Huck turned away from his image and cleared his throat. "You're blushing again. I'm flattered."

His voice was different. Deeper. Her first instinct was to coddle him, but Jude had told her not to. What should she say? Nothing would make him feel any better about what had happened. "Ready?"

"Yeah."

She helped him into the wheelchair and pushed him to the bathroom. He instructed her on how to tie the trash bags around his casts so they wouldn't get wet, although she already knew both from med school and the nurse's instructions. She obeyed without arguing. Best to let him think it was his idea. She wrapped his arm in the plastic then fitted a bag around his leg. Now what?

Arianne stood and crossed her arms. Dread barreled through her.

"Help me to the stool and I'll take care of the rest."

She nodded. Good idea.

Together they hobbled into the shower. "There are your fresh clothes." She pointed to the items she'd draped over the towel rack beside him. "Are you sure about this?"

"No," he said, his breath ragged. "But I'm halfway there. I'll holler when I'm done."

She couldn't flee the bathroom fast enough. So much for turning in early.

~*~

Arianne smoothed the hem of the crimson, chiffon bridesmaid's dress. She stood to admire her handiwork. The two women looked divine with the fabric draped across their shoulders that gathered to an empire waist.

One bridesmaid—a tall, voluptuous woman with sun-bronzed skin and dark, smoldering eyes—nodded her approval in the full-length mirror. "Beautiful work,

Arianne, simply beautiful."

Arianne's heart swelled. She'd worked on them most of yesterday, adding by hand the special touches the bride had requested. No matter how long it took, or how sore her fingertips were, it was always worth it to see her customers' satisfied smiles.

The woman looked like a runway model with her six-foot-long legs and the way the gown's lines cascaded down her perfect curves. She ran her palm along the silky fabric. "Arianne, your work is stunning. I'd like to speak with you about my upcoming wedding."

The woman held out her hand. A golf ball-sized diamond glittered under the fluorescent lights. Arianne whistled. "That's the most gorgeous ring I've ever seen."

Something familiar struck a chord in Arianne's brain when the woman smiled. She didn't think they'd ever met, but Arianne knew her somehow. The eloquent speech and sophisticated way the woman carried herself exuded a finishing school education.

"I'm Darcy Roberts." She paused as if that said it all.

The other bridesmaid rolled her eyes. "Great job, Arianne. I'm going to get changed and be on my way."

"Thanks for coming in." After a few moments, the woman's identity dawned on Arianne. The governor's daughter? She recalled seeing the woman's face plastered in newspapers and over local television. What was Miss Roberts doing in Arianne's shop?

Oh yeah, she was a bridesmaid. Why would Darcy want to discuss her wedding with Arianne when she could afford to go anywhere?

"It's a pleasure to meet you." Arianne shook her

hand. The ring had to weigh five pounds, judging by the weight of Darcy's grip.

"Likewise. I'm the bride's cousin. She's from Stone Harbor and happened to stumble into your shop. I'm delighted she did. I love this old Hollywood theme you have here."

Vintage. Finally, someone who understood.

"I can go anywhere for a bridal gown, but I'm looking for something unique. A gown made specifically for me. A design never worn by another bride before. Something classic. Do you know what I mean?"

Arianne's cup ran over. "I do."

"Now, I can choose any designer, but I see something in you, Arianne."

Was she breathing? The room started to spin, and she inhaled a deep breath. No, she hadn't been.

"Daddy's campaign is all about growing small businesses this term." Darcy examined the room with a slight scrunch of her nose. "This kind of publicity would do wonders for your shop. I think we'd work well together. What do you say?"

"I'd be honored to design your wedding gown."

Darcy clasped her hands together. "Smashing. Now make sure you tell everyone you know to vote for Daddy this fall. I'll contact you after Jillian's wedding so we can discuss a design before I leave town."

"Of course. I'm looking forward to it." Arianne forced herself not to squeal.

Darcy retreated to the dressing room like Miss America walking across the stage.

With a hand pressed to her lips, Arianne turned to the window. Was this a dream? She pinched her arm and winced. Nope.

She removed her rose-colored glasses and examined the boutique through Darcy's eyes. When she'd opened the place a few months after Adam left, she'd filled it with secondhand decorations from consignment shops and garage sales. She was a single mother, determined to accomplish her dream. She'd saved some money to redecorate, but then the economy dipped and her income slowed to a trickle.

Now the shop was in serious need of an update. Along with her life.

This opportunity could do wonders for her business. This one wedding alone might provide her with enough overhead to move out of this building and open another shop. A place where no one could force her out on a whim. Once women discovered that Darcy Roberts had used her shop, they'd all want to come here.

Renewed hope surged through Arianne's veins. No more scrimping and scraping. No more secondhand stores for her daughter. She was going to provide a better life. She'd work harder in the next year than she ever had and be rid of this place forever.

~*~

He'd never survive three to four more months.

Huck coughed and cringed from the pang in his ribs. Stiff, achy muscles complained from lying in bed so long. Every time he took his meds, they knocked him out. Taking a deep breath, he tightened his abs, and attempted to push his body up. Pain exploded in his chest. He collapsed against the mattress. The house was silent. Where was Arianne when he needed her?

Not that he needed her. She just insisted on

hovering over him, but now that he could use her assistance, she was gone.

He readjusted his pillow and gazed out the open window. A perfect July day. Bees foraged nectar from the geraniums in the window box. By the time he was well enough to run the farm on his own again, these workers would be deceased and new ones would have taken their place. They didn't live long, but they worked hard and lived every day to the fullest. As if they knew their days were numbered.

He felt like a bee trapped in a Mason jar, pining for flight while the world continued around him.

Girlish laughter came through the screen. Emma skipped into view of his bedroom window. Her giggles floated behind her along with the bubbles from her green plastic wand. Arianne chased the kid through the buttercups, sending bubbles and pollen puffs into the air.

They made a game of popping the bubbles and running after the ones that escaped. Mother and daughter linked hands and spun in a circle, all squeals and giggles. He smiled. Arianne released the kid's hand and wrapped her arms around the girl, twirling until she fell to the ground. The two held onto one another, laughing. He'd like to be out there too. And not just so he could run again.

He fixed his eyes on the ceiling. The narcotics were eating his brain cells.

Arianne was a good mother. It was evident from the first day he'd walked into her shop. She spoke quietly and patiently to Emma. Always gave the girl attention even when she was busy. He'd even heard Arianne tell the kid she loved her.

Adele Anderson-Jones-Brown-Tait-McFee-

Washburn-Johnson had only shown him affection when she wanted him to fetch her vodka and cigarettes or star in her latest scam. The revolving door of men she'd brought into their home had practiced parenting skills with their fists.

Huck scrubbed his hand over his wooly face. He hadn't thought about his childhood in years. Buried the memories with his mother. The reflection brought an ache to his chest.

Ever since Arianne walked back into his life, things he'd drowned long ago rippled back to the surface. Being near her made him feel things he didn't want to feel. Hurtful things. Wonderful things. She treated him as if he hadn't just killed a woman. She treated him like a friend.

He had to find a way to heal quicker, so he could send those two packing before he actually started to like having them around.

Henry Fonda, actor of over 96 films, kept bee hives on his grand Bel-Air estate for hobby. He enjoyed gifting jars of "Hank's Bel-Air" honey to co-workers and party guests. His unique honey blend was foraged from his groves of lemon, grapefruit, tangerine, apple, and orange trees.
—Ocala Star-Banner, *June 9, 1980*

12

"That should do it." Arianne placed a pillow beneath Huck's arm and smiled.

He relaxed into the cushions of his recliner. She folded a blanket over his lap, still wearing that goofy grin she'd held all through supper, even when gnawing on overcooked pork chops. How she was able to eat shoe leather and be happy about it was beyond him.

"Can I get you anything else?"

"Yeah, a beer."

The kid sprang from the couch and ran from the room. Wow. He didn't know she was trained to fetch.

Arianne stood taller. "There isn't any."

"What do you mean?"

"I threw it out."

"What? Why?"

She crossed her arms. "You can't mix alcohol with medication, and I didn't want to explain that stuff to my daughter when she asked me what it was."

His neck prickled with heat. "This is my house. What I drink is none of your business."

"Like it or not, for the next several months you are my business, and I'm yours."

Not by choice. "When she asks, you tell her to stay away from it. What's the big deal?"

"I hate the stuff." The fire in her voice and the steely gaze in her eyes told him it went deeper than dislike.

The kid skipped back into the room. "Here you go, Mr. Huck."

He examined the aluminum can in her hands. "What's this?"

"You said you wanted root beer." Her shoulders squared and she smiled.

Hard to be mad when she was so proud of herself. "Thanks, kid."

"You're welcome." She tip-toed through the wreckage on the floor.

What Arianne called fabric swatches, spools of ribbon, sketches, bridal magazines, pencils, and pastels littered his carpet like her bridal shop had walked in and thrown up. Emma's toy box had exploded in front of the TV. Like mother, like daughter.

Arianne reached down and popped the tab. Brown carbonation hissed into the air.

"I can open my own pop."

She glanced at her bare toes. "I know you're capable, but you've only got one good hand, and I didn't want to chance a mess."

He pointed to the floor. "You're concerned about *my* mess?"

She smirked.

"And another thing. You plannin' to finish me off

by torturing me with cartoons?"

Arianne put a hand on her hip. "You'll live. The movie doesn't have that much longer. Now, if you don't need anything else, I have things to do."

His fuse had run short with her ever since she'd gotten back from town. He'd decided to start looking right away for investors who might be interested in the space. By the time he chose a partner, took care of the necessary paperwork, made improvements to the building, and healed completely, Arianne's time would be up, and he could go on with his life. Not that he really deserved to.

He waved her away. At least she'd uncovered his moose.

She settled onto the carpet beside him and rummaged through her supplies. That gorgeous smile returned.

"What's with you?" He took a sip.

"What do you mean?"

"You're so happy."

As if it were possible, her grin widened. "Darcy Roberts came into the shop today."

"OK…"

"Darcy Roberts—the governor's daughter."

"Really? Hmm. Is she as hot in person as she is on TV?"

She threw a spool of ribbon at him. "Her cousin is a customer, and Darcy is one of the bridesmaids. I feel so silly. I had no idea it was her when the family came in for alterations a few weeks ago." She sat on her haunches and latched onto his good arm. "When she came in today for a final fitting, she said she loved my work and wants to use *me* to design her own, one-of-a-kind wedding gown. Can you believe it?"

No.

Her eyes shone brighter than the Portland Head Light. His lips twitched from her nails digging into his skin. But he liked her touching him so he let it go. "What's that mean?"

"This one wedding alone could mean enough money in my pocket to pay my debts and secure another building. Every woman in Maine will want to use the same bridal consultant as Darcy Roberts. By the end of the year, you could be rid of us forever."

The best news he'd heard in weeks. He ignored the pang in his chest. "Good for you." He meant it. He wanted her to succeed, and now he wouldn't have to worry about them when all this was over. He had enough baggage to carry around. "Now, about the cartoons…"

"The movie only has about twenty minutes left." She pointed to the kid and made doe eyes. Pouted those red lips. Was she attempting to coerce him with feminine wiles?

He was immune. "Fine."

She released her grip on his arm. "As soon as it's over, I promise you can have the remote."

"Thank you for your permission."

She fetched something from her purse that lay on the couch. "Here. It might make the cartoons more tolerable."

Whatever it was, she held it behind her back with excitement, like an owner does with their dog's treat. He refused to perform tricks for her.

Then, like a game show model, she presented a box of Reese's Pieces. "You used to snack on them while we studied. Are they still your favorite?"

She was the sweetest thing he'd ever met. "They

are."

"Good." Arianne returned to the floor.

He broke open the box and snacked while he watched animated sea creatures in HD. There had to be a football game or girls' volleyball match he was missing somewhere.

Bored, he stole a glance at Arianne. Her navy blue sweats were folded cross-legged. White threads dangled from the bottom of her thin Warrior's Hockey T-shirt. He was becoming quite a hockey fan. She squinted behind the nerdy glasses she'd slipped on and sketched subtle lines along her paper, tilting her head from side to side after each stroke. A #2 pencil was the only thing holding up her messy bun. He zeroed in on her top teeth brushing her full lower lip.

Huck cleared the gravel from his throat and shifted away. "Uh… So, what's going on with this blue fish?" He pointed to the screen. "Does she have Alzheimer's or something?"

Arianne laughed. "Short-term memory loss. She's helping the clownfish find his missing son."

"The clownfish who can't tell jokes. Funny."

"Mommy?" Emma sliced a plastic hairbrush through her doll's hair. "Is my daddy looking for me?"

Arianne's head jerked up. Her cheeks paled, and any spark of joy she'd had earlier vanished. She swallowed. "I don't know, sweetheart."

"What if he can't find us now that we've moved?"

Arianne lifted her eyes to the ceiling as if the answers were written there. "If Daddy wants to find us, he will."

Baby sea turtles covered the screen, recapturing Emma's attention. Arianne closed her eyes for a few moments. Her shoulders rose then fell. She glanced his direction before returning to her sketch.

The grief in her eyes punctured him. He knew she was divorced but didn't realize they'd been abandoned. Arianne deserved better than that. And no child deserved to grow up without a father.

The movie continued to play while he considered her ex-husband. Emma cheered when the father-son fish team united. Huck cheered that it was over. Now for some ESPN.

Emma brought him the remote. First the pop, now this? What else could the kid do?

Arianne told her to clean up the toys. Emma collected them in a small, pink suitcase with only half a picture of a Barbie left on the front. "Did you like the movie, Mr. Huck?"

He opened his mouth to answer as an air bubble rumbled through his chest and out his mouth. Emma giggled.

Arianne looked at him over the frames of her glasses. "You are such a Neanderthal."

"Thank you, but I prefer the term chrome-magnum man."

"It's *cro*-magnon. Their skeletal remains were found in caves in southern France. Scientists say they had long heads, broad faces, and sunken eyes." Arianne cocked her head. "Come to think of it, I do see the resemblance."

Who but Arianne would retain that useless information after all these years? "Be careful, Arianne. You're inner nerd is showing."

"I'm compensating for your inner dunce." She laughed, a sweet giggle contrary to her current geeky image.

Emma curled her fists on her hips. "Are you guys

fighting?"

"No, pumpkin, we're teasing. Tell Huck goodnight."

The kid walked to his chair. "G'night, Mr. Huck. When can I see your bees?"

"Tell you what. As soon as I'm able to get around better, I'll give you and your mom a tour of the whole farm."

Her mouth formed an *O*. "Can I watch you make honey, too?"

"I don't make the honey. The bees do that. I just bottle it and sell it."

The skin on her forehead puckered. "Do you squeeze the honey out of them?"

"What? No. Bees collect nectar and pollen from flowers. Then they take it back to their hive where they make the honey. When it's ready, I remove it from the comb."

"Like the kind you use for your hair?"

"Good grief, kid. Don't you ever go outside?"

Her shoulders dropped. "Not much."

He looked at Arianne.

"We've lived in the apartment above the shop for the past few years. The only place to play outside is the park across the street, but it's nothing to speak of."

The kid inched forward and wrapped her arm around his. She snuggled her head in the crook of his neck. "Thank you, Mr. Huck, for letting me play outside while we're here."

He stiffened. Her damp hair held the lingering scent of strawberry shampoo. "Uh...sure, kid, anytime."

She released his bicep and strangled her doll with her elbow. "Can we get a swing set?"

"All right, Emma, that's enough questions for tonight. Let's get you tucked in."

As Emma trudged away, Huck noticed that her tiny pajama pants ended four inches above her ankle. Her shirt was snug too. He'd worn clothes as a child in similar condition. At least Arianne was trying.

They disappeared to their side of the house. The room was estrogen-free. He already breathed easier. Craving normalcy, he flipped through the channels on TV. He wasn't sure how to handle all the female emotions ricocheting off the walls. There was nowhere to hide where he wouldn't get hit.

When Arianne returned, she cleaned up her things while he caught the last inning of a Cincinnati Reds' game. Half an hour later, she helped him to bed. Her fire was gone.

"Good night, Huck." Her voice sounded robotic. She pulled the blankets up to his chest.

"Night."

The light vanished and she closed the door behind her. He turned toward the window. A full moon brightened the darkness. He thought about Arianne and the kid living alone, struggling. He didn't know the pressures of being a husband or a father and never would. But a man would have to be loco to abandon those two.

~*~

Rain trickled down the kitchen windows. Arianne looked past the rivulets into the gray, clouded sky. Puddles collected in the yard, and the splash of water played the most beautiful music. Thunder rolled in the background so lightly it was barely distinguishable.

She loved an afternoon storm.

"You sure you know what you're doing?" Huck's voice broke her reverie.

"I've never been to beauty college, but I can manage a trim. I cut Emma's hair all the time." She grabbed the scissors and a fine-toothed comb from the kitchen counter.

He shifted in his wheelchair. "Where'd she take off to anyway?"

"Napping." Arianne fought a yawn. Her daughter had the right idea. She dampened Huck's hair and began to cut. His thick locks were soft against her fingers. The masculine scent of his soap followed her in every direction.

Huck squirmed.

"If you don't sit still, I'm going to mess up."

"I can't help it."

"What's wrong?"

"My leg itches."

She snipped another lock then stared at his cast. "I think I can fix that."

She put the scissors and comb on the counter, pulled several bags of frozen vegetables from the freezer, and spread them on his cast.

"What are you doing?"

"Cooling the skin helps relieve the itch. Skin cells grow continuously and die as they near the surface. On a normal basis, the outer layer rubs off on clothing or while you bathe. Under a cast, they've nowhere to go."

His brows arched. "I don't get it."

"Which part, genius? The skins cells growing or dying?" She continued to trim his hair.

"I understand that part, Yoda. What I don't get is why you quit medical school to be a bridal consultant.

You're so good with this stuff."

Arianne sheared the hair around his left ear. "I never wanted to be a doctor."

"Then why did you go to medical school?"

She switched to the other side. That familiar fear of disappointing her father crept into her chest. "To please my dad. He'd been saving for it since the day I was born."

He grunted. "He always did dictate your every move."

"What's that supposed to mean?"

"Nothin'," he mumbled.

She used to feel that way too, but ever since her father's unexpected death in the line of duty, she'd wondered if he'd known what was best after all.

Arianne finished trimming Huck's hair then lathered his face and neck, avoiding eye contact. She turned on the tap and rinsed her hands, letting the hot water build steam in the sink. She thrust his chin toward the ceiling and ran the razor upward along his neck.

"What happened with the kid's dad?"

Brave man to ask that when she held a razor so close to his jugular. "What's your sudden interest?"

"Just curious."

She swiped another path through the white foam.

"What happened?" His Adam's apple bobbed.

She ran the razor through the hot water stream, the temperature icy compared to her rising anger. "He left us. In the middle of the night. We went to bed together, and the next day he was gone. Left everything behind—clothes, car, *us*. Found a note saying he'd never be back." She looked away. "The only promise he ever kept."

Inhaling, she worked on removing the hair on his cheeks. "Is that what you wanted to hear?"

"No, it isn't."

Their gazes collided. Compassion flowed from his eyes and soothed her temper. Blast it, she was weak.

Arianne focused on her task, shoving away memories as stormy as the weather. "Emma's a great kid. She doesn't deserve what she's ended up with."

Truth be told, she didn't deserve Emma.

"Why did he leave?"

"Emma had colic until she was six months old. She screamed around the clock, but it got worse at night. I don't think that's why he left. I think it just pushed him to leave sooner."

"How long were you married?" His deep timbre vibrated the blade in her hand.

She rinsed it off and started on the other side. "Three years. I met Adam in a coffee shop in Cambridge while he was on furlough from the Air Force. I guess I got a little carried away by the uniform."

Loneliness she never allowed to consume her took over, and the words spilled out before she could stop them. She hadn't spoken Adam's name aloud in years. "We had a courthouse wedding and immediately conceived Emma. Dad was furious and refused to continue paying my tuition. But I didn't care. I was in love. So I quit school to be the wife my husband needed and ran him off in the process."

"Why weddings then?"

Her eyes grew misty. "I'd like to believe it's never too late for a happy ending." She concentrated on the last patch of facial hair to keep the tears from falling. "Leg feeling better?"

He nodded.

She rinsed the razor and patted his face and neck with a hand towel. Huck slid his hand into hers and gave her fingers a gentle squeeze. His calloused thumb rubbed circles on her knuckles. The tender gesture zinged electricity up her arm, shocking her to her toes. Lighting struck outside and thunder shook the house.

Arianne pulled away as rain pelted the windows. "I...I need to check on Emma."

She left the room.

Royal jelly is a high-protein substance fed to the young queen, which she will eat for the rest of her life. When ingested by humans, it helps to strengthen the immune system and balance hormones naturally.

13

On Sunday morning, Arianne plunked a steaming mug of black coffee in front of Huck. He rubbed the sleep from his eyes and inhaled the strong brew as he raised it to his lips. Dare he ask what she was serving for breakfast?

He glanced at the plate she carried toward him. Syrup dripped from three stacked waffles next to a golden pile of scrambled eggs. She placed the food on the table and went back to the coffee pot to pour herself a cup—in his favorite mug.

Icy fingertips touched his wrist. "Don't worry, Mr. Huck." Emma's whisper was loud enough to be heard in the next room. "They're frozen waffles."

Huck winked his thanks.

"I heard that." Arianne piled food on her own plate. As she swayed across the kitchen, her yellow skirt swished around her knees. Tucked in at the waist, her white dress shirt was rolled up to her elbows, and her hair covered her shoulders.

"You didn't have to get dolled up just to serve me breakfast, darlin'."

"Don't flatter yourself. I'm dressed for church."
She sat in the chair across from him.

He chewed a bite of buttery waffle.

"Are you going to church with us today, Mr. Huck?" Emma popped scrambled eggs into her mouth then made a funny face.

"'Fraid not, kid."

Her bottom lip pooched. "Why not?"

Why not? He hadn't set foot in a church in years, that's why. Not since he was eight and Mom had him sneak into the church's office to steal the money from the collection plate while she'd kept the reverend occupied. "I don't have any proper clothes that will fit over my cast, and I'm sure they wouldn't want me showing up in my pajamas."

Emma swallowed a sip of milk. "They won't care. The kids that come on the church bus wear their pajamas. It's real fun. We sing songs and learn about Jesus. And after the lesson we have juice and cookies."

"Thanks for the offer, kid, but not today."

Arianne stared at him from across the table, mouth in a straight line, eyes speaking something he couldn't quite hear. What he needed was peace and quiet to kick back and watch a ball game instead of cartoons or chick flicks.

Arianne flipped over the book she had spread on the table to hold her place. Emma picked at her food and wiggled in her seat, shaking her head from side to side, humming a tune Huck didn't know.

He drank his remaining coffee. What had ever possessed him to let these two invade his home?

~*~

"Go, go—ugh, come on!" Huck cursed at the TV. "We need a goalie not a ballerina!"

Gravel crunched outside. Through the window, he spied Arianne's car pulling up the driveway. Great. Now he'd have to keep it down. He wasn't in the mood for another lecture on why he had to watch his mouth around the kid.

A few minutes later, the door opened, and Emma ran toward him with a grin. "I made something for you at church, Mr. Huck."

She brought a piece of paper from behind her back. He glanced at Arianne who nodded as she slipped off her heels and closed the front door. He took the gift and turned it over to see the other side.

A crayon stick-figure lay on a narrow gray strip. A decent attempt at a motorcycle blended into the green bushes, and blue waves had been drawn by the road. It didn't take a genius to know this was him. The scene looked exactly like the crash site. How did she know what it looked like if she hadn't been there? Had she seen the footage on the news?

Yellow scribbles hung in the cloudless sky. She'd done so well with the rest, and she couldn't draw a circle? "That's a nice sun."

Emma pointed at the yellow blob. "It's not a sun. That's God. He's watching over you."

Arianne walked up and placed a hand on Emma's shoulder.

When he didn't respond, the kid continued. "Today we learned about how God watches over His children. Miss Hannah said that God is always looking down on us, so we should always behave."

Oh, not her too.

"She also said that God protects His children from

harm."

Did she think he hadn't been harmed? All she had to do was look at him.

He stared at the picture, unsure what to say. Unsure how he felt.

"I believe Huck likes it so much he's speechless." Arianne kissed Emma's head. "Why don't you go wash up for lunch?"

Emma skipped away, humming.

Arianne sat on the arm of his recliner, facing him. "Now that I know how to keep you quiet, I'll have her draw you pictures all the time." She smiled. "What's on your mind?"

Her light perfume hung in the air between them.

"You guys really buy into all this religious stuff?"

A groove formed between her brows. "What do you mean?"

"Do you really believe there's some supreme being we can't see controlling everything that happens?"

"I believe in God if that's what you're asking."

"Why?"

"Why not?"

He muted the TV. "Let's pretend God exists."

"I don't have to pretend that God exists. I know He does."

"If He's so great and loving, then why does He allow horrible things to happen to people? Why am I like this? Why did He let your husband leave you?" *Why did Giada die?*

She smoothed her skirt. "There is a purpose to all things under heaven." Arianne sighed. "I don't have all the answers, but I believe bad things happen sometimes to teach us a lesson, or to keep us from something even worse later on. It may be a consequence of our sin, and sometimes it's solely because people have freewill and choose to do wrong things. Each person's case is different, I guess."

She sounded just like Uncle Marty.

The tiny hairs on his neck bristled. He rapped his palm against his cast. "You believe this happened to teach me a lesson?"

Arianne shrugged. "Maybe. I know one thing. God was watching over you that day." She pointed to the picture. "He has a plan for you, Huck."

He stared at the yellow blob. "What makes you think that?"

She hooked a finger under his chin and guided his face toward hers. "Because you're still here."

"Life is the flower for which love is the honey."
—Victor Hugo

14

He loved sports just as much as the next guy, but this was getting ridiculous. The term *couch potato* now held a personal meaning, only instead of a sofa it was a recliner. And the leather now held permanent butt indentions.

Huck gazed at Emma through the living room window. That picture she'd given him had distracted him through most of the baseball game. Could Giada really have died because God wanted to teach him a lesson? If so, it wasn't fair to her, or to her family. He didn't want anything to do with a God like that.

Emma sat on her blanket beneath a maple tree, arms wrapped around her legs, chin on her knees. She stared straight ahead. What could a kid that young be in such deep thought about?

That's when he noticed her frown, the draw of her forehead. Was she thinking about her dad?

An image of himself, not much older than she, pushed its way into his mind. There'd been many days he'd sat alone, wishing his father—whoever he was—would show up on their trailer doorstep and take him away to a better life. To a home where people paid attention to him, told him they loved him, made him feel important. At least Emma had a mom who did those things. He'd had no one.

A butterfly soared above Emma's head and dipped as if deciding where to land. Oblivious, she rocked back and forth, pushing with her toes. His chest cracked like ice thawing in a frozen pond. Like him, a part of her was lost, searching for the piece she'd never find. Knowing a parent—or parents—didn't want you disintegrated the soul. Little girls shouldn't grow up jaded.

He couldn't fix the dad situation, but he could be her friend. It wouldn't hurt to make the kid happy while they were here. Would it?

~*~

Emma's giggles erupted into the summer air. "Higher, Mommy, higher!"

Arianne pushed harder. Her arms were getting a workout. "Just a few more minutes, and then I need to go inside and help the ladies in the kitchen."

Emma stopped pumping her legs and slowed to a stop. "All right, Mommy, I'll slide instead."

Scooping her doll off the adjacent swing, Emma snuggled it close to her orange sundress and climbed the stairs to the top of the slide. Arianne sidestepped a small blanket strewn with plastic tea cups and fake cookies. An open bottle of bubbles sat in the grass, and she bent to screw on the lid.

The aroma of grilling hamburgers caused her stomach to growl. Jude and his wife, Sherry, had orchestrated a cookout, along with two other beekeepers from their association. Huck had missed working his booths at the Lobster Festival in Winter

Harbor and the Machias Blueberry Festival that kicked off the month of August. Since he couldn't join the fun this year, the festivities had come to him.

Arianne yanked opened the screen door and stepped into the kitchen. Sherry stirred pasta salad, while her mother, Janet, supervised. "Sorry it took me so long. Emma can't get enough of that swing, and she hasn't quite figured out how to do it herself yet. How can I help?"

"No problem. They're only little once." Sherry glanced out the window with a wistful smile. "I brought some fresh lemonade. Could you get it for me?"

"Sure."

Arianne retrieved the lemonade and set it on the table, along with the soda and a gallon of sweet tea. "I can't believe Huck agreed to a swing set. It was generous of you both to lend us yours while we're here. I'm sorry to hear your son and grandkids had to move out of state, though."

Janet lifted a shaky hand from the purse in her lap, which could easily be mistaken for a small suitcase, and tapped the buff-colored device in her ear. She leaned toward Arianne. "They didn't lend you theirs. It's still in the backyard. Huck bought that one."

Arianne frowned. "I don't understand."

Sherry's face blossomed to a dark pink. "Oh, Mother. You promised."

Janet shrugged her bony shoulders and returned her hand to her purse.

Sherry rinsed off the rubber spatula and snapped the lid onto the bowl. She turned to Arianne and leaned an ample hip against the counter. "Huck didn't want you to know, but he gave Jude the money last week and asked him to buy Emma a swing set."

Arianne's mouth fell open. "Why didn't he want me to know?"

"You know how men are. Nothing they do makes sense. I told Jude if the truth came out, I wouldn't deny it."

Arianne looked out the window at the group clustered on the patio. Huck sat in his wheelchair at the picnic table. The skin around his eyes and nose was no longer bruised. He threw his head back and laughed at something that Matt, his "little brother" said, calling his dimples into action. Was this grouchy, ex-football star really capable of such a gesture?

Even Ebenezer Scrooge had a change of heart in the end.

Huck never said a word the other day; he'd simply watched Emma run to the swing set before he'd gone to bed saying he was exhausted from his first day in therapy.

Arianne would never figure him out. Though he was patient when answering Emma's questions about the bees, Arianne saw the vacant look in his eyes when her loving daughter would do something special for him or when they spoke about God.

"I can't believe you were willing to move in and take care of him," Janet said.

"Mother! How could say such a thing?" Sherry's cheeks darkened from pink to red.

Janet stuck out her chin, jiggling the loose skin on her neck. "There's something about that man that rubs me the wrong way."

Sherry waved a finger at her mother. "You said the same thing about Jude forty years ago."

"I still feel that way. The only man on earth worth

having was your father."

Sherry rubbed her forehead. "You'll have to forgive my mother, Arianne. She doesn't have filters."

Janet shrugged again.

Arianne swallowed her laughter. Though they teased mercilessly, their love for one another was evident. Would this be the kind of relationship she might've had with her mother, if she had lived? Arianne took the chair across from Janet. "We both had a need the other could fulfill. It hasn't been easy, though. I'll give you that."

Janet gasped in disdain. "The way women act these days is scandalous."

"She wasn't referring to *that*, Mother." Sherry glared at Janet. She tugged on a chair and plopped onto it. The wood groaned beneath her weight. "You're not the easiest person to live with, either."

Sherry winked at Arianne. "There are days when I'm tempted to tape her lips closed."

Janet shoved her glasses further up the bridge of her nose. "After agonizing in labor for three straight days, this is the thanks I get. Well, I took care of you for twenty years. Now it's your turn."

Sherry took her mother's hand. "We love each other. We truly do."

Janet failed to hide the smile on her lips.

"Tell me about your bridal shop." Sherry released Janet's hand and crossed her arms.

Arianne made it sound as glamorous as she could without fibbing. "Things are falling into place. I'm working with a high-profile client who'll bring in more revenue. I hope to relocate by spring."

Sherry patted Arianne's hand. "I'm glad things are working out. I don't think Pine Bay needed a bait and tackle shop..." Sherry winked. "But who am I to say? I'm just a woman."

Arianne opened a box of plastic utensils. "I don't think Huck cares what goes into the building as long as the bridal shop moves out. I can't decide which one he detests the most: me or the idea of marriage."

Sherry folded her hands. "In my long lifetime—"

"Ha!" Janet interrupted.

"Mother, behave." Sherry scolded Janet with a look. "I've learned that sometimes the things people are most opposed to are the things that scare them."

Janet nodded. The room grew silent as Sherry opened the napkins and stacked them in a perfect white cloud. "I've not spent much time around Huck, but I think he likes to pretend he's impartial to people and things, when he's really the opposite. The swing set proves that."

Janet placed her palm on the table. "Men aren't good communicators. You've got to learn to read between the lines."

Arianne had never been good at that. Whenever she thought she knew what they were thinking, she'd been proven wrong.

Jude came into the kitchen for a plate to put the cooked burgers on. As Sherry retrieved one from the cabinet, Jude gazed at his wife with longing in his eyes. The lovebirds shared a tender smile when Sherry handed him the plate, revealing secrets that made Arianne feel like an intruder. Would she ever know a love that special?

When the food was ready, they gathered on the patio, and Arianne called Emma from the playground to eat. Jude swiped off his hat and hushed the crowd to say grace. Everyone linked hands, and Huck glared at hers before he captured it. Infuriating man. One minute he was delicate with her and the next he was repulsed.

The evening passed with good food and laughter. Janet's blueberry pie, baked with lemon juice, was to die for, and she refused to reveal the recipe, claiming it was an old family secret. Sherry leaned into Arianne's ear. "The tapioca's the secret," she whispered. "I'll send the recipe over with Jude next week."

After Matt's mother picked him up and the other guests went home, Arianne swiped the sponge across the counter to clean off the crumbs. A breeze swept through the house, sending goose bumps over her arms. The overnight rain showers and cold front were moving in.

She fetched a sweater from her closet and a sweatshirt for Emma. Her daughter sat in a swing, barely rocking her little feet. Her head rested against the plastic-coated chain. Tired eyes rolled open and closed.

"Why don't you come in and let me tuck you into bed. It's been a long day."

Emma lifted her droopy eyelids. "I'm not tired."

Arianne laughed. "I think you are."

"I wanna sleep out here tonight."

"Well, you can't sleep outside. You need to sleep in the nice, cozy bed with Mommy."

Emma shivered and gripped the chains tighter. "Will my swing set still be here in the morning?"

Her daughter already knew too well how quickly treasures could be snatched away. "Yes, pumpkin, it will."

Grasping Arianne's hand, Emma slid off the swing and dragged her feet into the house. After a quick bath and fresh pajamas, Emma was snoring on her pillow within seconds.

The clock read eight when Arianne went outside to check on Huck. The air had cooled to somewhere in the low-sixties, and she wrapped her sweater tighter around her middle. She glanced around the yard. His wheelchair was parked by the footbridge. He stared at the setting sun reflecting off the water.

What was going on in that mind of his? He'd barely spoken a word to her in two weeks, ever since she'd told him God had a plan for his life. The statement somehow triggered his shut-down mode. Now on Sundays he avoided her altogether.

Grass rustled beneath her flip-flops as she moved closer. Birds chirped in the distance. Water lapped against the rocky edge of the inlet. If Huck was aware of her presence, he didn't look up.

She sank onto the cool grass beside him, pulled her legs close, and rested her chin on her knees. Post-Traumatic Stress Disorder was a real and serious thing, but he refused to see any psychiatrist or counselor. What could she do to help him heal emotionally, now that his physical healing was underway? The grief in his eyes was sinking deeper and bitterness feasted on his heart in a visible way.

If only he knew how much God loved him.

Arianne plucked a blade of grass that stood taller than the others and twirled it between her fingers. Sitting together in silence, they seemed to communicate more than they had all week.

~*~

Before the accident, Huck was content with his

life. Then Giada died, and in came Arianne with her mini-me, talking about God, angels, and heaven. It was all he could think about, since thinking was all he could do. He questioned his entire life.

If he had died in that wreck, there would be no one to leave his legacy to. That hurt. There was no one to go through his things and pick out a keepsake because he'd meant something. No family photos to sort. No one to stand beside his casket and say, "He was a good man. He'll be missed."

Huck looked at Arianne sitting on the ground beside him and twirling a blade of grass between her fingers, innocent as a child. The setting sun glowed around her in a halo of light. All this talk about a higher power. He'd always brushed it off before, but what if he had died in that accident? Where would he be?

If there was an afterlife, had he ruined his chances when Giada died? Where was she now?

Arianne tilted her head and smiled at him. "Thank you for the swing set. I haven't seen Emma this happy in a long time."

He turned back toward the water. "Don't make a big deal out of it, Arianne. Jude didn't want it anymore. He knew you were staying here, so he brought it over. That's all there was to it."

"I just wanted to let you know that we're grateful." She stood and brushed her palms over her backside. "Jude brought some wood for a campfire, and I've got marshmallows. Would you like to join me?"

Did he? It was either her, reruns on TV, or bed. He wasn't tired yet. "Sure."

Arianne tossed the grass and pushed his

wheelchair toward the fire pit. "Does it feel good to get outside?"

"It does." He sucked in a breath and caught the smell of rain in the air.

"How are you feeling?"

"Sore. Sergeant Sandy worked me pretty hard yesterday."

"She must've. You never left your bed after you got home."

The doc said his fingers, nose, ribs, and collar bone had healed. Though he still had a cast on his arm, he was no longer confined to a sling. His right leg and hip had six weeks left, but he was getting stronger every day. By October, he should be able to start on crutches.

As Arianne stacked the firewood in the metal ring, they argued over the best way to build a campfire. He was right, of course, but try telling her that. To his surprise, she got it going on the first try and looked to him for approval. He stared across the field. Beginner's luck.

She went inside and a few moments later returned with marshmallows, drinks, and blankets. When he declined the marshmallows, she handed him a one-pound bag of Reese's Pieces she'd hidden beneath the blankets, along with a sweet smile as she spread the quilt across his lap.

Hard to keep her at a distance when she knew how to get to him.

The sky was dark, and Arianne sat in a lawn chair that she'd angled so the fire would allow her enough light to read. She wrapped her legs beneath the other blanket and opened her novel. Every other page, she rewarded herself with a marshmallow.

She alternated between smiles and frowns as she

read deeper into the story. Arianne had changed so much over the years. Yet she hadn't. She still had a caring heart, still found joy in the little things. Still drove him unbearably crazy.

With her chin tucked to her chest, Arianne gazed at him over her glasses and caught him staring. Try as he might, he couldn't pull his gaze away. Firelight flickered off the side of her face. Desire swept through him. What would she do if he scooped her up in his arms, threw those hideous glasses into the fire, and kissed her until she couldn't take anymore? Impossible to do when he couldn't even walk over there.

"What's wrong?"

Huck cleared his throat. "That sweater."

"What's wrong with it?"

"It looks like it came out of 1970."

"It did. It was my mother's."

That triggered a memory he'd long forgotten. Her in that same sweater sitting close to him at her dad's kitchen table, books stacked around them. . .

"Can we take a break, Arianne? My brain can't handle any more laws and theorems."

"We're running out of time. If you don't pass your final—"

"I will." The alternative wasn't an option. He rubbed his eyes with the heels of his hands. "Got anything to eat?"

"If you'd quit thinking about your stomach, you might be able to comprehend Sir Isaac Newton."

"Studyin' in a kitchen makes me hungry. Every time I look up, I see the fridge and wonder what's in it."

She removed her glasses and rubbed her nose. "If I feed you, do you promise to work hard the rest of the evening?"

With her glasses gone, the dark, vivid blue of her eyes was unmistakable. He'd never noticed how attractive she was before...in a geeky, librarian kind of way. "Promise."

Her chair screeched along the vinyl floor as she got up and rummaged through the cabinets. He grinned when she stood on tip-toe to reach them. After a few minutes, she shrugged and went to the freezer. "We have Hot Pockets."

"Does it have meat in it?"

"Bacon."

"I'll take it."

The cellophane crinkled as she opened the end. Then she placed it in the microwave. Her fingers poked the buttons. The machine's whir was the only noise in the quiet house. Huck stood to stretch and walked to the fridge for a pop.

"Want one?"

She turned to see what he referred to. "Sure."

Huck grasped another can. He closed the door and a Polaroid of a pretty blonde with long, hippy hair caught his attention. Her smile was similar to Arianne's, and she wore bellbottoms and a fringed vest over a tie-dyed shirt. "Is this your mom?"

The microwave beeped, and Arianne pulled out the plate. "Uh-huh." She carried the plate to the table and pushed his book aside. "Here you go."

"Thanks." He settled back onto his chair. It was hard to imagine her mother as a free spirit, when Arianne was so serious and structured. "Are your parents divorced?"

She stared at her lap and shook her head. "She died of leukemia when I was seven."

The food stuck in his throat. Losing a mother hurt, even if she wasn't a good one. He swallowed. "I'm sorry. Do you remember her?"

She fingered the book. "Some things. Other stuff gets fuzzy as I get older. I remember she hugged me a lot and read us books every night before bed, even when she was so sick she could hardly talk."

His mother never did that.

"What about your mom?" she asked. "I heard she passed away, and that's why you moved here."

Huck shoved another bite into his mouth, a big one to give him some time. He nodded and swallowed. "She got killed in a car accident in Vegas."

He wasn't about to tell her that his mom didn't bother to let him know she was going. Just left a twenty with a see-ya-later note telling him she was getting married—again—and would be back in a few weeks. He'd found it when he'd gotten home from school. Twenty dollars didn't go far on a growing boy's appetite.

A groove formed between Arianne's scrunched brows. Her pink lips pursed. "I thought it would hurt less as time passed, but it doesn't."

He chewed the last bite. It did hurt. Not because of all the things his mom had done, but because of all the things she hadn't.

Their eyes met. Her loss collided into something inside him. Like Newton's Third Law of Motion, the force she acted on him, caused him to act with equal force on her.

Oh. Now he got it.

Unlike the girls he normally dated, who were only nice to a person's face, Arianne was beautiful inside and out.

They both sat frozen, heat crackling between them. Forget the food. He wanted to taste her lips. He leaned in, and she met him halfway, eyelids falling heavy. His mouth closed around hers. Her kiss was willing but timid. He put his hands on her shoulders, and she tensed. This was obviously her first kiss. He stopped at one, not wanting to scare her.

The front door slammed and they jumped apart. Heavy footsteps echoed through the hall. She slid the Physics book toward herself, cheeks so red they were almost purple, and started babbling about the law of gravity.

He chuckled, reached for his pop, and waved at her father as he passed, dressed in his police uniform. The sheriff scowled a warning, grabbed a beer from the fridge, and headed to the living room.

Huck tugged a pack of Reese's Pieces from his book bag and poured a pile into his hand, then gave her the rest. She picked one up with a shaky hand, a dumbstruck grin on her face.

The memory was sweeter than the candy on Huck's tongue. That might've been the clumsiest kiss he'd ever gotten, but it was also the purest. Full of truth. Trust. Something he craved more of. The flames licking the wood matched the wildfire raging inside him.

Arianne tucked hair behind her ear. "I know the sweater is ugly, but it's comfortable. Wearing it reminds me of her."

For the good of his sanity he needed a distraction. "What'cha readin'?"

She held up the book. A man and woman stood next to a horse, arms around each other, faces hidden behind the man's cowboy hat.

Lame.

"Romance, huh? I figured you'd be reading about Madame Curie and the periodic table."

She glared.

"Let me guess, they meet, they fall in love, and ride happily into the sunset on his horse."

"Well, I haven't finished the book, but...probably."

He made a gagging gesture with his finger.

She threw a marshmallow at him. It hit his ear and bounced into the grass. "Why are you such a cynic anyway?"

Huck laughed and popped some candy into his mouth. "It's crap. Things like that don't really happen. When it comes to marriage, very few people stay faithful to their spouse their whole life, so why make a promise you can't keep?"

She spread the book across her stomach and studied him with half disgust, half amusement. "You want to know what I think?"

"No."

"I think you refuse to fall in love."

"Yep."

Her mouth gaped, as if his answer was more shocking than Bill Clinton's impeachment. "And if your soul-mate should happen to come along—if there is a girl out there so dim-witted—how do you plan to keep from loving her?"

Like Sir Isaac Newton, Huck had his own laws of resistance: never date a woman with kids, and never say *I do*. Those kept everyone safe.

Until Giada. But her death didn't have anything to do with his philosophies. It just...happened. He was still working on figuring it out.

His rotten mood settled in again, and when he didn't answer her, Arianne shifted her attention back to her book. He tried to refrain from watching how the flames chased shadows on her body, but failed. He needed another taste of those lips so bad he couldn't think straight. Every time she pinned those blue eyes on him, telling him without words that she saw someone good, worthwhile, he was tempted to burn his rulebook.

"If the bee disappears from the surface of the earth, man would have no more than four years to live."
—Albert Einstein

15

Huck stared at his laptop screen, flicking an ink pen between his fingers. His accountant, Ray, knew some investors who might be interested in his bait and tackle venture. Good. It was time to get this ball rolling.

The smell of orange-scented furniture polish hung in the air. His office gleamed. It was nice to go into a room that was clean and organized. Two things he stank at. Movement outside his office window stole his attention.

Arianne stood at the makeshift clothesline she'd put up between two trees. He'd told her it wasn't necessary, that his dryer worked fine. She argued it would save on his electric bill now that more laundry was being washed. He appreciated her frugality, and she was mighty cute, balancing on her toes to hang his bed sheets on the line.

She bent and retrieved a pillowcase from the basket. Her hair clip fell to the grass when she righted herself. A mess of blonde went everywhere. She pinned his pillowcase to the line then shook out her hair.

Heat swelled in his gut. What would it be like to tunnel his fingers into—?

He wouldn't go there. Instead, he focused his attention to the blinking curser on the website's search engine box. At first he'd blamed those thoughts on the narcotics, but now he had to man up. Ibuprofen didn't cause such side effects. And he'd been having strange symptoms ever since the campfire episode last week.

Avoiding her all together was impossible, and the more he tried not to think about her, the more she invaded his brain. He couldn't afford to fall for her. She couldn't afford it. He'd have to double his effort during physical therapy so she and the kid could move back into their apartment.

His life had turned into a house of cards and every day the girls would blow on it, threatening his stability. Huck scrubbed his hand over his face. How could he get his life back to the way it was two months ago?

He couldn't.

The realization slammed into him as hard as he'd hit that guardrail. He was responsible for a woman's death. His life would never be the same.

The keyboard clicked as he clumsily punched the letters into the search field using the index finger of his left hand. This wouldn't change anything, but it was a start.

Arianne burst into the room. "I've got to make a run to the shop."

He rocked backwards, startled.

She scooped her hair into her hands and captured it in a ponytail. "Jude's here. Do you need anything before I go?"

A time machine. "No."

Her blue shirt looked delicious against her skin. "See you when I get back."

She smiled and his heart kicked. He faced the computer screen again where Giada's obituary had loaded. He scribbled her parent's names on a notepad.

Huck closed his eyes against the nausea swirling in his gut. He'd thought he had mastered relationships. Hang out, have a good time, exchange needs—all without getting too close. After all, those women were willing. But it had cost him. For Giada, the price was too much to pay. She deserved so much better.

So did Arianne.

~*~

Arianne gasped. She gripped Emma's hand tighter and stepped farther into the mess. Bridal shoes were strewn across the floor in front of the full-length mirror, obstructing the small platform that brides used to determine whether a gown suited or not. Cropped strings and white lint had been tramped into the carpet. Gowns hung sloppily on the hangers. Fingerprints smudged the glass door, each print highlighted by the sunlight filtering through.

This wasn't a burglary. This was Missy.

Arianne's blood boiled. As much as she'd wanted to believe Missy wouldn't let her down, she knew it would happen. She'd known it from the second Missy said, "I'm a big girl. I can handle it."

"Mommy, you're hurting my hand." Emma winced.

"I'm sorry, baby." Arianne let go. It was her own fault for entrusting her shop to someone else. For nursing an old crush who only weeks ago was kicking her onto the street.

She'd prayed for more time and God had been merciful in giving it. Albeit, in a tragic and strange way she never saw coming, but an opportunity all the same.

Her purse fell from her shoulder, and she caught it in the crook of her arm. Where was Missy anyway? She stomped to the office, but her sister wasn't there. Her nose curled. What was that smell?

"Mommy, I want to color Mr. Huck a picture." Emma pulled out the chair and tossed her backpack on the desk. The crayons crashed against the plastic box inside.

"That's fine. I'll be cleaning."

Hands squeezed into fists, Arianne dropped to her knees and started on the shoes. Ten minutes later, Missy waltzed through the door, to-go coffee in one hand and a muffin in the other.

"Where have you been?" Arianne shoved the last shoebox onto the rack.

Missy held up the muffin. "Getting breakfast."

At 11:45? "Are you just now opening the store?"

"Boutique." Missy dared to make air quotes around the items in her hands. "Yes. I had a late night, and nobody ever comes in on Thursdays anyway."

Arianne threw her hands up and slapped them on her thighs. She'd had a late night too, acting as cook, nurse, and maid. Somehow she'd still managed to drag her butt out of bed at six-thirty this morning.

"What are you doing here anyway?" Missy bit into her chocolate-chip muffin.

"It's my shop. Jude's with Huck this afternoon, and I thought I'd come by to catch up on things. I had no idea I'd be walking into this." She waved her hands around the room. "I left a detailed checklist of what needs to be done every day. How hard is it to push a vacuum?"

Missy swallowed her bite and raised a brow. "Oh, I see. My services don't meet Queen Arianne's expectations."

"No, they don't."

"So it's off with my head?" Missy plopped the cup on the glass countertop, splashing drops of coffee down the rim. "What do you want from me, Arianne? I help you with the cooking—God knows you need it—I run your shop when you ask me to. I'm nanny to your kid all the time. Tell me, what more do you expect from me?"

"I expect you to apply yourself and do a good job when you commit to do something. Become a good, responsible citizen and make your way in the world. I support you with a roof over your head, food in your stomach, and a little extra cash for watching Emma. So, what's the big deal if I ask for your help? It's not like I'm interrupting your career plans."

Missy blinked. "We can't all be Arianne Thompson."

"It's Winters. And what's that supposed to mean?"

Missy snatched her cup. "You wouldn't get it, would you?"

Tears stung Arianne's eyes. She hated confrontation. Especially with her sister. "No, I guess I don't. I'm not perfect. My life's proof of that. Don't be like me, Missy, struggling and scrimping and still not making ends meet. I want you to make something of yourself."

Arianne went behind the counter and grabbed the window cleaner from the cabinet. She sprayed the liquid on the glass and cleaned with vigor until her upper arm burned. "Darcy Roberts walking in here and asking for my business is the break I've been waiting on. I know this shop isn't your thing, but I'm only asking for your help for a little while longer. We're family."

"Playing the family card, huh?"

Arianne curled her fingers around the wet paper towel. "I shouldn't have to *play* it."

Emma skipped into the room, humming "Keep On the Sunny Side." Those Sunday school songs were putting Arianne in her place on a daily basis.

Arianne's nose tingled with a sneeze. "What's that smell?"

"Patchouli." Missy dropped the cup and muffin liner into the trashcan. She ripped off a paper towel, grabbed the cleaner, and sprayed the front door. "I couldn't find any more candles around here, so I bought one."

Missy left a candle burning when no one was here? Arianne bit her tongue from saying the words aloud. She rubbed her fingers across her forehead instead.

"Don't worry, Arianne. It's an electric warmer that melts wax tarts. I wouldn't leave a candle unattended."

That was a relief. Still, light floral tones or lavender scents calmed an overwhelmed and jittery bride. Not Patchouli. If Arianne didn't keep a closer eye on things, Missy might start burning incense in funky jars and stocking hippy gowns. If this place had any customers left by the end of her and Huck's agreement, it'd be a miracle.

~*~

Huck stretched beneath the blankets and stared at his dark bedroom ceiling. He couldn't sleep. Body restless. His mind tortured by the obituary he'd read and reread while Arianne had been out. A basket of hot wings and a beer on tap was yelling his name. If he could get out of this bed and make it over to Sharky's Tavern before dawn, he would.

The glowing numbers on his alarm clock said midnight. His foot ticked, making a zipping noise beneath the sheet. He couldn't shake Emma's disappointment at dinner when she'd invited him, yet again, to join them for church tomorrow and he declined. Worse than that, she'd insisted on tucking him in with a bedtime story.

How ridiculous. When he was a kid no one wanted the job. Now into adulthood, the role was coveted by a child.

A faint noise reached his ears. He raised his head and listened.

It came again.

Light flickered in the hallway, followed by faint sobs.

"Arianne?" He pulled himself up and swung his legs over the side of the bed. Was she hurt?

He pushed his body weight onto his good leg—torture!—and dropped into his wheelchair. Stupid casts. He fiddled with the wheels, guided by the dim light coming from the living room.

On full alert, he inched down the dark hallway toward the sound. The lights were off, but the TV provided enough light to see Arianne cross-legged on the couch in her pajamas, a tissue held to her nose.

"What's wrong?" He scanned the room for trouble.

She jumped. "I'm sorry. I didn't mean to wake you."

He wheeled closer and pushed to a standing position. "What is it?"

She raised to meet him. Tears filled her eyes. Even in the dimness, he could detect her red nose. She opened her mouth to speak but when her lower lip wobbled, she closed it. More tears spilled down her cheeks.

"Has someone hurt you?" His heart sped. Hands curled into fists.

She shook her head.

Relief swept through him. He opened his arms, and she buried her face in his shirt. Within seconds she drenched it.

"Shhh," he soothed, weaving his fingertips into her hair. Every bit as soft as he'd imagined.

Her body trembled. He held on tighter. His leg started to ache, but he'd rather lose it than let go. The fresh, cottony smell that was all Arianne welcomed him. Just being near her made him dizzy.

Her shoulders finally stopped heaving.

"What's going on?"

"I'm sorry." Her voice shook. "Daniel was in an accident, and Sarah, she…"

More crying.

He cupped her face, brushing away tears with his thumbs. "Take a deep breath." She obeyed. "Now, who are Daniel and Sarah?"

Arianne pointed to the TV. "Daniel, he's a farmer. He got run over by a tractor before Sarah had a chance to tell him she loved him."

A gold crown took over the television screen. He looked down at her in disbelief. "Daniel and Sarah aren't real people, are they?"

His hands moved from side to side with the shake of her head. "No. I'm a sucker for historical romances."

Oh brother. Huck dropped his hands. "You mean I almost killed myself getting out of bed to check on you, and you're crying over some dumb movie?"

More tears. "I'm sorry. It's been a bad day."

He laughed. The woman wasn't right. She really wasn't. Arianne started laughing too, and before he knew it, they were both standing there giggling like a couple of hyenas.

The lunacy subsided, but he couldn't take his eyes off her. He'd come in here prepared to fight a pack of wolves on one leg. Someone ought to just shoot him now. He trailed a finger along her jaw to her chin. Her eyelids slid closed as he brushed his thumb over her lips, tugging the bottom one slightly.

Knowing he shouldn't, he lowered his head toward hers.

She ripped herself from his arms and nearly pushed him over. "No, Huck. I won't do this with you again."

His neck burned with rejection. He stared at the light reflecting off the carpet. Of course she wouldn't want to. She knew how it'd end. When he looked up again, she was gone.

Huck sank into his wheelchair, gripping the armrests until his knuckles ached. His weakness for her had clouded his judgment.

A bride floated down concrete steps on TV, and he punched the power button, encasing the room in black. That's the kind of ending Arianne deserved. Wanted. His mind went back to the last day with Giada at the diner. She'd wanted the happy ending too. He'd stolen it from her.

He massaged his burning leg muscle until his eyes adjusted to the darkness. He found his way back to his room, stretched out on the bed, and went back to staring at the ceiling.

"Float like a butterfly, sting like a bee."
—Muhammad Ali

16

Huck sat on the bed and rubbed the sleep from his eyes. He grabbed the folded stack of clothes off his nightstand and slung them over the back of his wheelchair, then maneuvered into it and inched toward the bathroom. Each day got easier, but the process was slow and painful.

The house was silent. No girlish humming. No cartoons. None of the usual noises Arianne made while making breakfast.

No female tears or drama. Just quiet.

The bathroom tiles were cold against his feet. He reached into the shower and twisted the faucet. By the time he'd removed his clothes, steam filled the room like a sauna. He swiped a towel over the mirror and glanced at his back. The road rash had healed, leaving only a quarter-sized scar on his right shoulder blade. Come next year, no one would ever know by looking at him that he'd broken almost everything in his body. He secured a trash bag around his casts and staggered to the shower.

He peeled back the curtain and frowned at the bright-colored bottles. Large containers of shampoo and conditioner, smaller ones with cartoons on the label—strawberry scented and tear-free. A bar of white soap next to his. Purple, sparkly liquid, something called shower gel, a metal can of pink shaving cream, and an orange razor possessed one corner. How much stuff did it take to get a woman clean?

And why were they in *his* shower? She had her own. Wasn't it enough that she'd infected the rest of his house, including his TV? Now she had to have his bathroom too? He didn't want to know what things she'd stuffed in the medicine cabinet and under the sink.

Hot water pelted his back and shoulders, relaxing his stiff muscles. After he rinsed his hair, he threw his head back and let the spray run down his face. A light cottony smell lifted in the steam. He breathed it in. Why had he tried to kiss her?

Because she set his body on fire, that's why. The more he was around her, the more he wanted to be. A bad thing he couldn't get enough of. He scrubbed a hand over his face. Arianne was getting to him, more than any woman. She'd moved into his house, and now she was moving into his heart. Except there was no vacancy.

After his shower, he dressed and wheeled himself to the kitchen. The coffeepot gurgled the last drips into the pot. He inhaled something sweet. Sticky buns? Have mercy. How was he supposed to keep his feelings platonic when she kept doing things like this?

Huck pushed to the counter, balanced on his good leg, and opened the cabinet above him. Where was his mug? He'd watched Arianne closely as she emptied the dishwasher after dinner last night, so he knew it wasn't in there. He grabbed the nearest one and filled it. Took a sip. He swallowed and stuck out his tongue.

Arianne walked into the kitchen. "It's cinnamon roll flavored. You'll want to add cream and sugar." She rested her mug on the table—his mug—and breezed through the room.

The crayon drawings on his fridge rustled as she opened the refrigerator door. She brought him the cream and sugar. Now that the rancid taste had left his tongue, his attention zeroed in on the light blue dress swishing just above her calves. The style was old. Very 1950s.

Arianne babbled, which she did when she was nervous. Overcompensating for last night, he supposed. He didn't register a word she said. He was too preoccupied by the way her hips swayed as she moved around the room.

Her fingers snapped in front of him.

He blinked. "What?"

"I said it's good with whipped cream. Do you want some?"

He scratched his chin. "I don't drink girlie coffee."

Plus, he'd had his heart set on sticky buns. The talking vegetable cartoon theme song drifted from the living room.

"You don't know what you're missing." She poured herself another cup. Steam lifted around the rim. "Are you sure you don't want to go with us to church?"

"I'm sure."

Arianne looked down at her bare feet. "We, um…need to talk." She nibbled her bottom lip and scratched her head. "About last night."

Why did women always have to talk everything to death? "No, we don't."

One hand hugged the curve of her hip, and she

studied him over the mug raised to her lips. She was barely taller than him, and he was sitting down.

"Huck, I—"

"You tryin' to bring back the fifties?"

Her forehead wrinkled, and she looked down at her dress. "It was my grandmother's. I found it in the attic after my dad passed away. I had to repair a few things, but it was salvageable."

"You look like you belong in an episode of *Happy Days*."

"It's true vintage. Women pay big money for dresses like this." She lowered her long, black lashes. "Well, I like it."

He did too, but he wasn't about to tell her that. "Why is your stuff in my shower?"

"Oh, I forgot to tell you. There's a leak in our bathroom. I found it last night. It's made a terrible mess on the wall. I don't know anything about plumbing, but I managed to get the valve shut off. We moved everything into your bathroom temporarily."

"Fine, but I draw the line at fuzzy, pink toilet lid covers."

"Agreed."

"I'll call and get someone out here right away."

She placed the mug in the sink. "No hurry. I don't mind."

"Well, I do." The words left his mouth before he could stop them. "And quit using my coffee mug."

Immature, yes, but there wasn't anything in his house she hadn't fingerprinted. Couldn't a man at least have his coffee mug?

"We'll just be on our way." She stomped a cute little tantrum to the living room entryway. "Emma, turn that off, please. It's time for church."

With her stubborn chin held high, she passed him without a glance.

"And another thing. She watches entirely too much TV."

Arianne spun, mouth open. "When did you become an expert on child-rearing? You don't have children. You're not even married!"

"It doesn't take a marriage license to see she needs more than cartoons."

"Are you going to church with us today, Mr. Huck?" Emma bounced beside him.

Her dingy floral dress was a stark contrast to her bright smile. "Sorry, kid."

Emma slouched and gripped her tiny Bible closer.

Huck nudged her elbow. "I was just telling your mom how much fun you can have doing things outside. How 'bout after supper, you and I do some fishin'?"

Arianne's face puckered like a prune.

Emma squealed and danced on the toes of her scuffed, white shoes.

He grinned, looked at Arianne, and winked.

She clasped Emma's hand. "We need to go, or we'll be late."

They moved past him to the door. Arianne shoved her feet into her heels and snatched her purse and Bible. Emma went outside. Arianne followed, slamming the door behind them.

~*~

Ripples expanded on the glassy surface of the water. Arianne held tight to her fishing pole in one hand and rested her chin in the other. She'd agreed to this only because Emma was so excited. Otherwise, she'd have told Huck what to do with his fishing poles. How dare he tell her how to raise her child?

They hadn't spoken a word to each other since his tantrum this morning. Men. One minute they want to kiss you, the next, they insult you.

Something tugged on her line. She straightened. Another tug. She jerked the pole back and reeled it in. The line gave, flinging the hook out of the water. No fish, no worm. She sighed.

Story of her life.

Emma hopped up from her spot beside Huck. "Did you get one, Mommy?"

"No, he just stole my worm."

Emma sat back down.

"You don't have your bait on good enough." Huck never looked up from the water.

"At last, he speaks."

His Adam's apple shifted in his thick neck.

She'd show him. Arianne grimaced and lifted a wriggling worm from the container and impaled it. *Worm murderer.* She wiped her slimy fingers on the bridge and recast.

Water lapped over the rocks at the pond's edge. Emma hummed. Arianne dared to peek at Huck. She knew Emma's crooning irritated him, but he seemed unaffected.

What had almost happened the night before, however, affected her a great deal. She'd craved that kiss the way she was craving a cherry cheesecake right now. The fact that she'd come close to giving in to him… She couldn't get attached. Wouldn't. At the end of their deal, they'd part one way or another, and after taking care of him, the last thing she wanted to do was nurse a broken heart.

She had to protect her little girl too. Emma had already placed Huck on a pedestal so high he couldn't be seen for all the clouds. That's why she'd never let Emma around the few men she'd dated. There was too much to lose if it didn't work out. And it never did.

"Mommy, I need to go potty."

Arianne reeled in her line. "OK, I'm coming."

"I can do it by myself." Emma stood and passed Huck her pole.

"Are you sure?"

"I'm not a baby."

No she wasn't. Her little girl was growing up. Maybe that's what Huck was getting at this morning. "All right."

Emma's footsteps thumped along the bridge then quieted when she reached the grass. When she'd disappeared through the back door, Arianne stole the empty place beside Huck.

He visibly tensed. She recast and stared at the circles the water made when her bobber hit the surface. "About last night..."

Huck groaned. "A word of advice: when a man wants to talk about something, he will. Otherwise, let it be."

"If all women abided by that rule, nothing would ever get settled."

"Instead y'all nag us to death and wonder why we get mad."

"I don't nag."

"Yes, you do."

"No, I don't."

"You're nagging right now."

"I'm not nagging. I just want you to answer my

question!"

"What question? What do you want me to say? It was really poor judgment on my part, Arianne. It won't happen again. End of discussion."

That's what every woman wanted to hear after a man tried to kiss them. "There's more at stake here than just me this time—my business, my daughter."

She would not let him hurt her again.

"Are you still holding on to something that happened years ago?"

"What are you talking about?"

"You just said you won't let me hurt you again."

Embarrassment flooded her. She hadn't meant to voice that out loud.

He sucked in a deep breath. "I didn't stand you up that night because I wanted to."

Yeah, right. "I have no idea what you're referring to." No way would she give him the satisfaction of knowing she remembered. Or that it still hurt. She'd memorized the feel of the pale pink chiffon of her mother's old dress, the one she'd dreamed of redesigning for years, the one that would've made every girl at the prom envy her if she'd gotten the chance to show it off.

The muscle in Huck's jaw bulged. "I was getting into my car to pick you up when your dad and his posse paid me a visit."

"My dad? What was he doing there?" Stupid woman. She'd let him reel her in.

"To let me know I'd better think twice before taking out his daughter."

Arianne swallowed her shock. Daddy didn't like Huck which was why she'd told him she was going stag. How did he find out? The mantel clock ticked through her memory. She'd counted every one, waiting for Huck.

Huck shrugged, eyes trained on the water. "You know, it doesn't matter anymore."

Sure it did. "If that's what happened, why didn't you tell me then?"

"I couldn't."

"Why?"

"At the time, it was easier to make you believe I'd stood you up."

"Because of my dad? That doesn't make sense."

"He threatened my scholarship."

"What hold could he have possibly had over your scholarship?"

Huck stared at his lap. "Never mind."

"No. You said yourself it doesn't matter anymore. So tell me. I deserve to know."

"I was almost nineteen. You were a minor." He regarded her with caution. "It's best that he stepped in."

Was it?

She'd driven to the school that night in hopes she'd misunderstood and was supposed to meet Huck there instead. Her heart had hit the gym floor when a spotlight illuminated the couple in the middle of the room. Huck, in all reigning glory, had his meaty hands wrapped around the waist of a bosomy brunette wearing a glittering tiara.

What little contents were in Arianne's stomach threatened to re-appear. Chairs screeched across wood as couples left their tables to join the monarchy. She looked around the gym without really seeing anything.

In a daze, she stepped through the crowd. Huck's gaze locked with hers. His smile fell, along with his hands from the girl's waist.

The fairytale spell was broken. Tears clouded her view, but she blinked them away. The brunette turned to see who'd stolen Huck's attention. Ashlynn Evans smirked and pulled Huck closer.

He tugged her arms from his neck and started toward Arianne, looking...wounded. He was an excellent actor, however, making her believe he wanted to take her, even if it was only payment for his tutoring. Before he reached her, she fled to the car, escaping all the smiles and snickering.

She'd been vulnerable ever since. Determined to prove to herself she was worth having and that not all gorgeous men had a black heart. Daddy had tried to save her from the mess she'd fallen into with Adam. And what a disaster it was.

Arianne crossed her bare feet at the ankles. "For the record, if it hadn't been for my dad, you'd have taken me?"

~*~

He'd have been there early. Weeks in fact. "I'd have kept my end of the bargain."

The sheriff's words rang fresh in Huck's ears. "You're not fit to be around my daughter."

Two cops had pinned Huck against his waxed Mustang. Rage swelled in his chest as he tried to fight them off. The buttons on his white shirt strained along his chest. When he noticed them scratching the car's paint, he surrendered, swallowing past the grip the bowtie had around his neck. "This is illegal. You can't lay a hand on me without a valid reason."

And for once, the law didn't have one.

Laughter spewed from the sheriff's throat. "And who's the judge going to believe? You think I don't know about you?" He paced behind Huck. "I know you're a bastard child from Tupelo, Mississippi. I know your mother—if you can call her one—had a criminal record longer than the roach-infested trailer you both lived in. You've had more daddies than you can count with your fingers and toes."

The grip on Huck's hands released, and he pivoted toward the cops, rubbing his wrists. The sheriff's hot breath rolled across Huck's ear as Thompson placed his hand on the Mustang's hood and lowered his voice for effect. "I know all about what you did, son. Why you moved up here in the first place."

Huck stilled.

"I won't allow my daughter to be humiliated." Thompson backed away. "Hopefully, we both agree that it's best you stay away from Arianne. After all, she's a minor. I sure would hate to press charges when you've been promised that fancy football scholarship. A second chance at life might do you some good. We understand each other?"

It wouldn't matter what Huck said. The sheriff had made up his mind. "Yeah."

"Good, because I'm sure your uncle wouldn't want his past returning to haunt him, either."

Huck started toward him when two hands slammed into his shoulders and pinned them to the car. "What's my uncle got to do with this?"

"My beef with Martin is my business, boy. You just make sure you stay out of trouble and away from my daughter."

Thompson nodded toward the squad cars, and all three men fell away. Engines revved and pebbles spit from their rear tires, raining gravel on top of Huck and his restored classic.

His first instinct was to fire up the engine, beat the sheriff to his own house, and pick up Arianne anyway. But he'd worked hard to make a new name in this town. He was a school legend, scoring more touchdowns than any quarterback in county history. If he ever wanted to be somebody, he needed that scholarship.

Huck slammed the driver's side door and stormed into the house, shedding his tuxedo jacket as he went. How would he ever explain to Arianne why he didn't show up? He couldn't tell her the truth without exposing his past. His only option was to make her think he'd stood her up. That he'd played a part in the scheme.

That would crush her. He ran cold water in the bathroom sink, cupped his hands, and splashed his face. He dabbed his skin with a towel and took a long look in the mirror. She'd done so much for him. Believed there was something good deep inside his heart. No one had ever seen him that way before. He didn't want to kill that, but it was going to happen either way. Breaking his word was the lesser of two evils.

His jaws clamped together so tightly his molars threatened to crack. Love wasn't real anyway. The only person he could count on was himself. He needed that scholarship. So he'd go to prom tonight, but not with Arianne.

A pull on Arianne's fishing line brought Huck back to the present. He took it from her, and with a few turns of the reel, up came a big juicy bass fighting the hook.

Emma ran to him, curls springing every direction. "You got one, Mr. Huck. Gee, that's big!"

"It's your mom's." He handed the rod back to Arianne.

She tried to grip the fish and shrieked when it wriggled and sprayed water off its fins.

Emma giggled. "It almost as big as the one who ate Jonah."

Arianne smiled, finally getting the fish under control.

"Was Jonah a worm?" Huck changed positions in his wheelchair. He was ready to burn this thing.

Emma scratched her head. "No, silly. Jonah and the whale. It's a Bible story."

Arianne made faces as she worked the hook from the bass's mouth.

"So what happened?"

Emma placed one hand on his shoulder and another on her hip. "God told Jonah to do something, and he didn't obey, so he got eaten by a big fish."

She extended her arms in demonstration.

Huck reeled in his line. "That's not a very happy ending."

"You haven't heard the rest of the story." Arianne tossed the fish back into the water.

After the splash, Emma waved at the fish and continued. "He stayed in the fish's belly for three whole days, praying and asking God to forgive him. He promised to do what God had asked. From the bottom of the ocean, God heard his prayers, and the fish swam to shore and puked him up."

Sure. Huck raised the corner of his upper lip. "I bet Jonah needed a good bath."

Both girls laughed. He'd take whale spit over a

guardrail any day.

"Mommy, can I play on my swing set now?"

They'd only been fishing for thirty minutes.

"Sure, I can see you from here."

Emma sprinted up the hill.

Silence stretched between them before Arianne finally spoke. "I'm doing the best I can with her, Huck."

He turned, only to get drawn into her blue eyes. "Look, I'm sorry about this morning. I've no right to tell you how to raise your kid."

She nodded. "It's not easy doing this by myself. Playing mom and dad."

"It's even tougher on the kid, believe me."

"Are you speaking from experience?"

"Maybe."

Cold, lonely nights in juvenile hall when he was twelve crept into his memory. The bloodied, lifeless face of his cell-mate still haunted him at times. The horror of watching those thugs gang up on James, surround him and beat him to death with their fists. Huck's fault. Though he was protecting himself from something he didn't do.

Huck had caused some ruckus in his life, but he'd never witnessed such evil before. It'd scared the spit out of him. That's why he was a Big Brother now. He didn't want Matt, or any kid, to suffer the same fate. Huck had banished that nightmare to the darkest corner of his mind, but occasionally, like today, it would slip through the cracks.

"I'm no good, Arianne." She needed to know that so she could intervene on the days he was weak. Like last night.

Her fishy-smelling hand reached for his. "Giada's

death wasn't your fault. You had no control over that driver's heart attack. It was...her time to go."

Her words could sooth his open wounds if he'd let them. Emma's giggles floated on the air. She'd finally learned how to swing on her own. "Why do you really think Jonah got eaten by the whale?"

"He disobeyed God's instructions. There are always consequences to sin."

Huck nodded. God or not, there were always consequences.

There are thousands of kinds of bees, but only the honeybee can produce honey.

17

Why did some brides think that ruffles and lace and all-out gaudiness on their gowns made them more special on their wedding day? Arianne curled her nose at Darcy's sketch. The dress had everything the governor's daughter had demanded, down to the last pearl: sparkling white satin, strapless bust line, a sheath silhouette to hug every natural curve, and—heaven help them all—a twelve-foot, chiffon train that flowed from around her knees like a waterfall.

Who on earth needed a twelve-foot train? What a waste of expensive fabric. Sure, the dress would look fantastic on a model in a bridal magazine, posing in the middle of a forest in some artsy, unnatural way. Impractical in reality. Not to mention, between the fabric and her time, very expensive. Arianne quoted upwards of ten-thousand dollars. At this, Darcy hadn't batted an eyelash. Arianne couldn't imagine having that much money to spend on a single dress. Or a car for that matter.

With Darcy's classic beauty in mind, Arianne had sketched a gown more sophisticated, enchanting. A gown that would enhance her natural beauty instead of the dress stealing the spotlight. The fabric would've glittered under the reception hall lights and given the black-and-white bridal portraits an old-movie feel.

Darcy had hated it.

Arianne returned to the sketch in her hand. Instead, her client would look like a giant spool of ribbon that had unraveled and attacked her dress. It was Darcy's day, however, not Arianne's.

If it were hers, she'd wear a simple design with a fitted bodice and a scalloped, sweetheart neckline. Beige cotton tulle trimmed in gold embroidery, open back, and a sweep train to gently skim the floor. Homage to the decadence of 18th-century France.

The white pant suit she'd worn with Adam at their Justice of the Peace wedding slipped into her memory. She folded it away. Next time—if there was a next time—she'd have a real wedding, with a groom who actually loved her.

"Mommy!" Emma's voice drifted from the stairs.

"I'll be down in a minute." Arianne put aside the sketch and checked her reflection in the mirror as she sucked in her tummy. The outdoors offered great exercise. She should take advantage of it while she was here and give a good effort to shedding that extra twelve pounds she carried around. Today's humidity gave her hair enough frizz to make Medusa jealous, and...was that a wrinkle?

What did it matter? Prince Charming was taken anyway.

The main level was quiet. Sketch in hand, Arianne went to Huck's office and fired up his laptop, grateful he'd given his permission earlier in the day. She dropped into the leather chair. A puff of his cologne escaped, and she breathed it in. Heaven help her.

After the computer woke up, the last webpage

he'd used filled the screen. *Bangor Daily News*—Giada's obituary.

Her heart squeezed. Laughter filtered in through the window where Huck and Emma sat in what looked like a golf cart on steroids. His attitude had improved lately. He even joked and laughed on occasion, but the smile never quite reached his eyes. His tough-guy mask didn't fool her. He was hurting.

After she scanned the dress design and emailed it to Darcy, she shut down Huck's laptop and followed the noise coming from the kitchen. Emma extracted water bottles from the fridge and put them in a plastic bag.

"What are you doing?"

"Mr. Huck told me to come and get you and some drinks. We're going to see his bees." Emma shut the fridge and pulled Arianne along. "Come on, Mommy. He's gonna leave without us."

Outside, Huck waited in an open vehicle with heavy duty tires and a small bed. "You'll have to drive."

She climbed behind the wheel after Emma scooted to the middle and handed the bag to Huck. A spike in temperature, more common in July than the end of August, caused sweat to bead along her forehead and temples. Huck had to be smothering in that thick cast.

"Ready?" he asked.

Arianne gripped the wheel. "I've never driven a golf cart."

"It's a Gator—a farm utility vehicle. Just turn the key and drive."

"If you say so." The engine fired, and they all flew forward when her foot hit the gas.

"Woman." Huck gripped the dash with one hand

and the top of the frame with the other.

Emma giggled.

Arianne cringed. "Sorry."

She pressed lighter this time, and they coasted over the bridge and through the meadow, bouncing in the hot vinyl seats. Long, wispy grass rustled around the tires.

She glanced at Huck. Sweat glistened on his skin and soaked circles on his white T-shirt. The breeze floating through the cab brought his scent her way. If only she could bottle that smell and keep it forever.

He caught her staring and winked. "You might want to keep your eyes ahead of you."

She snapped her head forward. His laugh rolled in the wind.

~*~

The Gator slowed to a stop and Arianne shut off the engine. "What's that noise?" She tipped her chin, listening.

"The bees." Huck grinned as Emma's eyes grew round as bowling balls.

"What are they doing, Mr. Huck?"

"Humming."

"I like to hum too." Her heels thumped the floorboard with each kick.

Oh, he knew. He pointed to the white boxes tucked among the pines. "Pull closer."

Sweat rolled between his shoulder blades and soaked his shirt. It could be hot as the sun, and he wouldn't leave. He was back where he belonged.

Arianne drove until he instructed her to stop. Less than ten feet away, the hair on his arms and neck perked with the adrenaline rush that always got him when the bees were near.

"I don't know about his, Huck." Arianne leaned closer to his side of the vehicle. He rested his arm across the back of the bench seat.

"Feel that?" The air around them buzzed. Her ponytail brushed his hand, and he stroked the soft ends of her hair.

Arianne rubbed her arms. "I'm not sure about this. Will our being here make them mad? Emma's never been stung before. What if she's allergic?"

"Don't be such a downer." He could swim in those dark pools of blue looking to him for reassurance. "Trust me."

She blinked a few times then grabbed Emma's hand and nodded.

Worker bees by the hundreds surrounded the supers, flying in and out of the white boxes, slicing through the air with their tiny bodies.

"What are they doing, Mr. Huck?"

"You don't have to whisper. The ones hanging 'round those boxes are the guard bees. They protect the hive from danger. The others are collector bees. They're foraging—gathering food. They find flowers and other plants, collect as much nectar as they can carry, and then bring it back to their home. They transfer the nectar to the younger worker bees inside those white boxes, who turn it into honey."

Emma pushed a damp lock away from her sweaty forehead. "Where's all the honey?"

"It's in there." He handed her a water and pointed to the supers.

Bees buzzed around the cab. Arianne squealed when one landed on her arm and marched toward her sleeve.

He squeezed her shoulder. "Be still. She won't hurt you. She's trying to decide if you're a threat."

Arianne craned her neck away from her arm, but her gaze never left the bee. "How do you know it's a she?"

"All the workers are females. Male bees—drones—only wait around to mate with the queen."

"Can we see the honey, Mr. Huck?" Emma rubbed her temple with the cold bottle.

"Not today, kid. The heat makes 'em cranky, and I don't have my equipment with me. But it'll be ready to harvest next week. If your mom says it's all right, you can see it then."

Emma looked up at Arianne, who didn't look too sure. The bee flew away, and Arianne relaxed against the seat.

"I'll take you both to see the building where we separate the honey and bottle it. No bee threats in there. I'll even let you help if you want."

Something he never offered. He played with a damp curl at the nape of Arianne's neck. Her eyelids closed for a second, and her cheeks turned pink. "We'd like that."

If that made her blush, what else could he get her to do?

Arianne swallowed. "What do you say we head home? I made a fresh jug of blueberry lemonade this morning, and I'll cook a pizza for supper."

He and Emma exchanged glances.

Arianne frowned. "Don't worry. It's a frozen pizza from the store."

Emma slapped him a high-five, and Arianne gave them a mock scowl.

They cruised down the path through the field and over the hill. The ocean was a good five miles away, but he could smell the salt on the breeze, almost taste it.

His gut tightened as they neared the house. Home. Arianne had called his house *home*. It was starting to feel that way, wasn't it? Something stirred within him he couldn't define. As much as he knew she was off-limits, he couldn't help but be drawn to her, like a bee to a rare flower.

"Thy lips, O my spouse, drop as the honeycomb: honey and milk are under thy tongue..."
—Song of Solomon 4:11

18

The letter opener sliced the crisp, white envelope. Arianne fingered the check for seven-thousand dollars—Darcy's down payment for her gown. She squealed and grinned so wide it hurt. This small piece of paper was the start to a new life. The promise it held crept into her bones, along with an ache from the jog she'd attempted yesterday. She rested her palm in the small of her back and arched, stretching her pinched muscles.

Arianne placed Huck's letter opener in the desk's top drawer. His spacious office held a masculine charm with matching walnut furniture and simple décor. Outside, sunlight played peekaboo through maple leaves, casting prismatic rays of light into the room. White towels and washcloths on the clothesline danced in the breeze. September was Arianne's favorite time of year. Tepid days relinquished to cool nights, requiring extra layers of clothing.

On the corner of the desk sat a framed picture of Huck in his college football uniform, pumping his fist in victory. Beside it lay a loose, faded photo of him around age ten. He stood by an attractive blonde who appeared to have lived a lot of life for such a young age. Next to the woman, a dark-haired man with a mustache and wide grin gazed at her with love in his eyes, his hands resting on Huck's shoulders. The woman was clearly Huck's mother, but was the man his father?

She lifted the frame of Huck in all his jock glory and stared into the velvety brown eyes that made her body hum. Then it hit her. Her future life wouldn't involve him.

Her initial elation of a fresh start plummeted. She sank onto the leather desk chair. How silly. She really needed to kick this adolescent crush. At her age, it was ridiculous. Beyond the borders of pathetic. She was a grown woman for crying out loud, not a teenager. Then again, the longing she'd caught on his face lately—or at least that's how she'd interpreted it—and the stirring his simple touch invoked brought on all kinds of teen angst.

Arianne replaced the photograph and stood. This was Huck Anderson. Every woman up and down the eastern seaboard had the same reaction. He was an expert fisherman, using himself as bait. The female population swam straight into his net.

Well not her. Thirty waited just around the corner, ready to jump out, snatch her, and drag her up the hill, kicking and screaming. When she reached the top, she didn't want to look down and see another heartbreak on her list of life's mistakes.

And heartache would surely come with Huck. His gypsy heart didn't know how to settle down. How to love. Furthermore, he'd no desire to, saying as much that night by the campfire, which she only partly believed.

Had Huck's comment been a defense mechanism? A way of protecting himself from her—as if she were a threat—or from detaching himself from Giada's death, a subconscious way of coping? After all, he'd never sought counseling to help him grieve.

His motorcycle accident alone was a daily reminder of why he and Arianne were incompatible. Huck was insouciant and impulsive, and she was careful and…boring. But she liked boring. Boring was safe, and as a parent safety took priority.

He'd become such a part of their lives the past few months it was strange to think of a day without him. Except she couldn't let her heart think that way, no matter how integral his presence felt.

Arianne fingered the check, rubbing her thumb over the slick surface. Nope. Come spring, her bridal shop, her daughter, and her own semi-truck load of excess baggage were moving on.

~*~

After three weeks of grueling therapy drills led by Sergeant Sandy, Huck's reward was a completely healed arm, a lighter leg cast, and a pair of crutches. He could finally walk on his own—sort of. Anything beat that wheelchair. And once he was able to slip back into jeans, he was going to burn every pair of shorts he owned.

Little hands wrapped around his bicep. Emma snuggled against his arm. The wind blew through the Gator's cab and fanned her curls across her face. She closed her eyes and brushed the hair away. After a good yawn, she burrowed closer to his stiff arm. He gave in and steered with his left wrist through the meadow.

Another crayon drawing had graced his fridge this morning. One of his toothpick arms held a fishing pole, and the other held a shield. She stood next to him with her rod, dressed in a pink ball gown and gold tiara. A horse stood poised on the hill by her swing set. A yellow blob hovered over them from the sky. He'd known the picture held some deep meaning by the twist in the pit of his stomach.

A red, metal barn came into view. His attention drifted to his adult passenger in a blue shirt that fit her just right. She'd pulled her hair back into a messy bun he'd like to undo altogether. Purplish circles under her eyes hinted at the absence of sleep. He'd barely gotten a word out of her after she'd returned from getting the mail that morning. He wasn't sure what he'd done to upset her this time—probably breathed the wrong way—but she'd definitely built a wall.

"Here we are." He parked the Gator by the barn door and turned the key.

The building towered over them. He steadied his weight on the crutches and hobbled inside. His pith helmet and tools hung on racks by the door, and the warm, sweet scent of honey welcomed him home.

"What is all this stuff, Mr. Huck?" Emma's curious eyes observed the room.

The dehumidifier whirred. The noise mixed with their voices and echoed off the walls. "This is the honey house."

Supers stacked as tall as him swallowed the entire west corner. A few vagrant bees flew among the exposed support beams. Arianne craned her neck to look around, clutching the picnic basket she'd brought along.

Huck pointed behind her. "Through that door is a small office with a fridge. You can put our lunch in there 'til we're ready. There's a bathroom back there, too, should y'all need it."

The girls disappeared behind the office door, and he moved further into the barn. Jude emerged from the stack of supers with five wooden boxes balanced on his dolly. "You couldn't stand it, could you?"

Huck chuckled at the old man's grin. "It feels good to be back." He shifted on his crutches. "Even if it's just for the day."

"Jude!" Emma ran out of the office. "What are those?"

Jude tapped the boxes with his palm. "These are supers—where the bees live. They build their hives in these boxes, and when the honey is ready, we remove the bees, bring the supers back here, and rob the honey."

Emma's eyebrows wrinkled. "The bees aren't in there?"

"Not right now."

Huck heard Arianne's sigh of relief. Even the bravest folks got jumpy around a thousand bees. He moved between work tables that held white buckets. "We have to remove them to get to the honey."

Arianne followed beside him while Jude passed with the cargo. She wiped her damp forehead with the back of her hand. "Why is it so hot in here?"

"We keep the place between ninety and a hundred degrees. Warm honey flows faster than cold honey does, and we run a dehumidifier to reduce moisture and prevent fermentation."

"How do bees keep it from fermenting in the wild?"

Huck stopped and lifted a broken chunk of wax hexagons from a table. "The honeycomb. It seals and preserves the honey."

Arianne smiled. "Very smart."

Smart didn't cover it. "Honeybees create something unique in this world. Even the Ancient Egyptians appreciated their work by embalming their dead in honey to preserve the bodies for the afterlife." Huck's left crutch caught the table leg, and he tripped then caught himself. If there was an afterlife, he didn't want to take this body with him.

Emma tugged his T-shirt. "If you take all the bees' honey, then they won't have anything to eat, Mr. Huck."

"I don't take it all, and I always keep plenty on hand in case they get hungry."

They reached the uncapping machine. Jude started the implement, pulled a honey-glazed frame of honeycomb from a super, and placed it on the moving belt. "This strips the beeswax, and gives us access to the honey."

Arianne looked around at all the stacked supers and equipment. "You normally do all this by yourself?"

"Hardly. Harvesting is a big job. Twice a year, I call some guys to help me collect the supers and extract and bottle the honey. The rest I take care of myself."

He led Arianne to a machine where they worked together uncapping the frames while Jude and Emma manned the honey extractor. Huck divided his weight between the crutches, occasionally resting on a stool. Jude lifted Emma onto his shoulder, so she could watch the uncapped frames spin around the machine as it separated the honey from the combs. From there, a sump pump forced the amber liquid from the extractor through a filter and into large storage tanks.

As the afternoon wore on, hunger gnawed at Huck's stomach. He scooted next to Arianne to tell her he was ready to break for lunch. Bottom lip pinched between her teeth, she concentrated on removing an uncapped frame from the turning belt. Loose strands of hair played around her face. Her cut-off shorts gave her an entirely different look than her vintage dresses, but produced the same result. Irresistible.

He brought his lips close to her ear. "You've worked hard. Ready for a break?"

His breath stirred her hair. Goose bumps trailed from her honey coated fingers up her arms. Her eyelids slipped closed for a moment and she nodded. Huck backed away, grinning. She still had a thing for him, even if she wouldn't admit it.

They shut down the machines, returning the barn to the quiet whir of the dehumidifier. Suds collected in the utility sink as they each took their turn washing the sticky mixture of wax and honey from their hands. The girls retreated to the office to collect their lunch, and Huck shuffled behind them.

"Well…" Jude patted his gut. "If you've got everything under control, I think I'll head home for a few hours. Eat some lunch. Take a little siesta."

"A siesta?"

"Hey, I'm used to retirement. This old man needs to rest his arthritic knees."

The crutches clicked along the smooth concrete floor. Huck's arm muscles ached and his good leg burned. A nap might be the right prescription. "Take your time, Jude. No rush."

"I know you've got some guys coming in

tomorrow, but if you don't mind, I'd like to bring a buddy over to help too. I need to finish this up by the weekend. The missus has been begging me to take her shopping in Freeport. We'll be gone two days, but don't hesitate to call if you need anything."

Huck raised a brow. "You're gonna drive three hours to take her shopping?"

Jude shrugged and gripped Huck's shoulder. "And stay for two days." He shook his head. "Sometimes you've got to do things you don't like to keep them happy. That's the secret to a strong relationship—compromise." He held Huck's gaze as if needing to emphasize his point.

Wasted breath. Huck didn't need relationship advice any more than he needed a relationship.

Emma joined them, rubbing her heavy, red-rimmed eyes. Arianne closed the office door behind her.

"I'll be back later." Jude waved and moved toward the exit.

Arianne's cheeks, pink from the heat, lifted in a heart-stopping smile. "Tell Sherry I said hello. And thank her for the blueberry pie recipe."

"I'll do that."

A few moments later, Jude's old Mazda pickup rattled past the barn and the sound faded in the distance.

Huck stepped through the door and squinted as his eyes adjusted to the light. A refreshing breeze cooled his baked skin. Arianne grabbed a quilt from the bed of the Gator, and he led them to a large shade tree by the creek not far from the shop.

She spread the blanket, and he settled onto it, resting his back against the trunk. Every bone and muscle in his body sighed. Half a day's work and his joints creaked like the floorboards of a hundred-year-old house. He fought the urge to throw his crutches in the creek.

Emma passed him a turkey sandwich and a small bag of chips. Arianne placed chocolate chip cookies between them and handed him a cold root beer. He was getting used to the root, even if it wasn't his preferred beer. Apparently, the girls were as hungry as he, because they were both quiet as they ate their food. The soft twitter of birds in the slight breeze was the only conversation they needed.

Emma chewed her last bite of sandwich. "Mommy, can I go put my feet in the water?"

"It's going to be cold. Don't you want any cookies?"

"Not right now." Emma took off her beat-up tennis shoes and socks, walked to the creek, and slipped her feet into the water, yelping from shock.

Arianne sat taller to get a better view of the water. With a full belly, Huck leaned his head against the trunk and closed his eyes. His leg throbbed from standing so long. He dug three extra-strength Tylenols from his pocket and chased them down with soda.

"Thanks for bringing us with you. I never realized how much work goes into beekeeping. You've got an amazing set-up here."

His chest swelled at the compliment. He'd never taken a woman into the honey house before. A few had asked, but he'd refused. Too personal. The bees were his family, and he had rules about women and family.

Huck studied Arianne's profile while she lifeguarded from the blanket. He hadn't thought twice about bringing them here today. Her working beside him was as natural as the honey they'd bottled. His imagination teased him into seeing a future where they worked here together permanently.

"What made you get into beekeeping?" Arianne pulled a cookie from the plastic box and took a bite.

"Do you remember the genealogy report we had to do for Mr. Warren's class our senior year?"

"Yes."

"I actually did it."

Arianne chuckled. "By yourself?"

He grinned. "All by myself. I found out my great-grandfather was a beekeeper in South Carolina. Before that, beekeeping had been in the family since the Civil War."

He'd hoped the project would lead to clues about his dad, but it hadn't. He'd been embarrassed to tell Mr. Warren he didn't know who his father was and therefore could only complete half of the project. No judgment came from the man, only understanding. Huck had received an A.

Arianne brushed the crumbs from her hands and stretched her legs out in front of her, crossing her feet at the ankles. "Beekeeping skipped a couple generations, huh? What did your grandfather do?"

Huck downed the last of his pop. "He was a Kirby vacuum salesman."

Her laughter brought him along for the ride.

"What a rebel." She put her arms behind her, weight on her palms. "How long have you been at this?"

"Eight years. After college I traveled, working odd jobs here and there. When I decided to get serious, I joined the Maine Beekeeper's Association. That's where I met Jude and a few other guys who showed me the ropes. I got involved with some local colleges three years ago, and I teach classes on beekeeping and small business now and then."

Arianne lifted a hand to wave at her daughter. "What do you do in the winter?"

"I stay busy repairing equipment, filling honey orders, applying mite treatments to the bees and such. I also make flavored honey sticks, beeswax candles, lip balms…"

"Wow. You turned out to be quite the entrepreneur."

Huck flicked the tab on his empty can, voices from the past whispering in his ears. "Yep. Who'd have thought I would do something with my life."

Her lips fell into a serious line. She gazed at him with drowsy eyes, her brows knitting together. "I didn't mean that, Huck. I always knew you were capable of doing anything you wanted to."

Was that why she'd graciously offered her time all those years ago? He probably wouldn't have any of this had she refused to tutor him.

The gratitude he started to express was cut short by Emma trudging toward them with dripping, bare feet. "Mommy, I'm tired."

Arianne patted the empty spot beside her. The girl curled up in the fetal position and laid her head in her mother's lap. Water droplets clung to Emma's ankles and small blades of grass stuck to the soles of her feet. Her eyelids closed and after a few moments of silence, her body fell limp, her breaths slowed.

Was Arianne so angelic when she slept? He'd bet his last drop of honey she was a vision to wake up next to. He allowed his mind to wander in that direction, but a hollowness carved out his middle. He braced his weight against the tree and stood. Not possible. He was no good for her.

"If you need to go back to the house, go ahead. Jude can drive me back later."

Her lips pouted. "We're fine. Where are you going?"

Her confusion begged him to stay. "Back to work."

The misery in his leg had eased by the time he got back to the processing room. He started the machines, the rhythm hypnotizing him closer to that siesta. After a while, Arianne joined him. The woman worked faster than most professionals.

Guilt settled in. She had her own business to run, a life she should be living, and here she was helping him. Again.

He raised his voice to be heard over the noise. "Now that I can creep around, you won't have to babysit anymore."

"What do you mean?"

"I mean take a break. You've been at my side for three months now. Have some fun. Go on a date."

Why'd he say that? She should, but...

The corners of her eyes twitched, as if his words stung. "After my last experience, I'll be staying home from now on."

He frowned. "What happened?"

She stared into the vat of honey. "He turned out to be married."

Huck stood taller and clenched his fists. If he was in better shape, he'd pay the idiot a visit.

"I sure know how to pick 'em, huh?"

Honey strained through the filter.

"Where's the kid?" He didn't want to have this conversation with her listening ears.

174

"Sleeping on a blanket in your office." She nodded toward the corner door. "It was coolest in there."

"Where do you find these guys?"

"I don't. They find me." She waved it away with her hand. "So, I saw a picture of you as a child in your office. Are those your parents?"

Great way to change from one sore subject to another. "It's my mom and step-dad."

"Where is he now?"

"Don't know. Mom booted him out after he refused to be her puppet."

"That must've been hard for you."

Huck shrugged. "I got a new one three months later."

When Rick left, it ripped any hope of a real family right out of him. The man actually had tears in his eyes when he told Huck goodbye, the first time a man had ever hugged him. Their fishing trip would remain one of Huck's only pleasant childhood memories.

"Did he work out?"

"Nope. But the next one"—he snickered and shook his head—"he gave Mom a run for her money."

Arianne's shock was evident on her face. "How many were there?"

"Six."

"She had six husbands?" Her voice rose with each word.

He removed the uncapped frame and passed it to her. "She was working on her seventh when she died. They were on their way to Vegas to get hitched. Never made it."

The rattle of bones grew louder the further he opened his closet. Why was he telling her this? He'd never talked about his mom with anyone. He busied himself by adding another frame to the conveyor belt.

Arianne's stunned gaze bore right through him. She needed to know what he'd come from, that her dad had been right. It would give her a head start to sprint away, put an ocean of distance between them. Every day that passed left him weaker, and he was losing the will to do it himself.

When a colony becomes overcrowded, the queen lays eggs for another queen, then leaves the hive in search of a new place to live. This process is called swarming.

19

Voices filled The Crabby Tavern along with the flow of the tap. Laughter rumbled from the bar. Huck's accountant, Ray Meyers, stepped through the door. Huck waved him to the table. Ray's gray mustache lifted as he pumped Huck's hand. The lights reflected off his bald patch.

Ray tugged his khaki's further up his waist, where his crisp, green polo shirt was neatly tucked. "Huck, let me introduce you to Lamar Johnson."

A man with serious, dark eyes and curly hair sidestepped Ray to shake Huck's hand. His plaid oxford shirt and dress pants matched his all-business demeanor. A thick, black strap curled around Lamar's shoulder, and Huck followed it with his gaze to see where it ended.

Was that a man purse? He forced his thoughts off his face. This would never work. He couldn't open a bait and tackle shop with a guy who toted a man purse. It was sacrilegious.

After they exchanged greetings, Huck gestured to the open seats across the table.

A waitress took their orders and returned with their drinks a minute later. Huck sipped the foam from his golden stout, the rich texture gliding down his throat. Mmm…he'd missed that taste.

Lamar sipped his wine—figured—then set down the drink. "Ray showed me the location of your building, and I think it's perfect for what I've got in mind." He dug papers from his handbag and passed them to Huck. "I went in and looked around to get a feel for the place. By the time I left, the woman had almost convinced me to buy a wedding dress."

The purse probably had nothing to do with it.

He could see Arianne now, flashing Lamar her dazzling smile, fluttering her long eyelashes, and pouring on her feminine charm. "The bridal shop was my uncle's doing. Now that it's relocating, I'm ready to open something more practical."

Lamar folded his hands. "I understand. However, I want to make it clear that what I have in mind is more than just a bait and tackle shop. I'm talking a complete sporting goods store."

The blueprint layout was perfect, though it would have to be tweaked in order to accommodate the building's dimensions. Kayaks, backpacks, hiking boots, sleeping bags, tents, rods and reels, guns—he could picture it all. Purse or not, this guy knew what men liked. Huck nodded his approval.

"The building will need some repairs. I noticed cracked mortar between some bricks, and it needs new windows. The inside—"

"A complete remodel isn't a problem."

The waitress brought their food, and Huck ordered another beer to complement his "Marty's Monster Burger," named in honor of his uncle. Ray joined the discussion now and then, but Huck and Lamar did most of the talking. By meal's end, business had transitioned into casual conversation.

Ray flicked his wrist and glanced down at his Rolex. "I've got another meeting in half an hour." His chair screeched across the wood floor. "Take care, Huck."

"Will do." He'd better go too. Arianne was supposed to pick him up at two, and he didn't want her to have to wait on him. He stood, and the room went fuzzy. Pathetic. A few months without drinking, and he'd turned into a sissy. Two beers had never affected him before. He shook the men's hands.

"Will Sunday morning work for you?" Lamar waited for Huck's response.

The boutique was closed on Sundays. "See you then."

Huck tossed his money on the table and pulled his crutches away from the wall. He positioned them beneath his arms, glanced at Uncle Marty's picture on the Wall of Fame one more time, silently said goodbye to the man, and then moved out the door.

Taking Lamar through Arianne's shop—his building—replacing the sight with sporting goods... It felt wrong.

Ludicrous. He and Arianne had a deal, and she was excited about relocating. She'd even checked out a few available spaces lately.

The thought stung his flesh like a swarm of angry bees. It wasn't losing the bridal boutique that bothered him. He couldn't care less about that. But losing it meant losing Arianne, and that was not good.

Then why didn't he let her stay?

He waited for Arianne on the curb and watched the stoplight change colors. Cars drove past, a horn honked, a bicycle sped behind him. He stared at the empty parking space where he'd first seen Giada. He'd come here that night with a purpose and left with an altered future. Thinking totally of himself, as usual.

Was this sporting good venture just as selfish as his past decisions? Of course he'd make sure Arianne and the kid were taken care of, but he could let them stay. Then he'd have an excuse to see them from time to time. The knot in his chest loosened to a sensation he'd never felt before. Good grief, what was in that beer?

~*~

"How was your day?"

Huck's deep drawl filled the kitchen and curled around Arianne like a fleece blanket on a winter's night. He'd been so sweet to her ever since that day at the honey house. Thoughtful, patient… She turned and gave him a speculative glance.

The weasel must be up to something. "Wonderful. Yours?"

"Good."

Still, she couldn't help but enjoy it. They'd fallen into an easy camaraderie, a comfortable routine.

He came up beside her to examine the steaming casserole on the stovetop. He poised his finger. She slapped his hand.

"Ouch. That's no way to treat a guy who brings you a gift."

She spun to face him. His flannel shirt intensified the rich chocolate of his eyes. That crooked smile brought out his dimple and her weak knees every time. "A gift?"

Huck leaned his weight on the crutches and pulled a small glass jar from his back pocket. "Strawberry honey. We finished making the last of it today. Thought you might like to try it."

The rosy liquid made her mouth water. "I would. Sherry sent over some homemade bread. I'll put some on a slice at supper."

"Did she send that over too?" He licked his lips at the pan of steaming parmesan chicken.

"No. I made it."

His smile slipped.

"It's her recipe though, and I followed the directions exactly. It should be edible."

Maybe that was her problem with men—she couldn't reach their hearts through their stomachs.

His brows knotted, and he stretched out his hand to touch her arm, but then drew it back. They fell into silent chores, him awkwardly setting the table, her filling glasses with ice.

"How was church?"

Her hand stilled around an ice cube. He'd never asked her that before. If he was scheming behind her back, he should be a little less obvious. She dropped the ice chunk into the glass. "Great. Brock Taylor was there this morning. Remember him?"

Huck set down the last fork. "Tall, dark-headed, played basketball?"

"Yeah."

"What's he doing now?"

"Army. He just returned from his second tour in Afghanistan. His parents were thrilled to have him at church, everyone was, but he seemed pretty uncomfortable. He was polite when spoken to, but there was sadness in his eyes. I'm sure he's seen things the rest of us can't imagine."

The muscle in Huck's jaw twitched. "That's

tough."

"It is. I'll be praying that he finds a new normal. And a job. He's out of the service now, and his mom mentioned that he's having trouble finding one. Unsure what he wants to do from here." She wrapped potholders around the handles and carried the chicken to the table.

"Send him over. I have work for him."

"What if he doesn't know anything about beekeeping?"

"He can learn. It'd bring a steady income, and he can work alone, give him some time to adjust before getting back into the workforce. The government used beekeeping as a means of transition after World War I."

Arianne couldn't believe it. She'd just witnessed the Grinch's heart grow three sizes. It took everything she had to stay on her side of the table and not throw her arms around Huck's neck. She grabbed a plate instead.

He leaned his arms on the back of a chair. "Can I ask you something?"

"Sure."

"When did you get into all this church and God stuff?" Not a trace of snarkiness in his tone this time.

"Right after Emma was born. As a child I'd believed in God because people were always telling me that my mom was in heaven. We never went to church though, so I really didn't give it much thought. The night I had Emma, I stared into the face of such a beautiful, tiny miracle...and I just knew there was more to our existence. I wanted to do right by her. I started going to church. That's when I began a true relationship with God."

Huck's fingers wrapped around the chair's back so tight his knuckles turned white. "What about your husband?"

She shrugged. "He didn't want any part of church. That may have been what scared him off. I don't know. He never said, just left." She transferred a piece of chicken onto a plate. "I know one thing. If I hadn't known God when Adam took off, I wouldn't have had the strength to be standing here today."

Huck stared at her, his features blank. She cleared her throat and finished dishing out supper.

He stepped to the fridge and handed her a diet soda. Sighed. "I have an investor for the building. I took him through it while you were at church today. Except your apartment. We didn't go in there."

His words stole her breath. What was the motive behind his kindness lately? Her heart took a dip, even though she'd known it was coming. They'd made a deal, and she too had been looking at other places. What did she expect? For him to change his mind and beg her to stay? That'd be the day this dish runs away with this spoon. At least he was being honest with her.

"Thanks for telling me."

He pulled two root beers off the shelf and closed the fridge. "I won't leave you without anywhere to go. I'll make sure you've found another place before we start renovations."

She raised her chin. "It's fine. I'm making my own plans anyway. No worries." To her amazement, she sounded convincing. She almost believed herself.

Huck's chest rose in a deep breath. He crutched to the living room doorway and told Emma it was time to eat.

Arianne opened the bottle of strawberry honey

and dipped her finger inside. She brought it to her mouth. Tart and sweet melted onto her tongue, reminding her of life's joys and sorrows.

Emma followed Huck to the table. He pulled out his chair, sat, and then laid his crutches on the floor. Elbows on the table, he laced his fingers together and waited for Emma to pray.

Sometimes the sweetest things in life were the hardest to work for.

~*~

Emma hummed between bites. Arianne sat across from him. He'd gotten used to this routine, to the company. A normalcy he never had growing up. Pretty soon, he'd have the house all to himself again.

A strange feeling curdled deep in his core. For once, it wasn't dinner. The food was more than edible. It was good.

"Mommy, I like this."

Arianne's big smile made the sick feeling worse. He was torn between needing them to go and wanting them to stay. The stay part couldn't be what he suspected. Could it?

"Thank you, sweetheart. Sherry taught me how to make it."

Emma grabbed her mother's hand. "You're learning, Mommy."

Guess he was too.

"One can no more approach people without love than one can approach bees without care."
—Leo Tolstoy

20

Arianne opened the register and pulled out the day's revenue.

Missy locked the boutique door and flipped the sign. "Eight hours of staring at the four walls, and all I sold was a pair of shoes to a homecoming queen nominee and a veil to a forty-something woman who plans to dye it black for her Halloween costume."

One-hundred and twenty-three dollars. "The cup is half-full. Yesterday's sales were the largest we've had in a long time."

"You need to invest in some good advertising. I don't think anyone but the locals know you're here, and they're all married. Well, except us."

Arianne ignored the jab, closed the register, and made her way to the safe. "As I've said before, advertising costs money I don't have right now. Hopefully, one day soon."

That went for the marriage thing as well. But to do that again she'd have to trust a man, and with her record it wasn't likely to happen. *The cup is half-full. You don't need a man. The cup is half-full.* Maybe if she had a doughnut to dip in it, she'd believe.

"Mommy, is it time to go home yet?" Emma rubbed her eyes and yawned.

Home. Adjusting back to apartment life would be hard for Emma when the time came. For her too, really. "Yes, it's time."

The safe clicked the numbers of Arianne's birthdate. A no-no in the world of safe money keeping, she knew, but it was easy to remember, and a burglar would be disappointed in his efforts anyway.

Missy pushed the ancient vacuum over the shop floor. The thing was loud as a freight train and just as heavy. Emma followed Arianne to the glass counter where she'd stashed the mail that afternoon. Bill...credit card offer...grocery ad...bill...a letter for Missy.

Arianne waved her sister over. Missy turned off the vacuum and took the letter. Emma's reflection in the display window made faces back at the girl. Arianne laughed and played along, thankful the rest of the square had closed hours ago.

Signs of autumn decorated the town. Golden leaves dusted the tree tops with sprigs of red throughout. Pumpkins lined the porch railing and each step of the B&B on the square. The crisp air meant sweaters and jeans, hot cider, and apple pie. Nothing was more beautiful than New England in fall.

She patted Emma's head. "Let's go before people think we've lost our minds." She turned to Missy. "You got the rest?"

Missy's face was as white as the wedding gown behind her. She gaped at the letter, wide-eyed, mouth open.

"What is it?" Arianne reached for the letter but Missy pulled away.

"Nothing." Missy folded the letter and slipped it into her pocket. She shrugged as she reached for the vacuum. "Jury duty."

No one liked jury duty, but Arianne had never seen someone that upset over it. "Well, let me know when you need off, and I'll cover it."

Missy nodded and started the vacuum, keeping her back to them.

"Goodnight." Emma slipped her hand into Arianne's, and they walked to their car. A strange sensation floated on the breeze and traveled down Arianne's spine. She'd experienced this discomfort before and it never ended well.

~*~

Huck stood tall on the sidewalk of the doctor's office and sucked in a deep breath of crisp October air. Freedom. He'd missed his old friend. Now for the celebration campfire tonight with his crutches and wheelchair as kindling.

He stepped off the sidewalk and fought for balance. The Aircast Boot had him striding to his truck like a tipsy cowboy who'd been in the saddle too long. He wouldn't complain. He was back in his jeans, could legally drive, and he and Lamar had signed a contract last week to open their sporting goods store.

Huck maneuvered his pickup onto the highway. He flipped the heat on low to warm his foot, only protected from the cold air by a sock. The light up ahead turned yellow and he slowed the truck to a stop behind a semi. A Harley Sportster Forty-Eight pulled in the turn lane beside him; the driver was dressed in layers against the cold. Sunlight gleamed off the orange metal flake paint and chrome pipes. She was a beauty. The driver revved the engine. The light turned green, and with the same confidence Huck flaunted before his accident, the driver sped away, rattling doors and disturbing the peace.

No, freedom hadn't fully returned. He'd thought about getting back on a bike, but the idea scared him witless. And so did paying his respects to Giada. He'd memorized every word of her obituary he'd read it so often. At least a dozen times he'd picked up the phone to call her parents and apologize but hung up instead. He needed to tell Giada he was sorry, even if she couldn't hear him.

But he was a coward.

This whole turn of events—Uncle Marty's death, the accident, Arianne—hit him like a massive earthquake and crumbled the wall he'd spent years building around himself. Now that he was left with no defenses, one wrong move and a thief could take him down. Where fear was a robber itself, the real bandit had honey-colored curls, full red lips, and a heart of gold. Arianne scared him more than anything.

At the edge of town, the cemetery flag waved in the breeze, as if signaling him that now was the time to make peace. He gulped. Fingers shook against the steering wheel. Another four-hundred yards and he'd confront his biggest regret. He owed Giada that much.

A homemade sign on a pink poster board advertised free kittens. He slammed the brakes then whipped the truck into the driveway at the last second, shoved the gear into park, got out, and headed for the house.

~*~

Sharp, tiny claws dug into his skin. Huck gritted his teeth, pulled out the neck of his hooded sweatshirt, and peeked inside. "Knock it off, you little rat. I just saved you from the pound."

He shifted the kitten and held it tighter against him to keep it from using his chest as a scratching post. Not yet brave enough to attempt the front steps in his new boot, he entered the house through the back door.

A meaty aroma hit his nose. He sniffed his way to the stovetop where chili simmered. Steam lifted from the red juice. He loved coming home to this.

His sweatshirt meowed. "Knock it off, varmint. I'm taking you to your mama."

Female voices echoed down the hall. He followed them to his room. Arianne held his bare pillow under her chin and shimmied on a fresh pillowcase. He liked the way she kept the house clean, everything in its place.

"Hi, Mr. Huck!" Emma bounced over to him and strangled his legs. Her head leaned back to look at him. "Hey, you can walk."

"Sure can."

The welcome smile on Arianne's face dimmed, and she lowered the pillow to the bed. Huck cocked his head to the side and opened his mouth to ask her what was wrong, but the kitten nipped him. "Ah, you little devil."

Emma released his legs and stepped away.

"Not you, kid." It took him a few seconds, but he managed to kneel. "I gotcha somethin'." His breath hitched as he reached inside his shirt and yanked the claws from his flesh.

Emma leaned in to see. The hissing fur ball calmed

when it saw the light of day. "A kitten! Oh, Mommy, look. A kitten."

That smile was worth it all. "Be careful. I think it's part piranha."

The feline meowed during the transfer. Emma snuggled it under her chin and rocked back and forth. The evil thing turned to mush in the girl's arms. "Can I keep it, Mr. Huck?"

"It's all yours, kid."

Emma left the room, rocking the cat like a baby. Arianne's lips flattened into a serious line. Uh, oh. What'd he do now?

"You shouldn't have done that, Huck."

"Why?"

She offered him a hand up, then turned away and pulled a blanket from the laundry basket. "It's hard enough."

The scent of fabric softener filled the room as she flicked the blanket into the air and spread it over the bed. When she wouldn't meet his eyes, he stepped closer and touched her elbow. "What do you mean?"

Arianne sighed and concentrated on his closet door. "She's not going to take it well when we leave. She loves it here. And that cat's going to make it harder. We can't take it with us, and leaving it behind will break her heart."

"We'll figure it out. You're not going anywhere for a while and—"

"You're walking on your own now." She turned.

Sadness mixed with fear and desperation showed in her eyes. It rattled him.

"We'll be leaving soon. You don't really need us anymore."

Oh, but he did. Five months suddenly wasn't long

enough, and the thought of them leaving made him suffocate. "I...I'm not finished with physical therapy. I've got four weeks before I can walk without this boot."

"You'll be fine now on your own." She blinked several times as if trying not to cry. Would leaving be hard for her, too? His traitorous heart hoped so.

Arianne put her palm flat against his chest. "You've been so kind to her. But, please, no more gifts. You're the only man in Emma's life right now, and she's eating it up." She swallowed. "This is a business arrangement, and she won't understand at the end when we go our separate ways."

He wrapped his hand around hers. His heartbeat pounded beneath them. Blood pulsed in his neck and wrists. Intense longing flooded him. He'd never wanted a woman so bad in his life.

What if he told her he wanted this to be more than a business arrangement? Would she stay?

The words stuck in his throat. What if she didn't feel the same way about him as he did her? A fear he'd never really dealt with before. He rubbed his thumb across her fingers and nodded instead. She gave him a weak smile.

Arianne turned away and took her soft hand with her. "The nights are getting colder. I washed you an extra blanket this time."

"Thanks." His voice was husky.

"Supper's ready." Arianne propped the basket on her curvy hip and left the room.

Huck stared at his neatly made bed. Extra blanket or not, his nights just got colder.

"To make a prairie it takes a clover and one bee,
One clover, and a bee, and revery."
—Emily Dickinson

21

Clouds swept across a gunmetal sky. The wind blew crispy orange and brown leaves around the town. Arianne sat on a stool behind the register and stared out the window at the bleak world. The image mirrored her heart. As much as she tried to deny it, the thought of moving back upstairs tore her heart in two. Emma wouldn't be the only one to miss the wide outdoors. The comfort of a real home.

Huck.

She'd tried not to let him into her heart again, but his kindness toward Emma broke any iron-clad defenses she owned. The very reason she didn't refuse when Huck offered to take Emma to work with him today. Too many nights she'd lain awake, imagining them all as a real family. Easy to do when they'd fallen into a routine of asking about each other's day, laughing at the dinner table, tucking Emma into bed together. She never should've allowed that last one, but Emma had begged, and she couldn't bear to tell her no when the little girl had been denied so much already.

Huck had even taken to helping her clean the kitchen after dinner. He was different than before.

Acted as if he didn't mind them being there anymore. As if he wanted them there. Wanted *her* there. All this time, she'd tried to keep her distance so she wouldn't get hurt, but she'd end this thing broken-hearted either way.

What was she doing? She didn't have time to be depressed. Twenty more ruffles still needed to be sewn on Darcy's twelve-foot train. Besides, she should be happy. The sale she'd made this morning was a good one, even if she did have to compromise with the customer on the price.

Missy yanked the door open against the wind, sending icy air into the room. Arianne pulled her mother's sweater tighter around her and crossed her arms against the chill. Without a word, Missy put a cup of hot cider in front of Arianne. The spicy aroma raised her spirits a notch. "Thanks."

Missy looked at her with red-rimmed eyes as though she were seeing Arianne for the first time. Dark hair spilled from her knit hat and caressed her pink, chapped cheeks. Missy nodded solemnly and turned away.

"Miss, what's wrong?" Her sister had been acting melancholy ever since she'd been selected for "jury duty." Arianne's sisterly instincts knew that letter had nothing to do with appearing in court. Not as a juror anyway.

"Nothing." Missy headed up the stairs to the apartment.

Arianne lifted from the stool to follow when the phone rang. Missy disappeared from view, and Arianne reached for the phone. "Yesteryear Bridal Boutique. How may I help you?"

"Arianne, I've called four times in the last two

weeks. Why haven't you returned my calls?"

It took a moment for the voice to register. "Darcy? I'm sorry. I wasn't aware that you'd called. Is everything OK?"

"No, everything is not OK. I'm frantic. I'm getting married, and I can't reach the seamstress making my dress."

Missy. "I apologize. What can I do for you?"

"We…We've moved the date up."

Was Darcy crying? "No problem. What's the new date?"

"Mother insists on a Christmas wedding." Sniffles.

Christmas? This was a big problem. Now Arianne was taking deep breaths. She sank onto the stool and rubbed a hand along her jeans. "What's the exact date?"

"Christmas Eve." More sniffles.

Arianne glanced at the calendar. The cider in her stomach was about to reappear. "Darcy, that's only six weeks away."

"Is that a problem?"

Yes. A gown of this caliber required hand-stitched detailing. With her being the only seamstress, with four bridesmaids to outfit, plus the flower girl, ring bearer, the miniature bride and groom…

"Arianne, are you there?"

"I'm here." Her voice echoed in her ears, hollow and tunnel-like. "I wish I'd have known sooner. Are you sure you want a Christmas wedding? You don't sound so sure. I know you're under a lot of pressure in your position, but keep in mind this is *your* wedding. If you want to get married in the sunshine at Acadia National Park in June then that's what you should do. You only get married once."

Well, hopefully. She poured out her words thicker than corn syrup. No meddling socialite mother was going to ruin this for her.

"The date has officially been announced. And mother...Well, she's already made arrangements for everything elsewhere. What I'm trying to say is: I won't be needing your services anymore. I'm so sorry."

A blast of wind hit the windows. Leaves scattered down the road, leaving town. She'd lost this account as fast as the clouds headed west. The room grew foggy. Her head swam. Was she having an out-of-body experience?

"I am sorry, Arianne." Darcy's voice cracked. "I have no choice. Mother says to keep the money I've already sent you for your troubles."

Before Arianne could respond, the phone clicked.

This wasn't happening. Any minute she'd roll over in bed and punch the snooze button. She'd wipe the sweat from her forehead, laugh in relief, and put this nightmare behind her.

After several minutes passed without the blare of an alarm, she hung up the phone, fighting back tears. Now what? Darcy was her security blanket. She had a meeting with the bank tomorrow. Huck had already signed a contract for his store.

Despair gave way to anger. If she'd received the message the first time Darcy had called, she may have been able to work something out. Instead, her irresponsible sister just cost her everything. Arianne twisted the bottom of her sweater in a death grip. She pushed to her feet and marched up the stairs. In the dim living room, Missy was sprawled on the couch with an arm covering her eyes. Tiny speakers dangled from her ears to her iPod. Arianne flipped on the lamp and yanked them away.

"Hey, what are you doing?" Missy sat up, blinking.

"How could you?"

"How could I what?"

"I just talked to Darcy Roberts on the phone, the governor's daughter—my big client! She said she's called four times to let me know she'd moved her wedding date and, thanks to her overbearing mother, would no longer need my services. I never got the messages!"

Missy rubbed her eyes and yawned. "I did tell you. I called Huck's one night and told Emma to tell you. And I left you a note by the register the other day."

"You left an important message with a four-year-old?"

"You were in the shower!"

Arianne looked around. Dirty clothes littered the floor, food wrappers covered the coffee table, and dust two inches thick coated the entire room. Missy had burnt her last straw. "You cost me my future."

Well, in reality it was Darcy's controlling mother's fault, but someone was going to pay for this. If Missy had given her the messages, she might've been able to negotiate. "Darcy. No. Longer. Needs. My. Services."

Missy lifted her chin. "It's not my fault."

"We're not kids anymore, Missy. This isn't like when you left my favorite doll too close to the campfire and melted her face off. This is life. I just lost a huge opportunity because you're not responsible enough to relay a message. This was my chance."

Missy jumped to her feet and ripped the iPod from the strap on her arm. "Do you think you're the only person around here who wants to get out of this town? I have dreams, too, you know."

She started for the door, but Arianne blocked her path. "It's always about you isn't it? Tell me, Missy. What would those dreams be?"

"You wouldn't understand." Missy sidestepped Arianne and gripped the door handle.

"I don't get you." Arianne rubbed her throbbing temple. "I swear, sometimes it's like we're not even sisters."

Missy winced, and her eyes filled with tears. "Maybe we're not."

"What's that supposed to mean?"

After a slight hesitation, Missy said, "Forget it," snatched her coat, and pounded down the stairs. Before Arianne could reach the landing, the bell above the door jingled, and Missy was gone.

~*~

The crunch of gravel reached Huck's ears. He made his way out of the shed toward Arianne's approaching car. She was gonna get a piece of his mind. What was she thinking coming home three hours late without so much as a phone call? Anything could've happened to her. A blown tire. Mugged. Finding the man of her dreams and running off into the sunset.

He stopped in his wobbly tracks. All those chick flicks she'd been subjecting him to were poisoning his brain.

By the time he half walked, half swayed to the car, Arianne was doubled over, retrieving her purse. Emma ran out the back door holding a DVD. "Mommy." She threw her arms around Arianne's legs. "Can we watch *Dumbo*?"

Arianne swallowed.

Huck nodded. "Sure, kid. You get it started. We'll be in shortly."

Emma skipped inside the house, slamming the screen door behind her. Arianne slumped to the back of the car and lifted the trunk without a word.

Something was wrong, and he tried not to let his voice inflect the chaos going on inside him. "Why are you late?"

She pulled a pink box from the trunk and closed it. Her bloodshot eyes had makeup streaks around them. "I brought you dessert. The bakery in Stone Harbor is under new management, and I thought you'd like to try it."

Huck wiped his dirty hands on the rag he'd been strangling. "You went thirty miles out of your way to bring me dessert?"

She shrugged. Her lower lip trembled. "You're right. I went for me."

"What happened? Why were you late?"

Her hand covered her mouth as full-blown sobs erupted like Mount St. Helens. She shook her head, unable to talk. He wasn't good with tears.

Huck gripped the box and set it on top of the car. Without much coaxing, she fell into him and wrapped her arms around his waist. Her tears soaked his flannel shirt. He let her get it out, waited patiently, even though the cold air seeped through his clothes and started to numb his skin. He rubbed circles on her back until her sobs subsided to sniffles.

She pushed away and brushed her damp cheeks with her hand. "I'm sorry. I didn't mean to come home and blubber on you."

Home. He liked that. "What happened?"

"I had a fight with my sister."

She'd made him worry for the last three hours over an argument with her sister? "If you women would handle matters like men do and punch each other, it'd be done and over with and you could skip all the drama."

Arianne chuckled, swiping thumbs beneath her eyes. "As angry as I was at her, I considered that."

He couldn't picture it.

She grabbed the box and walked into the house. He followed and closed the door behind him, enjoying the warmth. He found Arianne in the kitchen with her palms on the counter, shoulders heaving. He itched to walk up behind her and wrap his arms around her waist.

He pocketed his hands. "I could be wrong here, but this seems like more than an argument with your sister."

One hand flew up to cup her mouth. Her shoulders continued to shake.

"You want to…talk…about it?" Dumb question. She was a woman. Of course she did. They'd be here all night.

She laughed through her tears. "You don't mean that."

He scrunched his face in pretend pain. "Sure I do." As long as she'd let him hold her close while she talked.

Arianne turned but hesitated. Did she doubt that he cared? Or did she still not trust him?

She looked down at her white socks and shook her head again, this time the gesture barely visible.

"I let you use my shirt as a hanky. You might as well tell me." He wanted more than anything to make the wrong in her world right.

She stared at him as if he were a life preserver, but she was afraid to grab hold. She sniffed, swallowed. "Darcy Roberts, the governor's daughter, fired me today."

Huck pulled his hands from his pockets and stepped closer. "Why?"

She leaned her hip against the counter, and crossed her arms over her stomach. "They've decided on a Christmas wedding instead of next summer. She called me four times to let me know, but because of Missy I never got the messages." She rubbed her forehead. "Darcy's mother has taken over everything, and they've decided they no longer need me."

"That's illegal, isn't it?"

Arianne gazed out the window. "Darcy paid the deposit which is non-refundable in a case like this, so she's technically fulfilled the contract."

Crap. He scratched his chin. "What will you do now?"

"I don't know." Arianne took a deep breath and lifted her chin. Her soft blue eyes had turned to steel. "Don't worry, I'll figure something out."

She stormed toward the living room.

"Arianne…" Huck grabbed her wrist.

She turned on him. "I'm true to my word. Come spring, I'll move out of the shop, and you can go on with your plans. Then I'll be out of your life and won't hold you back any longer."

"Don't say things like that." He didn't want her gone from his life. Panic seized his lungs.

Jude's wisdom filled his head. *Compromise builds a*

strong relationship. Not that he wanted a relationship. Well, he did. Oh, he didn't know how to define it, only that he didn't want to lose her. "We'll work something out. I'll talk to Lamar and see what we can do."

"Why?" Hungry eyes searched his for the right answer.

Because I love you.

The impact was as fierce as the Cadillac's. When had this happened? Was it love? He wasn't sure what love felt like. The woman had put a hex on him.

He cleared his throat. "I owe you for not keeping my end of the deal last time."

The spark in her eyes dimmed. Wrong answer. "It doesn't matter anymore."

She pulled away from his touch. "I need to stand on my own two feet. When Martin saw me struggling and offered the space rent free, it was an answer to prayer. But I can't expect it to last forever. Maybe this is God's way of telling me I'm in the wrong business."

Fresh tears trickled down her cheeks. "Maybe I'm not meant to have a happily-ever-after," she whispered. Arianne rifled through the cabinet for a plate, opened the box, and pulled out a red whoopie pie. "Take what you like. I'm off to drown my sorrows in a hot bubble bath and carbs."

She started for her end of the house.

"Your bathroom's out of order." And his only had a shower.

Arianne stopped and hung her head.

"I'll call 'em again. See what's taking so long."

She went back to the box, picked out the darkest iced brownie Huck had ever seen, added it to her plate, and disappeared into the living room with her desserts.

When a colony moves into a new home, they spray a particular scent from a gland on their abdomen to help lagging bees find their way.
—Bees: Tales from the Hive

22

Arianne heaved the last box into the trunk of her car. A spool of satin ribbon escaped and unraveled at her feet. She stomped her foot, picked it up, and spiraled the silky tape around the cardboard circle.

"What's wrong, Mommy?" Emma peered around the car.

Arianne forced a smile. "Nothing, sweetheart."

Except that Missy wouldn't answer her phone, and at some point during the night had cleaned out her things from Arianne's apartment.

She shouldn't have been so hard on her sister. They'd had plenty of arguments over the years, but they never lasted more than a few days. Arianne was tired of being sucker-punched at every turn. Her life was like circling a barren wilderness with lookout points over a beach resort she couldn't get to. Nowhere to cross. *What am I doing wrong, Lord?*

She threw the spool into the overloaded trunk and hoped the lid would shut.

"What are you doing?" Gravel flew as Huck kicked the brake on the Gator so hard it jerked him and the vehicle to a stop. His fleece-lined hoodie added to his bulk. She traced his broad shoulders with her gaze, his tender embrace from the other night branded on her skin.

He slid from behind the steering wheel and limped toward her. "What's going on?"

She looked at the trunk then back to Huck, wondering what she'd done wrong. "Now that I'm back to work full-time and not designing anymore, I thought I'd take this stuff back to the shop."

"You're not leaving though..."

Was that desperation in his voice? His eyes?

"Yes, but I'll be back." Arianne studied him, her heartbeat speeding.

Huck shifted to see inside the trunk. His gaze roamed the contents and landed on her open sketch book. "Is this the dress you designed for Darcy?" He pulled it off the top of the pile.

Heat flooded her cheeks. No, it was *her* dress. "I set a match to Darcy's sketch the day after she fired me. Those are some I've done for fun over the years. Nothing important."

He studied the design for a few moments then fingered through the rest. His face revealed nothing.

"These are really good." Huck turned to the next page. "I mean, I don't have a clue what I'm looking at, but you've clearly got talent." He looked them over again. "Have you ever thought about designing and selling your own dresses?"

She tugged the book from his hand and tucked it back into the box. "Only every day since I was five."

"So why don't you?"

She slammed the trunk lid, relieved when it locked into place. "That costs money I don't have."

He caressed her elbow. "Don't give up on it." Huck rubbed his palm over her upper arm and stepped closer, then let go. With an awkward gait, he sauntered back toward his vehicle, but not before she caught the tortured sheen in his eyes.

"You're getting around well by yourself now. Sergeant Sandy deserves a medal."

He stilled.

"See you tonight." She got into the vehicle and closed the door, smiling. That sizzle and pop she felt whenever he was near wasn't just in her imagination. Huck cared for her.

Arianne's heart dove as she looked over the storybook house by the sea. Her storybook.

She turned around in the drive. Fog from the exhaust clouded the scene in the rearview mirror. Emma hummed in the backseat. Arianne didn't know how to tell her daughter that after this weekend, they'd be sleeping in their old beds again.

~*~

The stack of towels that rounded the corner before Arianne did was Huck's cue. He grabbed his knee and waited for her to come into view. He ground his back teeth and let out a long, exaggerated moan.

Arianne dropped the towels in a crumpled heap and rushed to his side. "What's wrong?" She fell to her knees beside him. Her fingers gripped his wrists, and he wriggled in the kitchen chair, doing his best to convince her he really was in pain, though if he was, this isn't how he would handle it. But she didn't know that. She'd buy it.

"What happened?"

Her cute little forehead bunched, forming lines between her brows. Her concern made guilt swell in his chest. He didn't answer, only shook his head.

"Does it hurt badly?"

He shot her a callous glare.

"Of course it does. Let me get you some ice." Arianne sped to the freezer and grabbed an icepack. She returned to her post and placed it on his knee, pressing her hands on it to hold it in place. Her gray shirt brightened her blue eyes to match the ocean on a stormy day.

Huck refused to let the rising guilt drown him. After all, he was doing this for his own good. "I tripped on a rake in the shed. Lost my balance and fell." He made sure to gasp every couple of words.

Wooden legs screeched across the floor as she pulled a chair in front of him and lifted his still-healing leg onto it. "You shouldn't be working yet. I told you it was a bad idea, but no one ever wants to listen to me. I knew you weren't ready. Now you've gone and messed yourself up…"

He blocked out the rest. Normally, her nagging would raise his blood pressure. This time her badgering meant she'd be staying with him longer.

She removed the icepack to examine his kneecap with her fingers. Her pink bottom lip darkened as she nibbled in concentration. "Am I hurting you?"

Oh, yeah. "Be careful."

"Sorry." She replaced the icepack. "Everything seems to be in place, though you may have a sprain or fracture. It doesn't feel swollen."

The back door opened then closed. "Arianne, its Jude." The man's boots thumped closer. Great. Jude was going to blow his cover.

"We're in the kitchen," Arianne called over her shoulder.

"Hey, when you see Huck, will you tell him...There you are." Jude put his hands on his beltline. Huck had left him outside minutes earlier. "What are you doing?"

Huck opened his mouth, but Arianne spoke for him. "He fell in the shed."

Jude stepped closer. "Fell?"

Huck tightened the muscles in his face and acted brave, the way he would do if this situation were real. Jude would never buy his wailing like a girl. "I'm fine."

"No, you're not." Arianne squeezed his fingers and stood.

Jude leaned against the counter. "What'd you trip on?"

"A rake." This was starting to scalp his dignity.

Jude's mouth twisted the way it always did when he was thinking something over. "The rake? But it's—"

"Ooh..." Huck gripped his knee. Anything to keep Jude from revealing the rake was hanging on a wall hook.

"You need to rest." Arianne bent and wedged her body under his arm to help him stand. "I'm helping you to the recliner where you're going to stay. Got it?"

He honed in on her wrinkled nose, bunched in determination. *Yes ma'am.* "We'll see."

Huck muted her fussing as she helped him settle into the recliner under a blanket and then fetched him some Ibuprofen and a pop. He really should feel sorry for deceiving her. But he didn't.

~*~

Huck drummed his fingers on the arm of his leather chair. The birthday card he'd helped Emma make for Arianne last night lay open on the desk. She was turning thirty in a few days and hadn't said a word about it. He'd seen a letter in the mail forward-addressed to her, the right size and thickness for a greeting card, and the "Happy Birthday" postage stamp and balloon stickers gave it away. He'd searched the Internet, found the exact date, and then pretended not to notice.

She'd been studying her reflection in the mirror a lot lately, checking, he assumed, for gray hair and wrinkles. Crazy woman. She didn't need to fuss over that stuff. She was gorgeous. Every time she smiled, it took him back to eighteen—fast cars, football games, and her kitchen table the night they'd kissed.

This hippy daydreaming junk had to stop. He called the Big Brother office to let them know he was ready to come back; then he asked to talk to Matt.

"You ready to make up that basketball game, tough guy?"

Huck could hear the goofy grin spreading across Matt's face. "Sorry, buddy, no games just yet. I will shoot some hoops with you, though. As long as you promise not to rat me out."

"To whom?"

"My nurse."

"The blonde chick from the cookout? Please. If you're afraid of her, then you're a bigger wimp than I thought."

Turned out, he was.

They decided on Thursday, and Huck ended the call and dialed the registrar at the University of Maine.

On the fourth ring, he prepared to leave a message when someone answered. "Max Jordan, please."

After a transfer and more rings, Max answered. "You're not calling to cancel on me are you?"

The chair groaned as Huck leaned his weight against the back and propped his feet on the desk corner. "No, I'll be there."

Max had invited Huck to be a guest speaker in their agricultural class to reiterate the importance of proper pollination versus a good yield.

"Glad to hear it. What can I do for you, then?"

This was gonna hurt. Huck unclenched his jaw. "I had a question about a scholarship. I saw the college was offering one for design, and I have a friend who might be interested."

"Great. Graphic or interior?"

The old-fashioned dresses in her shop certainly weren't graphic. Interior? He didn't know. "Uh, she designs wedding gowns."

"Hmm. Currently, we aren't offering any scholarships for fashion design."

Ah, fashion design.

"Let me check with my colleagues, though, and see if I can get you some information for your *friend*."

Huck's neck warmed. Max better not be picturing him in a dress and heels. "Thanks, 'ppreciate that."

Huck kept talking, touching on everything from fly fishing to bear hunting to the mechanics underneath the hood of Max's Audi TT, in case Max was questioning Huck's masculinity.

He hung up, unable to believe he'd done that. More than anything, he wanted Arianne happy. Whether that included him in the future or not. For once he wanted to do something good for *her*.

He stood and braced himself on the crutches. Stupid things. A man had to be insane to use 'em when he didn't need 'em. Someone ought to lock him away in the nearest nuthouse.

He wasn't sure what frightened him more. The fact that she might disappear from his life, or the fact that he was sinking to such lows as faking an injury to keep her around.

It wasn't love. He'd decided that the other night as he stared at his ceiling, unable to sleep. Again. Huck Anderson didn't fall in love. But it was something. Until he fit all the pieces together, he had to do what he could to keep her here, because the idea of her *not* here was more painful than rehab.

~*~

Arianne's breath clouded in the air, mixing with the snow flurries. "Come on, Emma."

She rubbed her mitten-wrapped hands together and shivered while her equally freezing daughter climbed out from the backseat.

November was making quite an impression. Her car had complained when she'd started it after work, but the engine finally turned over. The heater warmed them enough to keep the frost away as she drove home—to Huck's.

She'd expected to be back into her apartment a week ago, but with Huck's regressing health, she couldn't leave. And to be honest, she was relieved for any excuse to stay. This place had seeped into the cracks of her dry soul.

Emma's knit cap bounced with each step up the walk. She'd failed her daughter again. The Darcy catastrophe had cost her a new building. They'd better enjoy their lives now. Once Huck started his sporting goods store, who knew what would become of them.

Warmth enveloped her as she opened the door and stepped inside. Arianne shucked her coat and mittens and helped Emma do the same. The faint smell of pine hung in the air. They followed the scent to the dim living room where wood crackled in the fireplace. The flame reflected on the coffee table where her latest book and a bag of Reese's Pieces sat. The cozy ambiance did nothing to lighten her weighted spirits. In fact, it made it worse.

She ran her hand along the hooded sweatshirt Huck had thrown across the recliner. Where was he anyway?

Emma trailed behind her to their side of the house. Light spilled into the hall. Male voices grew louder as they neared the bathroom. Inside, Huck leaned against the sink with his back to the door. A dark-haired man with a tool belt hanging low on his hips stood in the bathtub. A section of the wall by the shower had been removed, and the muscles in his back rippled beneath his shirt when he rotated a pipe with his wrench.

"Wow, what happened, Mr. Huck?"

Huck jerked away from the wall and snatched his crutches. His wide eyes flew straight to Arianne. "Uh, Jack here's come to fix your bathroom."

What was the deer in headlights look all about?

Jack swiveled his head, hands wrapped around the wrench. Arianne recognized him as one of the newcomers at church. He'd attended faithfully the last few months, but she'd only seen him from a distance. She smiled.

He released the tool and stepped out of the

bathtub, his boots crunching the crumbled drywall on the floor. "I'm sorry it's taken me so long to get out here. Since the house is owned by the municipality, we're the only one's allowed to do the work. It's just me and one other guy. We take maintenance requests in the order that we get them."

"No problem. We survived." Now that she spied him up close, she understood why the Double-Mint twins from the singles class had made such a fuss over him from their pew the other day.

He swiped his hand along his faded jeans before extending it to her. "Jackson Swift." His mouth curled in a crooked smile. Dark green eyes filled with recognition and a hint of amusement looked from her to Huck then back again. "I believe we go to church together. Arianne, right?"

He knew her name? A blush singed her cheeks, and she hated herself for it. "Yeah, I recognize you too."

Did that sound as lame to everyone else as it did to her?

"And this is Emma," Huck said. "Now that we all know each other, Jack and I have work to do."

That's when she noticed they were still shaking hands. More like holding, really. She swallowed and let go. Jack's gaze cut to his boots. Huck watched them with a snarl.

"You're not 'posed to work, Mr. Huck. Your leg's hurt again. Remember?"

Huck's face reddened, and Arianne bit her lip to keep from giggling.

Jack returned to his task. Slightly shorter than Huck, his presence was every bit as intimidating. And appealing.

Arianne patted Emma's shoulder. "Huck's supervising."

His glare intensified.

She winked. "Come on. Let's leave the men to their work."

Because two gorgeous men in one room was too much to handle. Especially since she'd sworn off men entirely.

"But Mommy, I'm a good helper." Emma's new blue-and-cream plaid shirt made her look older. Hopefully, any growth spurts would hold out for a while, so she could wear it plenty.

"I know you are, sweetheart, but you don't want to ruin your new clothes." She led her daughter out the door. "How do pajamas and some dinner sound?"

"Can I have a fluffernutter?"

"We might be able to work something out." The peanut butter and marshmallow cream sandwich was a comfort food favorite of hers as well.

She helped Emma change into her purple polka-dot pajamas. They went to the kitchen, where Emma insisted on making her own snack. Arianne cut it in half, got Emma settled at the table with milk, and went back to her bathroom to ask Huck if he was ready for dinner. She paused outside the doorway when she heard her name.

"So, are you and Arianne..." Jack's voice.

"No," Huck said. "We're old friends. She agreed to help me recoup, and I agreed to help her with the shop. Business partners. That's all. Why?"

Arianne sagged against the wall. She was stupid to hope otherwise. That's all they'd ever been. All they'd ever be. She knew this, yet it hurt to hear Huck say it aloud.

"I just wanted to make sure." Jack again, plus the sound of metal breaking loose. "Thought about asking her out sometime."

Huck's laugh grated. "Go for it. You might give her a couple years' notice, though. She's a homebody. Not the spontaneous type."

Arianne's mouth gaped open. What was he saying? That she wasn't fun? Heat spread through her. She was fun. Just not *his* kind of fun.

"That's good. Neither am I. The worst she can do is say no, right?" Jack grunted as another piece of metal broke free.

Arianne stepped away from the wall. The attraction between her and Huck lately—he was playing with her because she was here. He didn't really care at all.

She tip-toed back down the hall, sure to make noise as she returned to the bathroom. The men's conversation ceased. "I was about to start dinner and wondered if you'd like to join us, Jack." She forced sweetness into her voice as she tilted her head to the side and offered a flirty smile, praying she didn't look like an idiot.

Jack wiped his hands on a rag. "Uh, sure."

See? She could be spontaneous.

Huck stood taller. "You sure you want to do that, buddy? Arianne here's not the greatest cook."

She willed herself not to gasp out loud. If they'd been alone, she'd have clawed his eyes out. Jack must've noticed the horror on her face, because after clearing his throat, he said, "I'll take my chances. A home-cooked meal sounds nice."

Jack was looking better every second. "I'll let you know when it's ready." Arianne turned and put her hand on Huck's arm. "Your leg is never going to heal if you keep pushing yourself. Why don't you go sit down? I'm sure Jack is capable of handling the job by himself." She threw as much admiration into that last sentence as she could muster.

Huck's nostrils flared. She threw him a battle-lines-have-been-drawn scowl.

An hour later, she called everyone to a beautifully set table and peppered shrimp Alfredo—thanks to Sherry's step-by-step guidance over the phone—garlic bread, previously frozen from the store, and a pre-packaged garden salad. She'd make Huck a liar if it was the last thing she did.

Jack swallowed his mouthful. "This is amazing, Arianne."

"Sure is." Huck raised a brow. "You been holdin' out on me all this time?"

One more derogatory comment and that guardrail was going to seem like a pony ride.

Huck made polite jabs throughout dinner, and somehow she managed to make it through without killing him. He hovered over her every move, bumbling around on his crutches, while Jack helped her clean the kitchen. She was all too relieved when Emma asked Huck to tuck her into bed and read a story.

"Sure, kid. Me and your mom'll be there in just a minute."

Emma tugged his arm. "I want you to read it, Mr. Huck. You do all the funny voices."

Huck turned away, but not before Arianne caught the red in his cheeks.

"Go ahead, Huck. You need to get off that leg anyway. I'll be there shortly."

His crutches pounded the floor as he followed Emma down the hall. With him gone, she could breathe deeper than she had all evening.

"She's a sweet kid." Jack put the last clean plate in the dish drainer. "Thanks for dinner, Arianne. It was delicious."

"My pleasure."

Jack wiped down the counter and tossed the rag into the sink. "I'd like to return the favor. Will you go to dinner with me tomorrow night?"

She hesitated only a moment, ticking off the reasons a date with Jack made sense. One, Huck didn't love her. Two, Jack was a Christian. Three, he wasn't spontaneous, which meant boring, just like her. "I'd like that."

Another crooked smile crept up his face, crinkling the skin around his eyes. Why hadn't she noticed this guy before? In his work clothes and tool belt, he belonged with *This Old House*. Put the man in a suit and he could easily model for *GQ*.

"Pick you up at seven?"

She'd be ready by noon. "Perfect."

He cleaned his mess from the bathroom then said goodbye. Huck was finishing *If You Give a Mouse a Cookie* when she entered her bedroom. Emma's eyelids fluttered closed, and Arianne kissed her cheek.

Arianne turned on the nightlight then flipped off the main one, bathing the room in darkness except for the small glow that lit Emma's beautiful face.

Huck rounded on her as she closed the door, and she pressed her body against the wall. "Handy Manny go home?"

The air sparked with his close proximity. "What's your problem? I thought you guys knew each other."

"No problem. Just askin'."

He smelled so good. Her heart pounded harder. If he hadn't insulted her all night, she'd hope he'd leaned down to kiss her. The fire in his eyes told her he might. His gaze dropped to her lips. She sucked in a deep breath and fled to the living room. They were business partners. And he was only playing.

"Oh, there's a problem all right. A big one." She turned on him when he caught up to her by the fireplace. "I can't even count how many times you insulted me tonight."

"I didn't insult you. I was teasing."

"Ha! You were making me look as bad as you possibly could. Do you really think that poorly of me?"

He rubbed his forehead. "'Course not." Huck inhaled and stared at the flames dancing between the logs. "The guy mentioned that he wanted to ask you out. I thought I was doing you a favor."

"By making me look stupid?"

Wounded eyes gazed back at her. "I'm sorry. That wasn't my intention."

"Then why?"

He paused. "That day at the honey house, you told me you were done with dating. That every guy you picked turned out to be a creep. I thought I'd save you the trouble of fighting him off."

Oh. She had said that, hadn't she?

"Thanks, but I can take care of myself." She lowered her voice. "Jack asked me out for dinner tomorrow night. I accepted."

His jaw slacked. "What about the kid?"

"I don't know how to reach Missy, so I can't ask her. You both get along so well. I thought I'd leave Emma with you."

Huck took a step back and shook his head. "I'm not babysitting so you can go out on a date."

Arianne crossed her arms. "I don't see the problem. Unless you have another reason why I shouldn't go."

He stared at his socks. Arianne noted the white-knuckle grip on his crutches. "You're right. I'll watch the kid. You go have a good time."

Arianne uncrossed her arms. "Really?"

She didn't mean to sound so disappointed.

Huck lifted his head. "Really."

His Adam's apple bobbed. She tried not to let it affect her, but it didn't work.

A draft from the chimney shifted the flames, blowing in an intense level of awkwardness and the scent of cedar. Arianne wasn't a bit tired, but her bedroom was her only escape. "Well, then. Thanks." She picked up her book from the coffee table. "I'm going to bed. Do you need anything before I go?"

He sank into the recliner and laid the crutches beside him, his focus on the fireplace. "No. 'Night."

"Good night." She backed away, knowing sleep wouldn't come. Not from excitement over her date tomorrow night, but from the defeated, somber tone of Huck's farewell.

Russian author Leo Tolstoy enjoyed beekeeping. In War and Peace, *he compares the evacuation of Moscow to a "dying, queenless hive."*

23

"You look lovely," Jack said from behind her as they waited by the hostess stand.

Arianne blushed when Jack's breath brushed her ear. "Thank you."

He looked great too. The waitress led them to a table splashed in lantern light. The restaurant was attached to the oldest B&B in the area. Dark, hand-hewn beams, large plank flooring, and rustic décor made her feel as though she'd stepped back in time to a tavern frequented by the founding fathers.

Jack pulled out her chair, and Arianne tucked her legs beneath the table. Déjà vu hit her in waves as her date with Travis replayed in her mind, making her nerves sizzle. That night had started like this one—a handsome man, a nice restaurant way out of her budget. If Jack hadn't told her he was a widower on the car ride here, she'd be watching her back for another woman. Maybe she should anyway.

They both ordered eggs Benedict with ham and asparagus. Unlike the restaurant on her last date, this atmosphere was casual, and she felt relaxed in her dark jeans, cream tank, and red flyaway cardigan. She'd spent extra time on her hair, calling herself crazy the whole time. The men she dated never worked out. Why should Jack be any different?

"Pastor Dave's sermon on truth last Sunday was enlightening." Jack leaned forward, resting his forearms on the table. The plaid shirt beneath his gray crewneck sweater peeked out from the open buttons and around the sleeves he'd pushed up to his elbows. His forest-colored eyes sparkled in the lantern light.

"I agree. It really enforced the basics of truth and reminded me how God expects us to relay it to others. No matter the subject."

"Most of all, it made me see how I need to be more honest with myself. Sometimes I'm truly my own worst enemy."

"Me too." Only she was her own assassin.

"For a long time, I told myself I'd betray my wife's memory if I started dating again. Deep down I knew that wasn't true. It's what she would've wanted. Maybe I told myself that because I was afraid to get back out there, open myself up again. I don't know. Truth is I'm tired of going home to an empty house."

She understood that. At least she had Emma. He didn't have any children to love and honor his wife's memory by.

"Thanks for coming out with me tonight, Arianne. I don't have any expectations and certainly don't want to rush things. If anything, it's nice to have a friend."

Like a punctured helium balloon, all the nervous pressure drained away. She grinned. "You can never have too many friends."

Over dinner, he asked about her shop. She left out the gloomy details. No need to bring the night to a depressing halt. He was curious about Emma and laughed at the many antics Arianne relayed. The best part was he enjoyed the chocolate cake as much as she did.

When they reached Huck's house, Jack walked her to the door. Stars twinkled in the clear sky, and the chilly air nipped at her cheeks. Arianne burrowed further into her scarf, holding it tighter around her neck with her mitten-wrapped hands. "I had a great time tonight, Jack. Thank you."

"The pleasure was all mine." His breath clouded the air between them.

This was the moment where awkward farewells normally began. Only nothing about the night had been uncomfortable. She'd truly enjoyed herself.

She opened her mouth to ask Jack if he'd like to come in for coffee, but closed it when she remembered this wasn't her house and Huck was inside. Awkward.

Jack stepped closer, hands burrowed in his coat pockets. "I'd like to do this again."

She nodded, too cold for words.

"How's next Friday sound?"

"Good."

He pulled out a hand and grazed his thumb over her mostly numb cheek. Was he going to kiss her? Jack didn't seem the type. Exactly what she needed.

A crash inside the house stole the moment. She cracked open the door. "I'd better check on the children."

Jack laughed, lowering his hand. "Good night."

Arianne smiled as she watched Jack head to his car. A second date with a man she could discuss the Bible with, a man who understood marriage and its trials, was the best way to overcome her girlish obsession with Huck.

~*~

What idiot had installed this window at the right angle to hide any view of the porch? Huck picked the curtain rod off the floor and hung it back on its rickety perch. The front door cracked open and laughter filtered through. He fluffed the mussed curtains, jerked his crutches from the wall, and shoved them beneath his arms. He stepped away from the window so she wouldn't know he'd been spying, and a sharp pain wrenched through his heel. He ground his teeth and lifted his leg to find a Barbie high-heel stuck to his bare foot.

Arianne walked through the front door, all rosy-cheeked and starry-eyed. The goofy grin on her face made his stomach drop. They'd been making out—he knew it!

"You're late."

"I wasn't aware I had a curfew. Where's Emma?" She removed her coat and mittens.

"Asleep." He'd learned the hard way that candy, grape drinks, and four-year-old girls did not mix. She'd shot through the house like a rubber band, spilling milk and knocking things over, then crashed when the sugar-high wore off.

Arianne yawned. "Good idea. Did she behave?"

"We got along fine."

"Good. Would you mind watching her for me again next Friday night?"

She looked so beautiful in her red sweater-thing, he would almost agree to anything. Almost. "Why?"

"Jack asked me out again."

Good thing the crutches helped to keep his

balance. "The date went that well, huh?"

She clasped her hands. "He's wonderful."

The knife was in, now all she had to do was twist. "How so?"

Masochist.

She frowned at the crooked curtain rod and sank onto the couch. "Well, he's easy to talk to. He was open with his feelings about being a widower and not wanting to rush things."

No rushing. Good.

"He's a family man. He wants another wife someday. Kids. We discussed church and the Bible. Jack seems like a good man."

Huck's complete opposite. Jack had probably never been responsible for anyone's death, either.

Arianne covered her mouth and yawned again. "I'm beat." She stood and stretched. His gaze followed the length of her body. "See you in the morning."

Her sweater swayed behind her as she left the room. She'd taken extra care to look nice tonight. For Jack. Heat pricked his neck.

He'd thought volunteering to watch her kid while she went out would prove to him that he wasn't falling in love with her. In reality, he was downright—he shuddered—jealous. He'd never been jealous over a woman before. Never had to be. He always got the girl.

The crutches chafed under his arms. He gripped them both in one hand and walked to his bedroom, slapping off the living room light on his way out. He didn't know anything about being a family man, kids, or the Bible, but Arianne made him want to be a better man. He would try to be worthy of her.

He knew just where to start.

~*~

"What are we doing here?" Arianne parked the car and looked at the diner through the frosty-edged windshield. The neon *Open* sign glowed across her curious face.

"Some gal I know turned thirty today." He unbuckled his seatbelt and let it zip into place.

She pouted. "I was trying to forget."

He glanced at his partner-in-crime in the backseat. "Come on, girls. Dinner's on me."

Arianne stared at him, a smile in her eyes. That's what he was after.

The smell of greasy diner food welcomed them as they stepped onto the faded black-and-white tile floor. After crawling into a vacant booth with red upholstery, they read over the sticky, laminated menus. Not the fanciest choice for a birthday dinner, but it was the best in town.

Marge, his favorite waitress, sped to their table in her blue uniform. "Haven't seen you in a while, handsome. You haven't grown up and gotten married on me, have you?" Her cheeks rose, deepening the wrinkles around her eyes.

Arianne snickered.

"Forgot who I was talking to." Marge let out a raspy laugh and slapped his shoulder.

Cantankerous broad.

Marge threw a hand on her hip and turned to the birthday girl. "You look like a smart woman. What are you doing with this guy?"

She waved at Emma.

Arianne put down the menu and folded her hands. "He's my patient."

"Patient?" Marge's gray eyebrows disappeared beneath her bangs.

Arianne explained about the wreck. Marge's eyes grew wide. Shame burned Huck's face at the knowledge that the last time he'd been in here, Giada was with him. What was he thinking coming here? The excitement of surprising Arianne for her birthday overtook his common sense.

Marge laid her hand on his arm and squeezed. "I'm glad you're all right." She took their drink orders and disappeared into the kitchen.

"I like her." Arianne's lips curled in an impish grin. "She knows how to handle you. I take it you're a regular?"

Huck stared at her pink painted fingernails. "Used to be."

Giada's memory lingered over him. A haunting he'd never escape.

"What's wrong?" Arianne reached for his hand.

That's when he realized he was frowning. Her soft fingers brushing his gave him strength. Could he wipe his slate clean and start again? He'd never been the definition of good, but Arianne made him want to learn. What would she do if he opened up his hand and twined his fingers with hers? Only one way to find out.

Her breath hitched. Perfect fit.

"How does it feel to be thirty?"

Arianne's face turned a beautiful shade of pink. Her mouth hung open slightly and she looked from him to Emma, who was too busy coloring on her paper placemat to notice her mother was being admired. "Uh…"

She tried to pull away, but he held on. She looked

224

down at her lap, but not before he saw a tight-lipped grin on her face. "Just another day older."

A different waitress brought their drinks, giving Arianne an excuse to pull away. He leaned back against the booth, and they ordered their meals.

"Have you heard from your sister?"

"No. I wish I knew where she was staying. If she's safe. I've called everyone I can think of." She sipped her cherry-flavored pop. "I thought she'd at least call to tell me happy birthday. They get lonely sometimes, you know? Birthdays, holidays."

He knew. Even when he'd had a so-called family, he spent those times alone.

She gazed at him over the glass in her hands, lips hovering near the straw. "Thanks for not letting me spend this one alone."

If he had his way, she'd never spend another day alone.

A few minutes later, Marge brought out their burgers and fries. When Emma had eaten enough to satisfy Arianne, Huck ordered dessert for them to share. While spooning away the giant chocolate-chip cookie with ice cream, hot fudge, nuts, and whipped cream, Arianne reminisced about her favorite childhood birthdays.

He pointed to the candle lying in an ice cream puddle at the bottom of the dish. "What'd you wish for?"

Arianne shook her head. "If I tell you it won't come true."

"I didn't think you were the superstitious type."

She chuckled. "I'm not. What did you wish for on your thirtieth?"

He wiped his mouth with a napkin. "Guys don't

sit around wishing on candles and stars."

Arianne put her elbows on the table. "Fine then. What is something you'd planned to do by your thirtieth birthday that didn't happen?" Her face lit up with a mischievous grin, like a teenager playing Truth or Dare.

Another dead memory to haunt him. "Ride all of Route 66 on my motorcycle."

"It's not too late."

Huck nodded.

"It sounds like a good dream." She rested her chin in her hand. "Who knows? Maybe someday I'll be *spontaneous* and go with you."

He narrowed one eye. She'd spit that word with sass. Had she overheard him and Jack the other night?

The thought of her on the back of his bike, arms wrapped around his waist, the two of them heading for adventure was exhilarating. Then reality set in. "I don't think I'll be riding any more bikes."

Especially with a passenger.

Emma tugged on Arianne's sleeve. "Mommy, I need to use the bathroom."

Huck tossed the tip on the table and folded the ticket in his hand, glad the subject had ended. He stood and grabbed his crutches, angling them under his arms. Arianne handed him her keys so he could warm the car, and then she and Emma weaved through the tables to the restroom.

Marge met him at the register. He placed his crutches against the counter and leaned onto it. Her nimble fingers hit the keys, and she eyed him 'til he was downright uncomfortable. "She's the one, Huck."

"What?"

"Don't play dumb with me. You love her."

Did the woman have X-ray vision? He stood tall and scratched his jaw. "Did you take your crazy pills this morning?"

The register popped open and he passed her two twenties.

"Maybe I did, but a person would have to be blind not to see how you three fit together." She held out his change and smiled, revealing the lipstick on her teeth.

He blinked, not knowing what to say.

Huck took his change and dropped it into her tip jar.

"Thanks, handsome."

He headed for the door. Maybe the cold would shock him from his stunned state.

"Forget something?"

Hand on the doorknob, he turned to Marge. She pointed to his crutches leaning against the counter. He looked at his leg then back to her smiling face.

He could make all kinds of excuses, but what was the point? "Thanks."

Arianne left the bathroom, guiding Emma from behind. Huck shifted the crutches beneath him. A world-class dummy.

Marge waved to Arianne, who was helping Emma put on her coat. "You better get him home, honey. I think his leg is hurting something fierce."

With that, the ornery server walked away.

~*~

Arianne stepped into the warm house, lugging her sleeping daughter.

Huck locked the door behind them. "Get her to bed. I'll make coffee."

"This late at night?" She shifted Emma to keep from dropping her.

"Yeah. I've got a present for you." His intense gaze made her stomach tremble.

She put Emma to bed and paced her bedroom floor. What was with Huck tonight? Ever since she'd gone out with Jack, he'd been different. More attentive. Flirty, even. Could he be jealous?

Yeah, right. This situation made them close friends now. That's all. He was just being nice because it was her birthday. Except the fireworks that had exploded inside her when he'd held her hand made it more like the Fourth of July.

With a hand pressed to her middle, she closed the bedroom door behind her and met Huck in the kitchen. He poured coffee into two mugs and handed her one, along with a manila envelope.

She blew on the liquid. "What's this?"

"Happy birthday." His deep voice sent a shiver down her spine.

Arianne stared at the envelope, thought of a million bad things it could be. Good news never came in manila envelopes. Divorce papers and final notices—that's the kind of mail she always got. Maybe he'd found a place she could move to. Maybe he couldn't wait to get rid of her.

Huck reached for her mug, and she gave it to him. "Open it."

Arianne swallowed and pinched the envelope's metal clasp, lifted the flap, and pulled out papers. She skimmed the words, aware of his close presence beside her, his every breath. "A design scholarship?"

"It's a great opportunity."

Yes, it was. "I can't go back to school. The shop is

my only income. I can't afford employees right now. I can't afford a sitter for Emma."

He placed his mug on the counter. "It's a full ride to design school. Online. You could take courses at night, after you close the shop, and you wouldn't need a babysitter. If for some reason you did, you'd have me."

Hope filled her chest then deflated. "I do my alterations at night."

He pursed his lips in thought. "Do 'em when there's downtime at the shop. Take the simpler stuff home and do it while you study. If you want it bad enough, you'll find a way."

She stared at the papers. "I've always dreamed of designing my own gowns and selling them in my shop, but maybe that's all they're meant to be, Huck. Dreams."

Huck stepped closer and gripped her elbows. "Those dreams can be reality, but not if you don't try. All you've got to do is design something and enter. The judges pick the best one for the scholarship."

"But, it'll take time and money for fabric and…"

He tipped her chin with his finger. "Now that you're not working on Darcy's dress, you've got the time. You also have her money." His lips curled into his movie-star smile. "Now what other excuses are you gonna give me?"

"I want to…" *Kiss you.*

His grin transformed from debonair to devilish. "Good. It's all ready. Just sign the paper and mail it in. You've got exactly one month to design a dress." He looked at her lips. "I believe in you."

No man had ever said that to her before. The words wrapped around her like a warm blanket, pulling her closer to Huck. He released her, then picked up his mug, winked, and took a sip. "Better get busy."

A hive can only have one queen.

24

A design scholarship.

Arianne perched on the edge of her bed, the papers in her hand bathed in lamplight. A cocktail of emotions swirled, but she was stunned more than anything. Huck had taken her dream, tucked it into a crisp envelope, and placed it in her hands. She'd always followed this road alone—discouraged by a father who'd been furious with her for quitting medical school, duped by an ex-husband who'd taken the nearest exit, and discounted by a sister who didn't get it. A sister Arianne hadn't seen or heard from in two weeks.

She laid the papers on the nightstand, crawled beneath the quilts, and turned off the light. Arianne stared at the dark ceiling. Emma's body warmed her side. The girl's light snore joined the creaks of the settling house, serenading the night.

Huck supported her. The man who was booting her from his building because he abhorred weddings so much wanted to see her succeed. What was she to make of that?

The hunger in his eyes and his heated touch stayed with her. Friends didn't hold hands. Neither did business partners. His gesture, his recent actions…he wanted more.

Or did he? Was she misreading him entirely? She was good at that.

Then there was Jack. Though they'd had only one date, a future with a guy like Jack made sense. Huck was a run-away train. Fast, thrilling, dangerous, with the promise of disaster at the end of the ride. Jack had already been married and proven he was ready to settle into family responsibility.

But he wasn't Huck.

Arianne punched her pillow and rolled onto her side. Emma stirred, but her breaths quickly returned to a deep rhythm. People change, right? She'd seen Huck make several alterations to his life in their short time together. And by God's mercy and grace, she'd changed.

A chill brushed her skin, and she burrowed deeper into the blankets. Was Huck Anderson capable of loving anyone other than himself? There were times when she was sure she saw it in his eyes, with her and Emma. Like tonight, when he'd held Arianne's hand, given her his birthday present. That was…

Probably guilt. He wanted to ease his conscience by making sure she was steady on her feet before he moved on with his life. Like he'd told Jack, they were only business partners.

Besides, Huck wasn't a believer. She would not compromise her convictions for him. Her next relationship, if there ever was one, would be founded on God. Especially if it involved a movie-star handsome cowboy who sported heart-stopping grins and a southern twang that could melt a woman's heart into a puddle of mush.

~*~

A week before Thanksgiving, Huck stood in his kitchen by the coffee pot, waiting for the French vanilla roast to finish dripping from the filter. The sweet aroma filled the room and mingled with Arianne's cottony perfume as she greeted him with a sleepy smile.

She'd worked hard every night over the last two weeks, tucked away in the corner of the living room, the sewing machine thumping non-stop until it made him want to kick it over. Then she'd nibble her lip in concentration and weave the fabric beneath the needle, agitating him for different reasons.

A woman had never been so far from reach. Where human nature and need had always fueled his desire, it was more than that with Arianne. That was the only thing stopping him from coaxing her to his bed. She deserved more than that. She deserved to be loved, cherished. He didn't know if he was the man to offer her that.

Emma walked in, rubbing her eyes, her kitty following close behind. The ruffle on her princess nightgown swished about her ankles. A tiara Arianne had fashioned out of beads and pipe cleaners lay lopsided and tangled in Emma's hair. The girl needed a daddy. She needed to learn life wasn't a fairytale, to get her hands in the dirt, to learn where her food came from and how to change a tire. How to take care of herself. There was so much to teach her, and time was his enemy.

He'd fooled himself a few times, thinking he could do the job, but what did he know about being a father. He'd never had one.

The bum leg charade wouldn't last much longer. At his final appointment a week ago, the Sergeant had deemed him good as new. Once Arianne found out, she'd be gone.

Huck poured Arianne's coffee into his favorite mug and then emptied the rest into a thermos she could take to work. He rinsed the pot and started a batch of good, old-fashioned coffee.

He handed Arianne the flavored coffee as she swallowed the last bite of her jellied toast and licked her lips. She looked down at the mug and smiled. "I need to finish getting ready. I've got some alterations to finish at the shop today, and then I'll be ready to piece together the panels for the scholarship gown."

She laid her delicate fingers on his arm and squeezed. "After the whole Darcy thing I considered giving up. Thanks again, Huck. I never would've had the courage to do this on my own."

"You're welcome." His gaze traced the curve of her jaw to her lips, which held a faint smear of grape jelly.

This was maddening. He'd finally hit his limit. He leaned in for a taste…

Emma tugged on Arianne and asked for cereal. Arianne jerked away, kissed her daughter on the head, and made Emma's breakfast.

His coffee gurgled into the pot. He poured a cup, admiring Arianne's patience, her quiet strength. What would it be like to share every morning with her? Her nights? To tame a passel of rowdy kids at every meal? Blonde girls as beautiful as their mom and big sister, brown-haired boys as wild and mischievous as he was.

Insanity.

The phone conversation between Arianne and Jack

last night blasted through Huck's fantasy. They'd been talkin' a little too friendly. If Huck wasn't careful, those kids he'd just imagined would have tool belts and a daddy named Jack Swift.

~*~

Yikes! Arianne put down the needle and thread and squeezed her fingertip. Blood seeped through the hole she'd punctured. The phone beside her rang. She grabbed a tissue and placed it over the wound then answered the phone. "Yesteryear Bridal Boutique. How may I help you?" Silence. "Hello? Is anyone there?"

"It's...me."

Arianne inhaled a quick breath. "Missy?"

A sigh. "Yeah."

Arianne spread her palm over heart. "Are you all right? How've you been? Where've you been?"

"Around. I'm fine."

"But... How..." Arianne paused. No bombarding. "I'm glad to hear it."

More silence.

"Missy? Are you still there?"

"I just wanted to let you know I'm safe. And to hear your voice." Raucous laughter ricocheted through the receiver.

Hear her voice? Something was wrong. "Missy, please, come home. I'm sorry for everything I said. The Darcy thing wasn't your fault. I miss you. Emma and I will be moving back into the apartment soon, and you can have the bedroom. I'll sleep on the couch and—"

"I'm not moving back, Arianne."

"But...where are you?"

"Look, I've gotta go."

Arianne panicked. "Will you at least come visit us?"

"Soon." Missy's voice cracked. "I have plans tomorrow night, but maybe I'll come by Wednesday."

"Plans?" A job interview, a hair appointment, skydiving lessons—what plans? Arianne took a deep breath and tried for nonchalant. "A date?"

Missy snorted. Arianne didn't fool her. "Yeah, a hot one." Sarcasm dripped through the phone. "I really need to go."

No, you can't. But Missy was an adult, and the more Arianne smothered her, the further she'd stray. "Keep in touch, Missy, please. Don't let another month go by before I hear from you again."

"Sure thing."

"I love you."

"You too." The words had barely left Missy's mouth when the call ended. Arianne hung up the phone, sent up a prayer, and let the tears fall.

~*~

Huck shoved his foot into his boot and tugged his jeans around it. He stood, shifted his weight to the other leg, and prepared for the other boot.

Arianne called his name, and he jumped and grabbed the crutches. This was nuts. "You've gotta quit sneakin' up on me like that."

"Sorry. Sherry and Jude want to get together for dinner, and I wondered what time you'll be home."

Huck proceeded with his other boot, near impossible with crutches beneath his arms. He'd be home after he met her sister to discuss...whatever it was Missy wanted to discuss. She'd never explained herself on the phone that morning, simply said it was important that they meet up and not tell Arianne. Something was going on and whatever it was, if he could protect Arianne from it, he would.

"We'll have to do it another time. I'm not sure when I'll be home." He grabbed his coat from the hook and shoved his arms into it.

Her head tipped to the side, like a puppy who didn't understand its master's command.

"I'm meeting someone after work."

Arianne's eyes grew wide and she straightened. She cleared her throat and hooked her thumbs in her back pockets, trying to look casual. "Like a date?"

A flash of green ignited in her blue eyes, and Huck bit the inside of his cheek to keep from grinning. She'd made him suffer with Jack. Why not? "Yeah. Don't wait up."

He winked.

The rest of her looked a little green too. Nothing showed how a woman truly felt like a good dose of jealousy.

He opened the door, stepped into the cold air, and let a smile slide up his face.

~*~

The dainty fabric slipped over Arianne's skin, conforming to her body like a glove. She tugged at the zipper on the side and curled her lip at the paint peeling in the dressing room. So this is what it felt like to try on a gown in here. No wonder business was down.

The light flickered, making her silhouette difficult

to examine. She pushed open the door, relieved for the fresh air, and tip-toed down the narrow hallway to the three-way mirror at the front of the shop.

Five-thirty. The store was closed, but she prayed no one would walk past and see her trying on her own goods. With the scholarship deadline a week away, Arianne needed to see what the dress looked like on, so she'd have time to apply any final touches.

Arianne hitched the gown above her ankles and stepped onto the platform. The flowing fabric dropped with a whisper. She stared at her reflection; tears of bittersweet victory pooling in her eyes. Her dream gown. The one she'd always imagined making for her own wedding. Only now its purpose was to further her education. The fact left a sting.

To win the scholarship would be a dream come true, a sign from God. She turned to admire the scalloped back. Arianne swayed from side to side, studying the dress from all angles. Not a stitch needed to be added. She ran her hand along her waist. Even with her few extra pounds, it was perfect.

The bell jingled above the entrance. The lavender candle on the counter flickered in the mirror. She spun toward the door in horror. Huck's frame swallowed the doorway.

He stood on his crutches, a key in one hand, gaping at her. Arianne's pulse leapt. Seconds seemed like hours as his gaze traveled the length of her body then back up to her face.

She swallowed, trying to decipher his expression, and then reminded herself to breathe. After gathering her courage, she turned full circle. "This is my entry for the scholarship. I finished it this morning. What do you think?"

He blinked.

She froze.

Huck dropped his crutches and ate the distance in a few unwavering strides. His eyes held a fierce hunger she'd never seen before. Almost animalistic. Her blood rushed, thumped in her neck. His fingertips stroked the seam at her waist, searing the brocade. Her bones quaked as he pulled her against him. He took his time trailing his hand up her arm and curled his fingertips into her hair. Alarm bells blasted in her head, but her heart was oblivious. He held her face with his other hand, brushing his calloused thumb along her jaw, her lips. His feather-soft touch drove her wild. If he didn't kiss her soon she'd explode.

She tipped her head back and closed her eyes.

His lips covered hers, soft, controlled. The pleasure of it hammered into her. It'd been so long since she'd been kissed. A moan escaped her throat, fueling the fire. He leaned into her, deepening the kiss. She engaged submissively, arched into him on tiptoe, and matched his intensity.

She broke for air. Huck's mouth roamed her neck, the sensitive spot where her jaw met her ear. Heat filled her belly. More bells rang. She pushed her palms against his chest and opened her eyes. A figure blurred in her vision. Couldn't people read the closed sign?

"Sorry to interrupt."

The familiar voice sobered Arianne. Missy?

Her sister stood inside the door, chin hitched, arms crossed around her as though she were prepared to defend herself. Arianne was so glad to see Missy, but her sister had the worst timing.

Or maybe the best.

Arianne swallowed. "Missy. It's good to see you."

She didn't trust her legs, or she'd walk over and hug her sister.

"You too." Missy's smile was unsteady as she gazed from Arianne to Huck. "Ready to go, Huck?"

Ready to go? Where were they going? Didn't Missy have a date tonight? Wait, didn't Huck?

Arianne's mouth dropped open as the pieces fit together. Huck squeezed his eyes tight and rubbed the back of his neck.

No.

Huck cleared his throat and fished his keys from his pocket. He tossed them to Missy. "Truck's around back. I'll be out in a minute."

Missy looked at her with a pathetic half-grin. "Uh, we'll catch up later."

She left.

Arianne turned to Huck. Why was she always second best?

He rubbed his jaw. "I can explain."

"No. You can't."

She lifted the dress enough to step off the platform.

Huck turned her around by her elbow. "I didn't mean for you to find out this way."

Arianne's skin grew hot, and her sight dimmed around the edges. She tore away from his grip and went to the door. "Get out."

"Arianne, please, I—"

"My sister?" Her voice sounded far away, like it was echoing through a tunnel. "How can you kiss me like that when you're dating my sister?"

His brows slammed so close together they were practically one. "Dating Missy?" Then his eyes rounded. "Wait, no. You've got it all wrong."

She'd heard that before.

Arianne bent over and snatched the crutches—the crutches he no longer needed—and the key he'd thrown to the ground. How else had he been deceiving her? She flung open the door so hard she nearly knocked the bell off. "Get. Out."

She thrust the crutches at his chest, and he caught them with an *oomph* before she shoved him out the door and locked it.

"And all they of the land came to a wood; and there was honey upon the ground. But Jonathan heard not when his father charged the people with the oath: wherefore he put forth the end of the rod that was in his hand, and dipped it in an honeycomb, and put his hand to his mouth; and his eyes were enlightened."

—1 Samuel 14:25, 27

25

Huck threw his crutches in the truck bed. His secret was out. He yanked open the driver's side door and climbed inside.

"Trouble in paradise?" Missy's sarcasm filled the cab.

He slammed his door, jarring the entire vehicle, and rubbed his cold hands together for warmth. "Your timing stinks."

"I didn't expect to walk in and find you devouring my sister." She waved her hand in front of her face in a fake swoon. "Whew! That one must've been building for years."

He rolled his eyes and fired up the engine. "I doubt you'll have to worry about walking in on us ever again."

"Why? Is she mad?"

Like a wino in a dry county.

He nodded. "She thinks you and I are dating."

"What?"

"Don't look so insulted."

"Sorry. It's just that…" Missy sighed. "Why would she think that?"

He let out a breath, cursing his stupidity. "Long story. I'll handle it later."

He could handle it now. After all, locking him out was silly when he had a key, but it might be best to let Arianne cool off and find out what Missy was up to.

"You were handling things pretty well before I showed up."

"What do you want, Missy?"

The amusement vanished from her face. She stared at her high-maintenance fingernails. "Drive."

He pulled away from the curb and drove out of town.

For the next twenty minutes, Missy remained silent with her elbow against the window and her lips pressed against her fist. He drove along the coast, each mile taking him further from the only woman he wanted to be with tonight. Whitecaps swelled angrily toward shore. Mist clung to the windshield and iced over. He flipped on the defroster and wondered if Arianne would warm up to him again after she learned the truth.

When they passed a sign announcing five more miles to Stone Harbor, Missy finally spoke up. "Be careful with my sister. She's been through a lot."

"You're one to talk. You've put her through misery the last month, disappearing and not answering your phone." He clamped his teeth together and reined in his temper. He forced the edge from his voice. "What's this about, Missy?"

She twisted her purse strap until the fake leather

squeaked. After a long pause, she tossed it aside and rubbed her palms down her jeans. "Do you have any idea why your uncle would leave me something in his will?"

Huck floored the brake. "What?"

Tires squealed, and they jolted forward.

Missy grabbed the dash. "Maybe you should pull over."

Good idea. A convenience store lay ahead. He pulled into the parking lot and angled the truck into the first available space. Missy gripped her purse and bolted out the door. He opened his. His leg wasn't strong enough for a chase, but if that's what it came to...

When Missy entered the building, he relaxed against the seat and closed the door.

A few minutes later, she returned with two foam cups. The heater blasted lukewarm air through the cab, and he made a mental note to check the heating coil. Missy handed him a drink.

"Thanks."

She nodded and pressed her lips to her straw, suctioning red liquid through it. She swallowed and traced the lid with her finger. "Your uncle remembered me in his will. Which is really weird, since I've never met the man. I wondered if you could tell me why."

Had he heard her right? His brain was still a little fogged from that kiss. "No idea. Are you sure it was my uncle?"

She bobbed her head. "Martin Eugene Billings, resident of Trenton."

The one and only. Uncle Marty had taken care of every detail with his lawyer as if he'd known when he was going to die. Since the will was all settled, Huck hadn't questioned it.

He eyed her warily. "What'd ya get?"

She played with her straw as if deciding whether or not to light this stick of dynamite. "Cash from the sale of a 1967 Chevelle."

His jaw dropped. "*You* got the Chevelle?"

Missy shrugged. "In a manner of speaking."

The classic flashed before his eyes. The shiny orange paint, the glimmering chrome. He was gonna need something stronger going down his hatch than this pop. "How much did it sell for?"

She hiked her chin. "None of your business."

Why would his uncle leave something like that to a stranger? He didn't even get to say goodbye.

"So you have no clue whatsoever why your uncle would leave me money?"

"No."

Neither said a word. Customers entered and exited the store. Nothing in Uncle Marty's will had made sense. None of it.

"I could see him leaving Arianne something, I guess." Missy broke the silence. "They knew each other. Spoke often. But, why me?"

The dots connected. "You're M. Thompson."

She nodded and took another sip. "So, tell me about Martin Billings."

"Why?"

"I'm curious about the man who left me a small fortune for no apparent reason."

Huck gazed out the window. "He was a regular Joe. Known in the community, not showy or wealthy." He looked at Missy. "An all-around good guy."

Quiet returned to the cab, and he sipped his drink. As far as Huck knew, his uncle hadn't left anything to

Arianne. Why would he leave something to her sister?

The boutique windows were dark when they returned to Pine Bay. Streetlights bathed the truck and allowed enough light to see around the cab. Missy wrapped her fingers around the door handle. "Please, don't say anything to Arianne about this."

Huck put his hands in the air. "Oh, no. I'm not keeping any more secrets. She's mad enough already."

"Please. If she finds out, she'll want answers I can't give. I promise I'll tell her as soon as I figure this out." She put a hand on his arm. "I know you care about my sister. You have to agree there's no need to upset her until we know the facts. She worries enough. She's big-hearted and delicate and—"

"I'm not making any promises." He'd wanted to protect Arianne from whatever this was, but it backfired instead. "You need a ride?"

She shoved open the door, inviting in the cold air. "I have a ride. Thanks."

He watched Missy jog to a sedan down the block. Fog escaped the exhaust after a minute; then she pulled away.

The entire ride home, Huck's mind reeled. News of the Chevelle and that smokin' kiss with Arianne were almost too much to handle in one day. And how he was going to explain his miraculously healed leg? Maybe he could claim it was an answer to her prayers.

Gravel crunched beneath the tires as he rolled up the drive. Arianne's car was parked beside the back door. The hazy porch light illuminated the contents of her open trunk.

Suitcases.

~*~

Arianne willed herself not to shed anymore tears. Emma was having a hard enough time as it was.

"Mommy, will Mr. Huck be back before we leave?" Emma pumped her legs on the side of their bed.

Not if she hurried. Arianne shoved the last of Emma's clothes into her bag. "I don't know, sweetheart."

"I don't want to leave." Her little voice trembled.

"We have to, honey. Huck's all better now, and we can't stay any longer." Arianne hoisted the bag onto her shoulder and left the room.

"I didn't think he could get any hotter." Missy's comment the day she'd run into Huck at the shop grated Arianne's nerves worse than a fiddle severely out of tune.

Her sister? He'd aimed straight for the jugular.

What a fool she'd been, falling into his arms when he had other women waiting in the wings. She wasn't the closing act. She was intermission.

Oh, what did it matter? It was just a stupid kiss. People gave away meaningless kisses every day. Arianne stopped at the end of the hall. Not her. She didn't even know she could kiss with such reckless abandon. And she'd certainly never been kissed that way before. Not even by her ex-husband. Huck's kiss had been full of rugged passion and vulnerability…

Enough! He was out with Missy right now, probably kissing her the same way, giving her the same false, giddy feeling. She continued toward the boxes stacked by the door. Arianne heaved one onto her hip and struggled for balance. She'd fallen for this twice. Twice! Only this time, the other woman was *her sister*.

She kicked open the door. It swung back and crashed against the house. Wild, free-spirited, unpredictable—wouldn't they make the perfect couple?

She walked into the cold night and jolted at Huck's image standing by her car, coat zipped to his chin, hands buried in his pockets.

"Are you trying to give me a heart attack?" she snapped.

He looked to her open trunk. "Where're you going?"

She moved toward her vehicle. *"Home."*

"Arianne, I know you're angry, but, please, hear me out."

"Mr. Huck!" Emma flew past Arianne and captured Huck's legs in her arms.

"Hey, kid." He rubbed circles on Emma's head with his palm, never taking his eyes off Arianne.

"Are you going with us, Mr. Huck?"

He stared at Arianne. A raw desperation radiated from his eyes, begged her to say yes. When Arianne didn't invite him, he said, "Not this time."

Emma released his legs and hung her head.

Arianne stormed to the car and threw the box and bag into the trunk. Her daughter would suffer the most, and it was all her fault. "Emma, will you please go inside and gather up all your dolls?"

"Yes, Mommy." Tears shimmered on Emma's lashes, and she trudged into the house.

Huck pulled his hands from his pockets and joined her by the car.

Arianne slammed the trunk. "How's the leg?"

"Fine."

She threw a hand on her hip. "Care to tell me how

one second you're hobbling around on crutches and the next you're miraculously healed?"

His mouth turned up. "Your kisses have healing powers?"

This was no time for games. "Did you tell that to Missy too?"

"I'm not dating your sister."

"Yeah, right. Yesterday on the phone, Missy told me she had a date tonight. You said this morning that you had a date tonight, and then Missy shows up asking if you're ready. I'm not stupid." She started past him, but he caught her arm.

"You have my word, Arianne."

She yanked away from his grip. "What good is that?"

He winced like she'd slapped him.

Maybe she should. "You've watched me worry myself sick about Missy for weeks now, knowing good and well this whole time where she was."

"Until this morning, I hadn't talked to Missy since high school. When she called, she sounded upset. All she wanted to do was meet and talk."

"I bet."

"Think about it, Arianne. Missy would've reacted a lot differently if we were dating and she'd walked in on me kissing another woman."

Arianne opened her mouth only to close it again.

True. Missy had seemed distant not angry.

Huck shook his head. "Uncle Marty remembered her in his will, and she wants to know why, since she's never met him. She asked me not to tell you until she's figured it all out, but I didn't make any promises." He inched closer. "I'm not dating your sister. Or anyone."

Marty had left her sister something? Why did

Missy want to keep it a secret?

Huck closed the space between them. "I came by the shop to tell you I was meeting Missy because I felt guilty for hiding it from you. Then I saw you in that dress and…"

He scratched his jaw.

"And what?"

He gripped her elbows and pulled her closer. "And I forgot why I'd even walked in there. All I could think about was how beautiful you looked." He rested his forehead against hers. "And how badly I wanted you."

Arianne jerked away. Oh, he was good. He'd had practice over the years to know exactly what to say to a woman to make her heart sing. She couldn't trust him. He'd still lied to her and she was tired of being deceived. "What's your game, Huck?"

"No games."

"Then why did you lie about your leg?"

"I didn't want you to leave."

"Why, because you'd miss your housekeeper?"

He shook his head. "I'm not sure how to go back to the way my life was before."

"Well, that's your problem. We're leaving." She stuffed her hand into her coat pocket and pulled out her keys.

His fingers dove through his hair. "Please, don't leave. I'm sorry for not telling you about your sister. I'm sorry I lied about my leg, my date. I'll be completely honest with you from now on. Please, Arianne, don't leave."

Her instincts told her the crackle in his voice was genuine, which probably meant he was lying his face off. "Why? Give me one good reason why I should stay."

His warm hands encased her face. "Because I..." His eyes grew wide. A few seconds passed and Huck let go. He hit his palm against the car's metal frame. Rubbed his hand over the back of his neck.

That's what she'd thought. "It's called Florence Nightingale syndrome."

He looked at her. "What?"

"What you *think* you're feeling. It's when a patient develops romantic feelings for their caretaker. You're grateful for what I've done for you, confusing your psyche into believing it's something more. That's all this is."

Huck stared off into the distance with a slight shake of his head. He'd figure it out eventually. She opened her door and started the car. It sputtered but turned over, sending a cloud from the exhaust. She got out and shut the door.

Huck stood there, hands in his coat pockets. "It doesn't matter what I say, you're going to leave. Aren't you?"

For a moment she saw him as a small boy watching one dad after another walk away. She'd never seen such a crumpled mix of anguish on one person before, the shrapnel of abandonment. Except in her own reflection. Her heart screamed for him, but her head told her she was a fool. Someone needed to fight for her for a change.

Her boiling anger had dropped to a simmer. "I have to. You're healed. It's no longer appropriate for us to be here."

Emma slunk from the house, dragging her Barbie suitcase. Arianne took it from her and threw it into the backseat. "Come on, Emma. It's time to go."

Sobs erupted from her daughter, twisting Arianne's heart. Emma didn't remember much about her dad, but this scene, she'd remember.

"I don't want to go, Mommy."

Arianne turned her back and pressed a hand to her mouth. Tears welled up in her with the force of Niagara, and though she closed her eyes tight, a few managed to escape.

Huck's soft voice carried to her ears. "It's all right, kid. I'll be around. You be good and go with your mama, and maybe you both can come back to visit sometime."

Emma sniffled. "But I want to stay with you, Mr. Huck."

A beat of silence. "Now that we're good friends, I think it's time you just call me Huck."

Another sniffle. "We're friends?"

"The very best."

His voice was deep, full of emotion. Arianne wiped her frozen cheeks. She turned and found him kneeling in front of Emma. He stared into Emma's eyes with a tenderness she'd never witnessed in him before.

Emma slipped her arms around his neck. "Goodbye, Huck."

Huck wrapped his arms around Emma. He closed his eyes and swallowed. "Goodbye, Emma."

Tears poured down Arianne's cheeks. He'd finally called her daughter by her name. With every cell in her being, she longed to throw her arms around them.

Arianne swallowed the tennis ball-sized lump in her throat. "Emma, it's time."

Huck released her. "Be good."

"Mommy says we can't take Baby Kitty tonight. Will you take good care of him for me?"

"I will."

Emma rubbed her eyes and followed Arianne to the car, sobbing all the way. Arianne buckled Emma in, kissed her daughter's wet cheek, and closed the door. Huck's gaze locked with hers for several seconds.

Arianne realized she'd overreacted about Missy. But Huck's past behavior had her spooked and she was tired of being a doormat for men to wipe their shoes on. Besides, the way she'd reacted to his kiss—she needed to move out.

Finally, Huck backed toward the door. "Got everything?"

"Yep."

He looked down at his feet then up again. "Take care."

"You too."

Arianne slid beneath the steering wheel and put the car in drive. Huck watched them leave until the dark night swallowed him in her rearview mirror.

*Male bees, called drones, don't have stingers to protect
themselves.*

26

The drafty apartment was dark and depressing.
Walls closed in on her. Breaths weren't deep enough.
Air wasn't fresh enough.

The company wasn't masculine enough.

Arianne put down her fork. Missy and Emma
picked at their food too.

Emma hadn't smiled since they left Huck's last
week. She missed her kitty. Missy had called yesterday
to reconcile, but she, too, lacked enthusiasm tonight.
Arianne wouldn't ask why. She'd promised Missy over
the phone that she wouldn't mother-hen anymore, and
that she'd let Missy live her life without interfering.
She'd manage, grateful to have her sister safe and
relieved that Missy and Huck had no romantic interest
in each other.

Arianne pushed back her plate with a sigh. "How
about we forget the pasta and go straight to the
cookies?"

Missy and Emma both shrugged, staring at their
plates.

Arianne retrieved the cream-filled cookies and
placed a gallon of milk on the table. The bag crackled
as she tore it open. These wouldn't solve her problems,

but they'd make her feel better for a few minutes.

Until they were all gone.

Arianne poured a glass of milk and drowned a cookie.

"You and your sweets." Missy pushed her uneaten pasta to the side.

Arianne slid the double-stuffed delights in Missy's direction. Missy shook her head, so Arianne ate one for her. "I can't help it. I get it honestly. You know how Mom loved her sweets."

Emma reached for one.

Missy dropped her chin in her hand. "No, I don't know. I don't remember anything about her."

"Really?" The cookie broke in half and sunk to the bottom of Arianne's glass. She grunted, munched on the salvaged end, and took another one.

"I was two when she died. I can't remember what she looked like, much less her personality."

"I should've done more to help you remember her."

Missy shrugged and scooted from the table. "It doesn't matter."

"Of course it does," Arianne said through a mouthful of mushy chocolate.

Missy forked her spaghetti into the trash. "Everywhere we went, people said, 'Arianne, you look just like your mother.' You and Dad hung out, did things together. I was the odd one out."

The plate splashed into the sudsy sink.

Arianne swallowed. "I didn't know you felt that way."

Missy shrugged. "You were too busy living the life Dad had mapped out for you to notice." Her voice cracked.

Arianne wiped her hands and mouth with a napkin and led Missy into the living room. She searched her sister's teary eyes. "What's brought all this about?"

"Didn't you ever wonder why Dad had big plans for you and nothing for me?"

"He had greater expectations of the oldest child, I guess."

"But he didn't have *any* for me. Why?"

Arianne drew Missy close and squeezed. "I'm sure he did."

"No, he didn't. He never once mentioned me going to college. When I brought it up, he chuckled like, *Yeah right. You, go to college?*"

"I'm sure that's not what he was thinking."

Missy pulled away. "What do you know? You were in medical school at the time. You don't know what went on around here."

Arianne crossed her arms. "I know Dad didn't mistreat you."

"Not physically."

"Then, what?" Fear clutched Arianne's throat. She'd never heard her sister speak in such a way before.

"Come on, Arianne. He never looked at me the same way he did you. He always looked right through me." Missy crossed her arms around herself as if she needed protection. "I don't look like Mom or Dad. Or you. I've never had anything in common with any of you. It's like…like I'm not even a member of this family."

Arianne huffed. "What, do you think you were adopted? Dropped on our doorstep by aliens? I was there. I remember the day you were born."

A single tear trailed down Missy's cheek. "No, Arianne. What I'm getting at is that maybe I'm not Dad's kid. Maybe that's why he couldn't stand me."

Arianne uncrossed her arms and threw her hands on her hips. "That's absurd. Dad loved you, and to say something like that is to insinuate that Mom had an affair."

"After you moved out, his drinking got worse. Sometimes he'd look at me like...like he didn't know what to do with me. I think Mom did have an affair."

Arianne gasped. "Have you lost your mind? Mom loved us, loved Dad. She'd have never done something like that."

Would she?

"And you're such a great judge of character."

Though the words weren't hostile, they hit their mark.

Missy sagged against the wall. "My inheritance didn't make any sense. I had to leave. Link the pieces to this puzzle."

Her sister's gaze focused on something far away, nonexistent. A chill ran down Arianne's spine, despite the warmth blasting from the ancient baseboard heater. "What do you mean?"

"People don't just leave strangers money when they die. I knew there had to be a reason." Missy closed her eyes and took a deep breath. "I found out that Mom and Martin Billings used to be engaged. They were high school sweethearts."

Air *whooshed* from Arianne's lungs.

"The Washington County public library has their engagement picture on file from an old newspaper dated May 4, 1969."

Milk and cookies curdled in Arianne's stomach.

Her legs trembled. She made it to the couch. "Why didn't they get married?"

"I don't know. I'm still working on that one. But I've heard they always kept in touch."

Like a light bulb blazing in the darkness, Arianne recalled what Lucy Cosgrove had said to her at the hospital that first day. *I forgot you two were related. Cousins, right?*

Arianne was about to see her dessert again. "What are you saying?

Missy dropped next to her and leaned her elbows on her knees. "I think I'm Martin's illegitimate daughter."

~*~

Huck ran his fingers through his damp hair and padded across the cold kitchen floor. The house was too quiet. He gripped the freezer door handle and yanked it open. He missed the pictures Emma used to color for him. Arianne had taken them all. Except the very first one of his wreck and the angel. That one never left his office desk.

Salisbury steak or meatloaf? He reached in and grabbed whatever was on top. Food tasted as bland as his existence, and it had only been a week since they'd gone.

It was like an episode of *The Twilight Zone* in reverse. Unlike the characters that couldn't get back to their old lives fast enough, he wanted to stay. His former life played in black and white, but Arianne had shown him Technicolor.

Baby Kitty, as Emma had originally named him, wound around his ankles, dropped on its side, and bit

Huck's toe. "Yeow!" Huck nudged the cat away with his foot and slammed the freezer door. He tossed his dinner into the microwave and moved to the cabinet to pick his poison. He stared at three amber bottles. They hadn't helped the night Arianne left. Or eased the loneliness of spending Thanksgiving alone. He doubted they'd help now.

Distraction. That's what he needed.

Huck removed his pajama bottoms and pulled on jeans and a sweatshirt. He left for Sharky's Sports Bar, ignoring the frozen dinner spinning in the microwave.

His truck tires squealed into a parking space. He turned off the engine, got out, and strode toward the bar. Voices clamored, bottles clinked. The smoky atmosphere stung his eyes. He took a deep breath, and then coughed into his fist.

The regulars greeted him, asking him where'd he'd been. Worley, a crusty old man with yellow teeth, slapped Huck's back and bought him a round. Yep, this was exactly what he needed, to get back to his old life. He hadn't thought of Arianne once in the last—he glanced at the neon clock that read, *It's always time for beer*—fifteen minutes.

A group of guys next to him balked at the hockey game on the wide-screen. Huck tried to keep up with the score, but it reminded him of Arianne in the mornings when she'd greet him with coffee and her sleepy eyes, wearing an NHL shirt.

Tilly invited him to join their poker game, but he'd never been a card player. Besides, he hadn't touched a deck since his and Emma's last game of Go Fish. He moved his glass in little circles on the bar, swirling the brown liquid. Those two females had brainwashed him.

He threw back the contents of the glass and ordered something stronger.

After two hours of mindless yapping and a six-beer and whiskey shot buzz, Arianne slipped from his mind. He scanned the smoky room, and his gaze landed on Jessa, a voluptuous red-head he'd kept company a few times. She winked. Before he knew it, she'd left her chair and swayed his direction, sporting a provocative smile and a low-cut blouse that had his full attention.

She stood close, leaving no space between them, one elbow on the bar, the other on his arm. "I thought you'd abandoned us."

Her perfume and lipstick both needed to be turned down five notches. She didn't look natural or smell fresh like Arianne. Huck shook his head to clear his thoughts and gulped the last of his whiskey.

"It's been lonely around here without you."

He knew lonely. Huck motioned to the bartender. "I'll take another."

Tack's eyebrows raised. Or at least Huck thought they did. Everything was rising and falling right now.

Jessa reached into her blouse and removed a few bills that she slid across the bar. "Give him one more, Tack. I'll make sure he gets home safe."

With that statement, she ran a long fingernail on his thigh. Was the fire alarm going off, or were the bells in his head? Huck looked around the room. No one else seemed to notice, so it must be him.

Tack slid him another shot. "That's it."

Old habits consumed and Huck gulped it down in one swallow. A deep belch escaped from his gut. He moved the glass toward his lips again, disappointed to find it empty.

Jessa tugged it back down. "You trying to pass out on me before I even get you home?"

Sweat rolled down his temple. "You know I don't take anyone to my place."

"I wasn't suggesting we go to your place."

Huck willed the room to stop spinning. Something about this scenario made his skin crawl. He'd tried this before, and though it was great at the time, it left him empty.

If only the room would stay still, he could think.

"Why don't I get you out of here?" Jessa's whisper purred in his ear.

Her lips brushed his earlobe. Once. Twice. He turned his head and kissed her. Hard. She tasted like liquid smoke and mint chewing gum.

Jessa pushed at his chest. Four eyes glared at him. He blinked. No. Two eyes, and they weren't happy.

"Who's Arianne?"

"What?" Had he said her name out loud?

"Who's *Arianne*?"

A pang hit against his chest. Must have. A crooked grin crept up his face. "Jessa, are you drunk?"

"No, but you are. And you didn't answer my question. Who's Arianne?"

Hearing her name made his heart physically hurt.

Jessa's mouth fell open. "Don't tell me you've fallen in love with this woman."

Arianne had left him. "Course not."

Jessa's arms wrapped around his neck. "Prove it."

He stood and nearly hit the floor. He held Jessa's tiny waist for balance, then moved his arm around her shoulders and stumbled out the door.

When bees believe their hive is under attack, they release alarm pheromones to alert the other bees. Smoke masks these pheromones and confuses the bees. This allows the beekeeper to work the hive.

27

Daylight stole the darkness from the back of Huck's eyelids. A war drum beat in his temples. He cracked an eye open. Searing pain shot through his head. He closed his eye again. What happened?

Cold air seized his lungs as he took a deep breath. He shivered. Why was it so cold? Remnants of the night burst like balloons in his mind.

Oh.

Huck shielded his eyes and forced them open, prepared to find Jessa beside him. His stomach rolled.

A beige glove box cleared in his vision. A dashboard. Windshield. He reached beside him, and his fingers met the leather seat. His truck. Fog escaped his lips, and he shivered again. Why was he in his truck?

He pushed to a sitting position, and the drum beat louder, harder. A blanket fell from his shoulders into his lap. The gray-and-black-striped wool one he kept behind the seat for emergencies.

Huck swallowed and cleared his throat. His vocal chords rubbed together like sandpaper. What was that stench?

Frost glazed the windows, but Huck could see enough to know he was in the bar parking lot. His was the only vehicle left. Where was Jessa? Had they…?

His gut churned like waves at high tide. Huck thrust open the door for air and stepped down on the concrete. Right into—

He cursed. Now he remembered. Jessa had shoved him in the truck after he'd let loose all over her new shoes. Those must've been some nice shoes too, because the words she yelled would've made a sailor blush. She'd also made it clear that her name wasn't Arianne. His ears were still ringing.

All that root beer had made him soft. Wimp. Then again, it kept him from making a mistake he'd regret. Arianne's doing, even if she didn't know it.

He eased over to the crunchy grass to clean the sole of his boot. Jessa's brash kiss still lingered on his lips. Had things gone further, it would've appeased him for the night, but it wouldn't have quenched his thirst. Jessa hadn't felt right in his arms. Huck thought he could drown Arianne from his mind, but he'd failed.

Arianne wasn't in his head. She was in his heart.

Huck raised a palm to his throbbing forehead. Now what? How did a man who was in love—and he could no longer deny he was—when he didn't want to be, get back to his old life? Huck's stomach dived, and he blew out a slow breath.

Did he even want to go back to his former life? It seemed so empty now.

An icy breeze blew across his chest through his unzipped coat. He tugged the zipper, and his hand met something wet. He looked down. It matched the mess on the concrete.

Huck crawled into his truck through the passenger side and scooted behind the wheel. No. He didn't want to go back to his old ways. But where did he go from here?

The engine hesitated then turned over. He revved the motor a few times to warm it up, willing the heat to work faster. A few minutes later, he backed out and drove home. John Wayne would go get the girl. After a shower, some sleep, strong coffee, and more sleep, Huck believed he'd find his inner cowboy.

~*~

Should he follow them in?

Huck gripped the steering wheel until his knuckles turned white. It had been almost two weeks since they moved out. How would Arianne react when she saw him?

The stragglers in the parking lot thinned. He opened his truck door, eased out, and closed it quietly, afraid the noise would finish knocking his world off its axis. His boots thumped across the cold pavement. His heart pounded even louder. He ran his palm over the back of his head. He felt naked without his hat.

Huck turned around at the double doors. He couldn't do it. Wasn't ready. No confounded woman on earth was gonna make him—

"Hello, sir. Glad to have you today. Did you leave something in your vehicle?"

Huck groaned softly. *Yeah, my sanity.* He turned to spout some lame excuse and met the eyes of a man not much older than himself. "I, uh…"

"Welcome to Pine Bay Baptist Church. I'm Pastor

Dave." The man thrust out his thick hand and shook Huck's with the grip of a grizzly bear. Lean, broad-shouldered, and slightly gray-headed, this pastor in trendy glasses banished all Huck's preconceptions. Huck introduced himself and before he could sneak away, the pastor ushered him into the church.

This was a really bad idea.

The pastor led him into purgatory—or so it felt. They stood in the doorway that lead to a room full of pews. Huck confessed he was Arianne's visitor, and the pastor pointed in her direction. Of course she'd chosen a front row seat.

On shaky legs, he walked down the aisle. Halfway there, the pianist broke out in song as if she were commemorating the occasion. Were everyone's eyes burning holes in his back, or did it just feel that way? Most of the congregation probably knew him by reputation and were wondering if hell had frozen over.

Come to think of it, he was too.

As Huck neared, Arianne hunched over and dug around in her purse. His gaze locked with Jack's all cozied up beside her. Huck puffed out his chest, nodded, and slipped onto the pew next to her.

Arianne looked up at him, wide-eyed. She touched his arm as if she were unsure whether she was hallucinating. Then she tilted her head and broke out the most beautiful smile he'd ever seen.

Heaven help him; he loved her.

~*~

Sweat beaded along Arianne's temples as the heat from both Huck's and Jack's bodies warmed her sides. Huck. In church. Was he finally opening his heart to

God?

The temptation was too much to resist. She turned her head and sneaked a glance at him from the corner of her eye. Huck tugged at the collar of his blue dress shirt and ran his palms down the legs of his jeans. The motion stirred the scent of his cologne. She breathed it deeply. He always smelled like leather and sunshine.

Huck turned his head and met her gaze. The intense longing in his eyes brought back the moment in the wedding gown. Her heart beat faster. Then she remembered they might be related—sort of.

Jack closed his song book and placed it beside him. The deep timbre of his last note crooned in her ear. Jack always smelled good too, like designer cologne and wood chips. She couldn't compare anything else. Jack hadn't kissed her yet, but she doubted it would be anything less than wonderful.

Pay attention to the message. Every time she tried, she found her mind wandering off again.

When the service ended, she introduced Huck to several church members. He rocked his weight from one foot to the other and unbuttoned his collar, revealing a sliver of white T-shirt underneath.

"Huck!" Emma bolted through the sanctuary, clutching her Bible, her red dress flapping around her knees. Curious faces followed the stomp of her black dress shoes. Emma swelled like a helium balloon, filled with so much happiness she might fly away.

Huck scooped her up. "Hey, darlin'."

Emma hugged his neck so tight his face turned pink. "I missed you. How's my kitty? Can we go to your house and see him today?"

Huck patted her back. "Sounds like a plan."

Arianne's heart squeezed at the sight of Emma in

his strong arms. It had been days since her daughter had shown any happiness, and she hated to disappoint Emma. Jack's hand on the small of her back made it inevitable. "I'm sorry, Emma, but we can't today. We promised Jack that we'd spend the afternoon with him."

The duo frowned at her.

"But, Mommy...my kitty..." Emma's chin quivered.

Arianne stroked her daughter's cheek. "We'll visit your kitty soon. I promise."

Emma turned her face away and buried it in Huck's neck.

"Tell you what," Huck said. "I happen to know your landlord, and he said it's OK to let the kitty live at your house. How 'bout I bring him over one night this week?"

Emma lifted her head and placed a chubby hand on Huck's face. "Will you stay too?"

"For a little while. Then I'll have to go back to my house."

Emma nodded, her lips turning down at the corners.

Jack's hand moved up Arianne's back to her shoulder. "I'll warm up the car. You girls come out when you're ready." He released Arianne and shook Huck's hand. "Good to have you, Huck. Come back any time."

"Thanks." Huck's narrowed gaze followed Jack until he disappeared out the door.

Arianne set her purse and Bible in the nearest pew and unwound her coat from her arm. Huck put Emma down and took it from Arianne. He held it up, and Arianne slipped her arms inside. He left his hands on her shoulders and his touch seeped through the wool. "I've missed you," he whispered.

His breath stirred her hair. A tingling sensation ran through her body, as if it had been asleep and was waking. "Huck, I..." She turned, and he dropped his hands.

Longing played across his shaven face. It started in his ticking jaw and poured from his eyes. After a moment of silence, Huck looked down at his boots and shoved his hands in his coat pockets.

"Emma, go find your coat, please. We need to go."

Emma trudged toward the foyer. Arianne smiled, knowing how hard it was for Huck to come to church. It stirred all kinds of things inside her. "How's Friday night?"

He looked up at her.

"You can bring the cat, and I'll make dinner." *And we'll discuss the idea that you and Missy might be cousins.*

"Depends. What'cha makin'?"

She swatted his arm.

His deep laugh filled the space between them.

~*~

Huck waved to his girls as they left the church parking lot in Jack's BMW. The cold air bit his ears. He made his way to the truck. Jack was a good guy, but he needed to buzz off. Huck couldn't tolerate another man flying in and threatening his hive.

The truck door moaned. Huck climbed in and started the engine. While he waited for it to warm up, he opened the folded paper Emma had given him on their way out of the church. A lopsided Christmas tree filled the paper. A stubby stick-figure with pigtails stood beside the tree, wearing a ball gown and holding a taller female's hand on one side and a cowboy's hand on the other. Bees flew around the pine tree, while presents filled the space beneath. One present was open, with bright sunlight spilling out.

Did Emma draw pictures for Jack too?

Huck folded the paper and placed it in the seat beside him. He turned on the heater and left the parking lot.

When they'd lived with him, he had the advantage over Jack—spending time with them when Jack wasn't around, stepping in when things between Jack and Arianne looked too serious, teaching Emma to be tough. Now that they weren't on his turf anymore, it was all out of control. He was out of control. He'd have to fix that. He could be good like Jack.

Come Friday, he'd prove it.

"One who is too wise an observer of the business of others, like one who is too curious in observing the labor of bees, will often be stung for his curiosity."

— Alexander Pope

28

Frost coated the windows in Huck's kitchen. He poured coffee into his thermos and screwed the lid on tight. He missed Arianne's sleepy-eyed chatter in the mornings and the patter of Emma's bare feet on the linoleum. Though the silent house drove him to near madness at times, other than leaving for work, he'd stayed home and out of trouble all week.

Last night in the quiet darkness, he'd considered marriage for the first time in his life. He doubted he'd be good at it, and he wasn't too sure he wanted to go there, but he knew he couldn't let Arianne go to another man. If he didn't step up to the job, someone else would.

He stared at Emma's latest picture hanging on the fridge. Christmas was in two weeks. He'd make sure it was the best one they'd had in a long time.

He went to work with his mind in a haze. Hours passed as slow as cold honey through a spigot. He applied mite treatments and antibiotics to the bees, filled orders for beeswax candles, and filed paperwork in his office. He picked up the electric bill from his desk to file it away and a yellow sticky-note caught his eye. In his handwriting were Giada's parents' names, their address, and the cemetery where she was buried.

Six months had passed, and he still hadn't visited her grave. Seeing her name engraved on the headstone would make it real. It was real, but without visual proof it was too easy to pretend it didn't happen.

Huck rubbed the knot that formed between his brows. He'd deal with that later. Right now, he had somewhere to be.

He stood, rolling the chair across the floor. He grabbed his truck keys from his bedroom dresser, put on his coat, secured the pet carrier with the kitty inside, and pointed his truck toward Pine Bay.

Huck parked in front of the boutique and walked past the shop. From the corner of his eye, the mannequin danced. He came to an abrupt stop and stared at it. *What in the world?*

He opened the door to jingling bells and stepped inside. The mannequin's dress bubbled out and moved, swaying the statue from side to side. Two human feet peeked out from beneath the white dress.

"Arianne?" He set down the pet carrier.

"Just a sec."

Fabric flew in all directions as she tried to shimmy the dress over her head. Finally, she got down on all fours and crawled out. Huck laughed. The barrette in her hair lay lopsided in a mass of static curls. Cockeyed glasses perched on the end of her nose.

Arianne pushed them back into place and stood. "I'm so glad you're here. Can you help me with this?"

Huck removed his coat and tossed it on the counter. "What do you need me to do?"

"The lining is caught, and I can't get it situated

with all this...dress." She reached down, grabbed the bottom of the gown, and hauled it up to reveal two wooden legs that looked like they belonged on a table. "Can you hold this up for me while I straighten everything out?"

He took over. "Shouldn't you at least introduce us first?"

Arianne swatted his arm and giggled, then ducked beneath the fabric.

The dress hung over her like an umbrella. He glanced around the place, envisioning the remodel he and Lamar had approved. Replacing this girly stuff with sporting goods would be a welcome sight. This was no place for a bridal shop. He'd make sure Arianne and Emma were secured elsewhere.

"Got it." She backed out from underneath the dress.

He let the dress fall and watched her smooth it into place. A long, white string clung to her hair. He pulled it out, letting his fingertips brush the silky strands.

Her gaze fell to his lips.

He grinned. "Miss me?"

Her throat worked as she swallowed. He'd missed her unbearably. He stepped closer, putting his hands on her waist. His mouth hovered close to hers, giving her a chance to back away.

She didn't. He leaned in.

"Kitty!" Emma pounded down the stairs.

Arianne backed away. She locked the door and turned over the sign while he helped Emma release the cat from its prison. The girl snuggled it close to her chin and it purred. Arianne rubbed the girl's head and smiled, clearly flustered. "Let's go upstairs."

They led him to their apartment. The walls surrounding the stairs were dingy and scuffed. The door rubbed the frame when it opened, revealing an equally repulsive living room. The apartment was clean, but it needed a serious overhaul. He had no idea they lived like this. What had Uncle Marty been thinking letting them move in here? They deserved better than this.

The kitchen was a joke. It needed to be gutted completely. He wanted to pack up their things and take them home with him right now, but Arianne would never let him. Instead, he set the table while she scooped dinner onto plates.

They gathered around the small table, and Emma said grace, thanking God for bringing her kitty home. The girl's meal-time prayers had become such a habit, he'd caught himself several times over the last few weeks, bowing his head before eating. Then he'd mentally slap himself since he was alone and wasn't sure what to say anyway.

Huck dug his fork into his beef and noodles and savored the bite.

Emma sipped her milk. "Mr. Jack is bringing me a Christmas tree."

Food stuck in Huck's throat and he swallowed to dislodge it. "That so?"

Arianne kept her gaze riveted to her plate.

"Uh-huh. He said every kid should have a tree at Christmas."

They should. But the ones who didn't, survived without them. As a kid, he'd loved walking through town at night in December, spying the colorful lights on the houses, looking in the windows at the decorated trees, wishing he had a real home. A real family.

That his mom hadn't been cruel and told him Santa wasn't real when he was four. Was it so wrong for him to believe in something good?

He cleared his throat. "You have plans already, then?"

Arianne raised her head with a half-grin. "Not really. Jack's flying to Pittsburgh to spend the week with his parents. Who knows what Missy's doing."

Huck's tense shoulders relaxed. "Spend it with me." Resting his elbows on the table, he pointed his fork at Emma. "There's a white pine behind my house that would make a mighty fine Christmas tree. And since you've been such a good girl all year, helpin' your ma take care of me and all, I heard Santa was bringin' some presents for you to my house."

Emma's face broke into a wide smile. "Can we, Mommy? Can we?"

Arianne's mouth hung open as she looked from him to her daughter. "Well...I..."

Huck winked.

Arianne smiled. "We'd like that."

After dinner, they cleared the table, and Huck washed dishes while Arianne gave Emma a bath. Splashing noises and laughter echoed from the bathroom. Sounds he'd missed. He dunked his hand under the soapy water for a plate and noted the chipped porcelain sink. Streetlights blurred through the fogged window in front of him, blocking any view with the condensation trapped between the old panes. He remembered Arianne appreciating the view out his kitchen window at the fields beyond. How could she stand this?

After her bath, Emma snuggled beside him on the couch while he endured some cartoon about a girl who kissed a frog. Her little-girl scent hit his nose. Her damp hair soaked his sleeve. Halfway through the movie, Emma's head drooped, and he glanced down to find her asleep. Arianne turned on the bedroom light, and he placed Emma in bed, tucking the blankets around her shoulders. If only he could do this every night. He turned on her nightlight and closed the door on his way out.

"Thanks for bringing the cat." Arianne nodded to the pest curled in a ball in the corner.

"Believe me, it's no problem."

She smiled and fidgeted with her ugly green sweater.

He'd known her long enough to know she was hiding something. "What is it?"

Arianne sucked in deep breath. "I..." She blew it out.

"Spill it."

She walked to the couch and sat, patting the cushion beside her.

He obeyed, though he didn't like it. He preferred to take bad news standing up.

"Martin—your uncle—and my mother were engaged. Missy discovered it in a newspaper dated 1969."

The news knocked him against the couch back. Uncle Marty never mentioned that. Math had never been Huck's best subject, but that would've made his uncle pretty young. "Wow." He rubbed his chin. "Why didn't they get married?"

"We don't know." Arianne picked at her fingernails.

He studied her. "I have a feeling you're not done with this story."

She nibbled her bottom lip. "Missy thinks she's Martin's daughter."

"What?" Huck stood. "That's crazy. Besides, she's younger than you are. Your mom would've been married before she was born. There's no way."

Arianne's cheeks burned dark red. "Maybe they reunited."

If it was true, that would make him and Missy cousins. Where did that leave Arianne? He shook his head, remembering a conversation between him and Uncle Marty while they worked on Huck's Mustang one night. "Uncle Marty couldn't have kids. I think that's why Aunt Faye left him."

Arianne gave up on her nails and started picking at a loose thread on the couch. "That doesn't mean he couldn't produce children. Some people just aren't...compatible."

He narrowed his eyes in thought, searching his memory for that night, bringing the smell of WD-40 and the warmth of kerosene heaters in the small garage along with it. Uncle Marty leaned over the open hood of the Mustang laid up on blocks, waiting for new wheels. Huck dug through the toolbox for a three-quarter-inch wrench.

"I'm sorry your mom let you down." Uncle Marty twisted the rusty bolt on the carburetor with a grunt. "She should've done better by you."

Huck shrugged and closed the toolbox, uncomfortable with the subject. "Whatever."

Uncle Marty released the bolt and leaned his arms against the car. "I'm no psychiatrist, and I won't force you to talk about your feelings, but I'm here if you ever need to sort things out."

Wrench wrapped in his fist, Huck headed toward

the exhaust. "What made her so crazy?"

Uncle Marty sighed. "She didn't start out that way."

Silence followed, as if his uncle's mind had gone back in time or he was choosing his words carefully. Huck couldn't tell which, since he was now lying beneath the car.

"Somewhere along the way, she traded in her pigtails for sex and drugs. We all did. It was the sixties." Another bolt groaned, and so did Uncle Marty. "That's no excuse. Frankly, I'm ashamed."

"Of the sex and drugs or your pigtails?"

Uncle Marty chuckled. "Very funny, smart mouth." The spray of WD-40 followed by a cough. "You don't have to make the same mistakes your mom did. You've got a fresh start here, a clean slate."

Huck dropped his arms from the exhaust and stared at the car's frame.

"Like this car—she's gone places, seen and done a lot of things, and has the dents and motor damage to prove it. With some care, a few new parts, and shiny paint, she'll be like new. But leave her out in the weather, drive recklessly, and she'll be right back in the same ugly shape she's in."

The meaning behind Uncle Marty's words was similar to the ones the warden had told him. Huck continued working. "If you're so good at this, why didn't you have kids?"

"That's a sore subject, son." Minutes ticked by before Uncle Marty spoke again. "I can't. I've got the car, but no gas. Makes it hard on a marriage."

Huck made a face. That was way more than he wanted to know. "Is that why Aunt Faye left?"

"Bad relationships run in our family like a curse.

There were a hundred reasons. That was one."

"Why didn't you get married again?" Mom always did.

The toolbox opened and metal clanked. "I don't ever talk about this. With anyone." Silence. "I was engaged before Faye. Came up here to work on a fishing boat for the summer and met a woman. Bad timing with the war in Vietnam. I joined the Army to do my part. Got real sick. Found out I couldn't have kids."

The heater whirred. Nothing else was said.

Huck's arm burned from the awkward position in his attempt to release the bolt. He let it rest. "What happened to the girl?"

"You ever heard the saying, 'If you love something, you'll let it go'? She wanted to be a mother more than anything. I didn't want her settling for me when I couldn't give her what she wanted. I let her go."

"And married Aunt Faye."

Uncle Marty's wry laugh. "And married Aunt Faye."

How Huck missed the old man's laugh now. He put his hands low on his hips and looked at Arianne. "Uncle Marty couldn't have kids. He told me."

Arianne rested her elbows on her knees. "Did he have a medical condition? Maybe he was just saying that to protect my mother."

Was that why the sheriff hated him and Uncle Marty so much? Why he didn't want Huck around Arianne? If this was the reason, why not say so? Unless, the sheriff didn't want the dirty secret revealed either.

"We're not related." He waved a finger between

them.

"You and I aren't. I was the reason my parents married so quickly. But if you and Missy are cousins, then we would be related, sort of."

Huck sank onto the couch and rubbed his forehead while he classified facts. Could this be right? If so, why didn't Uncle Marty say as much? He'd always been a straight shooter. It wasn't like him to be so cryptic.

But why else would Uncle Marty leave a hefty inheritance to the daughter of his ex-fiancée? Huck rested his head on the cushions and stared at the ceiling. *What's this about, Uncle Marty?*

"Honey, I'm home."

—anonymous

29

Arianne scrunched her nose at the stale smell in the storage closet. There was barely enough room for herself in here, much less Missy and Emma too. "What are we looking for again?" Missy asked.

Arianne stood on tiptoe to reach a box on the top shelf. "Our old Christmas ornaments. Jack brought over a gorgeous Douglas fir last night, and Emma can't wait to decorate."

Missy frowned. "You're still seeing Jack? I figured you and Huck were exclusive after walking in on you guys—"

"Ahem!" Arianne pursed her lips and nodded toward her daughter.

"Resuscitating." Missy chuckled.

That word described it about right. Huck's kiss had awakened something dead inside her she could no longer ignore. But she had to. He'd yet to declare any real intentions, and she enjoyed spending time with Jack.

Jack wasn't intimidated by the fact she had a child, and he was an intelligent man. They never seemed to run out of things to talk about. The more they were together, the more he proved he was the best choice.

Then why had she been so relieved last night

when he'd pulled her into a lingering hug instead of moving for her lips? Her prayers for such a wonderful man appeared to have finally been answered, so why wasn't she embracing this relationship with her whole heart?

"It's complicated."

"I guess it must be." Missy opened another box, shook her head, and put it back.

Though Jack would be gone for Christmas, Arianne had promised to spend New Year's Eve with him.

Emma opened the box nearest her. "Is these them, Mommy?"

They all peeked inside. A Bruins sweatshirt, an autographed hockey puck, some photos, and a man's watch.

Arianne groaned. "No."

Emma started to slide the box back into place, but Arianne picked it up and tossed it out the closet door. "Trash." She looked at Missy and mouthed the word *"Adam."*

They continued the search. Missy pushed bridal magazines aside and grabbed the box behind it. Inside were some certificates, newspaper clippings, a fishing hat with rust-colored stains, and a police badge. Arianne swallowed the lump in her throat. "Dad's things."

Missy stared into the box, biting her bottom lip. "I didn't know you'd kept anything."

"Stuff I couldn't part with."

"Hey, look what I found." Emma held up a white shoe with a broken heel.

Arianne chuckled. "Trash."

Emma's eyes lit up. "Can I throw it like you did

that box?"

"Go for it," Missy and Arianne said in unison.

Emma chucked it into the hallway with a giggle.

Missy reached into the box and rubbed her thumb over the worn badge. Then she fingered Dad's fishing hat with a large hook sewn onto the bill. Dried blood stains spotted the fabric. Arianne remembered offering to wash it for Dad after his Canadian fishing expedition in '98, but he'd set her straight on that. Something about a seaman ritual, yet another thing she'd never understand about men.

"Do you care if I take this stuff with me?" Missy closed the box and turned away.

"Sure. Can I ask why?" Arianne's sister instincts were buzzing.

Missy's fingers curled into fists, and she closed her eyes for a moment. "The blood stains might be a way to test for paternity."

Air fled Arianne's lungs. This whole thing was nuts, yet scarily possible. "It could be fish blood. Or the test results could be inconclusive. Are you sure you want to do this? What if...?"

Missy stood tall. "I have to know."

Arianne nodded.

"I found the decorations." Emma's smile chased the dark cloud from the room.

~*~

Emma squealed and flung tissue paper into the air. Like little parachutes, they descended to Huck's living room carpet.

He laughed. "Like it?"

The girl ran to him, jumped in his lap, and threw

her arms around his neck. "It's 'zactly what I wanted."

That made all the embarrassment of asking the store clerk for help worthwhile.

Arianne shook her head. "Huck, those things are outrageous."

He shrugged. "It's what she wanted."

Emma released his neck long enough for him to catch a breath. "Did you like your present?"

Huck glanced at the framed picture of him waving from the doorway of a beehive. She'd said it was his honey house. "I do. I've always wanted to live in a beehive."

She hopped down from his lap. "Me too. Maybe someday we can all live in one together." Emma picked up her doll and admired the red velvet dress, unaware of the gravity of her words.

He'd love that.

Arianne rose from her spot on the floor and started picking up tissue paper, then paused when something caught her attention on the muted TV.

"What're you gonna name her?" Huck pointed to the doll.

"She already has a name. It's Sydney." Emma whispered something in the doll's ear then put its plastic mouth up to her own. "Sydney wants to see my old bedroom. Can I show it to her?"

"Go ahead. It's probably cold on that side of the house, though."

Doll in hand, Emma skipped away, a hum trailing behind her.

Huck tossed the gift bag on the couch and joined Arianne by the TV. Her face had paled, and unshed tears clouded her eyes. He put a hand on her back. "What's wrong?"

She swallowed. "Darcy."

He turned up the volume in time to hear the reporter say the footage was previous coverage from Darcy's Christmas Eve wedding at a historic Portland parish. The ending clip showed a bride and groom dodging birdseed as they hurried down the concrete steps to their waiting limo.

"My dress." Arianne sighed and swiped a tear. "That's my design."

"She can't do that."

"She did."

Huck took a breath and blew it out, knowing there was nothing they could do now. "She looked fat."

Laughter spewed from Arianne's lips. He pulled her against him and gently rocked, aching for her. Arianne was too talented to allow someone else to steal her creativity.

"Will I ever win?"

He kissed the top of her head. "Don't give up. If you don't get the scholarship, we'll find another way."

She pulled back just enough to see his face, her arms remaining circled at his waist. "We?"

He catalogued every line on her face from her slender nose to the dip above her upper lip. He wanted nothing more than to lean over and prove his love without words, but not until after he'd offered his gift. "We."

Reluctantly, he released her and walked to the tree poised in the center of the large window, revealing small flakes drifting in the air. This was the first Christmas tree he'd ever owned, and there wasn't anyone he'd rather share it with.

He plucked a small box from between the branches twinkling with white lights. Heart in his throat, Huck offered it to her, nervous about how she'd react.

"What's this?" she asked, voice shaky and breathless.

"Open it."

Her fingers trembled as she clasped the box and opened the lid. "A key. I...I don't understand."

"It's the key to your new shop."

She searched his face with an intense gaze. Did he detect disappointment?

Huck brushed away a thick strand of hair that had found its way into her shirt collar and let his fingers play with the ends. "It's not much. More of a shack really. 'Bout the size of your apartment. But it's in great condition and right on the highway. I got a good deal on it."

He'd only had to use the insurance money from his busted motorcycle and a chunk of his savings to make the down payment. He'd also promised the blueberry farmer who owned it free hive rental for his crop from now until the end of the century. Thankfully, the hospital was allowing him to make interest-free payments on his bill so he'd been able to afford the building.

Arianne remained quiet, unmoving, staring at him as if he'd committed a crime. What was running through that mind of hers? Wasn't this the answer to her dilemma? The longer the silence, the more uncomfortable he grew. He stood tall and shifted his weight from one foot to the other. "Merry Christmas."

Why wasn't she jumping into his arms? Or at least smiling?

"You won't have to worry about rent. Do whatever you want with it. It's entirely yours."

Emma's humming echoed down the hall as she made her way back to the living room.

Say something.

Arianne looked down at the box and fingered the key. "Why would you do this?"

Blast it, the woman was gonna force him to get mushy and the things he wanted to say he couldn't say in front of the kid. "I appreciate your help after my accident and all. It's not the first time you've been there for me when I needed help. I wanted to return the favor. Make sure you had a nice place to relocate."

She nodded, slowly, and turned to face the window. His gut twisted. Why was she displeased?

He glanced at Emma, entertained with the tiny tea set that came with the doll, and ran a hand up Arianne's back until it reached her neck. He massaged, attempting to chase the tension away, hoping she'd see how much he cared for them. "What is it?" he whispered.

She put a hand to her stomach and shook her head as though clearing away the fog. "I'm just shocked. Thank you. I...don't know what to say."

"You don't have to say anything." He kissed her temple, breathing her in before he pulled away and continued rubbing her shoulders.

In the window's reflection, Huck saw Arianne close her eyes and her body started to relax. Uncle Marty had brought them all together for a reason, and Huck believed he was starting to understand.

~*~

"She didn't make it." Arianne pointed to Emma asleep on the floor, curled up in a blanket, still wearing her New Year's party hat.

Jack tipped his mug to swallow the last drops of his hot cocoa. "She gave it good effort."

He leaned forward on the couch. The ceramic cup rested with a *clunk* against the coffee-table-turned-snack-buffet. Two open potato chip bags, a bowl of half-eaten chip dip, cookie crumbs, and four empty soda cans were all that was left of their feast.

Jack was handsome tonight in his brown sweater with a small zipper at the neck and his brown and red plaid shirt peeking from around his sleeves, neckline, and waist. His left hand rested on a leg of his dark jeans. Arianne marveled at the missing ring. How was this guy not taken?

The mass of bodies gathered in Times Square swept across the television screen, noise-makers, cheers, and music emanating from the speakers. Five minutes to go. Colored bulbs from the Christmas tree reflected on the wall.

She glanced at Jack whose face had grown serious. The skin between his brows creased, and his eyes narrowed. She suspected even though he was looking at the TV, he wasn't really watching it.

He turned his head and locked those green eyes with hers. "I missed you while I was in Pittsburgh."

Arianne's heart shifted into second gear. She'd missed him too, but she hadn't been lonely for him. "How are your parents?"

"They stay busy, I'll say that. Between Mom's quilting classes and bridge club and Dad's bowling league, I hardly saw them the whole time I was there." He stared at her hand, then reached for it and laced his fingers with hers.

A tingle ran up her arm. "What about your

sisters?"

His mouth pursed. He seemed discouraged that she was more interested in his family than telling him she missed him too. Why wasn't she saying it? He was a good, steady man, a hard worker, devout Christian. She had missed his company.

"Same as they've always been. I got to meet my new nephew for the first time. He's a tiny thing—head's smaller than my palm."

People bundled in hats and mittens holding homemade posters told the home viewers where they were from. The emcee chose random spectators to chat with. One couple, whose sign said, "Louisiana woman, Mississippi man," held hands as he knelt and proposed. Mississippi reminded Arianne of Huck. Where was he spending New Year's Eve?

Oh, who cared? Though his gesture was huge and much appreciated, it had *business partners* stamped all over it. He could open his sporting goods store now guilt-free.

She'd mentally told herself she was moving on and would stop caring where Huck went and who he spent his time with. After all, she had a good man sitting right next to her who desired a relationship that could potentially lead to marriage. Now she was just waiting for her heart to catch up.

She hadn't told Jack about the building yet. They were still getting to know each other, and it's not like they'd declared any kind of status. Besides, it almost felt like Huck's and her secret, and that pleased her way more than it should.

The tenderness in Huck's gaze that day, his soft touch seemed to say he wanted more than friendship. But if that were true, why wouldn't he say so? What was holding him back?

Two minutes to go.

Jack's hand squeezed tighter around hers. "I enjoyed the time with my family, but when the house got quiet, I'd think about you."

His thumb brushed the inside of her wrist. Goose bumps covered her arms. She could be happy with Jack. He was nice, attentive, responsible. Sometimes love didn't come right away. Sometimes it grew over time. She'd be an idiot to pass this by.

The emcee announced one minute left.

Jack held their entwined hands against his hard chest, studying her so fully that she wondered if he could read her thoughts. "I really missed you, Arianne." His deep voice was barely above a whisper.

The crowd gathered in Times Square counted down the seconds. "Ten, nine, eight…"

Jack's gaze fell to her lips. She didn't pull away. This was it. He was going to kiss her for the first time, and it'd be so wonderful she'd never think of another man again. His warm lips met hers as he wound his fingers in her hair and pulled her closer, deepening the kiss. Tranquility washed over her like a bubbling surf swishing around her ankles as she stood on the shoreline.

Where was the spark? Where were the fireworks? The bells of Notre Dame?

They were all on TV. Cow bells, horns and sirens blared…from Times Square.

Jack broke the kiss and rested his forehead against hers, his thick fingers cupping the back of her neck. "Happy New Year."

Arianne forced a smile through her disappointment. Huck's kiss had ruined her.

She was so stupid. She craved a happily-ever-after. The best prospect she'd had in a long time—possibly ever—was holding her in his arms at this very minute, and all she could think about was her lackadaisical reaction to his kiss? Relationships didn't survive on such things. If they did, she'd still be married to her ex-husband.

That's what was wrong. The past three years had been so full of turmoil, she couldn't find her balance. Life had blindfolded her and spun her by her shoulders until she was so dizzy she couldn't stand. Then, when the blindfold came off and she'd found her footing, her equilibrium couldn't catch up. She refused to sabotage this just because Jack's lips didn't cause her to go into cardiac arrest. She kissed him again. "Happy New Year, Jack."

What would this one bring?

After Jesus' resurrection, his disciples offered him fish and honeycomb.

—Luke 24

30

Huck twisted the doorknob and stuck his head inside Arianne's new shop. "It's me."

"Come in." Arianne's muffled voice drifted from another room.

He stepped inside and closed the door behind him. The temperature inside wasn't much warmer than outside. Her footsteps from the next room grew louder.

"Hey." Pink dusted Arianne's cheeks and nose. Her hat sat low over her ears, and she rubbed her mitten-wrapped hands together.

Before he could ask why the place was so cold, she grabbed his arm and dragged him from room to room. She told him her plans with animated gestures like Emma on Christmas morning. He didn't try to hide his amusement, or the fact that he enjoyed her touch.

Daylight spilled into the windows in the main room, illuminating the dust on the dark laminate floor. Arianne patted the light gray wall, trimmed in white. "After a fresh coat of paint, Jack's going to build shelves for me and stain them to match the floor."

Huck's smile fell.

She tugged him to the window by the front door. "Jack's also going to help me redo these flowerbeds.

He said the ground slopes at an odd angle and needs to be restructured to prevent water from pooling around the foundation."

Whoa. When did Jack weasel his way into this? Huck tugged her hand to spin her around. "If you need shelves, I'll build them."

Her head tipped to the side. "Thanks, but Jack said he'd make them."

This property didn't fall under Jack's jurisdiction. Neither did Arianne. "I know how to build shelves, Arianne."

His voice came out rougher than he'd intended. Her excitement wilted, as did her grip on him. "I wasn't insinuating that you couldn't. Jack wants to help, and you've done more than enough already."

Apparently not. "Where's squirt?"

Arianne crossed her arms against the cold. "With Missy."

Her words were barely above a whisper. He'd just won the Jerk-of-the-Year award. But Jack wiggling in on his plans smarted. It was Huck's job to see that the girls were secure and happy. Not Jack's. "How's Missy doin'?"

Arianne shrugged. "She's so obsessed with finding out who her father is, it's almost scary."

He spread his feet shoulder width apart and tucked his hands in his coat pockets. "What do you mean?"

"She goes off on these strange escapades, looking for clues—including going through my things." She made a face. "It's weird. She's talked to everyone in town who's ever known Dad or Martin. There's this desperation I don't understand. It's eating her alive."

"Do you think she's Uncle Marty's daughter?"

She gazed out the window at the bare, gnarled branches of an old oak. "I don't know. Martin was a good man. I don't think he'd have children and not raise them. He adored Emma and detested the situation Adam left me in. Martin didn't seem the hypocritical type." Arianne pinned her eyes on him. "Then again, people surprise me every day."

The comment was obviously directed at him, but was it a compliment or an insult?

"Why's it so cold in here?" Huck glanced around the former coffee shop and bookstore, satisfied with his purchase.

Arianne buried her hands in her coat pockets as well. "I haven't had the utilities turned on yet." She wouldn't meet his eyes.

"Why not?"

Arianne sighed. "Because my tire blowing the other day was an unexpected expense. I'll get them turned on soon. I promise."

"Your tire blew? Why didn't you call me?"

She suddenly found his boots interesting. "Jack picked us up and fixed it."

That did it. Couldn't she see how *he* felt about her? He'd bought her a new shop for crying out loud.

It was this whole stupid mess with her sister. She'd started retreating as soon as the ridiculous paternity issue had popped up. He'd get it settled and bury it along with Uncle Marty—before a life with Arianne vanished like his uncle's ghost.

~*~

"He didn't tell you?"

Huck paced in front of the window in his office.

"No."

Ice glazed over the glass, along with the bare tree branches from the maple beside the house. The wind howled, pushing a slight draft past the trim and into the room.

Daryl Peavey, Uncle Marty's lawyer and childhood friend, blew out a loud breath on the other end. "This goes against oath, but..." Another sigh. "He had mumps."

"He died of pneumonia."

"Yes, he did. Marty contracted mumps while overseas during Vietnam."

Huck sank into his leather chair and propped his socked feet on the desk. "And you think that has something to do with why he couldn't have kids?"

"It was a bad case from the start. For him, the virus caused swelling and inflammation in his reproductive system, which led to scar tissue damage. Not long after he arrived home from war, he showed up at my house in a drunken stupor and told me everything. I think that haunted him more than the flashbacks. "

"If you love something, you'll let it go." Words Uncle Marty truly lived by. The chair groaned as Huck settled his weight against the reclining back. "I had no idea."

"I'm surprised he didn't tell you."

"Me too." Though Uncle Marty had come close that night in the garage. Huck couldn't imagine giving up Arianne. How did his uncle do it?

Huck ran a hand down his face. "So you think this paternity case is bogus?"

Daryl released a loud breath. "Nothing's impossible. Each baby is a miracle and they happen every day."

Miracles. Huck stared at Emma's framed drawing of his motorcycle accident. Did miracles really exist? "And he didn't give any reasons why he left Missy a random inheritance?"

"Marty was of sound mind, so I didn't ask. But I do know he never stopped loving Karin. They kept in touch. Even saw each other from time to time. Of course there were rumors, but you know how those go. I can say he was never the same after she died."

Huck nodded, saddened his uncle was tormented by a life never lived. "Thanks, Daryl. 'Preciate your time."

He hung up the phone and glanced around his office. In some ways, he could sympathize with his uncle. This house had been alive when the girls were here. Lately, when the loneliness threatened to devour him, he imagined rowdy children running in the hallways, a soft, feminine body pressed against his at night. The same body every night. Forever.

Crazy. He'd never given a second thought to having kids. Or taking a wife. But his entire life overturned the first day he walked into Arianne's shop. And it was time he told her. What happened from here would determine whether it changed for the better.

~*~

Arianne admired the way Jack held a drill steady in his hands. The tool bit into the drywall and whirred. Then Jack dropped it into his tool belt like a Wild West gunslinger dropping his Colt .45 in its holster.

Jack caught her staring at his profile and gave her

a sexy, lopsided grin. Winked.

He was amazing in every way, but something was lacking. A…a… She didn't know. Maybe, a southern accent?

Arianne frowned. This triangle was spinning her in circles and making her dizzy.

"What's wrong?" Metal clicked against metal as Jack dug around in his tool belt.

"Nothing." She smiled.

He studied her a moment then went back to hanging her new shelf.

She paced the room. The space might be small, but utilities were cheaper and the building was in much better condition. Huck had agreed to let them stay in the apartment until he and his business partner were ready to convert it into offices. He hadn't liked the idea, argued that it wasn't a fitting place for them to live and he'd help her find a new place. She'd countered that they'd lived there for three years and had survived.

The drill zipped the screw into place. With quick movements, Jack attached the shelf he'd made to the wall. Arianne ran her palm across the perfectly level surface. "It's beautiful."

"Yes, she is."

Arianne turned to Jack. There was no mistaking that look. Heat flamed her cheeks.

He chuckled and pulled her against his chest. Her cheek rested against his soft flannel shirt. He smelled like cologne and woodchips. But her skin didn't hum. "Valentine's Day is next week. If you don't already have plans, I'd like to spend it with you."

Arianne hadn't spent that holiday with a man in years. She couldn't help her smile. "I'll try to get a sitter for Emma."

"Bring her too." His deep voice rumbled in her ear. "We'll keep it casual."

She relaxed into his strong arms. How long had it been since someone—

The front door swung open. "Arianne?"

Huck's voice boomed in the doorway. Arianne jolted, tempted to pull away from Jack. She didn't. Huck had never made any declarations, and probably wouldn't, even though she suspected he wanted to be more than friends. Or business partners. Possibly relatives. Certainly not husband and wife.

Huck's initial grin faded to a frown as he stared at them, arms wrapped around each other. He swallowed. Then his back straightened and his face turned stoic. "How's it goin', Jack?"

"Good." Jack released her. "Just hanging Arianne's new shelf."

Anger—or jealousy?—flashed in Huck's eyes when he glanced her way. He blinked and it disappeared. "It looks great." He walked toward the shelf for a closer look. "Did you make this?"

Jack nodded.

"That's quality craftsmanship there." Huck's smile and stance revealed nothing, but Arianne knew him well enough to detect the strain in his tone.

Huck shook Jack's hand. "It's nice of you to help her out."

Jack smiled at Arianne. "My pleasure."

Arianne clasped her hands together, trying not to choke on the tension in the air.

Huck cleared his throat, removed his mask, and seared Arianne with a look of agony. "I came by to talk business, but it's nothing that can't wait. We'll catch up later."

Jack bent and latched his toolbox lid closed. "No need." He gripped the handle and stood. "I have to get going anyway." He gazed at Arianne tenderly, caressed her face, and leaned in for a quick kiss. "See you later."

"Bye, Jack." Her voice cracked, and she watched him walk out the door to his truck.

Huck scratched his jaw that had sprouted a healthy day's worth of growth. "Where's Emma?"

Arianne shoved her hands in her back pockets. "Making cinnamon rolls with Sherry."

The muscle in his jaw pulsed. "You and Jack looked comfortable."

She turned away and pulled the furniture polish and an old rag from a box. Ten minutes ago, her traitorous heart conjured Huck here. Now, all she wanted to think about was her Valentine's date with Jack. After all, it wasn't like Huck was professing any undying love. Her feelings bounced back and forth, colliding like a desktop pendulum. "What did you want to talk about?"

~*~

Huck raked his fingers through his hair. It took all his self-control to stomp his temper when he walked in on Jack groping Arianne. How would that pretty shelf hold up with Jack's face buried in it? He unclenched his fists and exhaled. That would only push Arianne away. Like Uncle Marty had suggested, Huck was wiping the slate clean. He had to prove to Arianne he was good enough for her.

"I, uh, wanted to see how things were going." At

least it was warm in here this time.

Arianne climbed on a stepstool and sprayed the furniture polish on the shelf. "You said we had business to discuss."

A lemony scent filled the room. "We do, but it doesn't involve the shop."

Her hand stilled on the dust rag. Morning light pooled into the windows and illuminated the drops of polish hanging in the air. "Why do I feel like you're about to deliver bad news?"

He'd thumb away the knot she'd created between her eyebrows if she were close enough. Huck offered his hand. "Sit with me."

Arianne glanced at the shelf then back to his hand. She linked them together and climbed off the stool.

He lowered onto a nearby stack of boxes. "Uncle Marty caught an extreme case of mumps during Vietnam. It hindered his reproductive organs."

She pressed her lips together. "I remember learning about mumps in medical school. Poor Martin."

"Yeah, I thought they had vaccines against that kind of stuff."

"They didn't back then. The MMR vaccination wasn't deemed safe and offered by the government until the early '70s."

He chuckled. "You're a walking encyclopedia."

She grinned. "Not really. It's that I'm a mom and I research what's going into my child's body." She leaned over and rested her elbows on her knees. "How did you find out?"

He mimicked her stance. "A friend of his, but his doctor confirmed it. He'd signed a consent form a few years ago giving his doctor permission to share his medical records with me. I didn't know that until I called."

Arianne exhaled. "Well, now we know he's not Missy's father."

He placed her hand in his, palm to palm, and enjoyed the feel of her. "It's not likely, but not impossible either." *Miracles happen every day.* If so, he could use another one right about now.

She looked at him for answers. Answers he was finally ready to give. He kissed her fingers, allowing his lips to linger. He itched to pull her into his arms and show her just how much she meant to him. This clean slate thing was harder than he thought. He'd never hesitated to charm a woman into bed before. But he wanted something pure and beautiful with Arianne. She made him want to be a better man.

"Huck?" she whispered. "What is this between us? I need to know where I stand with you."

With a mouth full of cotton, he faced her until their knees touched, prepared to give her his raw heart. He had to before it was too late. "Arianne, I…"

A cellphone rang. Arianne hesitated then stood, pulled the blasted thing from her sweatshirt pocket, and held up a finger.

Huck gulped his words, tucked his heart back inside his chest. If that was Jack…

"Missy?" Arianne walked to the window. "I can barely hear you. What? You're where? What on earth are you doing in California?"

Apitherapy is the art and science of using products of the honeybee for therapeutic and medicinal purposes.

31

"What are you doing in California?" Static crackled in Arianne's ear. "Missy? Are you there?"

"I'm here."

Huck stood and stepped away from the box he'd been sitting on. Arianne covered the phone with her hand. "Sorry," she whispered.

He waved to dismiss it and moved closer. "We'll finish talking about this later." He ran his fingers along her jaw, eyes so full of longing it made her blush. He turned to go, and she refocused her attention back to Missy. "What are you doing in California?"

"Martin was stationed here in Monterey. I came to see what I could find out."

When the door clicked, Arianne knew Huck was gone. From the window, she watched him huddle against the wind, climb into his truck, and drive away. Arianne shook her head. "Missy, you've got to stop this rabbit chase."

A pause. "I'm not Dad's."

Arianne stared at the headlights of a passing car and waited for Missy to say she was joking. When she didn't, Arianne said, "How did you find out?"

"I got the paternity test back yesterday. They tested the blood from his fishing hat. The results proved the sample to be human blood, and the possibility of being his daughter is so slim it's practically non-existent."

Her sister's words were as cold as the air outside.

"How do you know it was Dad's blood?" After all, he'd filleted dozens of fish on that trip.

Missy sniffed. "Because you match it with 99.8% accuracy. I sent a hair from your hairbrush."

Arianne's legs gave out, and she lowered onto the floor, leaning her back against the wall. The room turned black and fuzzy. She tucked her head between her knees. *Breathe.*

Arianne exhaled. Inhaled. Lucy's comment from the hospital that day resurfaced to haunt her again. How had everyone else known except her and Missy? How had they managed to avoid the gossip, the condemnation all these years? Arianne had only been seven when their mother died and coped by throwing herself into her studies and avoiding people, that's how.

No wonder Daddy hadn't liked Huck. It all made sense now. "I...I don't know what to say, Miss."

"I don't either. I've no way to test Martin's paternity, though it's quite obvious. I guess I'll never really know."

Arianne's vision cleared, but the sickness in her gut continued. "Why don't you come back home, and we'll move forward from here."

"I'm not coming back." Missy's tone was as hard as granite.

"Why not?"

"I've never felt at home there. Even more so now. I'm staying."

"What are you going to do in Monterey?"

"I don't know, but it's warm. That's a nice change. Maybe I'll get an apartment. A job. I've always wanted to leave Pine Bay. Here's my chance."

Softball-sized panic clogged Arianne's throat. "But Pine Bay's your home. With me."

"You've played my mother long enough, Arianne. It's time to let me go." Missy voice broke.

Tears burned Arianne's eyes. "I don't know how."

"You'll find a way. I'll keep in touch."

"Miss?" Warm droplets slid down Arianne's cheeks. "I love you."

A pause. "I love you too."

The phone beeped, ending the call.

Arianne glanced around the mostly empty shop. The scent of fresh paint lingered in the room from the wall she'd painted a few hours earlier. Boxes stacked three layers high filled the back corner. Nothing would be the same without Missy. Who would keep her on her toes? Help her with an encouraging word? Bring her hot chocolate or coffee in the middle of her mundane day? Be the other adult body sleeping in the apartment to remind her she wasn't alone in the world.

She was being selfish. This was about Missy. Not her.

Arianne brushed away the tears with her sleeve. Truth was she needed Missy more than Missy needed her. She'd smothered her sister since childhood because it helped fill the gaping hole inside. But it wasn't fair to Missy. Her sister was an adult now. Missy needed to find her own way. So did Arianne.

If only Arianne didn't get lost so easily.

~*~

Huck stared at the big screen in the upscale Portland bar, watching the Colts intercept the ball at the fifty-yard line. Their defensive lineman sprinted across the green, dodging one Patriot after another. The men at the table behind Huck pumped their fists and roared over the touchdown.

Huck would've joined in, but his mind was 175 miles away with two blonde beauties who were spending the evening with his tool-clad nemesis. He'd come close to telling Arianne he loved her yesterday before Missy's call interrupted. A part of him had been glad. Her half-empty shop wasn't the most romantic place for such announcements. Only now, picturing her cozied up on the couch with Sir Fix-a-lot, he regretted procrastinating. Huck popped a fried pickle into his mouth. It turned to dust on his tongue.

Lamar made his way back to their table and slipped his phone into his man purse. "Sorry about that." He shucked his suit coat, rolled up the sleeves of his beige dress shirt, and loosened his matching—probably silk—tie. "When the missus calls, I answer."

The guy looked like every other big-city dandy in here. A room full of male socialites in a fancy historic tavern on Valentine's Day made Huck nervous. Huck nodded. "Gotta keep 'em happy. You sure she's not upset about spending tonight alone?"

Lamar laughed. "She's not alone. She's out shopping and having drinks with her girlfriends. Besides, she's always tolerant when she knows it means more money coming her way."

Ouch. Huck had known women like that. Mainly, his mother.

"I've scheduled a crew to start renovations in two weeks."

Huck nodded again and took a swig of his pop. He'd help Arianne finish relocating by then.

Lamar's voice droned on about construction and inventory. *Jack better keep his hands off her tonight if he wants to keep 'em intact.*

"Is something wrong?"

It took a minute for Huck to register that Lamar had changed the subject. "I'm good. Just listening."

A basket of onion rings and a refill later, Lamar stood and stuck out his hand. "See you March first."

Huck pumped his hand. "See you then." He paid the waitress, told her to keep the change, and stood to pull on his coat. A hand on his arm stopped him.

A pretty brunette with hard green eyes and a wide smile fluttered her eyelashes. She reeked of money earned with dirty old men and cheating husbands. "Taking off so soon?"

He shrugged away her grip and put on his coat. "Yep."

She did her best to change his mind with her pouty pink lips. "You're not planning to leave alone, are you?"

Her invitation was as clear as the cleavage exposed from her low cut dress. Huck assassinated the part of him that already had them leaving together, though it wasn't easy. He was used to women throwing themselves at him, and he'd always handled it the only way he knew how.

He took a deep breath. "I sure am."

Huck zipped his coat in preparation for the cold walk to the hotel and stalked to the exit. He had a fine woman back home, and was going to make the right decision this time. He loved Arianne. Even if another man was keeping her company tonight.

~*~

Jack braked in front of her apartment, and Arianne glanced toward the backseat. Emma was asleep, as usual. The air outside was frigid, and Arianne hated to leave the car's warmth. "And they said Phil predicted an early spring."

"He can't always be right." Jack put the car in park, reached for her gloved hand, and laced his fingers with hers. He leaned against the headrest and turned to her. "I had a good time."

"Me too." His body heat seeped through her glove.

"It's been awhile. Valentine's day is always a little rough for me."

She squeezed his hand.

"I really enjoyed spending it with you and Emma."

Snow flurries danced in the beam of his headlights. The street was dark, abandoned.

Jack looked at Emma from his rearview mirror. "Can I ask what happened to her father?" he whispered.

Shame burned her cheeks. She shouldn't be ashamed, since it all happened against her will, but telling Jack made her uncomfortable, embarrassed. And after witnessing his wife's memory stamped all over his house from the wall colors to the beadwork in the homemade throw pillows, Arianne knew if they ever pursued this relationship to the altar she'd have some giant shoes to fill. She swallowed and opened the closet door in her heart wide, so she could clean it all out now and wouldn't have to enter it again for a good long while. Hopefully, never.

When she finished the whole story, Jack nodded and folded his other hand around hers. "I care for you both. A lot." He stared out the windshield into the dark night. "I wondered if I'd ever be able to open my heart to a woman again." He pinned his gaze on hers, the dash lights highlighting the side of his face. "With you, I believe I can."

His words choked Arianne. Could she ever *fully* open her heart to him? She wanted that capability. Jack was the ideal man. But her thoughts always went back to Huck. They'd yet to finish their lets-define-this-relationship talk, and she was impatiently anticipating his answer. She was growing weary of spreading her emotions between two men.

Jack leaned over the console, tugged her closer by the lapel of her coat, and kissed her in a way that left no doubt as to how deep he'd fallen for her. She kissed him back, guilt seeping into her core. Jack was an amazing man, but the truth was if Huck wanted all of her, forever, she'd take that life raft.

The pilfering of honey from a weak colony by other honeybees or humans is called robbing.

32

The sun burst through the storm clouds. Arianne tipped her face toward the sky, let the rays of sun envelope her, and allowed it to thaw the last frozen patches in her soul. After the news she'd received this morning, nothing could ruin this day.

"Ready to go?" Huck's deep drawl rumbled in her ear. She opened her eyes and clutched the box tighter in her arms. He stood behind her, so near she could smell his cologne. She couldn't wait to tell him her news, but wanted to wait until they were alone.

"I'm ready." She placed the box in the bed of his old truck with the others. A slight breeze rustled her hair. The forty-five-degree day held the assurance of an early spring, just as the groundhog had predicted.

Huck leaned his hip against the truck, one elbow propped on the bed. His crooked grin and rich brown eyes held depth she'd never seen before. She was horrible at reading other people, but not even she was able to mistake a difference in Huck. For the first time since his accident he seemed truly happy, more attentive—ever since he returned from his meeting in Portland last week.

They stared into each other's eyes for what seemed like minutes. She wanted so badly to reach out to him.

Ask him if they could finish that conversation. He carried a magnetism she couldn't resist. "Mommy, can I ride with Miss Sherry and Mr. Jude?"

Arianne tore her attention from Huck and focused on her daughter.

Sherry emerged from the former boutique's open door with an I-caught-you smile. "We'd love to have her, if it's all right with you."

"Of course." Arianne kissed Emma's head. "Be good."

Huck handed Arianne the keys. "Let it warm up for a minute. I'll lock the door."

Jude left the shop with the last box. "You're not letting her drive, are you?"

Huck stopped on the sidewalk and raised a brow at her. "Want to?"

Arianne shook her head. "As much as I'd like to see Huck squirm, I don't know how to drive a stick."

Everyone looked at her as if she'd said something ridiculous.

"You've never driven a manual transmission?" Huck continued to the door, kicked the wedge into the building, and then locked up.

"No."

Huck's boots thumped the pavement on his return to the vehicle. "Then it's time you learn. Hop in." He nodded to the truck.

Jude made a sour face. "You won't even let me drive it." Sherry patted her husband's back in sympathy and chuckled all the way to their car.

"Come on." Huck opened her door.

Arianne climbed aboard, settling herself behind the giant steering wheel. Huck walked around the front of the truck and joined her on the bench seat. The vehicle felt so big from the driver's side. "I don't know about this. What if I do something wrong?"

"You will."

"I'm nervous."

"She's simple. You won't hurt anything. I'll guide you. Now, push in the clutch and start her up."

Arianne obeyed. Jude and Sherry's sedan drove around them and headed down the vacant street.

Huck slapped his palm on the stick protruding from the floor. "This is the gear shift. You push in the clutch every time you need to switch gears. Got it?"

"I don't think I'm that coordinated."

"You can do it." He issued a few more instructions.

She did as commanded, biting her lip. The truck jolted forward. Died.

"Try again."

Arianne started over and produced the same result. Huck went through it all again, using his hands as an example. This time, the truck jolted but remained running. She tugged the wheel to the left and started down the street at a crawl.

"Now press in the clutch and move into second gear."

Grinding.

"Let off the clutch!"

She removed her foot. "Sorry. Did I hurt it?"

"No. Steady now." His palm rested against the dashboard. "We're leaving town. Shift it into third."

It went a little easier this time. They bumped along for a few miles as he continued to guide her. Her stomach calmed. This wasn't so bad.

Huck relaxed against the seat. "Where's Bob the Builder today?"

"*Jack* is supervising an addition to the municipal building. And what's up? I thought you guys were friends."

A curve lay up ahead.

Huck grunted. "I forgot about this. Apply the brake slowly, press in the clutch, and downshift."

More grinding. The truck wasn't slowing down.

"Release the clutch. Release the clutch!"

She looked down at her foot and removed it from the pedal.

"Whoa, stay on the road." Huck slid across the bench seat. His hip bumped into hers and his arms came around her to grip the wheel. He jerked the truck back to position.

Arianne's heart raced. "See? I can't do this."

He exhaled. "Pull over."

She did. A gunshot pierced the air. Arianne screamed.

Huck laughed. "It just backfired. Calm down."

Once they were stopped, she laid her trembling hands in her lap. He rubbed the tense knot between her shoulders.

Slow breaths in...out. Arianne closed her eyes and slowly melded to the seat. The heater whirred. Her shoulders sang from his touch. Why didn't Jack affect her this way?

Because Huck had stolen her heart years ago. That night at her kitchen table. She wasn't sure how to get it back. If she didn't, a future with Jack would be difficult. Especially with Huck as her landlord.

But a future with Jack was looking to be the better possibility. Huck didn't do forever.

His calloused palm paused on the back of her neck. His thumb rubbed the sensitive skin where her jaw and earlobe met. Like she'd been zapped with a cattle prod, her eyes popped open, and she jerked away from his touch. "I'm ready to try this again."

Wow, was that her squeaky voice?

"Arianne?" Huck remained silent until curiosity got the best of her and she looked at him.

Huck jerked the gear shift into neutral and turned the key, killing the engine. "About...us." He wagged a finger between them.

"I won the scholarship." She hadn't meant to blurt it out, but what if he'd planned to tell her they had no future together?

Dimples carved deep grooves in his cheeks. He pulled her to him, his big hand palming the back of her head. "I'm proud of you. I knew you had talent."

Words anyone might say. Not a hint to foreshadow the direction of his answer. Her stomach clenched, and she inhaled a deep breath. "Your turn."

He held her at arm's length, his face growing serious. He ran his palm down his jeans, and shifted in the seat. Opened his mouth. Closed it. Shifted his position again.

Her heart wilted. He was trying to find a way to let her down gently.

"I..." He cleared his throat and scratched his jaw. "I don't know how serious you are with Jack, but... Well, he..."

She lowered her forehead to the steering wheel. "Get it over with."

"I'm in love with you."

"What?" Arianne faced him.

Huck caressed her face. The truth in his eyes held a swath of pain. "I'm not good at this. I've never said it to a woman before." He exhaled. "I love you."

Her heart stopped. Could a person actually die from surprise? If so, she'd be in the morgue by lunchtime.

Huck blinked. Waited.

A horn blared as a car passed, making them both jump. The driver shook his fist at them.

"Say something. Please." Huck dropped his hands and stared out the windshield, brows knit together.

She tried to return his words but struggled to untangle her emotions. Ecstatic. Apprehensive. For years she'd longed to mean more to Huck than a tutor or a thorn in his heel. The image of them as a real family in his big house flashed through her mind. Cold winter nights curled on the couch together by the fireplace. Emma yelling "Daddy" and running into his arms when he got home from work. More kids. *A home.*

Arianne drank in Huck's strong profile. He might love her now, but could he love her forever?

Huck shook his head. Red flared into his neck and cheeks. "I'm too late." He nodded to himself. "Switch me places."

His tone sliced like a paring knife to her heart. "Huck…"

"It's fine, Arianne. We better get over to the shop before Jude sends out a search party."

He wouldn't look at her. It was as if she were on a tightrope, and no matter which way she moved, she would fall to her death. But if it weren't for Huck, she wouldn't have her new shop, the scholarship, her dream. "You've never said that to a woman before?"

The question seemed to take him by surprise. "No."

She reached for his hand.

He accepted. "I know I'm not good enough for

you, but I want to be."

"Huck—"

"Let me finish." He laced his fingers with hers. "I should've told you this years ago… I couldn't stand you being mad at me after prom. Truth is your dad also threatened to expose my past if I took you. No one here knew the things I'd done. I was ashamed for anyone—mostly you—to find out. It was easier to let you think I was a jerk than to let you find out the trash I came from, what I'd gotten into.

"I haven't made the best decisions. I still don't. But I'm trying." He moved closer and wrapped his strong arms around her waist. "We have a lot to work through, but there's something good between us. There always has been."

No matter what else she was feeling, she couldn't deny that. Arianne closed her eyes, barely nodding as she slipped off the tightrope.

"I know you're seeing Jack, but give me a chance. I can be the man you need. The man Emma needs."

Spoken that way, burrowed against him, she could believe anything.

~*~

Arianne fit perfectly in his arms. Huck trembled, an odd mix of relief and fear rushing through him. He'd just scooped out his bleeding heart and handed it to her. He pressed his forehead against hers. Closed his eyes. Oddly, this was enough—simply being near her. "Take a chance on me."

He couldn't lose her.

"What if it doesn't work out?" Arianne's whisper cut through moments of silence. "I can't go through it again, wondering if I'll be evicted from my store, if we'll have a place to sleep."

He kept his eyes closed, needing to stay in the moment. "You'll never be evicted. The building's paid in full and deeded in your name."

Her hands pushed against his shoulders.

He opened his eyes. "I'm talking forever, Arianne. But I want to do this with no strings attached. If something happens, you're safe."

She smiled brighter than the sun spilling through the cab. "What a relief to know you don't have a cocky nephew who'll swoop in and boot me out."

Huck laughed. "I was...wrong." He tried not to cringe as he said it.

Arianne pressed her ear against his mouth. "I don't think I heard that. Can you say it again, please?"

He nipped her ear.

She squealed and rubbed her fingers over her earlobe.

He could definitely do this every day—hold her, aggravate her, kiss her. Huck guided her face toward his and leaned close.

She turned her face so his lips landed on her cheek. Questions and uncertainty rolled over her face like a dark cloud. She still hadn't returned his confession. If she'd just give him a chance to show her how much he loved them. "We'll go at your pace. No expectations."

She considered it, met his gaze. "We won't rush things?"

Huck shook his head. He'd do whatever she wanted.

Arianne brushed the end of her nose against his. "OK, cowboy."

His lips grazed hers. Fire ignited his veins. Before he could actually taste her, she stopped him. "None of that," she whispered, almost breathless. "I have someone else to talk to first. And I have to figure out what to say."

How about, hit the road, Jack? "Whatever you need."

~*~

Huck lowered the pith helmet over his head and grabbed the bee smoker from the Gator. His flannel shirt kept him plenty warm as the sun thawed the ground. March storms in the Midwest the last few days had caused a freakishly warm fifty-eight degrees along the coast.

He ignited the bee smoker, emitting a cool, white cloud through the nozzle. Bees traveled in and out of the hive, content to fly free. He walked to the first stack of supers and checked the colonies' conditions. Satisfied with their honey stores, Huck went on to the next stack.

As he worked down the line, his mind wandered to his girls back at the house. He'd called to tell Arianne good morning and discovered Emma had woken with a fever. Arianne was leaving her store in the hands of her new part-time employee for the first time, and the construction noise beneath their apartment made it impossible for Emma to rest. He'd rushed over, picked them up, and brought them home.

Emma's pink cheeks had been hot against his chest as he carried her in the door wrapped in a quilt. She'd snuggled close and fussed when he'd tried to lay her on the couch. So he settled into the recliner and rocked her.

Arianne stood in the kitchen doorway, watching them, arms and ankles crossed, sunlight pouring through the windows behind her. In that moment, something shifted inside his chest, like a puzzle piece locking into place. Before three days ago, he'd never have believed something could feel so right.

A weak voice sounded from his arms. "Will I be sick on my birthday?"

Arianne pulled away from the wall and stopped beside their chair. "Your birthday is two weeks away. You'll feel better by then. You just have a little bug."

The girl stuck out her lip and rubbed a weepy eye.

"What do you want for your birthday?" Huck asked to take her mind off bugs. He was beginning to sweat from the combination of her feverish body and the thick blanket.

"A puppy."

Arianne gave him a stern look and shook her head.

Huck winked at Arianne. "Give me some other ideas, Emma. What do you want more than anything else in the world?"

"For you to be my daddy."

Raw fear and pure joy swept through him. He dared to look at Arianne, who'd paled to the color of a corpse. He couldn't read her face. Huck rocked harder and tugged the quilt further around Emma's shoulders. He'd love to give her that for her birthday, but he'd promised Arianne they'd take things slowly, work things out one day at a time. "Close your eyes and get some rest."

Now, as bees droned around him and smoke lifted in the air, Huck allowed Emma's words to penetrate his heart and grow roots. The idea still scared him numb, but he'd give his left leg to wake up to those two every morning. To keep Arianne warm at night.

Slow. *Slow.*

He added more fuel to the smoker and moved to the next hive, stomping away the effects of that last thought.

Three bees lay dead at the entrance. The buzz of activity was missing. Huck pulled out the frames to find the colony MIA. He removed his helmet and scratched his jaw. Squinting, he peered down the tree line. Where did they go?

He grabbed the bee smoker and shuffled through the short grass, the smell of decaying leaves and moist dirt filling his nose. His ears caught the faint noise of buzzing wings. He continued through the trees to the old fence line. A blob of moving insects clustered on a rotten post.

They were swarming. Why, he wasn't sure yet. If he could get to the queen underneath, protected by the colony huddled around her, they'd follow her scent back to the hive. After an investigation, he could fix what had caused them to swarm.

Huck put the helmet back on and smoked the buzzing mass. In sheets, bees fell away until he was able to locate her highness. He remembered a class he'd taught on bee folklore last year. One of the many examples he'd used was from a *Courier-Journal* article from 1890 that detailed beekeeping superstition. If a colony was found swarming on dead wood, it was considered a sign of impending death.

He found the queen, gently squeezed her between his thumb and forefinger, and considered the rotten fence post. Huck shook his head and walked back toward the hives. Good thing he wasn't superstitious.

*My son, eat thou honey, because it is good; and the
honeycomb, which is sweet to thy taste: So shall the
knowledge of wisdom be unto thy soul…*
—Proverbs 24: 13, 14a

33

Tell him.

Guilt speared Arianne as she stared into Jack's
face. She'd created a lame excuse every day for the past
two weeks for why she hadn't told him about Huck.
Jack was a widower and had lost the love of his life. It
had taken courage to open his heart again. He cared
about Arianne, no doubt. How could she break his
heart?

And this whole thing with Huck was so new. They
were spending time with one another, getting to know
each other—past and present.

Huck hadn't kissed her since the day he said he
loved her. He vowed because of his shaded past, he
wanted to prove he respected her and wouldn't move
further until she was ready. His love was exactly what
she wanted, but she couldn't shake the fear of *what if?*

A muffled train whistle sounded through the
boutique's closed windows. Jack pulled his hands from
his pockets and wrapped his arms around her, guiding
her to him. She rested her palms against his brown,
cotton shirt to keep some distance. He was dressed

nice for a spur-of-the-moment flight to Philadelphia. She prayed for his mother's healing from her unforeseen stroke.

He reached up and toyed with her curls. "I'm going to miss you while I'm gone."

Her mind went numb. She opened her mouth to tell him about Huck, but all she could think of was his deceased wife and how Jack had entrusted Arianne with his mourning heart only for her to reject him.

"Say good-bye to Emma for me."

"I will." Emma was excited to be making Huck cupcakes with Sherry right now and doubted her daughter would flinch.

Emma wanted Huck to be her daddy. The thought knocked Arianne flat every time it entered her mind. She wanted the same thing, but she'd fallen into bad judgment before and had barely clawed her way out.

"How's your mom doing?" Arianne asked, ignoring the bone-crushing ache that began whenever she thought of Huck breaking her heart.

But not telling Jack was unfair. She needed to tell him now...or maybe she'd wait until he got back. He had enough to worry about with his mother so ill. Maybe waiting would be the charitable thing to do.

Jack shrugged. "Better. The doctors are running more tests." He glanced at his watch and then tenderly cupped her elbow. "Life's short, Arianne."

He looked away. When he turned back, his eyes held a rawness that froze her pulse. "I hope you know by now that I don't rush into things. That I look ten times before I leap." He swallowed. "I'm leaping."

Jack removed his hand from her waist. A platinum gold ring with a large, flawless diamond appeared between his fingers. She covered her mouth. Her lungs refused to cooperate. The room dimmed.

"Will you marry me?"

Tell him! Tell him now. The mantra played in her head but her lips were paralyzed.

Jack's grin wobbled. "Don't answer me right away. I want you to think about it, pray about it. That's why I'm asking you now, so you'll have space while I'm gone to make a wise decision."

He took her hands in his and she managed to close her mouth.

"Can you do that for me? Pray about it?" He pressed the ring into her palm and touched her lips in the softest of kisses.

Tears filled her closed eyelids, but she couldn't decipher their motive.

"I love you. I'll call when I get to Philly."

Jack slipped into his coat and left her shop.

She pressed her fingers to her lips and watched his car exit the parking lot and disappear down the highway. Emotion clogged her throat. Jack wanted to marry her. No doubt he'd be faithful, a devoted helpmeet. She slipped the ring onto her finger. A perfect fit.

Tears fell. If she married Jack, she'd forever separate herself from the man she truly loved. If she didn't, she'd break Jack's already fractured heart. Jack was someone she could grow to love like she loved Huck. Right?

The clock ticked on the wall behind her. She sank onto the chair beside the rack of bridal shoes. Her heart wanted Huck. Her body responded to Huck like no other. She loved him soul-deep. There was no question, no doubt; but a decision couldn't be made based on her needs or wants. She had to do what was best for

Emma. Her daughter needed stability. Could Huck offer them that?

She stared at the ring and admired how the light caught every facet of the diamond. "A wise decision," she whispered.

~*~

"Mommy, Mommy! He's here. He's here." Emma clapped her hands and bounced on her tiptoes.

Arianne issued an apologetic smile to her customers and walked over to the birthday girl. *Five.* Where had time gone? She pitied Adam. He didn't even realize what a treasure he'd left behind or how much he'd missed.

Huck breezed through the door wearing an olive-colored fleece pullover and faded jeans. Emma ran to him and he scooped her up. Girlish giggles echoed through the store. Arianne playfully held a finger to her lips then pointed at him in a scold. Huck winked and flashed his dimples at the customers who were making their way to the veil display. The two women melted like butter at a picnic on the Fourth of July.

Arianne knew the feeling well. "Let me get our coats, and we'll be ready."

Huck followed her to her office, carrying Emma. The two made quite a pair.

She'd prayed hard the past three days about Jack's proposal. A clear answer had yet to come, though the uneasiness wrapped around her whenever she thought about either man. Right now, in this moment, seeing Emma's little arms hugging Huck's neck, Arianne knew exactly where she desired to be. But was that where she was supposed to be?

"What's wrong?" Huck's brows knit together.

"What do you mean?" Her words came out too rushed to be convincing as nonchalant.

"You sighed."

"I did?" Arianne grabbed her coat and handed Emma hers.

"Yes, you did." Huck set Emma down so she could put it on. He gripped Arianne's chin between his thumb and finger, his gaze intense, concerned. "What is it, baby?"

How could one simple word make her want to jump in his arms and never leave?

"Nothing," she whispered.

Everything.

He studied her a moment more before his gaze dropped to her lips. She physically ached to pick up where they'd left off last time. But Emma...

She pulled away, and Huck groaned as he dropped his hand from her chin and balled it into a fist. He stepped back, putting distance between them. His eyes never left hers. "Ready, Emma?"

Arianne watched as her daughter struggled with the zipper. "Here, sweetheart, let me help you."

"I can do it, Mommy. I'm five now."

Yes, she was. And tomorrow she'd be twenty-five, coming here to pick out her own wedding dress. Which man would be there to walk her down the aisle?

Huck patted Emma's head. "It's not that cold out. You keep workin' on it while we head to the truck."

Emma left the office. Huck shook his head and chuckled, throwing his arm around Arianne's shoulders. He turned off the light and closed the door behind them.

Braelle, her first and only part-time employee,

stood at the veil rack, helping a customer choose a veil that best fit her face shape. She flipped her long, chestnut hair off her shoulder as she explained the importance of a veil in addition to a stunning gown. The girl had a passion for weddings equal to Arianne's.

Arianne fished the register key from her pocket, confident Braelle could close up on her own. She'd gone over the routine with the girl twice.

Braelle left the customer to try on the merchandise. Arianne handed her employee the key. "If you have any questions, don't hesitate to call."

"I will." Braelle's smile accentuated the freckles on her nose.

Huck guided Arianne by the small of her back to the door. Emma held his other hand, humming the happy birthday song. They strolled to the truck like The Three Musketeers.

More like The Three Stooges.

A white SUV peeled into the parking lot. Tires screeched as it swung into a vacant space. Arianne and Huck exchanged glances. Amy Mason, the first customer she'd had at the new location, jumped from the vehicle, opened the back, and pulled out a wedding dress protected in a clear bag.

She sprinted to Arianne, tears dripping down her cheeks, mascara streaked beneath her eyes. "My dress. It's ruined!"

Arianne froze. Amy's wedding was tomorrow. "What happened?"

"We had our rehearsal this morning, since we have so many guests coming in tonight for the wedding. My aunt was pressing napkins when the flower girl bumped into the ironing board and the iron fell on my gown." Sobs interrupted. "The fabric's melted. It looks awful. Can you fix it?"

Her heart broke for Amy, but it was Emma's birthday. Arianne had fulfilled her contract. She could say no, but her conscience wouldn't let a bride walk the aisle in a burnt, crispy gown. She sighed inwardly. "The damage can't be repaired, but it can be covered. Take it in. I'll see what I can do."

Amy jogged into the boutique.

Arianne moaned. "If I hurry, I can at least make it to the party." She fought tears of frustration. Emma's special day was ruined.

Huck pulled her into a hug, knowing exactly what she needed. "Let me go ahead and take her. It's not fair for her to sit behind a counter on her birthday. I'll take her to the honey house as planned. That'll give you time to finish the dress, and we'll see each other at the party."

Bless Sherry for having it at her house and insisting on doing all the work. "All right, but keep her bundled up. And don't give her too much sugar."

"It's her birthday."

"Remember what happened last time?" She grinned, recalling the first time he'd watched Emma.

"Oh. Yeah." He opened the truck's passenger side door and bowed to Emma. "Your carriage awaits, princess."

Emma climbed inside, and he buckled her seatbelt. Arianne took his place to kiss her daughter goodbye and yanked on the seatbelt to double-check. "Be good. I'll see you at the party."

"OK, Mommy."

Arianne closed the door. Huck gave her a mock scowl. "I saw that."

"What?"

"You checked to make sure I know how to use a seatbelt."

"It's an old truck. I was testing it."

He moved toward her, acting angry. She played along and backed against the truck bed. He trapped her against it with his arms, one on each side of her, his fingers curled around the metal. "This old truck didn't come with seatbelts. These are state-of-the-art. Installed them myself." He rested his forehead against hers. "Don't you trust me by now? I won't let anything happen to that little girl."

His nearness made her dizzy. "Of course I do."

He lowered his head, hovered his lips beside her cheek. His warm breath tickled.

Huck kissed her cheek, blazing a trail closer to the corner of her mouth, setting fire to her belly. She turned to give in, and he backed away. If her arms had been long enough, she'd have shaken that smug look off his face.

He chuckled. "Bring your party hat."

~*~

The wind played with Emma's hair as they drove over the bridge toward the honey house. She'd propped her little feet on the dashboard. Her shoes were wearing thin at the toes. She needed a sturdy pair of boots. He'd see to that.

When they reached the honey house, Huck parked beneath the oak tree, remembering the picnic they'd enjoyed there over the summer. Emma hopped to the ground and pointed to the hives stacked amid the tree line. "Those are supers. Where the bees live."

Huck smiled. "Very good."

"Can we see them now?"

His chest swelled at his protégé's enthusiasm. She'd be so excited when she saw what he'd bought her. "Soon. First, we have to get their protein supplements ready and then you'll open a birthday gift."

"Can I open it now?"

"Soon."

Emma frowned and followed him to the door. "What's a protein supplement?"

Huck opened the door and flipped on the lights. They hummed for a moment then flickered on. "Remember how I told you that when bees forage for nectar, a yellow powder from the flowers and trees stick to their hairy bodies?"

She nodded.

"That yellow powder is pollen. It gives the bees protein—energy—to be strong and work hard. Since they're not foraging much right now because of the cool weather, we need to give them protein, so they'll be ready for spring."

"Can we take the bees to my party?"

He unzipped her coat and hung it on the peg beside the door. "No, but when we open the hives later, I'll show you the queen."

"Can I be the princess?"

"That's what your party is for." He put a finger on the tip of her nose. "You'll get to be the queen bee."

Huck shed his coat and led her to the supply room where he kept bee antibiotics, mite treatments, supplements, and extra equipment. They prepared the protein supplements and placed everything they'd need in a wheelbarrow. Then he took her to his small corner office where her wrapped gift waited on his desk.

Emma eyed it warily. "What is it?"

He viewed the gift from her perspective. The box was distorted and the pink, polka dot wrapping paper had more creases than a bulldog's snout. He'd tried. "Open it and find out."

Paper ripped and collected on the floor. She lifted the lid and peeked inside. "My very own bee mask?"

He nodded. "That'll protect your face and neck when you help me with the bees. There's long gloves in there too."

She grabbed the items, dropped the box, and danced on the loose wrapping paper.

He laughed. "Let's suit up and get busy."

Huck's cellphone rang. He pulled it from his pocket and glanced at a number he didn't recognize. "Give me a sec."

Micah Rollings, a member of his beekeeping association, was frantic. His bees were dying at an alarming rate, and he couldn't detect a reason. Huck scratched his chin. "Have you checked for mites?"

Micah grunted. "Of course. That's the first thing I did."

Stupid question. Micah'd been a beekeeper longer than Huck had been alive. The man knew about mites. "Pesticides?" Though no one should be using them this time of year.

"I checked that avenue too. None of my neighbors have used any, and the county hasn't either."

Hmm. He pulled the phone away from his mouth. "Emma, give me a minute. I need to help this guy on the phone, and then we'll go out."

"Ooo-kaaay." She dropped onto a chair, hung her head, and kicked her feet back and forth.

Huck ransacked his file cabinet for an article he'd saved from the Department of Agriculture on a study done on the diminishing bee population. As he looked, they discussed other possibilities that hit dead ends. He knew he'd kept the article. Was it in his home office?

After a thorough search, he came across a phone number for one of his contacts at Berkeley. "Give this guy a call, see if he can shed any light. In the meantime, I'll keep searching for that article and get back with you."

The cabinet closed with a bang. Huck turned off his phone and shoved it back in his pocket. "Ready?"

Emma's chair was empty.

He glanced around the office.

"Emma?" His voice echoed through the building as he searched. Where had she gone?

A draft swept into the room. The open door swayed in the breeze. Emma's coat hung from the peg where he'd left it. Arianne would kill him if she found out she went outside without her coat.

Huck stepped outside. "Emma?"

No answer.

He stalked the perimeter of the building, shouting her name. Water trickling in the brook was his only response. Panic kicked his gut. Was she playing a trick on him? If so, it wasn't funny.

Branches creaked in the wind above the Gator. Instinct told him something wasn't right. He looked around. A purple lump by the trees caught his eye, crumpled on the ground by the supers. "No!"

Huck sprinted to her, bile clogging his throat. The super lid had been lifted. Angry bees swarmed the still body in the dirt. They thwarted her to defend their colony, alerting more bees of the danger. They attacked her in waves.

He reached her and scooped her into a ball, protecting her with his body. Her new helmet slipped from her grip and crashed to the ground. Stings pinched his skin, but didn't slow him down. He jogged back to the honey house and laid her on the floor. His bad leg screamed. His breaths labored. He yanked his phone from his pocket and dialed 911. Bee corpses collected around her little body.

"911—what's your emergency?"

"I need an ambulance. Now!" He rubbed his forehead and rattled off his address.

The dispatcher assured him one was on the way and asked the nature of the emergency.

Swollen welts covered Emma's face and neck. He'd no doubt a hundred others marred her little body. Tears burned his eyes. "My little girl. She's been attacked by bees, and she's unconscious."

Why had he insisted on teaching her about bees?

"Does she have a pulse?"

He reached down and touched the side of Emma's neck. "Barely." He needed to get her to the house. "Her lips are turning blue. I don't think she's breathing."

Mortician bees carry dead bee corpses away from home to keep the hive hygienic.

34

No, God. Please. Not my daughter.

Arianne burst through the emergency room doors. Her cheeks were stiff from air-dried tears. The sobbing had started at a stoplight on the way there, but she'd forced herself to be strong for Emma. She had to get there, to hold her daughter and be assured everything would be all right.

She ran to the nurses' station. The glass window was closed. Behind the thin pane, a gray-haired woman snacked on chocolate at a computer.

Arianne banged on the glass. "Where's my daughter?"

The woman lifted her head. Annoyance flashed from her pale blue eyes, betraying her stoic expression. It seemed to take forever for her to slide open the window. A sigh. "Patient's name?"

"Emma Winters." Arianne swallowed the fear rising in her throat as the robotic woman pounded her thick fingers on the keyboard. Seconds, minutes, hours ticked by as Arianne waited. Was Emma stable? Scared? Crying for her? Arianne drummed her fingers on the desk and tapped her foot. "Please, hurry. I need to see my daughter."

The woman raised her pencil-drawn brows. "Ma'am you need to calm down."

Emma was in this hospital, possibly dying, and the woman wanted her to calm down? Fury filled her face and neck. "My daughter is back there somewhere, and I need to get to her." Her voice rose with each word until she practically yelled.

The woman pursed her lips. "Ma'am, I understand your concern, but you need to calm down, or I'll ask you to leave."

Leave? Arianne raised on her toes to go after the woman when strong hands gripped her shoulders, gentle yet secure. The woman now stood behind the computer, clinching her fists.

"Arianne, let's step outside."

She whipped around. Huck. "I need to get to Emma."

The agony in his eyes matched her own. "They're still running tests. Let's go outside, get some fresh air, and I'll tell you everything I know."

"I..." She looked from Huck to the woman's glare, then back to Huck. From the corner of her eye, she noticed she'd drawn people's attention in the waiting area, heard whispers. Tears blurred her view.

Huck kissed her head. "Come on, baby."

"No, I...paperwork...Emma."

Another nurse approached the window. "The doctor is running an MRI right now. Why don't you take a few minutes to calm down, and you can go back and see her as soon as they're done. We'll worry about the paperwork later." She smiled, her soothing voice calming Arianne's fire.

Huck put his arm around her shoulders and led her outdoors.

A fog settled around her as they moved down the sidewalk, the kind that appeared when something bad happened and the brain was combatting shock. They walked to the end of the sidewalk.

"Emma." Nausea sent the lowering sun in the pink sky spinning.

Huck gathered her in his arms. "I'm sorry, Arianne. I'm so sorry."

His smothering touch grated. She pushed him away. "What happened?"

He turned his head. "One minute she was there, and the next she was gone." His hair stood in wild tufts, as if he'd been pulling on it. The skin around his eyes and mouth sagged.

"What. Happened."

Huck scrubbed a hand down his face and closed his eyes. "I found her by the supers. She'd lifted the lid, stirred them up. I told her not to go without me." He opened his eyes, paced. "I called 911. She wasn't breathing."

A glimpse of her precious daughter with purple lips, struggling for breath, tortured her. Arianne released a moan before she could stop it. What if God took her? Emma was all she had left. *Please, God. Don't take her.*

The next thing she knew, Huck had her in his arms again, rocking her. "I'm sorry, baby." His voice broke. "It's all my fault."

"Don't you trust me by now? I won't let anything happen to that little girl." His words from earlier that day rang in her ears. She was such an idiot. A sexy grin, a few flattering words, and her loneliness played into dangerous men's hands every time. Only this time, it might cost her daughter's life.

Rage erupted—boiled and spewed. She wiggled from Huck's embrace. "Yes, it was. How could you? That little girl loves you, trusts you."

I did too.

Huck stared at her. "I…it was an accident. I was on the phone and—"

Everything inside her burned with a fierceness that terrified her. "I'm so stupid for leaving her with you. Every time you have an *accident* someone ends up dead."

Huck paled. Stumbled back.

The instant the words left her mouth, she hated herself for them. But this…this other Arianne had taken possession of her body, and she couldn't stop. Emma was all she had.

He concentrated on something in the distance. His eyes took on a glazed, faraway look. Then they started to glisten.

She moved to go around him, but he caught her elbow. "Baby, please, I—"

"I am not your baby." She tore away from him.

The kind woman from the nurses' station appeared from the doorway and called to them. "Mrs. Winters? The doctor would like to speak with you."

Arianne raced to follow her inside when heavy footfalls sounded beside her. She stopped and pointed a finger at Huck. "Not you. You've done enough. Go home."

He inhaled. "Arianne. You need someone here to support you. Provide for you and Emma."

"I'll call Jack."

She turned and took another step toward the door.

"*Jack?* No." He reached for her hand.

Arianne spun to face him. "We're through, Huck.

Jack proposed. And I'm accepting." Her stomach rolled. "I never want to see you again."

He grimaced as if she'd stabbed his heart and twisted the knife.

She rushed through the door with Huck beside her. Apparently, he didn't understand how serious she was. She stopped and poked a finger in his chest. "You're not family. You have no right to be here. If you don't leave and stay gone, I'll call the police. Understand? Go. Home."

With that, she caught up to the woman and the doctor standing in an open doorway marked *Staff Only*. This time, she walked alone.

The doctor directed her down the hallway. "Right this way, Mrs. Winters."

A loud click of the door echoed behind them, like the one permanently closing between her and Huck. She'd think about that later. "How's my daughter?"

The florescent lights reflected off the doctor's gold-rimmed glasses. He was tall, and his caramel-colored skin appeared darker against the stark white lab coat. "I'm Doctor Blevins, pediatric specialist. Your daughter is stable, but very sick. We'll talk in here."

He led her to a private room for consultations. Her legs grew weak from the fading adrenaline. She sank onto a chair and braced herself.

The doctor sat across from her and crossed his legs. How could he be so casual when her world was falling apart?

"Emma suffered over a hundred stings, which sent her into anaphylactic shock. The EpiPen used by the man who called for the ambulance helped counteract some of that until the paramedics arrived. But the poisons are attacking her kidneys. We have her on dialysis and a strong antibiotic. We're still running tests and will closely monitor her condition."

Arianne's bottom lip trembled. "Is she going to make it?"

"We're doing everything we can."

She slapped a hand over her mouth to cover her sobs.

"We just got her settled in ICU. Third floor. We ask that you let her rest, and when she does wake up, avoid too much stimulation."

Arianne nodded.

"Do you need a nurse to walk you there?"

"No. I'll be fine."

She prayed, begged God to heal Emma as she took the elevator and walked the hallways to her daughter's room. The metal bed swallowed Emma's body. Tubes and cords stretched to a dozen different machines. She grabbed her baby's cold, limp hand as tears poured down her face. Emma was swollen, and angry red knots covered her normally porcelain skin.

Sooner or later, everything she loved got ripped away from her. In the past, she'd moved on, continued to love. Did what she had to do to survive. But losing Emma would kill her. "Please, God," she whispered. "Save my baby girl."

~*~

Arianne fought against the pull of sleep. She needed to stay awake, but her eyelids were heavy, her body weighted with lead. A door opened. It took everything she had to crack one eye open. A blurry figure stood in her vision.

"Arianne," a deep voice whispered.

She forced herself awake. Her sight cleared. Jack stood before her with red-rimmed eyes, clutching his brown coat. Sleep faded. She rose from the bedside chair. "Jack."

He tossed his coat onto the chair and embraced her in his warm, safe arms. Stable arms. "Oh, Jack."

She cried into his T-shirt.

Jack rubbed her back, soothing. "Shh. It'll be all right."

Emma lay asleep, breathing softly. The welts on her body had calmed dramatically overnight. A golden sky peered through the slits in the blinds.

Arianne lifted her head. Jack's presence made her feel stronger. "Thanks for coming."

He took her face in his hands and thumbed away her tears. "I left as soon as you called."

"How'd you get here so fast?"

"I couldn't get a flight, so I rented a car and drove through the night."

"But your mom—"

"She's fine. We got her home, and my sisters are taking good care of her." He looked over at Emma and furrowed his brows. "What happened?"

She told him about Emma's fascination with Huck's bees and Huck's plan to surprise Emma for her birthday by teaching her how to care for them. Then she explained about the ruined wedding dress and how foolish she was to let Huck take Emma alone. The rage from yesterday began festering again. "The jerk thought a phone call took precedence over my daughter, and the next thing he knew, she was gone."

Jack's mouth fell into a serious line. "I'm sure he didn't mean for anything to happen to her."

He was defending Huck? Whose side was he on?

"Huck should've been more responsible."

Jack nodded. "Agreed."

He looked down at his shoes. Her anger fizzled, like water thrown on hot coals. She trembled. "They'll run more tests today to check her toxin levels. If she's improved, we'll discuss reducing the sedation medicine."

"Come here." After picking up his coat, Jack settled onto the chair then pulled her onto his lap. He held her like a child, covering her with his coat. She burrowed against him, relishing the warm cocoon he'd created.

This man loved her and Emma. He hadn't used flattering words to convince her to love him back, hadn't manipulated her feelings. He'd simply done his best every day to be the man God wanted him to be. God. He believed in God. Huck didn't. Maybe that was why she hadn't heard an answer to her prayers yet. The answer was staring her in the face all along. She needed to be with a godly man. A Christian man.

Whether or not Jack's touch created enough magic to shame the Northern Lights, she was going to marry him.

She slipped her arms around Jack's neck. "I'm so glad you're here."

~*~

Morning mist clung to Huck's windshield. The sun cast a golden glow over the budding trees. Birds chirped.

He stared at the gray stones that stretched the hillsides. They were all the same, yet each unique. Some larger than others. Some held miniature flags at the base, flapping in the breeze. Some had fake flowers stuck in plastic vases. Others were void. All had the same end result.

Reality sucker-punched his middle. What would hers be like?

Huck leaned away from the truck, uncrossed his ankles, and walked down the paved, narrow path. An eerie chill crawled up the back of his neck, as if the spirits below ground could sense his presence. He passed one stone with a birth and death date only a year apart. Huck stopped and stared at it. It wasn't right, this death thing. Never knowing when it would strike. He wanted to believe what the pastor had said in church about a life after death, about heaven. But how could he believe in something he couldn't see?

He continued on, gaining ground toward the area where Giada was at rest. Was she? The fact that he was responsible for her being here tore his chest wide open. His precious little girl in the hospital could be next.

Who was he kidding? She would never be *his* little girl. Arianne was marrying Jack. He'd lost them to a better man. Rightfully so. No matter how hard he tried, he'd never be good enough. Not good enough for Arianne. Not good enough for Emma. Not good enough for God.

A yellow finch, perched on a granite headstone, cheeped as if calling to him. Beneath the bird, a name. *Giada Roselli.* Huck stopped. There she was.

Emotions clogged his throat. He inched to the grave and knelt. Giada's laughter catching in the wind filled his memory. Her vibrant smile. Her zest for life.

Resting his palm on the polished rock, he whispered, "I'm sorry."

Tears stung his eyes, a reaction he was unfamiliar

with. The world went still. No birds. No sounds. He let the tears fall, let his emotions pour out of him as he grieved this young life he'd ended with his destructive choices. He cried for Giada. He cried for Arianne, the woman who taught him to love, and little Emma, who believed he was worthy of her adoration. But Arianne was gone, and Emma would never be his daughter, no matter how much his heart broke for them.

Suddenly, it became clear. Uncle Marty had stood in the shadows and mourned the loss of a life that could never be his. If he couldn't provide for those girls in life, he made sure he provided for them in death. The old dog knew Huck had been in love with Arianne since high school. Must've known that by throwing them together, Huck would do the right thing, take care of her. Love her. The way Uncle Marty wanted to with her mother.

Except Huck had failed. The one thing he was good at.

Emma couldn't end up like this because of him. She couldn't. His heart cried out. *God, please. If you're there, please…*

Nothing.

Huck tipped his wet face to the sky, gazing into the clouds. Either God wasn't there, or He couldn't hear Huck.

Wiping his eyes with his coat sleeve, he stood, disappointed. He didn't know what he'd expected. Maybe a sign that God was really there. He wanted God to exist. To believe someone could love him unconditionally despite his faults.

Huck sniffed and leaned forward, giving the headstone one last grip. He mentally said goodbye to Giada and turned. A black-haired woman in her fifties with olive skin and big dark eyes stared back at him. A heavy set man with more gray in his hair than brown held her hand.

Embarrassment washed through Huck. He'd hogged the space like he was the only one who'd ever lost someone. "Pardon me."

He nodded and stepped carefully around the nearby stones.

"What's your name, son?" the man asked.

Huck knotted his forehead. Why did it matter? "Huck Anderson."

The woman gasped. The man placed his hand over his heart. "We're Alberto and Bellina Roselli. Giada's parents."

And I have said, I will bring you up out of the affliction of Egypt…unto a land flowing with milk and honey.
—Exodus 3:17

35

Huck's blood froze. The woman standing before him, Bellina, had Giada's hair and stature. The man, Alberto, stared at him, eyes wide with fear as if Huck were a ghost.

They must hate him. Huck's eyes burned. What could he possibly say for what he'd done?

"I'm so sorry." He knew it wasn't enough, but it was the truth. "I never meant to hurt her."

No, he'd just slept with her, toyed with her emotions. Used her. He swallowed past the lump in his throat and looked at his boots.

"Of course you didn't." Bellina's words were soft. Kind. The opposite of what he'd expected.

Huck's head came up. Instead of contempt on their faces, he saw compassion. How was that possible when he'd murdered their daughter? "The car was in my lane. I tried to avoid a wreck, but lost control. I…"

His own voice sounded far away, unfamiliar.

Bellina released her husband's arm and walked to Huck. She stared up at him, tears filling her eyes, and gripped his arm. The wind shifted her long, black hair. "It was an accident."

Grief etched her face. Her motherly touch, her soft

words, radiated forgiveness. Bile rose in Huck's throat. He shook his head. "I shouldn't have had her on my bike. Shouldn't have been going so fast."

Shouldn't have been ready to throw her out like yesterday's leftovers.

He looked at Alberto, who wiped his face with a handkerchief. Giada had been this man's child—his little girl. And Huck had used her for his own pleasure. If a man ever treated Emma that way... Yet he was that kind of man.

"We cannot change what God wills." Bellina's thick, accented whisper filled the air.

Why wasn't she angry? She should yell at him, slap him—he'd know how to handle that. He backed away from her tender grasp. "It's my fault. I could've done somethin' differently. I'm sorry."

Alberto stepped forward, tucking the handkerchief into his coat pocket. "We know it was an accident. Bellina and I forgive you."

Huck shook his head. The man had no idea how Huck had treated Giada. He clenched his teeth to keep from yelling.

A single tear rolled down Bellina's cheek. "Did you force her onto your motorcycle? Did you make the other driver have a heart attack? Did you mean to lose control?"

"No." But it was his fault. Somehow. It always was.

Another of Bellina's tears followed the first. "We forgive you. You must forgive yourself."

A sadness like he'd never felt before welled up from deep inside him. Huck ran his fingers through his hair, once, twice. If he didn't escape now, he'd drown in it.

Huck strode to a nearby concrete bench and dropped onto it. Leaning his elbows on his knees, he lowered his face in his hands. How could they possibly forgive him?

A body stirred beside him. "We have prayed for you," Bellina said.

"Why? How can you forgive me for killing your daughter?" Sobs wracked his body. The more he tried to suppress them, the more they spilled out like waves. He hadn't been this weak since he was seven, begging step-dad number two to stop pummeling him with his fists for digging a hole in the yard to bury his cat. He'd decided that day that caring for others hurt. He'd never allowed himself to again.

Until Arianne and Emma. They'd climbed his wall.

"You did not kill her. Life and death are in God's hands."

"I don't deserve forgiveness."

"None of us do." Alberto drew out his weary, Italian accent and closed in on Huck's other side. "But that's the beauty of God's love. If Jesus could look down from the cross and forgive those who crucified him, we can forgive an accident."

Huck leaned back and wiped his wet palms on his jeans. All this God stuff. He wanted to believe it, but it confused him.

Bellina handed him a tissue from her purse. "I won't lie. Most days are hard. We do not know if Giada ever asked Jesus into her heart. We can only pray that she waits for us in heaven."

Huck scrubbed the tissue down his cheeks then blew his nose. He'd thought if he started being good, helped people, stayed out of trouble, he could make it into that place called heaven. Had Giada thought that too? Truth was no matter how hard he tried to be good, he just wasn't.

The flames of hell were licking his feet this very minute.

Bellina held his hand and squeezed. "If you are on your way to heaven, you will see her again also."

Huck gazed at the headstones. No. This is where it would end for him. "I wish it were possible—to apologize to her, but I won't be there."

Alberto shifted. "Why not?"

Dread coiled inside Huck and sealed his fate like the crack of a judge's gavel. "I'll never be good enough."

Bellina nodded. "None of us will be. 'For *all* have sinned and come short of the glory of God, being justified freely by His grace through the redemption that is in Christ Jesus.'"

Huck remembered hearing those verses at church. But that didn't really mean *all* could be redeemed, did it? It couldn't mean him. It meant people who used good to change the world, like Mother Teresa or the disciples.

Huck released Bellina's hand and folded his together, returning his elbows to his knees. "If that verse is true and none of us are ever good enough, then what's the point?"

She placed her hand on his back. "Jesus died for our sins on the cross. Those who accept him are covered by His blood. Goodness does not get us into heaven. Only through Jesus can we enter."

This was the part that never made sense. Covered in blood? "How do we go *through* Jesus?"

Bellina splayed her hand over her chest. "You cry out to Him, ask for forgiveness of your sins, and ask

Him into your heart."

He'd felt this tug before, this connection to something unseen. Like he was missing a person he'd never met, or yearning for a food he'd never tried. But there it was—that longing for something bigger, better, something...more. Could what Bellina said be true—could it be as simple as that to make peace with God?

Alberto cleared his throat. "And then the real work begins: learning to trust Him." His gaze drifted to his daughter's grave. "Even when we do not understand. I am glad I am not required to be perfect, because I would fail."

The pull grew stronger. Yesterday's events, his lack of sleep, confusion—they all hit Huck at once, striking panic and bone-deep weariness. He'd come to make things right with Giada. But nothing could be right as long as the woman he loved sat by the bedside of the little girl he wanted for his own, waiting for her to die. He couldn't let it happen.

Huck stood. "Again, I apologize. Giada was a sweet woman. I didn't appreciate her near enough."

Huck stalked to his truck. His boots rustled the dewy grass. If Emma survived, how would he ever move on with life knowing Arianne and the little girl he desperately wanted to raise as his own belonged to another man? If Emma didn't, how would he live with himself knowing her death had been his fault?

~*~

Arianne clung to Missy. "I'm so glad you're here."

Her sister's arrival brought comfort amid this awful situation. Missy smelled like California sunshine and suntan lotion. Her skin glowed a beautiful bronze.

346

"How is she?"

Arianne pulled away, and they both looked at Emma's pale body lying in the bed. Her eyelids fluttered in sleep. She'd woken for a few minutes that morning, looked at Arianne with glazed eyes, then fallen back asleep. "She's holding on."

How her body could produce any more tears Arianne didn't know, but they rolled down her face all the same. "The stings caused toxic buildup in her kidneys. They have her on dialysis. Without it, her kidneys will fail. The doctor's putting her on a donor list, but it could take months, even years. I'm not a match."

Missy held her hand over her mouth, releasing air beneath it.

The gravity of it all made Arianne ill. "I'm her mother. How can I not match?"

Missy pulled her into another hug. "I'll have them test me too."

"I've already called our family doctor. You don't have the right blood type. Neither does Jack."

Her sister stepped back and gripped Arianne's upper arms. "Why would Jack be willing to donate a kidney?"

Arianne searched Missy's incredulous face. Jack had volunteered for testing, though Arianne detected his reluctance. She'd seen it on his face, a silent hopefulness when he'd added, "I doubt I'll be a match." She couldn't blame him. Emma wasn't his child. But wouldn't a man who truly loved them, wanted to raise Emma as his own, be willing? She concentrated on her sister. There wasn't time to analyze that right now. "He's asked me to marry him."

Missy dropped her arms. "What? When?"

Arianne brushed the tears from her cheeks. "A couple of weeks ago. I promised him I'd pray about it and let him know."

Missy grabbed Arianne's bare left hand and stared at it. "Did you accept?"

"I haven't answered him yet. I need to get through this first. But I'm going to marry him." There was that bowling ball in the pit of her stomach again.

Stunned, Missy shook her head, walked to the chair in the corner, and sat down. "Are you sure? Like, a hundred percent?"

"Yes." More like eighty-five.

Missy rubbed her forehead, clinking her gold bracelets. "Arianne, it's your life, but you haven't known this guy very long. Are you really in love with him? I don't want you reliving what you went through with Adam."

"Jack is nothing like Adam."

"I know." Missy rubbed her forehead. "What about Huck?"

Hearing his name was like a metal bow on rusty violin strings. She gestured to Emma. "He's the reason she's in here. Huck is no longer in the picture. I don't care what he does with his life."

Which couldn't be true since her heart ripped from her chest every time she remembered how upset he was about Emma and how devastated he looked over her announcement about Jack. How Huck's EpiPen probably saved Emma's life.

Missy turned her head and stared at Emma. "Promise me you'll give this more thought before you answer Jack. Don't let your emotions and circumstances cloud your head again."

Her right-on-target words peeved. Arianne

crossed her arms, forcing control over her rising temper. "It's unlike you to play mother hen. Why the sudden role switch?"

Missy inhaled and leaned back in the chair. "I won't be around to pick up the pieces this time. Come July, I'm leaving for Haiti. I'm going to minister to children orphaned by the earthquake."

Now it was Arianne's turn to sit down. Aggravation morphed into shock. She seized Missy's arm. "When did you decide this?"

"Look, we can talk about this later."

"No. I want to talk about it now."

Missy took in a long, slow breath. "There's a little church down the block from my apartment that I started attending not long after I moved in." Missy's eyes flickered to Emma then back to Arianne. "A missionary visited last week and spoke about his ministry in Haiti. They need volunteers to help. There are so many orphaned kids that need to know about Jesus."

The shock fog Arianne had lived in the past two days grew thicker. "I still don't understand."

Missy grabbed her hand. "I never felt like I fit in with this family. And all this with Martin—I'm an orphan myself in a way. No mother, a father who could hardly look at me, one that denied me until his death. In my quest for answers, I discovered what I needed in that little church with that missionary. I'm going to love those children and teach them that God is the Father of the fatherless."

What was Arianne supposed to say to that? She stared at Missy. Overnight, her little sister had grown up. After all these years of praying that her sister would heed the things of God, Missy finally had. It was bittersweet. She'd miss her sister terribly. Missy's face glowed with a surety that only came from the Almighty. A part of Arianne was jealous. "I'm happy for you."

"Hit me for this if you want to, but you're good at jumping into things when the right solution isn't clear. Please, *please*, make sure marrying Jack is the right thing before you do it."

~*~

Huck opened the door and walked to his living room, exhausted. He shed his coat and tossed it on the couch next to Emma's doll, the one he'd bought her for Christmas. Her gift. It reminded him of all the gifts he'd never been given by a mother who didn't love him and a string of step-dads who never cared. That tug he'd shoved away earlier set his heartbeat loose. How could he long for gifts he'd never gotten? A father he'd never known?

An eternity he wasn't sure existed.

Just because he didn't have a traditional, happy family didn't mean there weren't any. He'd seen examples from kids he'd gone to school with, families he'd recently attended church with. There were dads out there who trained their sons to be good men, even if he didn't have one. Could he long for something like God and heaven even though he couldn't see them? Could eternal life be as easy as accepting a gift?

He sank onto the couch and picked up the doll. He'd done all the work—hunted the toy down, forked out the cash, wrapped it. Just to see the smile on Emma's face. All because he loved her. He didn't expect anything back, only wanted his gesture to show he loved her in hopes she'd grow to love him in return.

Was that how this whole God/heaven thing worked?

Huck ran his finger along the doll's crooked braid. He'd stopped by the hospital on his way home, but the nurses had refused to release any information about Emma. So he'd called Jude, knowing he and Sherry had planned to visit that morning. Jude confessed things didn't look good. Huck's grip on the doll tightened. He looked up at the ceiling. "God, please don't let her die."

Silence. If God was there, why didn't He answer?

Pastor Dave had said that prayer was how we spoke to God, but the Bible was how God spoke to us. Maybe there was something in there that would explain how he could help Emma.

He put down the doll and went to his closet where he kept Uncle Marty's Bible—the one he took to church then returned to the closet when service was over. He sat on his bed and flipped through the pages. A church bulletin fell to the floor. The cover had a Christmas tree with presents on the front and Romans 6:23 printed in the background. *"For the wages of sin is death, but the gift of God is eternal life through Jesus Christ our Lord."*

Gift. Huck thumbed through the thin pages, seeking the verse Bellina had quoted earlier. He stumbled upon Romans 10:13 instead. *"For whosoever shall call upon the name of the Lord shall be saved."*

Whosoever. Him.

The tug in his chest pulled so strong it made him weak, like he was swimming against a raging undertow. He couldn't fight it anymore. There was nowhere left to hide.

Huck dropped his head, vulnerable, exposed. "All

right, God," he said aloud. "You've got me. I believe."
Heat enveloped him. "I believe. Please, forgive me."

Emotions equal to those he'd experienced at the
cemetery swallowed him. His body trembled. The heat
disappeared, taking with it a massive weight from his
shoulders he hadn't known he'd carried. He finally
calmed down enough to stand. For all his solid weight
in height and muscle, he felt lighter than a helium
balloon.

Clean.

His cellphone vibrated in his pocket. He didn't
recognize the number but answered anyway.

"It's Missy," she said.

As she explained the reason for her call, his heart
twisted, and his stomach rolled.

"I'll be right there."

"...Ye shall inherit their land, and I will give it unto you to possess it, a land that floweth with milk and honey: I am the Lord your God, which have separated you from other people."

—Leviticus 20:24

36

Arianne lay next to her daughter, careful not to disturb any tubes connected to Emma's body. Her little chest rose and fell in quiet breaths. Some of Emma's color had come back, and almost all of the welts had vanished. What Arianne wouldn't give to see her daughter running around, healthy, laughing.

She'd left Missy in charge while she'd gone home to shower and eat. Now she stretched out on the hospital bed, wrapped in her mother's old sweater with Emma's favorite book in her hands, reading *Jonah and the Big Fish* aloud. The sun's evening rays poured through the window over a sleeping Jack, who was slouched in the chair in the corner, snoring softly.

Emma stared at the pictures as Arianne turned the pages. Occasionally, Emma would give a slight nod in response to her favorite parts. It reminded Arianne of the day when they went fishing with Huck on the footbridge. Emma had spoken openly to Huck about the importance of trusting God and the consequences of disobedience.

Oh, to have faith like a child. It was hard, during times like this, to trust that God would work things out for the best. Missy's words tumbled through her brain. *"You're good at jumping into things when the solution isn't clear."* What did Missy know?

Missy had never been abandoned by a husband who'd promised to love her forever. Never raised a child on her own, playing Mommy and Daddy. Never received eviction notices or felt the shame from not having enough money to pay her bills. Never had to live off Ramen noodles for days on end. Arianne wasn't a reckless person. Every decision she'd made had been in her and Emma's best interest.

Soon, the man sleeping across the room would help shoulder her burdens, fill those empty places. That solution was the best for everyone.

So, why did her chest squeeze every time she thought about it? Arianne closed the book.

"Again," Emma croaked, and then coughed.

Arianne shoved the future away and turned back to the first page. She read how Jonah fled from God's will. How he was afraid—of the future, the unknown. Afraid the task was too great. But his disobedience endangered not only his life but others. God blocked Jonah's path and reminded Jonah that His plan was perfect, even if Jonah couldn't see it.

Emma's eyelids closed. Arianne lowered the book to her lap. Was this Arianne's whale?

She'd opened the shop with the meager amount of her dad's life insurance that was left after his funeral. She'd accepted Martin's support, concocted the deal to help Huck in exchange for rent, dated Jack. Chose to marry Jack. Along with a million other decisions in between.

Sure, she'd prayed about those things, but looking back now, she hadn't waited for God's direction. She'd decided for herself what was best. Though she'd put her trust in God for salvation, she'd failed to put her trust in Him for everything else. Like Jonah, she'd been running in fear. Fear of the unknown. Afraid God's will wouldn't line up with hers.

So like the Israelites, freed from the bondage of slavery and led by Moses to the Promised Land. The land of milk and honey. Only because of their disobedience, their failure to trust God's plan, they wondered the wilderness for forty years, unable to live the lives God intended for them.

Most times her life felt as barren as a wilderness. Perhaps the life she led wasn't the one God intended. Either way, she realized that she hadn't been seeking God with her whole heart or trusting that He knew best.

Her throat burned with emotion. Tears filled her eyes. *I'm sorry, Lord. Please forgive me.*

Jack stirred in the chair but remained asleep. She stared at his kind face, strong hands. *Lord, why don't I have peace about marrying Jack? He's everything a woman could ask for.*

Squeaky wheels on a dinner cart passing by filled the room. She reached over and held Emma's little hand in hers. *Jack isn't what you have for us, is he?*

No.

God's answer was as clear as the shriek of that dinner cart. That's why that thorn in her gut burrowed deeper every time she thought about spending forever with Jack. He wasn't who God wanted for her life, even if it didn't make sense. And if she were honest with herself, Jack wasn't who she wanted to spend forever with, either. No matter how wonderful he was.

She blew out a shaky breath. What if God didn't intend for her to have a husband at all?

As the bridegroom rejoiceth over the bride, so shall I rejoice over thee. I'm enough for you. The words poured into her and spoke softly in her soul. Not her own thoughts. And they brought her to her knees.

Lord, You are *enough for me. Help me to trust You.* Arianne lightly clasped Emma's hand. *Please, heal my baby girl. She means more to me than a dozen proposals.*

Arianne stood and kissed Emma's tiny fingers. She leaned against the pillows, closed her eyes, and prayed for forgiveness, pleaded for her daughter's life.

A door opened. Arianne jumped, glancing at the clock on the wall. She'd fallen asleep. Sitting up, she rubbed her eyes and yawned as the doctor entered the room. Jack, too, stirred awake. He leaned forward in the chair and rested his elbows on his knees, yawning.

Doctor Blevins adjusted the stethoscope hanging around his neck. "Sorry to wake you, but I have good news. We've found a donor."

Arianne shot out of the bed. "So soon? You said it could take months. It's only been five days. How? Who?"

The doctor smiled and put his hands on his narrow hips. "Organ donors remain anonymous, and, yes, this is rare. Very. We'll be using an adult kidney. Therefore, I'll have to take a different approach to the procedure. I'd like to go over everything with you first thing in the morning for surgery at two o'clock. However, I wanted to stop in and tell you the good news. If Emma's body accepts the kidney, she has an excellent chance of living a normal life."

Arianne's heart swelled to bursting. "Thank you,

doctor. Thank you so much."

Doctor Blevins nodded. "Goodnight."

She cupped a hand over her mouth in disbelief and looked at Emma, still asleep. Someone had died so her daughter could live. Had it been a car accident? Did they have a spouse and children mourning them this very minute? She prayed for the donor's family.

Warm hands turned her shoulders. Jack moved her against him and held her to his chest. "Praise God," he whispered.

Arianne breathed in his masculine scent and shivered in his strong arms. God knew what He was doing. His plans were perfect. "Yes, praise God."

A tear rolled down her cheek and absorbed into Jack's shirt. *Lord, I don't deserve Your grace and mercy. You delight in giving your children the desires of their heart. Please, help my desires match yours.*

Emma was getting a second chance, but that wouldn't make turning Jack's proposal down any easier.

~*~

Huck woke to someone tugging on his hand. He opened his eyes to a blue curtain and turned his head to the nurse.

"Feeling better today?"

He grunted.

"Doc says you can go home, but you've got to take it easy for a few weeks."

He flinched as she pulled the IV from his hand. "I'll do anything for a large cheese pizza."

Why did hospitals think that if their patients had defective body parts, their taste buds must be defective too?

She placed a cotton ball on the spot where the needle was and applied pressure. "After what you just did, you deserve a lifetime supply."

The nurse had glossy blonde hair and a sweet smile. A woman like her used to spark his interest. Now, he couldn't care less if he ever looked at another woman besides Arianne. But she'd made it clear she never wanted to look at him again. The doc should've cut out his heart along with his kidney. Then maybe it wouldn't hurt so much.

The nurse removed the needle from the IV tube and slipped it into an orange box marked hazardous. "The nurse said you were getting around pretty well last night. How about breakfast, and then we'll work on your release. Do you have someone that can drive you home?"

"Yeah."

Missy had offered yesterday when she'd stopped by to check on him. She'd also confirmed his worst fear—Arianne was marrying Jack. He'd prayed Arianne had only said it out of anger, but apparently that wasn't the case.

Huck maneuvered from the bed and walked a few laps up and down the hall. He was sore and weak, but not enough to regret what he'd done. If Emma lived, that was all that mattered. Like Jesus had given His life for Huck, Huck would willingly give his life for that little girl if it came to that. He finally understood.

By the time he'd eaten, dressed, and signed a hundred papers, Huck was exhausted and ready for a nap. He complied with being pushed out in a wheelchair, since the nurse said he didn't have a choice. But the second they turned the corner, he had

Missy stop and ditched the wheels, having his fill of such things after the accident.

She wrapped her arm in his, and they slowly made their way to the main exit. "Thank you, Huck. For everything."

He shrugged, starting to accept the idea this woman might be his cousin. "I'd do anything for them."

"I know. You should tell Arianne what you've done."

"No. I don't want her to feel like she owes me anything. She's made her choice. I want her to be happy."

The pain meds made him dizzy. His tennis shoes rubbed on the shiny floor, and the waist of his track pants irritated his incision. "Tell me you didn't park in the back forty."

She chuckled. "I'm parked just outside the door."

They turned the corner by a small fountain and a wall mosaic of a forest in autumn. Just a few hundred more feet, and he could finally sit down. He should've taken the wheelchair.

The automatic doors opened. In stepped Arianne, carrying a canvas bag and fast food sacks. She stopped when her eyes caught his. Her gaze dropped, and she shifted the food. "What are you doing here?"

Her words hit their mark. Square in the center of his chest.

He saw Jack through the window, coming up the sidewalk, dropping his car keys into his pocket. "Nothin'."

Huck tore away from Missy's grip to keep moving. He had to get past Arianne and out the door before Jack entered. Couldn't watch the woman he loved walk away with another man. He ground his back teeth in pain as he took strides too fast and wide.

Missy jogged to his side. "Take it easy. Are you all right?"

"Fine," he groused.

Arianne's eyes narrowed. "Why wouldn't he be?"

"Because—"

He clamped a hand on Missy's arm. "Never mind."

Jack strode through the front door. His steps slowed. He nodded.

The room tilted. Huck's stomach rolled. He stared deep into Arianne's eyes, hoping to convey everything he felt for her but couldn't voice at the moment. "Let's go, Missy."

They started forward. Arianne handed the bags to Jack. "Huck, wait."

She grabbed his wrist. The plastic bracelet cut into his skin. The nurse had forgotten to take it off. Arianne looked down at the plastic band peeking from beneath the cuff of his long-sleeved shirt. She peeled back the fabric, her brows knotted.

"What's this?" Her words were slow, cautious.

Missy put a hand on Arianne's elbow. "Meet Emma's donor."

Arianne gasped. All color drained from her face. She tipped her head back and searched his eyes. He didn't say a word. Would she be thankful? Or angry that a part of him would always be linked to Emma? The pain medicine made him weaker by the second. He needed to sit down before he passed out.

Huck turned away and walked through the automatic sliding doors toward Missy's car.

~*~

Home at last.

Arianne closed Emma's bedroom door, thanking God once more that her daughter's body was accepting the kidney. If Huck hadn't swooped in and saved the day, Emma would still be on dialysis, waiting for an organ that may or may not come.

Her heart ached with a constant fierceness. She'd attacked Huck like a viper, spewing enough venom to take down an army. She'd accomplished what she'd set out to do, because when she'd announced she was marrying Jack, his face had contorted as if she'd cut him off at the knees.

And like a good soldier, he'd come to their rescue.

When the initial shock had worn off, she'd sought him out to apologize and thank him. But he wasn't at his usual places. She'd tried his house, but he wouldn't answer his door. Lamar, Huck's business partner, said Huck was recovering nicely but probably wouldn't be at the shop, since he wasn't involved in overseeing the reconstruction. Still, she'd watched for him. When he wouldn't answer her calls, she'd asked Jude what he knew. Jude had thrown his hands up and said he wasn't getting in the middle.

Huck had sacrificed for his love for Emma, and now that the job was done, he was leaving their lives like she'd ordered him to.

Only it wasn't what she really wanted. The scales had fallen from her eyes, and it was all clear now. In the face of adversity, she'd done the same thing to Huck that Adam had done to her—run.

Now she could say goodbye to a future with him in fifty different languages because he didn't want anything to do with her. Tears began to surface, but she pushed them away. There'd be time for those later.

Arianne met Jack in the kitchen and sank into a chair. He handed her a diet soda from the fridge and took the seat beside her. She smiled. "Thanks. I'd offer you something to eat, but I haven't been to the store in a while."

"I'm not hungry." His voice sounded deeper. He'd been keeping distance between them ever since they found out Huck was the donor. It seemed like deep down, Jack knew what was coming.

The can hissed as Arianne pulled the tab. A fine mist rose into the air and rained down on the can. She took a sip and wished the sweet liquid would wash away her troubles.

Jack looked at the hand he rubbed nervously on the table. "You're not going to marry me, are you?"

Though the question shouldn't have taken her by surprise, it did. Arianne set the can on the table. Condensation rolled down the metal and pooled at the bottom where it met the table. Her stomach clenched. "I'm sorry, Jack. I can't."

He lifted his chin and nodded as if he'd expected her answer. "Can I ask why?"

She didn't want to break his beautiful heart. Arianne blew out a breath, slowly. "I've prayed about it, like you asked me to."

"You love *him*. I saw it written on your face the day we saw Huck leaving the hospital." He stared at the table for a moment then stood. "I guess I've always known it. I really thought in time, though, you'd grow to love me, instead."

Arianne's bottom lip quivered, and she rose from her chair to block his exit. "I do love you, Jack."

A fake grin curled his mouth. "An 'I love you but I'm not *in* love with you' thing. I get it."

She winced. The man had already lost a woman he loved. Now she was causing him more pain. "Jack, I'm so sorry. I think . . . no, I *know* it's not God's will for us to marry." She stepped forward and gripped his arms. "I should've told you sooner, but with everything going on, it wasn't the right time. I'll miss you, Jack, but I believe you'll come to realize this is for the best. I thank you...for everything you've done."

He nodded as though trying to convince himself. "Yeah, for the best."

Her shoulders shook as tears rolled down her face. Jack stepped toward her and put his big hands on her cheeks. He stared at her with misty eyes and swallowed. "Goodbye, Arianne."

Jack kissed her forehead. His lips lingered. Then he walked around her and out the door.

"And the honey, and butter, and sheep, and cheese of kine, for David, and for the people that were with him, to eat: for they said, The people is hungry, and weary, and thirsty, in the wilderness."

—2 Samuel 17:29

37

Huck followed along in his Bible as Pastor Dave read aloud from the opposite side of the desk. Sermon notes, books, pencils, and highlighters cluttered the top. The small church office shrank with them in it, but Huck was at home in the humble space. He'd come to look forward to their meetings. He was halfway through the passage when his back pocket vibrated. The metal chair buzzed with every silent ring of his cellphone.

Pastor Dave looked up from his Bible. "If you need to get that, we can take a break."

Huck balanced his Bible in one hand and dug his phone from his pocket with the other.

Arianne.

He shook his head, pressed the power button to shut it down, and returned the phone to his pocket. "No, it's not necessary."

The pastor continued, and Huck had to force himself to concentrate on the lesson. It was torture not to answer her calls. Especially after Missy had phoned him two weeks ago after she'd returned to California to tell him Arianne and Jack had split. At least a hundred times a day, his fingers itched to dial Arianne's number, so he could hear her sweet voice. But he wouldn't. Not yet. He had some messes to clean up first. With the pastor's help, he was starting a new life. Only this time, it wasn't for Arianne. It was for him.

After the meeting, they scheduled their next counseling session and shook hands. Huck had yet to make it back to a Sunday service. The pastor understood when Huck had told him the circumstances and recommended another local church he could attend for a while. They would continue counseling together privately in the meantime, and Huck never missed the sermons broadcast on the radio.

He rounded the hallway to the foyer and collided with a soft, female body. He gripped her upper arms to steady her. "Sorry. I didn't know anyone was here."

Janet Hargrave, the cute brunette from the single's Sunday school class, smiled up at him, pink flooding her cheeks. "It's fine."

He usually ignored her efforts to gain his attention, but that was impossible at the moment. He let her go and looked around. Flower pots lined one wall, along with several closed umbrellas in different colors. "What's all this?"

She tucked her hair behind her ear. "It's my month to decorate the foyer. Since our Sunday school lessons have been about trials and the blessings that come from enduring them, I chose the theme 'April showers bring May flowers.'"

May. The last month had gone by so fast. "Ah, that explains it. You plannin' to open those inside?" He pointed to the umbrellas.

Janet nodded and let out an annoying giggle. "I'll take my chances."

He nodded. "Well, goodnight."

He hadn't made it three steps before she stopped him.

"Would you mind helping me carry in the flowers? I promise not to take up too much of your time." She batted her eyelashes. Her attempt to coat the request with honey was flattering, but it left the aftertaste of artificial sugar.

"Sure." Huck followed her to her car. He wasn't supposed to do any heavy lifting yet, but how much could a few flowers weight?

Her sandals clicked against her feet as they walked toward her open trunk. "I haven't seen you around for a while. I thought maybe you'd started going to church somewhere else."

"Been busy." That was an understatement.

The sun blazed orange as it lowered behind the pine trees. He reached her trunk and lifted a flat of violets. The sound of a loud exhaust approached. Huck turned toward the noise, and the flowers tipped off balance. Janet lunged, saving them, one hand on the box and the other on his arm.

A silver jalopy rattled into the parking lot. Air whooshed from his lungs. The brake lights of Arianne's car flashed before jolting to a stop. How did she know he was here?

Her window rolled down. The breeze blew her hair slightly, and her mouth hung open as if she were as surprised to see him as he was her. Her eyes were red rimmed. He'd seen that look often enough. And like those other times, he longed to fold her into his chest, tunnel his fingers into her thick curls, and tell her everything would turn out all right. Instead, he stood there, staring at her. Wanting her so bad it physically hurt.

Something squeezed his arm. He'd forgotten about Janet. Her brows lifted, wrinkling her forehead. "You OK?"

No.

He searched for Emma's head in the backseat, but didn't see it. Had something happened, and Arianne needed his help? But he'd talked to Jude right before his meeting with the pastor, and he'd said Emma was doing great.

Arianne gaped at him, opened and closed her mouth as if she wanted to speak but was unsure what to say. She seemed genuinely surprised to see him here, not frantic like something was wrong. He needed to move, to say something, but his muscles were as paralyzed as they were after his accident.

"Hi, Arianne." Janet removed her hand from the flowers to wave, but kept hold of his arm with the other. "How's Emma?"

"She…she's getting stronger every day. Thank you." Arianne could barely be heard over the rattling exhaust. He'd need to fix that.

"I'm so glad." Janet's hand crossed over her heart.

"I…" Arianne swallowed. "Huck—"

"Let me take these inside for Janet, and I'll be right back out." There was too much to say, and he wasn't doing it in front of an audience. He shrugged away from Janet's claws, lifted the second flat of violets in his other hand, and walked toward the church.

Janet chatted and giggled like a school-girl. Judging by her looks, he figured she hadn't been out of school too long. She opened the door for him, and he set the flowers on the pew along the wall.

"Is that it?"

Her pink lips parted in a smile. "Yes. Thank you."

"You're welcome. See you around." He fled before she had a chance to object.

Huck pushed the glass door open and stepped into the parking lot. His truck and Janet's car were the only ones there. Arianne was gone. He rubbed his jaw. Just as well. Now wasn't the time or the place. He had a few more things to do before he fought to win her back.

~*~

Arianne fingered the letters in her hand. "Here."

She handed an envelope to Braelle, her newly promoted and first-ever full-time employee.

"What's this?" Braelle tossed her hair away from her shoulder before opening the envelope.

"A thank you for all your hard work. I don't know what I'd have done without you while Emma was sick. You are truly a godsend."

Braelle pulled out the card. Her lips moved as she read silently.

The shop was warm with the sunlight spilling through the windows. White gowns glistened on the racks like diamonds. Business was thriving. Emma was on her way to recovery. Design school classes would begin next month. Her relationship with God was stronger than it ever had been. Only one thing was missing—the addressee from the other letter she gripped between her fingers.

The shock of seeing Huck last night still filled her veins. She'd driven to the church to sit in the dark, quiet sanctuary to search for answers. For the past month, she'd tried desperately to contact Huck. She wanted—no, *needed*—his forgiveness. And then, there he was, standing in the parking lot with the young and lovely Janet Hargrave, her manicured hand wrapped around his bicep. The sight cracked her heart open like an egg, and the opportunity to make amends soured. So she'd driven away.

Now she wished she hadn't.

Braelle's hazel eyes sparkled. "Wow. I don't know what to say." She brushed her thumb along her bonus check.

"You don't have to say anything. I'm the one who's grateful. You've helped take this place to a whole new level."

Braelle shrugged, scrunching the freckles along her nose. "All my friends are getting married and want to use your shop. Thank you."

Arianne patted her shoulder. "Thank *you*. It's well deserved."

She glanced at the clock. She'd run this letter out to the mailbox then call Sherry to check on Emma.

Traffic sped down the highway toward Bar Harbor. Tourist season was upon them. She breathed in the fragrant spring air, a mix of pine, flowers, and salt, soaking in the sun's warmth. The mailbox lid groaned as she tugged it open. She looked at the letter one last time, her eyes roaming over the address, the *Love* stamp. Probably inappropriate for this situation, but it was the only kind she had. She thought about the words she'd written inside and prayed they'd find their way into Huck's heart. Prayed her heart would accept that God didn't intend for Jack or Huck to be in her life. With a deep breath, she placed the letter inside the mailbox, closed the lid, raised the flag, and walked away.

~*~

Huck tapped his finger on the card. Arianne wanted his forgiveness. Didn't she realize she had it when he willingly gave away an organ? He hadn't been avoiding her out of anger. At first, he'd kept his distance to recover—his body and his heart. After all, she was marrying Jack. Then, when he discovered she wasn't, he'd stayed away to work on being a man worthy of her in God's eyes. If the good Lord was handing him a second chance, he certainly wasn't going to mess it up.

He propped his foot on the dash of the Gator and looked across the field. Rich, green grass sprouted from the soil. Daffodil buds dotted the meadow and would soon turn the acreage into gold. Bees buzzed all around, warming their wings in the sun. He read the card again.

Arianne thanked him for all he'd done. Not only for saving Emma's life, but for supporting her dreams and buying the building for her new shop. She'd found a small house to rent close to her work and would vacate his apartment on Saturday. Lamar would be thrilled, since the renovation to convert the upstairs into offices was the only thing left to do before the grand opening in mid-June.

Lastly, she wished him well, said she would pray for him, and hoped they could be friends. Impossible. They'd been friends for sixteen years. He had enough friends.

Soon, if Arianne would have him, they'd be so much more.

~*~

The buttery aroma of a flaky pie crust and creamy lobster filled Arianne's new kitchen. Boxes stacked in two neat piles filled one corner. The house was small but had more square footage than their apartment. She folded a dish rag and placed it in the drawer. "It smells heavenly."

Sherry smiled and patted Arianne's shoulder. "Your first night in a new home deserves a good meal."

Arianne folded another dish rag. "I really appreciate all you and Jude have done to help me."

The oven timer beeped. Sherry opened the door and lifted the lobster pie in her mitted hands. "I know."

Steam lifted from the golden crust, making Arianne's mouth water. She tossed the empty box aside and opened another, this one containing drinking glasses. One by one, she dunked them in the sudsy sink water. Her thoughts drifted to Huck. Five days had passed since she'd mailed the letter and still no word from him. She promised herself she wouldn't try to contact him anymore. He knew where to find her. If he'd wanted to talk, he would've by now. Tears threatened to drip into the sink.

"Arianne?"

It took a moment for Arianne to realize she'd stopped washing the glasses and was staring into the bubbles. She blinked and turned to Sherry.

"What's wrong, hun?"

The motherly lilt in her voice started the waterworks. Arianne shrugged, unable to speak.

"Is it Huck?" Sherry asked.

Arianne nodded. "I've tried every way possible to

apologize for being so awful, to tell him how grateful I am to him, but he won't speak to me. I can't blame him." She hiccupped. "I saw him last week in the church parking lot. I went there to pray. He was with Janet Hargrave. Carrying flowers. What was he doing there? With her?"

She didn't want to believe what gossip Harriet Jenkins had told her about Huck and Janet dating. She snatched a towel to dry her hands. "He paled when he saw me like I was the ghost of Christmas past. They were so chummy. Why was he there?"

Sherry sighed and dropped onto a chair, patting the one beside her. "Jude demanded I stay out of this, but only a woman understands another woman's heart. I don't know anything about this Janet lady, but I know why Huck was at the church."

Arianne sniffed and wiped the moisture from her cheeks. Sherry rested her thick hand over Arianne's. "Huck's been taking new convert classes with your pastor twice a week. He's given his life to Christ."

Goosebumps crawled up Arianne's arms. She swallowed. "He...he did?"

Sherry nodded.

Joyous tears clouded Arianne's vision. She'd prayed for him for so long. To know he placed his troubled childhood, his hurt, his fears in God's hands made her speechless. He was part of a family now. Her family.

The events of the past year became clear. She'd studied the Israelites journey out of Egypt the past few weeks. Despite all God had done for them, the miracles they'd seen, they failed to truly believe He'd do what He said He'd do. When tough circumstances came, they complained and determined to do things their way. It wasn't until they trusted and had true faith that they were able to enter the Promised Land.

She had no doubt Huck would be as successful at his new Christian life as he was in everything he did. He'd fall in love and marry a sweet girl like Janet, and she'd watch them drive off into the sunset together. The scent of the lobster pie now turned her stomach.

"Arianne?" Sherry squeezed her hand and leaned close.

"Praise God," Arianne whispered. And she meant it.

~*~

The bell in the shop doorway jingled. Arianne handed Emma the tissue paper. "Keep doing it like I showed you, and I'll be back in a few minutes to help you with the next step."

"OK, Mommy." Emma grinned at Arianne. The sun had turned her cheeks a nice healthy pink, and her energy levels were slowly climbing. Their schedule had changed, and the medicine cabinet looked like a pharmacy, but having her daughter was all that mattered.

She adjusted the satin panel on the dress form she was working on, and stabbed the needle into it for later. "I'll be right back."

Arianne grabbed the notebook with her list of things to accomplish in June and headed for the shop floor, excited that Braelle had returned from the craft store to help Arianne in crossing off number one. She rounded the doorway, stopped, and dropped her notebook. Huck stood in the middle of the shop, a short-sleeved, cowboy-style dress shirt with pearl buttons tucked neatly into his fitted jeans. He wore his best pair of boots. No hat.

Arianne gripped the wall trim to steady herself. His good looks put every other man to shame. She fumbled and picked up the notebook.

A corner of his mouth curled in that sexy, crooked grin she loved. "Hey."

Breathe.

She inhaled and found her voice. "Hey." Oh, how she wanted to throw her arms around him and stay there permanently. "You come to get fitted for a tux?"

He tucked his hands in his pockets and shifted his feet. "Actually, I did."

Her heart hit the floor with a jolting thud. She hadn't expected that response from her light, teasing words. "Oh."

She searched for signs in his face that this was a sick joke. His eyes were steady, his mouth firm. He was serious. Why would he come to her shop after all this time? Was this payback for hurting him?

An image of Janet in a wedding dress flashed before her eyes. It was her own fault for saying she wanted to be friends. Emotions clogged her throat, and she forced them down, determined to act professional. "Here is a catalogue of what we offer." She handed him a binder of photographs of men dressed in various styles of tuxedos. "Pick out the one you like, and I'll get your measurements."

Arianne ducked behind the register to compose herself. The wedding must be soon if he was ready to be fitted. He'd only known Janet, what—two months? Then again, they called it *love at first sight* for a reason. Hadn't she done the same with him the first time she spied him in his football uniform?

She bent down to get the tape measure which purposely hid her face. She couldn't refuse to do this for him, even though she wanted to. After all, he'd bought the place for her, given her daughter a second chance at life, and she did send him a letter pleading for friendship. *Stupid!* Why wasn't Braelle back from the craft store yet? Arianne needed to pass this off to her.

"I like this one—for a monkey suit."

His deep drawl curled around her from behind the counter. Arianne squeezed her eyes shut. *Huck isn't who you have for me, and You, God, are enough. But I can't do this without You.* She stood and walked to Huck on unsteady legs. He pointed to the tuxedo. It sure would bring out the velvety brown in his eyes.

She snatched a triplicate order form from the shelf along with a pen. "Hold out your arms, please."

He obeyed.

His rock hard shoulder rippled beneath her fingers as she held the measuring tape to it and stretched the tape to his wrist. She avoided eye contact for fear she'd crumble.

"How'ya been, Arianne?"

Miserable without you. "Good. Emma's doing well." She breathed in his woodsy scent she loved so much. Lifting her chin, she met his gaze. "Thank you. You'll never know how grateful I am for what you did."

His Adam's apple bulged against his collar as he swallowed. His gaze was intense. Yet almost…amused? She couldn't tell.

Trying to make as little contact as possible, she wrapped the tape measure around his thick chest. His heart beat against her fingers. She'd never be close enough to feel it again. Tears leaked into her eyes. She would not cry. She wouldn't.

Arianne pulled the pen from her pocket and distracted her brain by filling out what she could on the form. Unfortunately, she ran out of information. Sucking in a deep breath, she knelt in front of him to measure his inseam. "Spread your legs shoulder-width apart, please."

This was going to be awkward.

A mischievous grin lit his face.

Distraction. "Congratulations. When's the big day?"

Yes, she was torturing herself, but it was a question on the form. She would *not* ask who the bride was.

He cleared his throat. "Soon, I hope. I haven't exactly asked her to marry me yet."

Arianne dropped her hold on the tape measure and looked up at him. "What?"

Huck reached down and pulled her to her feet. He kept hold of her wrists, staring deep into her eyes with a love-struck look she'd only seen in the movies. What was going on? Her heart beat faster, and she twisted the tape measure with her hands. Huck yanked it away and threw it over his shoulder.

He lowered to one knee.

Her vision grew black and fuzzy at the edges.

"Arianne, I've loved you for a long time. Years. I just never knew how to show you." He dropped his head, glancing at his boot, then lifted it again. "I've done things I shouldn't have. Things I'm ashamed of. But I'm a new man. I've been workin' real hard to start over, to get where I need to be before I risked this."

He released her wrists long enough to tug something from his pocket. When a glistening, flawless diamond appeared before her eyes, her legs collapsed, and she dropped to the floor in front of him.

"I'd give anything for you to be my wife. Will you do me the honor?"

"You're not marrying Janet?" A tear trickled down her cheek.

He thumbed it away and frowned. "No. I only want you for the rest of my life."

She opened her mouth to scream "yes" but stopped. No more making decisions on her own. *Lord, what do I do? I thought a life with Huck wasn't what You wanted for me.*

Blinding sunlight burst through the windows, blanketing them. A pure and definite peace filled her heart.

It wasn't then. Now it's time.

The skin around Huck's eyes crinkled as he concentrated on her. "Arianne?"

Without a word, she crept closer, wrapped her arms around his neck, and kissed him with everything she had. A low groan escaped him when she pulled away. "Is that a yes?"

"That's a yes."

He kissed her again, pulling her as close as she could get, tunneling his fingers into her hair. She broke for air. "I love you," she whispered.

Something crashed into them and nearly knocked them over. They pulled apart, and Emma hooked an arm around both their necks. She bounced on her tiptoes. "Can I be the flower girl?"

They laughed.

Huck carefully picked up Emma and sat her on his knee. "If you'll let me be your daddy."

Emma placed her dimpled hands on his cheeks.

"I've always wanted a daddy. Will you stay?"

"I promise I'm not going anywhere." His voice was low, gruff, as if he was struggling to remain strong.

"Does that mean I can have my swing set back?"

He chuckled. "Yes."

"And baby kitty can live with us at your house too?"

"If he has to."

Huck slid the ring onto Arianne's finger. It fit as perfectly as the three of them did together. "Wait, isn't today your grand opening?"

He nodded.

Arianne glanced at the clock. "You better get moving, or you're going to miss it."

He brushed his thumb over her hand, admiring the ring, and squeezed. "I just got you both back in my life. I don't want to leave."

Arianne palmed his cheek. "We're in it to stay. You've worked hard for this. Now go before you're late. We'll see you tonight."

Huck sighed. "Promise?"

"Promise."

Huck kissed Arianne's lips then kissed Emma's forehead. He looked at her daughter with pride and affection. "I love you too."

Emma hugged his neck. Huck stood her on her feet and strutted toward the door. He winked at them over his shoulder and closed the door behind him.

Epilogue

One year later

A warm June breeze swept across the field, bending the buttercups into submission. Huck tugged at his tight collar and stretched his neck. He couldn't wait until after the ceremony so he could shed this blasted tuxedo. Among other things.

Beyond the footbridge, his new motorcycle waited with a *Just Married* sign and streamers attached to the front.

Jude clamped a hand on Huck's shoulder. "Not having second thoughts, are you?"

A baby whimpered from the audience then let out a squall. Huck looked over his shoulder at Jude and grinned. "Not a chance, buddy."

Pastor Dave joined them, clutching his Bible. He shook Huck's hand then waved to Missy who was managing the bridal party in a flower-draped tent.

Two violinists began to play a song Huck didn't know but Arianne loved. His gut tightened in anticipation. He glanced at Marge sitting on the front row. His favorite waitress wore a blue dress and a lipstick stained smile. She gave a thumbs-up and winked.

Emma, a vision in her white, princess gown, walked down the aisle, and sprinkled yellow rose petals on the clipped grass.

Missy followed a few feet behind in a pale green, strapless gown, her dark hair swept over one shoulder with tiny yellow roses and something Arianne called baby's breath tucked in there.

When they reached the pastor's other side, the musicians held the last note for effect then paused. Bows slurred across the strings into the beginning notes of the wedding march. The crowd stood, blocking the view of his bride. Sweat rolled down his neck. He walked down the aisle to meet Arianne, so she wouldn't have to walk alone.

How he wished Uncle Marty could be here in the flesh. Huck liked to think his uncle was here in his own way, watching from the best seat available.

Arianne materialized, stealing his breath. The white, lace gown hugged her curves perfectly. The neckline draped around to her tanned collarbones, ending high on her shoulders. She'd insisted on designing a new one he hadn't seen yet. Bad luck and what not.

Her navy blue eyes gazed at him behind thick black lashes, red lips teasing him beneath her gauzy veil.

"You are stunning," he whispered.

He held out his arm, and she hooked her fingers in his elbow, her grip loosening as they marched closer to Pastor Dave. She handed her colorful bouquet to Missy, and they linked hands to begin the vows.

Huck couldn't take his eyes off her. He'd never seen anything so beautiful. Nor had he ever heard a clergyman so long winded. He wished Pastor Dave came with a fast-forward button. He had a honeymoon to get to.

Arianne squeezed his hand. The pastor had

stopped talking, Huck's cue to speak. "I do."

Jude handed him the ring.

Pastor Dave viewed the exchange then said, "Repeat after me: with this ring, I thee wed."

Huck repeated the vows, meaning every single word. Arianne's eyes misted and a smile curved her lips.

Missy passed her his ring, and Arianne repeated the vows. "For better or worse…"

This precious woman had certainly loved him at his worst. They'd worked out a lot of issues over the past year with Pastor Dave's help and were starting their marriage on solid ground.

The pastor nudged his elbow. "Son, you may kiss your bride."

'Bout time.

Huck lifted her veil and folded it over her head. He cupped her face in his hands and kissed her like there wasn't an audience watching. The crowd cheered. Someone whistled. He pulled away and looked at his bride. Him, a husband. He never would've thought.

Author's Note

I hope you enjoyed Huck and Arianne's journey as much as I enjoyed writing it. Thank you for taking time from your busy life to visit the fictional towns of Summerville and Pine Bay, Maine.

When I began researching beekeeping for this book, I never expected to fall in love with honeybees. They're truly amazing creatures made by God to pollinate the plants and trees we need to survive, as well as providing healing and nourishment through the substances they make.

The honeybee population diminishes each year due to pesticides, mites, and weather. So how can you help the bees? Plant flowers and fruit trees and don't use anything around your home or on your plants that can be harmful to bees.

Did you know that honey has enough vitamins and nutrients to sustain life? Honey has been valued for centuries, even by God whose perfect plan was to lead the Israelites into a land flowing with milk and honey. That's why I chose to symbolically incorporate their wilderness journey into my own fiction story. My prayer for you, reader, is that you'll step out of the wilderness and give your heart and life to Christ (if you haven't already done so). Like Huck realized, salvation is a beautiful gift that cannot be earned but simply has to be accepted.

Sound simple? It is. Check out these short Scriptures for proof. Romans 3:23, Romans 6:23, Romans 5:8, John 3:16, Romans 10:13 and Romans 10:9.

I love to hear from readers! You can contact me through my website at www.candicesuepatterson.com.
God bless!

Thank you

We appreciate you reading this White Rose Publishing title. For other inspirational stories, please visit our on-line bookstore at www.pelicanbookgroup.com.

For questions or more information, contact us at customer@pelicanbookgroup.com.

White Rose Publishing
Where Faith is the Cornerstone of Love™
an imprint of Pelican Book Group
www.PelicanBookGroup.com

Connect with Us
www.facebook.com/Pelicanbookgroup
www.twitter.com/pelicanbookgrp

To receive news and specials, subscribe to our bulletin
http://pelink.us/bulletin

May God's glory shine through
this inspirational work of fiction.

AMDG

You Can Help!

At Pelican Book Group it is our mission to entertain readers with fiction that uplifts the Gospel. It is our privilege to spend time with you awhile as you read our stories.

We believe you can help us to bring Christ into the lives of people across the globe. And you don't have to open your wallet or even leave your house!

Here are 3 simple things you can do to help us bring illuminating fiction™ to people everywhere.

1) If you enjoyed this book, write a positive review. Post it at online retailers and websites where readers gather. And share your review with us at reviews@pelicanbookgroup.com (this does give us permission to reprint your review in whole or in part.)

2) If you enjoyed this book, recommend it to a friend in person, at a book club or on social media.

3) If you have suggestions on how we can improve or expand our selection, let us know. We value your opinion. Use the contact form on our web site or e-mail us at customer@pelicanbookgroup.com

God Can Help!

Are you in need? The Almighty can do great things for you. Holy is His Name! He has mercy in every generation. He can lift up the lowly and accomplish all things. Reach out today.

Do not fear: I am with you; do not be anxious: I am your God. I will strengthen you, I will help you, I will uphold you with my victorious right hand.

~Isaiah 41:10 (NAB)

We pray daily, and we especially pray for everyone connected to Pelican Book Group—that includes you! If you have a specific need, we welcome the opportunity to pray for you. Share your needs or praise reports at http://pelink.us/pray4us

Free Book Offer

We're looking for booklovers like you to partner with us! Join our team of influencers today and receive at least one free eBook per month. Maybe more!

For more information
Visit http://pelicanbookgroup.com/booklovers